OUT OF THE ASHES

Lori Dillon

AMARI PRESS

Amari Press

Back cover photo: Public domain photo courtesy of Ken Thomas at www.KenThomas.us

ISBN-13: 978-0-6155-8588-8

DEDICATION

For my husband, Knox, who dared me to try.

ACKNOWLEDGMENTS

I'd like to thank my wonderful critique partners,
Donna Dalton, Liz Lincoln Steiner and Mary Ann Clark
who helped me brainstorm and revise Ashes
from beginning to end.

I'd also like to thank the tremendously supportive and
innovative authors at IndieRomanceInk who gave me the
courage and knowledge to send this novel out into the world.
You rock!

PROLOGUE

"Bingo!"

Marsha looked in dismay at the cards before her—five Bingo forms, four with only one space left to fill. She glanced over her shoulder and glared at the excited woman bouncing up and down in her chair, clapping her hands in glee.

"Drat that Clarice. She always wins."

"There now, dear." Hershel patted her hand. "You know you've won plenty of times, too."

"She wins more," Marsha grumbled. "I think she cheats."

"Cheating's not allowed up here, and you know it." Hershel glanced at the cloud ceiling over his head. "*He* sees everything."

"Hrmph." Marsha tossed her marked-up sheets onto the growing discard stack in front of her. She pulled out five fresh ones and spread them out on the table for the next game.

A loud, crackling sound startled her so badly, she dropped her Day-Glo orange marker, leaving a vivid fluorescent streak across the top of the table.

"Paging Hershel and Marsha Baker. You're wanted in the Senior Guardian's chambers at once."

"Oh, my." Marsha glanced at Hershel and tried to slow the rapid beating of her heart. "We've never been paged before. I wonder what he wants?"

Hershel shrugged and scooted back his metal folding chair.

"How should I know? Maybe it's standard practice. After all, we are new to this position." He cupped Marsha's elbow, helping her to stand. "Come along, dear. We'd best not keep the man waiting."

Almost instantly, Marsha and Hershel found themselves

1

standing in the waiting room outside the Senior Guardian's office.

"Hershel and Marsha Baker?" the secretary asked in an overly cheerful voice. Her wide smile revealed bright pink lipstick coating her two front teeth. "He's been expecting you. You can go right in."

They stepped up to the wooden door floating suspended in the clouds. The words *Senior Guardian Angel Smithers* were emblazoned in shining gold letters on the frosted glass window.

Marsha gave Hershel's arm a nudge, indicating with a nod for him to knock on the door.

"Enter," said a deep voice from the other side.

Hershel opened the door, allowing Marsha to go in before him. For once, she wished he weren't so darn polite.

SGA Smithers, a very intimidating man with snow-white hair and a crisp pinstriped suit, sat behind a massive wooden desk. He thumbed through a stack of papers, reading over them with amazing speed.

"Sit," he said, without looking up.

Like trained dogs, Hershel and Marsha plopped down on the two leather chairs positioned in front of his desk.

Marsha glanced around the large office. Thick, puffy clouds made up the walls, floor, and ceiling. Diplomas and certificates in heavy frames decorated the room, each hovering in mid-air. The frames floated up and down as the clouds billowed, making her already unsteady stomach churn a bit more.

A life-sized nude statue of Apollo stood sentinel in the corner behind Smithers's desk. She gazed at the intricately carved face, so realistic that even a woman of her years could not help but admire his beauty. Her eyes traveled down the well-sculpted torso, each muscle defined to near perfection. Her appreciative gaze continued lower, passing slightly cocked hips to his...

Marsha shifted uncomfortably in her chair, forcing herself to tear her eyes away from the accurately carved anatomy pointing directly at her. Tugging her gray cardigan sweater tight over her frail chest, she dared a second peek, as if her tiny, grandmotherly body might tempt the stone Apollo to come to life and ravish her on the spot.

She glanced in Hershel's direction. His balding head bobbed on his chest as he fought off the effects of missing his afternoon nap. In all their mortal years together, she could only recall seeing him in the altogether on very rare occasions, and in her faded memory, he certainly hadn't been as well en—

The scrape of metal on metal drew Marsha's attention back to her boss. An open file cabinet drawer had appeared beside Smithers's desk, although there was no file cabinet to be seen. He extracted a folder from it. Just as quickly, the drawer slammed shut, and disappeared back into the clouds.

Smithers's gravelly voice startled her when he finally addressed them.

"You two are in charge of mortals Female 5923 and Male 2028, correct?"

Hershel's head popped up, and he glanced at Marsha.

She cleared her throat.

"Yes, we are."

Smithers eyed them, a bushy white brow arched in question.

"And how are they doing?"

Marsha grinned, relief relaxing her rigid pose. Obviously, the meeting was just for a status report. She waved her hand in the air, as if brushing away the anxiety brought on by this sudden summons.

"Oh, they're doing just fine. Why, they just met not too long ago. Had to do a little intervening there for a bit— thought the poor dear was going to faint dead away before she'd had a chance even to notice him. But our girl did as I thought she would, and everything is just fine."

"Really?" Smithers clasped his hands on his desk, eyeing both of them with avid interest.

"Oh, yes. Why, there were sparks right away between the two of them. I could tell. Weren't there, Hershel? Hershel!"

Hershel jumped in his seat, the sudden question startling him back from another attempt at his nap.

"Hmm? Oh, yes. Sparks. Definitely sparks."

"Sparks, you say?" Smithers nodded, appearing satisfied. "Well, let's review the situation, shall we?"

With a click of the small remote that suddenly appeared in his hand, a white screen dropped down out of the air. The clouds on the screen parted, and Mount Vesuvius spewing a tower of ash and rock high into the air nearly blinded them all.

As the scene played out, Marsha and Hershel looked nervously at each other.

They were in big trouble.

I stood within the city disinterred;
And heard the autumnal leaves like light footfalls
Of spirits passing through the streets; and heard
The Mountain's slumberous voice at intervals
Thrill the roofless halls;
The oracular thunder penetrating shook
The listening soul in my suspended blood;
I felt the Earth out of her deep heart spoke…

Percy Bysshe Shelley,
from *Ode to Naples,* 1820

Chapter I

August, A. D. 79
Pompeii, Italy

He was afraid. So very afraid.

Sweat beaded on his neck, running in tiny streams down his bare back. He shivered, not from the damp walls closing in on him, but from the fear. The fear of dying.

A roar rose from the crowd in the arena above, signaling the end of another contest. The joyous Romans cheered for the victory of one man and the death of another.

Dacian looked up at the grated hole in the ceiling of his tiny stone cell, the meager light filtering in a teasing reminder of a life that might be out of his reach this day.

His hands clutched his bare knees, making the leather covering on his right arm and shoulder creak in protest. Today he would have to kill or be killed.

The lots had been drawn. Who would be his opponent? Would it be a stranger, or would he face a friend across the field? Would he be forced to kill someone he'd trained with, or would his own life end this day? The decision was one he didn't want to have to make.

The bolt slid free outside the heavy wooden door. It swung open, and two Roman guards stood sentinel outside.

"Rise and follow. Your match is next."

Dacian stood and surveyed the cramped confines of the cell once more. Perhaps this would be the last time he saw it. The thought gave him little comfort.

The guard led him down a darkened corridor and shoved him into a cramped holding pen already crowded with several other gladiators. The sandy floor reeked of urine where those before him had relieved themselves on the ground, either in preparation for the fight to come or from the fear of their impending death.

One of the soldiers handed him a round shield and a *gladius*. This was the only time he was allowed to have a real weapon, and the steel blade felt heavy in his hand.

He gazed down at the weapon, realizing that in holding the short sword, he held his own life in his hands. The blade seemed incredibly small for such an important task, almost as useless as the wooden one he practiced with while training.

The door behind him closed with a thud, cutting off any hope of escape. Putting on the golden helmet with a fish embossed on either side to signify his role as a Myrmillo gladiator, Dacian took a deep breath and waited for the portal in front of him to open and reveal his fate.

Moments later, grating chains raised the heavy wooden door. The bright light of the sun nearly blinded him through the slits in the visor covering his face. As he stepped into the arena, he could not help but take note of the battles going on as the crowd of thousands cheered from the stands.

Nearby, a Secutor fell to a Thracian. In a distant area of the arena, two Velites fought valiantly, each tied to the other with a leather strap so they could never move completely out of harm's way. To the side, a man dressed as Charon, the underworld ferryman, dragged a defeated gladiator through a portal by sharp metal hooks impaled in the dead man's chest. Young African slave boys rushed behind them, raking up the trail of blood left behind in the sand.

Dacian turned away, feeling the piercing hooks imbedding in his flesh as surely as if he had already lost his own battle.

Walking to the center of the arena, Dacian faced his opponent, a Retiarius holding a trident in one hand and a large casting net in the other. The net fighter's only other protection was a leather shoulder piece similar to his own and wide leather straps around his legs. The dark-skinned man was large and intimidating.

He was also Dacian's friend.

"Bellator," Dacian said in greeting.

"Dacian?" Genuine surprise registered on the man's face. "Is that you?"

"Yes, it is I." Dacian nodded. "It seems the lots have drawn an even match today."

"That they have." Bellator grinned, his teeth a blinding white in his black face. "I cannot recall which one of us has won more matches on the training field."

"It does not matter. Only one of us can win this day, I am afraid."

The cheerful smile vanished from Bellator's face. "You speak the truth. I will do you proud, Dacian, but I do not intend to lose today."

"Neither do I, my friend. May the gods be with you."

The trainer standing nearby motioned for the contest to begin. Dacian and Bellator crouched into fighting position, slowly circling one another.

Bellator made the first move, tossing out the net with expert aim. Only through sheer speed did Dacian avoid getting entangled in its web. Dacian lashed out with his sword, leaving a shallow cut on Bellator's unprotected arm.

In retaliation, Bellator jabbed with the trident, poking Dacian in the ribs. Glancing down at his injury, Dacian was more surprised than hurt. It was obvious they were both trying to spare the other unnecessary pain.

A sharp crack filled the air, followed by a searing pain lashing across Dacian's back. He shot a swift look to the side to see the trainer grinning smugly, a slave holding a leather strap standing obediently by his side.

"You will have to put on a better show than that, or you will both be food for the lions tomorrow."

Dacian looked up in time to see Bellator receive a jab in the side with a hot metal iron brandished by another slave. The crowd hissed, voicing their displeasure with the poor display.

"They want blood." Bellator gathered up his net in preparation of resuming the battle. "We must give it to them. One of us will die either way."

"Then so be it." Dacian growled low in his throat, damning every Pompeian who stood ready to watch him die.

Lashing out, his sword sliced into Bellator's unprotected shoulder and sent blood racing down the man's arm. A cheer rose from the crowd.

They continued to circle each other, slashing and jabbing, blood mingling with the sweat and sand that covered their bodies. The crowd in the stands went wild, their shouts roaring in Dacian's ears, nearly drowning out the drumming of his own heart.

The match went on for what seemed an eternity, both men fighting with everything they had, each coming close to the point of victory, but neither willing to land the killing blow.

Dacian was tiring fast. He felt it in every muscle, heard it in his own labored breathing. The sword that had once looked so small now felt too heavy to lift. The shield that protected him dragged his weary arm down lower and lower, opening his body to danger. The sun beat down mercilessly on his sweat-soaked body, baking his own blood onto his skin.

It was a match well fought, but one that somebody eventually had to lose.

A stranger Dacian could defeat. He wouldn't care if a stranger lived or died. But this was his friend.

Bellator had told him stories of his childhood, whispered in the dark of night between their cells when the guards were asleep. He spoke of parents long gone and a sister sold into slavery at the tender age of seven. He told Dacian of the woman he loved and the child who waited for a father to return.

Dacian had no such ties, no one to miss him when he was gone.

And with that single thought, he made his choice.

Bellator tossed out the net, and Dacian dodged, but not far enough. His feet tangled in the netting, and he crumbled to the ground.

Let the end be quick, my friend, he thought as his tired body thumped onto the packed sand. *At least I will not have to fight any more.*

Dacian rolled over, his body tensing for the last time, and stared up into the face of death.

ᛈᛟᛗᛈᛇᛁᛁ

Sabina swallowed back the bile rising in her throat.

The August sun was unbearable. The awnings drawn over the arena to shield the crowd of twenty thousand Pompeians from the glaring sun did little to abate the heat. If she had to watch one more gladiator die, she might very well lose what little food she had in her stomach.

Try as she might, she could never find much enjoyment in the games. Even though most of the gladiators were criminals or slaves, it still made her uneasy watching their blood spill onto the sand.

Save him.

Startled, Sabina glanced behind her, wondering who could have spoken. The crowd cheered in their seats, entranced with the contest below. Turning back around, she rubbed at her aching temples. The sun was truly getting to her today, making her hear voices that were not there.

Save him.

Sabina felt a sudden chill, as though a cold wind had swept down through the arena and wrapped itself around her exposed shoulders. The voice whispered inside her head, a faint teasing sound she could barely make out over the thunderous shouts of the crowd.

The scene in the arena below drew her attention. The Myrmillo sprawled on the ground, defeated, his proud body slick with sweat and blood, the sand sticking to his skin. The victorious Retiarius stood over him, the point of his trident poised over the fallen man's heart, awaiting judgment from her uncle, the Giver of the Games. The Myrmillo's chest rose and fell rapidly, as if each beat of his heart would be its last.

Save him now!

She jumped to her feet.

"No!"

Silence fell over the spectators near her as they turned to gawk at her.

Sabina pushed her way in front of her father to kneel before her uncle, her hands gripping his plump knees as she used to do as a child.

"Dearest Uncle, as Giver of the Games, I beg you to spare the Myrmillo."

Gallus gaped at her with a puzzled look on his pudgy face, his arm suspended in midair, the thumb pointing neither up nor down.

"He lost the match."

"Yes," she conceded, "but he fought well."

"The crowd wants to see blood. That is what they came for."

Sabina gazed around them. The crowd no longer placed wagers on the combatants, but on whether her uncle would allow the loser to live or die. Half the people were hissing and booing, their thumbs pointing to the ground, blood lust evident in their dispassionate eyes.

"Only some. Look around you." The other half waved white pieces of cloth, their thumbs raised skyward in judgment of mercy. "The Myrmillo fought well for you this day. Spare him that he might fight again and bring victory to your name."

"Well..."

"Show the citizens of Pompeii you are a man of wisdom and mercy," she pushed on. "There has been much blood drawn today, and there will yet be more. What is one man's life? Prove to the people—your people—that you are not as heartless as Caligula of Rome once was."

Gallus frowned, his forehead creasing in deep furrows, and Sabina knew she would have to use her position as his favorite niece in the final thrust to win him over. She opened her eyes as wide as they could go and pouted in the way she knew he couldn't resist.

"Please? For me?"

He visibly melted at her plea. Shaking his head in admission of defeat, he raised his thumb in the air and spared the gladiator's life. The stands shook under her feet as the crowd went wild.

Her shoulders sagged in relief.

"Thank you. You will not regret your decision."

"I hope not, Sabina. I would not want the people to think I am too lenient. It could cost me the elections next year."

She chuckled. "It will not, Uncle, and you know it. If anything, your show of mercy has just earned you a thousand more votes."

"I certainly hope you are right." Gallus rubbed the first of his two chins and winked at her. "Perhaps I should make you my campaign advisor?"

Sabina grinned. "Perhaps you should."

She stood, ready to make her way back to her seat, when movement in the arena below caught her eye. The fallen gladiator rose on unsteady feet, and the crowd around her fell silent once more, anticipation thickening the air.

Sabina stood frozen, unable to tear her eyes away from the Myrmillo. Although his face was shielded from view by his helmet, she sensed him staring at her, his gaze boring deep into her soul.

A shiver rippled over her skin. Though he stood far below, she felt as if the gladiator had reached up and touched her.

Thumping his sword on his sweaty chest, the Myrmillo raised it high in the air and pointed it at her, breaking custom by saluting Sabina and not the Giver of the Games.

The crowd roared at the drama unfolding before them, but she barely heard them. All her senses were focused on the gladiator. She could almost feel the point of his sword piercing her heart, the hot metal vibrating with an unseen power inside her chest as her heart pulsed around it.

Finally, the gladiator severed the connection between them. He thumped his sword once more against his chest and pointed it at her uncle. Sabina felt weak, as if a string that had been holding her up had suddenly been cut, leaving her to drop limply to her seat.

"Well, I hope you are happy, Sabina," her father chided as both exhausted warriors were led away through a gate, only to have more gladiators enter the arena to take their place, "making a spectacle of yourself in front of all these people gathered in your uncle's honor."

"Oh, it was really not so bad. And she is right." Gallus chuckled as he smoothed the front of his white toga over his protruding belly. "After all, it did give me a chance to show my generous side, although I am not sure I like his arrogance, bowing to Sabina the way he did."

"You should have him lashed for losing, beaten at the very least for his insolence in the face of your leniency," her father said.

Sabina felt the blood drain from her body at the thought of the proud young gladiator suffering any more pain because of her.

"Yes, perhaps I will." Gallus returned his attention to the next match in the arena. "It will teach him to win next time, or there will not be a time after that, I can assure you."

POMPEII

She stood alone in the stands, the Amphitheatre empty except for the man in the arena. A dry wind blew across the field, the dust swirling in tiny storms across the sand.

With a will of its own, Sabina's arm lifted, her thumb poised midway. Her arm felt oddly detached from her body, as if she no longer had any control over her own limb. Yet she knew that she alone had the power to determine the gladiator's fate. With a simple twist of her wrist, she could decide whether he lived or died.

Bright bursts of light reflected off his gold helmet as he stared up at her, his eyes piercing her through the slits in the metal faceplate. He stood in the center of the arena, his arm stretched out to her. Then the raised sword in his hand crumbled to sand, the grains trickling through his fingers and drifting away on the wind.

The breeze carried his voice up to her, softly at first, growing louder until the vast stadium seemed to vibrate with the sound of his words.

"Sabina, save me."

She awoke with a start, her heart pounding, his voice ringing in her ears.

"Save me..."

She was back in her own familiar room. Yet the dream seemed so real, she almost expected the gladiator to be standing at the foot of her bed.

She tossed the covers aside and walked to her dressing table, her bare feet silent on the cool tile floor. Her legs felt leaden, her arms heavy, as though invisible chains weighed them down. She splashed cool water on her face from a shallow basin, trying to shake the last vestiges of the dream.

A dark-skinned woman entered the room bearing a tray of watered wine, bread, and honey. Sabina sat on a small stool, and the woman began brushing her hair with a comb delicately carved from bone, as she did every morning.

The wide leather belt the woman wore around her waist bore Sabina's father's name, marking her as a slave of his household. She had been Sabina's personal servant her entire life, and yet Sabina knew very little about her.

Picking up a mirror of polished silver metal, Sabina studied her own reflection as perplexing thoughts ran through her mind.

"Lidia, how did you come to be a slave?"

The woman paused in mid-stroke. Her large brown eyes met Sabina's blue ones in the mirror, revealing her obvious surprise at the direct question.

"I was taken from my home when I was but a child."

"Do you remember being free?"

"Some, but it was a long time ago."

"And what of your family?"

Lidia resumed combing, the strokes noticeably more forceful as she tugged at Sabina's scalp.

"My father and brother were killed when the slave traders attacked our village. My mother and sisters were taken, too. I have not seen them since I was put on the ship and brought here."

"I am sorry."

"I am no longer sad." Lidia shrugged. "As I said, it was a long time ago."

Sabina watched the slave's face reflected in the silver mirror. Though her words revealed little, if any, emotion, the sadness in her eyes showed the woman's secret torment. Lidia continued dressing Sabina's hair, pinning up the wavy russet strands with hairpins made of gold and jade, hiding her pain in the ritual of duty.

"Are you happy here, Lidia?"

"It is the only life I know."

"But are you happy?"

Lidia put down the comb and handed Sabina the cup of wine.

"Like any slave, I would like to be free someday. Free to make my own way, to marry and have children." Lidia turned away and pulled a *tunica* and *stola* from a chest at the foot of the bed. "But it is a foolish dream."

"Why is that?"

Lidia slipped the saffron *tunica* over Sabina's head and adjusted the folds so it draped her body.

"Because it will never happen. I have been a slave in your father's house for twenty years. It seems the Fates have decided that I shall die a slave."

Sabina did not know what to say. The possibility of never knowing freedom? To have no choices, no will of one's own?

Unbidden, the gladiator from her dreams crept into her thoughts. Did he have the choice to fight or not? Was he free or slave?

As Lidia wrapped a fine chain of gold links around Sabina's waist, Sabina gazed at the beautiful fresco painted on the plaster walls of her room. The bright greens and reds gave one the illusion of being surrounded by a peaceful garden, since no windows allowed in the outside world. But if she dared to look beyond the wonderful artist's painting, high stone walls surrounded her with no way out except through one small door.

She looked away as the walls closed in, her room feeling more like a prison than a sanctuary. Uneasy desperation drove her to escape the suddenly oppressive confines.

She stood and walked through the door, free to go about as she pleased. But that liberty did little to ease the guilt building inside her.

Guilt for what? For being born a free woman? Life had always been that way—there were slaves, and there were masters.

Crossing the open center courtyard of her father's house, Sabina found it difficult to draw in a full breath, even in the fresh early morning air. She could not shake the strange feeling that had come over her since the games.

What had happened to change things?

But if she were truly honest with herself, Sabina already knew the answer.

Somehow, *she* had changed. And in some way, she knew she might never be the same again.

These thoughts weighed heavily as she listened to Lidia's soft footsteps following quietly behind her, a human symbol of everything Sabina had always taken for granted.

Chapter II

Sabina strolled through the open-air market in the center of the city with no particular destination in mind.

As she passed a public fountain, two women, voices raised in anger, caught her attention. The marble basin to catch the water was dry, only a single drip falling reluctantly from the spout of the stone lion's mouth. The water no longer flowed freely through the aqueduct system under the city, and the women were arguing over the reason. One said it was the pipes, broken again from the recent rumbling of the ground. The other swore it was a sign from the gods that Pompeii's time of plenty was over.

Wondering briefly why that one and several other fountains in the city had gone dry in the past few days, Sabina shrugged and moved on. She could not be bothered with such mundane thoughts as the city's plumbing.

Instead, her thoughts returned to the gladiator. Even a long steam and a plunge in the *frigidarium* had done little to chase the dream from her mind. What was it about him? She had yet to lay eyes upon his face, did not even know his name, and yet she felt... drawn to him.

Was it merely because she felt responsible for having spared his life? Or that he had then risked that very life by paying tribute to her in front of twenty thousand spectators?

Sabina stepped up to a merchant's shop, picked up a terra cotta lamp, and feigned examining it. She would not allow the gladiator to creep into her thoughts anymore. She had done what she felt was right, and it was over, the entire incident best forgotten.

Why then, wouldn't the memory of him leave her alone?

Why did she feel as if he were calling to her?

"Stop it! I will not listen to you."

The shopkeeper eyed her suspiciously. Grinning to cover her embarrassment, she returned the lamp to its shelf and continued her stroll.

Sabina walked to another merchant's shop where urns of incense and precious oils filled the air with exotic scents. She picked up a bottle and removed the stopper to sample the spicy fragrance.

Did he hurt from the wounds he received during the match? Had he been lashed as her uncle had threatened?

"No!"

She slammed the bottle down, spilling the oil over her fingers and the tabletop.

"What do you think you are doing?" the shopkeeper yelled.

Sabina looked at the mess she'd made.

"I am sorry. The bottle slipped out of my hand. I will gladly pay for it."

The shopkeeper took her money, the pricey oil costing her every coin she carried. She hurried away from the shop, cursing the man for disturbing her thoughts.

Before she realized it, Sabina found herself outside the gladiator barracks on the far side of the city, the sound of clashing swords and shouting men coming from the practice field inside.

How had she come to be at this place? She had never had any intention of coming here.

Sabina made her way to the front gate. The iron bars of the door gave her pause, evidence of the violent men they kept within. A shiver raced up her spine, but that didn't stop her from seeking the posted results of yesterday's games painted on the plaster wall.

Scanning the lists, she noted many names marked with a *P* for those who had perished, while a *V* indicated the victors of the day's events. Her eyes skimmed over those, only reading the names marked with an *M* for *missus*—fighters who had lost, but been spared to fight another day. There were few who had been so lucky, and only one of them had been a Myrmillo. A gladiator named Dacian.

A guard stepped up to the gate, startling her.

"What do you want?"

Before she could think better of it, the words sprang out of her mouth.

"I wish to speak with the Myrmillo Dacian."

The guard looked at her in surprise, then stepped closer, a smirk on his scarred face.

"Oh, you do not want to consort with the likes of him. Why, he is just a filthy slave trained at fighting. Would you not rather dally with one of the free gladiators instead? They are accustomed to the ladies coming to visit and know how to treat them."

Sabina cringed at the thought.

"No, I wish to see Dacian."

The guard's smirk disappeared, and he eyed her up and down.

"Fine, but it will cost you. The slave gladiators are not allowed such liberties. They cannot be trusted."

She tried to comprehend what the man was saying. Did he actually want payment to allow her to speak with a gladiator? She had spent all her money on the oil she spilled. There was nothing left...

Sabina followed the guard's gaze to the metal band encircling her upper arm. She pried it off and handed it to him. The guard bit into it, noting it was made of polished brass and not the fine gold he expected.

"This will let you talk to him—through the gate. If you want to spend *private* time with him, you will have to bring something more next time." The guard tucked the armlet into his tunic and walked away.

Next time? Was she truly even considering that there would be a next time?

Just when Sabina began to suspect that the guard had taken her jewelry and left her to stand out in the hot sun all day, he appeared with another man in tow.

The gladiator was brought forward, his chest bare and sweaty from the morning training session, suspicion evident on his stoic features. She was shocked at how young he was. He couldn't be much older than nineteen or twenty, yet the strain of his profession had left its mark in the lines of his face, aging him beyond his years. Black curls surrounded that hard, yet handsome, face—curls a slave labored for an hour each morning to replicate on her father's balding head. He would be envious to see such perfection wasted on a gladiator.

Dark brown eyes studied her, showing no emotion at a strange woman wishing to see him. Then his eyes widened, and when he finally spoke, his voice was deep and strong.

"You are the girl from the games yesterday."

"Y-yes," she stuttered, surprised that he recognized her. "My name is Sabina."

He nodded. "I am called Dacian."

"I know. I saw your name posted at the gate."

Sabina glared at the guard standing next to Dacian. The man snorted, curling his upper lip in disdain before he moved a few steps away. Obviously that would be all the privacy her armlet would buy them.

She turned her attention back to Dacian, and they stared at each other for a long time, the silence growing as awkward as the iron bars that separated them.

"Why have you come here?"

"I had to see if you were all right. To see if…" Sabina stepped closer, wrapping her hands around the bars. "Father said you might be punished for losing the match during the games."

He remained silent.

"Well, were you?"

His lids lowered, casting his eyes into shadow under his long, dark lashes.

"No."

Sabina sighed in relief. When the silence became unbearable once more, she struggled for something to say.

"Do you like being a gladiator?" She cursed herself, realizing the ridiculousness of the question after she had spoken it aloud.

He laughed, the sound devoid of humor.

"How can you possibly believe men get pleasure from killing one another?"

"There are some who do."

"Only the free gladiators who are paid to fight, or those who sit safely tucked away in the stands, watching as other men die for their enjoyment in the arena."

"So you are not here by choice?"

"No, I do not choose to kill. I am forced to do it."

Sabina's exposed skin chilled. She'd always known of the slave gladiators, but she never considered how they felt about what they were required to do.

Embarrassed that she had ever been a spectator to such sport, she tried to justify it.

"But that has always been the way of things, has it not? It is how we rid ourselves of criminals and the unwanted in society."

"So does that make it just to pit man against beast? Man against man?" Dacian stepped closer, resting his hands above hers on the metal bars. "And what of an innocent man, guilty only because he was born a slave and sold into the gladiator school as a child? A man who committed no crime other than that of being born to the wrong family at the wrong time? Had my father been a privileged Roman…"

His anger and pain reached out and wrapped around her heart. She thought of the money her uncle spent so easily to sponsor the games, paying for men like Dacian to die so that he might win favor with the people and votes in the next election.

"I guess wealth means power and freedom, does it not?"

"*That* has always been the way of things." His hands gripped the bars, causing his knuckles to turn white.

"How much would it cost for your freedom?"

A look of hopelessness aged his handsome face before her eyes.

21

"More gold than I could ever hope to win in the games."

Sabina watched his gaze trace every feature of her face, his look so intense she could almost feel it caressing her skin.

He reached through the bars, fingering the indentation the armlet had left on her arm.

"Is this then the price for a gladiator?"

Sabina looked down to where his finger rubbed slowly back and forth over the mark on her skin, and a shiver raced through her body.

"No," she whispered. "Merely the price to speak to one."

A sharp crack pierced the air as the guard slammed a heavy stick down on the fingers of Dacian's other hand.

"Do not touch the girl. You are not worthy."

They both jumped away from the bars. Dacian cast his eyes on the ground, cupping his bruised fingers with his other hand.

The guard grinned at Sabina through the bars.

"It looks like your visit is over for today. Remember, if you wish to see him again, you know what is expected."

The guard grabbed Dacian and led him away, but not before Sabina saw the deep red lash marks streaking across his proud, young back.

POMPEII

Sitting in his dark cell, the wall cool against his ravaged back, Dacian struggled to ignore the pain. He tried to think of pleasant things to deaden the burning of the freshly striped welts that marked his flesh, overlapping the unhealed wounds from his lashing the day before for losing the match against Bellator.

The one image that kept returning to his mind was Sabina as she looked at him through the iron bars of the gladiator barracks. Soft amber curls framed her lovely face, and her eyes, big and blue, reflected a wealth of emotion for one so young. He shook his head. She was so pure and innocent, a rarity among the Romans.

Why had she done it? Obviously a privileged daughter of a prominent Pompeian, she'd not only risked a great deal during the games, but she had risked her very reputation by coming to see him, a lowly slave gladiator.

She would never realize it, but that one small act of kindness meant more to him than anything he could remember. He would hold tight to that memory, knowing he might not experience the feeling again anytime soon.

The bolt grated in the door, and Dacian looked down at his portion of boiled barley, grown cold. He realized he had been dreaming the day away and had not finished his noon meal. He stood, prepared to hand over the simple clay bowl. A spoon was never provided for fear he might find a way to use it against his guards.

When he looked up, a vision stood in the doorway, as if she had been conjured straight from his thoughts.

"Sabina." He spoke her name in a whisper, fearing if he said it too loudly, the vision might disappear.

Glancing first at him, then at the tiny confines of his cell, she smiled tentatively. When she finally stepped through the doorway, Dacian didn't know what to say. He didn't know how to react.

Sabina turned away, and he wondered if she had changed her mind and intended to leave. But instead, she spoke softly to the guard.

"You may leave us now."

The guard looked at her warily. "I do not think that would be wise. He is dangerous. You should not be left alone with him. You should not even allow yourself to be within arm's reach of him."

Placing her hands on her hips, she stiffened.

"I will be perfectly fine. After all, I spared the man's life not two days ago. I do not think it likely that he will take mine now. Now, I paid you good gold. Close the door and give me my time with him."

Amazing. This wisp of a girl stood there with the regal bearing of an empress, ordering the guard about with confident authority as if she did such a task every day and fully expected to be obeyed. Dacian had never seen anything like it.

The guard's beady eyes darted between the girl and Dacian before he bowed his head slightly, his lip curled in contempt.

"Whatever the *lady* wants."

His tone on the word "lady" made Dacian bristle. Given the chance, he would gladly kill the guard with his bare hands for the insult to Sabina's character, insinuating he knew exactly why she had come—the only reason any woman would visit the barracks.

The guard snatched at the satchel Sabina carried, opened it, and rooted through its contents. He withdrew a covered jar, removed the top, and sniffed it. Seemingly not satisfied, he shoved his finger into it and stuffed a glob of white paste into his mouth. No sooner had he closed his lips around his finger than he spat the paste out on the stone floor.

Sabina chuckled. "I could have told you it was not food, had you the decency but to ask."

The guard growled at her, and Dacian feared the man would make her leave. Instead, the guard shoved the bag and its contents into her hands and slammed the door. The bolt slid shut, effectively trapping Sabina in the cell with Dacian.

He stared at her back, afraid to move, afraid to make a sound. She seemed so small, like a delicate bird trapped in a wicker cage. He did not doubt the guard was right. If he wanted to, Dacian could kill her with a single blow of his hand. Killing was what he'd been trained to do. He sensed she realized that, but for some reason, she chose to trust him. Why? Why, of all the gladiators in Pompeii, did she choose to seek out him?

Sabina turned, a tentative smile touching her face.

"Hello, Dacian."

He set his half-eaten bowl of boiled barley on the floor slowly so as not to frighten her and wiped his greasy fingers on his dirty tunic.

"Why have you come here?"

The pleasant smile left her face, replaced by a piqued look that made her appear older than her years. "You lied to me yesterday."

"I did?" Confused, he tried to recall every word of their conversation.

"Yes. When I asked if they had beaten you for losing, you said 'no.'"

Dacian shrugged in a casual manner, belying the rage he felt at the injustice life dealt him every day.

"It is the price to pay for losing in the games."

Concern quickly replaced the look of displeasure on her pretty face.

"You did not get into trouble when they took you away yesterday, did you?"

"No." He shifted his feet, the pain of the fresh lashes under his tunic calling him a liar.

"Let me see your back."

Her request surprised him. Did she really wish to see the lashing he received because of her visit?

"I think it would be better if you did not."

Indicating the satchel she carried, Sabina approached him.

"I brought a salve that might help you. I risked a great deal in coming here today and had to spend a goodly amount of my own gold to do it. Now, are you going to remove your tunic or not?"

Heat rose to Dacian's face. "I do not wish to offend you."

"I have tended wounds before. The sight will not offend me."

"That is not what I meant."

Realization washed over Sabina's face, her mouth curving into a silent "oh." The filthy tunic was all Dacian wore.

Without hesitating, she removed the white *palla* from around her shoulders.

"Here, you may cover yourself with this."

Handing the lightweight shawl to him, she turned her back as if the decision were final.

Dacian nearly laughed. There he was, a trained killer, and yet he felt intimidated by this tiny girl. He removed his slave belt, then pulled the tunic over his shoulders, wincing as the coarse material scraped across his raw back. If she wished to see the ugly side of being a gladiator, so be it.

He took her *palla* and wrapped it around his hips, the material so thin and sheer it barely concealed him.

"You may turn around now."

Sabina turned slowly and eyed him from under long lashes, almost as if she did not trust him to be fully clothed. When she saw he was, the stiffness in her shoulders eased, and she seemed to relax.

"Please sit." Sabina indicated the stone slab that served as his bed. He did as she ordered. When she sat down next to him, he stiffened, unaccustomed to having anyone so close who didn't want to kill him.

"Now, let me see." Turning him with just the barest touch of her fingers on his shoulders, she angled his back toward the meager light coming in through the small barred window in the door of his cell.

Dacian braced himself for her reaction.

He heard her swift intake of breath. "By the gods, look what they have done to you!"

He craned his head to peer over his shoulder. "It probably appears worse than it feels."

"It looks awful. Why did they lash you again?"

"The guards are always ready to remind the slaves of their place."

Sabina sat silent for a long moment.

"Was it because you touched me yesterday?"

He hesitated before telling her a half-truth.

"Among other things."

"Then this is my fault. I caused you this pain."

His hand covered hers where it rested on his shoulder.

"No, Sabina. Do not blame yourself. You did not wield the whip. It was not your hand that laid these lashes across my back."

Her large blue eyes pooled with tears ready to overflow down her pale cheeks.

"But if I had not come—"

He shifted slightly so he could see her better.

"If you had not come, they would have found another reason to do it." Dacian watched her struggle with the unfairness of it and searched for the words to ease her guilt. "And if not for you, I would not have had a reason to bear it."

"I am sorry." She paused, worry furrowing her brow. "Will they punish you again because I have come?"

Dacian let his arm drop and shook his head.

"No. Since you paid them good coin, they will not hurt me in the hopes of receiving more if you come again. Besides, with the next games so close, they could not risk damaging me so much that I can no longer fight."

He watched as inspiration sprang alive inside her.

"But what if you are so injured that you could no longer fight? Would they set you free?"

Sweet, innocent Sabina. She had no idea of the way of the world.

"A gladiator who cannot fight is not worth keeping alive. If I can no longer compete in the games, they will pit me against the beasts, and both you and I know which will win in the end."

The room grew cooler as the hope faded from her eyes.

"Yes, I know." He watched her gaze rake over his scarred back. "Still, they should not have beaten you for a mere touch. It is not as if you meant to do me harm."

"No." Dacian looked deep into her eyes. "I would never hurt you."

She smiled. "I know that."

"How? How do you know, when you do not know me?"

Sabina shrugged. "I just do."

She looked down at the jar of salve in her hand and winced.

"However, you may not say the same of me once I am done with you."

Contrary to her words, her fingers stroked gently across his ravaged back. So unaccustomed to another's caring touch on his skin, he wanted to weep at the tenderness of it.

Reluctant to break the peacefulness of the moment, Dacian asked the question that had plagued him since the games.

"Why did you save me in the arena?"

He felt her pause.

"You fought well. I did not think you deserved to die." Sabina quickly resumed her ministrations, smoothing the cool cream on his skin just above where it met the barrier of the shawl.

"There are gladiators who fight well every day. Men who fall, hour upon hour, who do not deserve to die."

"I know."

"So why me?"

She sighed heavily. "There had already been so much blood and death that day. I thought maybe... I wanted to save one."

Dacian snorted at the futility of it.

"But you cannot save us all."

Sabina paused again.

"But I did save you, so do not dare tell me you were not worth it."

He had no answer for her. He remained silent and enjoyed her touch. Her fingers glided over his skin, tenderly applying the healing ointment to the cuts on his back.

"There, I hope it did not hurt too much."

Disappointed when her fingers left his skin, Dacian turned to her and took her hand, running his thumb over the tops of her fingers.

"I would gladly suffer the lash every day if it meant you would touch me with kindness again."

Sabina blushed and pulled her hand away. She passed him his tunic, then turned her attention to resealing the jar and replacing it in her satchel.

"You risk a great deal by coming here," Dacian said as he stood and dressed.

"I know."

"Do you really, Sabina?"

He stared down at her as she sat on his stone bed in her pure, white gown. She looked so young and naive. As much as he hated to do it, he needed to warn her of the folly of coming to the barracks, even if it meant he would never see her again.

"You risk not only your reputation, but perhaps any chance at a good marriage. Only women seeking a lover come to visit the gladiators."

She finished wiping the salve from her fingers with a cloth and stared down at her hands.

"I am aware of that."

"Is that why you really came?" Dacian held his breath, the thought sending a wave of heat through his body. He stepped toward her, his cock stiffening under his tunic at the possibility of her desiring him that way. "Is that what you want of me?"

Sabina's head shot up, her eyes wide while a telling blush crept up her cheeks.

"I... no. No, of course not. I only wanted to help you." Snatching up her satchel and *palla*, she stood and turned for the door. "I am sorry I came. I will not bother you again."

Dacian panicked and reached out to stop her. He grabbed her upper arm, his fingers encircling the delicate limb where the mark from her armlet had been the day before. Her skin was so soft, he ached to touch her more, but he didn't dare.

"Wait. Please do not leave just yet."

Sabina stopped, but she would not look at him.

"I am sorry." Desperate to take back the careless words he'd spoken, he faltered. "I... am glad that you came. Just by doing so, you have made my sad existence a little more bearable, if only for a day."

She turned, a wealth of emotion vivid in her eyes. With his hand still cupped around her arm, she stepped closer. They stared at each other for what seemed like an eternity, the silence of the cell broken only by the sound of their breaths drawn in unison, mingling in the air between them.

The grate of the bolt jarred them back to the moment.

"Your time is up," the guard said from the doorway. "You will have to come back tomorrow if you want to see him again."

Dacian looked at her, probably for the last time, knowing the regret he saw on her face was likely reflected in his own.

"I thank you for coming, Sabina, but do not come again. You risk too much."

She smiled shyly.

"Only my heart."

Dacian watched as the guard led her away, locking him back in his cold, lonely cell.

CHAPTER III

Sabina's gladiator now had a face—and a name.

Dacian.

Wrapped in the *palla* he had covered himself with the first time she'd gone to him in his cell, his scent surrounded her. Strong and musky, the smell brought him vividly to her mind.

Every day Sabina had managed to slip away to visit him, and each time it cost her more. Once her coin was gone, she began bribing the guards with various pieces of jewelry, but before long all that would be gone, too. Soon she would be forced to steal from her father if she wanted to continue to see Dacian. But see him she did, and each time, the look on his face made it all worthwhile.

In the dark confines of his cell, they spoke of small things— how well the grapes grew on the fertile hillsides of Vesuvius or the philosophy of Seneca and the writings of Pliny the Elder. They talked of the past—how Sabina's wine merchant father had raised her since her mother's death and how Dacian had worked at the laundry as a child before he'd been sold into the gladiator school.

They never spoke of the future—of Dacian's dreams if he were ever free or of what might happen between them should they be able to see each other outside the confines of his cell.

And they never spoke of the games or of what might happen when Dacian would have to fight again. The thought was unbearable for them both, and yet, the next games were only days away.

Time was running out.

These thoughts weighed heavily on Sabina's mind as she entered her father's solar. She approached him warily, not quite certain what she was going to say.

"Father? I wish to speak to you about the gladiator."

Busy tallying the day's wine sales, her father looked up from his wax tablet.

"Gladiator? What gladiator?"

"The Myrmillo from the games Uncle sponsored."

Her father looked momentarily confused, then pinned her with a stern look.

"The one you had Gallus spare? What of it?"

Sabina ran her finger across the front of her father's table. What she was about to ask was unthinkable.

"I was wondering if we could buy him."

He stared at her as if she'd just asked him to dump this year's wine harvest into the sea.

"Buy him? Whatever for? I have no need of a gladiator."

"I do not mean to buy him so that he may fight for us, but so that we may set him free."

Her father snorted at the very thought of it. "And throw away good coin? I think not, child."

"But he is a good man. He does not deserve to die."

He looked at her suspiciously. "How do you know so much about this gladiator?"

Realizing her error, she scrambled for an explanation. "Only what I have heard others say."

He waved his writing stylus at her.

"Sabina, I know you have a tender heart, but do not grow overly fond of this gladiator." He sighed heavily, shaking his head at her in the way that meant she would always be a child in his eyes. "I realize you may feel responsible for him after having his life spared, but you cannot save him each time. After all, gladiators die—it is their lot in life. It is best not to get too attached to them." Her father went back to his figures. "I do not want you carrying on like you did when that cat of yours got run over by the wine cart."

"Father!" Sabina ground her teeth in frustration. "I was only five when that happened. And besides, he is not a cat. He is a man."

He slammed his tablet on the table, causing her to jump. Pressing both hands on the wooden surface, he rose and leaned over the table until his face was only inches from hers.

"No, Sabina, he is not. He is like the cattle and fowl slaughtered for our meals. He was born for a purpose, and that is to perform in the arena, not to be your charity case. He is a creature put on this earth for our amusement. You cannot think of him as a man, because he is not."

"He certainly looks like a man to me," Sabina grumbled.

"What was that?"

"Nothing, Father." She bit her lip, cursing herself for voicing the observation out loud.

Her father cocked his head and stared at her with an odd look in his eye. He pushed himself away from the table and clasped his hands behind his back, making his protruding stomach stick out all the more.

"You will be seventeen this year, will you not?"

She rolled her eyes. "I turned seventeen last month."

"Did you? Well, then, it is definitely past time to find you a husband. You will accompany me on my next trip to Rome, and we will find you one. With your lovely face and figure, we should have no problem finding a suitable match, perhaps even a senator or praetor. Your uncle would be pleased at that."

"Marriage?" The word stuck in Sabina's throat.

"Yes, marriage. As soon as possible, I should think. Seems to me you need something to occupy that busy little mind of yours besides some worthless gladiator."

POMPEII

"I asked my father to buy you."

Shock seized the air in Dacian's lungs, turning it to ice.

"You did *what*?"

Did she even realize the risk she took in making such a request?

"I had to do something. The thought of you here, locked up in this place like an animal..." Sabina wrapped her arms around her narrow waist, "… or in the arena, fighting for your life. I cannot bear it."

"What did he say?" He waited, already knowing what the answer was by her forlorn expression, but hoping against hope that it would be otherwise all the same.

Her shoulders slumped.

"He was so angry that I would even contemplate such a thing." She paced the cramped confines of his cell. "He started questioning me. I had to lie. If he were to find out that I came to see you, he would forbid me from ever coming again."

A hollow, gaping hole punched through Dacian's chest, as if an invisible hand had reached in and ripped out his heart. What he had long dreaded—what he knew he would eventually have to do, but had avoided until now—had to be done. Though he longed for her friendship and craved the very sight of her, she couldn't return. Not after what she had done. Now it was beyond dangerous for her.

"Perhaps it is for the best."

"What do you mean?"

He heard the waver in her voice, the confusion at his cold tone. He steeled himself, knowing what he was about to say would drive her away. He hated to hurt her, but to protect her, he would.

"This is no place for someone like you." He straightened and nearly choked on the lie of his words. "I do not want you to come back. I wish to never see you again."

She inhaled sharply. He walked to the back of his cell, turning his back on the pain he was deliberately inflicting on her.

He ran his finger along the mortar between two stones, choosing his words carefully. The desire to see her and the need to shield her were tearing him apart. But he couldn't let her come to care for him, to feel for him what he was beginning to feel for her. Because if she did, it would destroy her to have to watch him die.

"When everything in life is pain, then the horror of it is always the same, and it does not seem so bad. But when I have a glimpse of what happiness can be, it reminds me how hopeless everything actually is."

He turned to look at her and prayed that she would understand. Every day, the joy of her being here followed by the desolation of watching her leave was killing him as surely as if he stood in the arena without sword or shield.

"Being with you makes me want something I can never have."

She sank down on his bed. "Is there no way out for you? No way for us to be together?"

He leaned his back against the wall.

"Only if I can stay alive and win at the games, then I might earn my freedom. But that takes years, and each match I win means another man loses, another man dies. I do not know if I can keep killing, even if it is to save my own life."

The color leached from her face. "But you must stay alive."

"Why? What life would I have outside the arena, even if I could gain my freedom? You know as well as I that slave gladiators are treated with no more respect than the lowest of whores. I have been trained to kill. That is all I know."

"What will you do then?"

Dacian shook his head, looking off into the distance, anywhere but at her pleading face.

"I do not know. The last time I was in the arena, I had given up. I was ready to die." His gaze returned to lock with hers. "But you stopped it. You took the choice away from me just as surely as these walls take away my freedom."

Sabina jerked as if he had struck her.

"I am sorry," she said, her tone curt. "I thought you would want to live."

"And I thought I wanted to die. But when I looked up and saw you standing there, so brave and proud, for a moment I thought maybe there was a reason for me to go on. A reason to fight to live." He raised his arms, indicating the confines of his cell. "But then they brought me back here, to these cold stone walls to wait for the next games, the next chance to die, and I wondered again if I should not just give up."

"Dacian, no." Sabina rose to her feet. "Do not give up. Do

not ever give up."

She reached out and touched his arm. He flinched, like an animal unaccustomed to human contact. He pulled away from her, because he was—nothing more than a caged animal.

"No matter what happens, I care. I care whether you live or die."

"Why?"

The single word a challenge. He still did not understand it, why someone like her would care for someone like him.

"Why not? What makes you less worthy than any other man?"

"I am not like other men." Dacian snorted, his lip curling in disdain. "You should be with some senator's son, eating figs and drinking wine. Not locked in a filthy gladiator's cell with a trained killer."

"You sound just like my father." Sabina stalked a few steps away. "It appears we are both trapped in our own prisons."

Something in her voice made him pause.

"What do you mean?"

"My father intends to find me a husband the next time we go to Rome." She fisted her hands at her sides. "I could just scream at the irony of it all. You cannot buy your freedom, and mine is about to be sold."

She spun around and waved one hand up and down the length of her body. "Behold, a piece of merchandise to be auctioned off to the highest bidder who can cushion my father's purse and improve my uncle's career. Like you, I have no choice in my own fate."

He could feel Sabina's desperation and hopelessness, and it nearly mirrored his own. Even though he hadn't the right, he wanted to howl at the thought of her in another man's arms, another man's bed.

"So you see, I am just as trapped as you are. I know how you feel. The very thought of being possessed by a man I do not love makes me wish for death, too."

Cold rage coiled within him that she would think to embrace so casually that which he faced every day. He reached

Sabina in two strides.

"You know nothing of death." Dacian grabbed her by her shoulders and shook her. "Not until you have faced it, smelled its breath, and tasted it in your mouth. Not until you have seen fear reflected in another man's eyes as you spill his life's blood onto the sand of the arena. You may be trapped, but your prison has gold bars and silk pillows. You sleep on a soft bed and awake each morning to know that you will live another day. You want for nothing in your life."

Sabina struggled within his grasp. He knew he was scaring her, but he didn't care. She should be afraid.

"Stop it!"

"You little fool. How can you even begin to think about dying? Long after I have lost my last battle in the arena, you will be secure in your life, happy in your marriage and the children it will bring. You will have everything you could possibly want, living in your fine villa with your powerful husband."

"But I don't want any of that!"

"Then what do you want?" he growled.

She tried to pull away from him, but he would not release her. Instead, he pulled her closer until they were chest to chest, and she was forced to look him in the eye.

"What is it you want, Sabina?"

"You!"

She instantly stopped fighting him. They both stood still, frozen by the meaning behind that single word.

"I want you, Dacian." She spoke the last words so softly, he wasn't certain she'd said them at all.

All the air was ripped from Dacian's lungs. He found it difficult to breathe, and the sound of his blood pounding in his ears nearly drowned out the thunderous beating of his heart.

He could not believe the fates would torture him so.

She leaned into him, so close that he feared she could feel him tremble, that she would know how her words made him want to drop to his knees from the need of her.

Sabina reached up, gently touching his lips with her fingertips.

"I want you," she whispered.

Dacian groaned and pulled her into his arms. He knew it was wrong, that he should send her away and beg her never to return. But if he never saw her again, if he were to die tomorrow in the arena, at least he could take this one moment with him.

Bending his head forward, Dacian touched his mouth to the beautiful lips that had just spoken words he never thought to hear. So soft, Sabina yielded to him, opening herself up to the long-dead emotions pouring out from the depths of his soul.

Unable to restrain himself, his tongue traced the fullness of her lips, then plunged inside to taste the honey of her mouth. Pure pleasure shot through him as her tiny tongue darted out to explore him, too. She moaned, the sound echoing the feelings raging inside his body. He felt her quiver and knew his own body shuddered with the power of the kiss.

Then the rumbling sound came to his ears, and he realized it wasn't just her kiss that affected him so.

The very ground beneath their feet had started to shake.

Chapter IV

"By the gods, what is happening?" Sabina cried out.

As quickly as it came, the trembling stopped. Dust filtered down from the mortar in the stones, dancing in the last beam of light coming through the barred window in the door.

"I do not know."

The door to the cell flew open and crashed against the wall, startling them both. The guard stood outside, his face a pasty white.

"What is it?" she asked.

"I must secure all the gladiators. You must leave now."

Sabina looked back at Dacian. Alarm mixed with the simmering fire still dancing in his eyes, and she felt cheated that her time with him had been cut so short.

She started to leave, then turned back and threw herself into his arms, squeezing him tight. He returned her embrace as if he were holding onto hope itself.

"I will return. Tomorrow."

"You should not."

"I know." She smiled as she darted out the door. "But I will anyway."

No bright sunlight blinded Sabina as she left the barracks. Instead, the sky was a dark gray, hinting at an impending summer storm.

Shouting came from the streets where vendors and merchants had their shops and homes. The tap-tap-tap of small white pellets falling like rain on the cobblestone street puzzled her.

Something was terribly wrong.

A man rushed past, knocking her down in his haste. Sabina

stumbled to her feet and started to run. She had to find her father. He would know what was happening. He would know what to do.

Rushing through the crowded streets, Sabina arrived at their villa to find the slaves rushing about, throwing household belongings into sacks and crates. Broken crockery littered the tiled floor, abandoned where it had been dropped.

Sabina found her father in his chamber, frantically tossing some of their most precious items into a large satchel.

"Father, what is happening?"

He looked up, relief easing the creases on his brow.

"The gods are angry. They are throwing stones down from the skies upon our heads. We must leave the city at once."

"Leave?" Alarm traced icy fingers down her back.

"Yes. Quickly, pack your things. One of the wine carts has been readied and is standing outside. We will head for Rome."

"But, Father, it was just the earth rumbling. It has been happening for weeks. Why do we leave now?"

Her father pointed at the ceiling as if she could see through the clay tiles to the sky above.

"Look to the sky, Sabina, and you will see the wrath of the gods. They warned us ten years ago when Pompeii was nearly crushed by the moving of the earth. I do not care to be here when it happens again."

Thinking of Dacian locked in his cell and her promise to come back to him, Sabina tried to make sense of what was happening.

"When will we return?"

"I do not think we shall. We will go to Rome, where it is safe and civilized."

Dread seized her. "But we cannot leave Pompeii forever. What of our family and friends?"

What of Dacian?

Her father pushed past her, lugging the bulging sack to the main atrium where the slaves were stacking anything of value to be loaded into the waiting cart. Sabina followed quickly on his heels.

"Can you not see?" He pointed out the open door where people dashed back and forth in the street like frenzied ants. "Everyone is abandoning the city. If we do not hurry, the inns in Rome will be filled when we arrive. Now, go and pack your things. We leave within the hour."

She would be leaving Dacian. She would never see him again.

No. It was too soon. Not when she had just found him.

Sabina ran to her room and grabbed any item of value, anything with which she might bargain—a silver goblet and tray, her combs carved from mother-of-pearl, the wooden box containing the last of her mother's gold jewelry.

Throwing it all into her *palla*, she folded up the cloth and raced to the front of the villa.

"Sabina!" her father called out as she darted past his chamber. "Where are you going? The cart is out back."

"I have to go to Dacian."

He followed her down the hall and grabbed her by the arm, spinning her around.

"Dacian? Who is Dacian?"

"He is the gladiator I told you about."

"*A gladiator?*" Anger mottled his sweat-beaded face. "He is not your concern. The guards will take care of them."

Sabina remembered the fear on the guards' faces. She did not have such faith in them.

Her father shoved her in the direction of the back of the villa.

"Now, stop this nonsense, and pack what you can."

"I have to go, Father."

"Sabina, we cannot wait." Her father pointed at the entrance of their home. "Look, now the streets are nearly covered. Soon we may not be able to get out of the city with the wagons."

She looked out the open doorway. The stones fell heavier, their sound muffled by the growing layer of white ash that covered the cobblestones.

"There is time. I will return soon."

"No. We must leave now."

"Then, go without me. I will catch up to you when I can."

"I forbid it!" Her father grabbed at her, but she slipped out of his reach.

She backed away, shaking her head and regretting the hurt she saw on her father's face.

"You cannot stop me. I have to go to him."

Looking one last time at her father, she turned and dashed out into the crowded street.

ᛈᛟᛗᛈᛖᛁᛁ

Sabina reached the barracks, only to find the gate locked. She shook the iron bars in frustration.

"Let me in!"

Desperation tasted as bitter as the dust that lodged in her throat. What if the guards had already fled? How would she get to Dacian?

Then she saw men on the training field, guards and gladiators alike in their fear, running about aimlessly.

"Open the gates!" she shouted at them.

Finally, a young guard appeared before her.

"Let me in."

"You cannot enter now. We are all leaving."

Hope surged within her. Was it possible that they were going to set Dacian free?

"The gladiators, too?"

The guard shook his head.

"Only the free ones. The slaves and prisoners will be locked in until it is safe to return."

Sabina gripped the iron bars tighter.

"But you cannot just leave them here!"

"We cannot take them with us. We do not have enough men to keep them under control outside the gates. It would be our heads should even one escape. They will be safe enough in their cells."

She thrust the *palla* through the bars, holding it open so that he could glimpse the small treasure inside.

"I will pay dearly for the Myrmillo Dacian's freedom. Let me in, and all this is yours." Seeing the indecision on the guard's face, Sabina pushed on. "It is enough so that you can live comfortably for years wherever you go. You will never have to return to Pompeii to face the consequences of one missing gladiator."

The guard looked hesitant. The earth trembled again, and his decision was made. Throwing open the gate, he grabbed the bundle from her hands.

"Go. Find your lover," he shouted over his shoulder as he shoved past her. "And may the gods have mercy on you both."

Sabina raced across the training field, surprised to see some of the free gladiators—trained warriors and killers in the arena—running about with terror on their hardened faces. She made her way to the slave area of the barracks and found Dacian's cell with surprising ease despite the madness. She slid back the bolt, and Dacian was in her arms before the heavy wooden door fully opened.

"You came back."

Feeling safe and secure for the first time in what seemed like hours, she squeezed him tighter.

"I told you I would."

"But how—"

Sabina grabbed his hand and pulled him through the door.

"We must hurry. Everyone is leaving the city."

Dashing out onto the shadowed portico surrounding the training field, Sabina could hear the desperate cries of the prisoners and slave gladiators left behind, locked in their cells.

Dacian stopped, looking at the barred doors lining the columned walkway.

"We have to help them."

"There is no time."

"We must try." Charging to a cell door, Dacian slid the bolt back and released the man inside. With only a moment's hesitation, Sabina rushed to the next door. As the ground trembled again beneath their feet, the terrified men stumbled out onto the practice field, confused at the sudden gift of freedom.

Dacian staggered back as he threw open the last door at the end of the portico.

"Bellator!"

Sabina looked inside the cell to see three gladiators sitting on the dusty floor, straining at the chains that bound them to the stone wall in punishment for some forgotten crime. One of them appeared to be Dacian's friend.

Dacian found the lock at the end of the chain, but unlike the cell doors, it required a special tool to remove the pin. She glanced around, but no such key was to be found.

"I cannot get it open," he roared in desperation as he tried to pry the iron nail from its hole with his fingertips. "The pin will not come out."

A fierce rumble shook the barracks. The wall behind them collapsed, and dust filled the air, making Sabina choke. She pulled on Dacian's arm.

"It is no use. We must leave now."

Dacian shook his head. He wasn't ready to give up yet. He wedged his foot against the wall and pulled at the chains where they attached to the stones, trying to release the men with the strength of his bare hands. Sabina watched the muscles of his neck and arms tense from the effort, sweat beading on his forehead.

Finally, he stopped straining, exhausted. He shook the iron links in frustration, as if by doing so they might crumble to dust as easily as the unsteady walls around them.

"I cannot leave them here. They will not have a chance."

"But we do not have the key. Dacian, please. You cannot save them all." His own words echoed through her head, words he'd spoken to her the first time she came to him in the dark confines of his cell. *You cannot save us all.* This time, she knew it to be true.

She glanced at Bellator, and they shared a look filled with remorse. *I am sorry.* Sabina mouthed the words to him, and the gladiator nodded, bravely resigned to his fate.

Dacian looked at her, his face devoid of hope, full of agony and misery at the futility of it all. What would become of his friends, these men in chains?

"Go," Bellator said to him in a voice calm with the acceptance of death. "Perhaps you will be one of the lucky ones. Go, my friend. Do not look back."

Dacian squeezed Bellator's arm in silent regret. Then he grabbed Sabina's hand, and they ran.

POMPEII

As they dashed down the cobblestone streets, people bumped into one another from all sides, trampling those who could not keep up.

Terrified mothers grabbed for their children, and men rushed to gather what belongings they could carry. Others took advantage of the confusion and pillaged the merchants' shops and villas. Food sat on vendors' stoves, pots boiling over, unattended. Urns and lamps were knocked into the street, their flames spreading in the spilled oils.

Sabina led Dacian down the street toward the *Porta Stabia*. Overturned carts blocked the road at the narrow passageway. Abandoned by their masters, frightened oxen and mules pulled in vain at their twisted harnesses. There would be no escape from Pompeii through there.

Backtracking, Sabina and Dacian pushed against the crowd toward the *Porta Nuceria*, the falling stones and ash now rising to their knees in some places. They passed dogs howling to be released from the chains tethering them to the houses they had been left to guard.

Dacian glanced up at a sky grown dark with thick clouds holding back the sun. The afternoon turned as black as night, adding to the confusion in the streets. The pungent smell of sulfur filled the air, making them cough and choke.

He jerked to an abrupt halt as Sabina stumbled and fell. Her crumpled body lay on the ground, her hand still clutched in his. Her dazed eyes stared at the ground, and blood trickled from a wound on her head where a falling rock must have struck her.

Leaning down, he lifted her into his arms. He needed to get

her away from the crowds of frantic people. He needed time to think. Having never been outside the walls of the gladiator barracks on his own, Dacian wasn't sure how to get out of the city.

People dashed within the chaos, while others lay deathly still in the streets, unlucky ones who, like Sabina, had fallen victim to the stones tossed down from above.

Dacian darted into a merchant's shop, the vendor's wares abandoned as if the shopkeeper had just stepped out for a moment. He carried Sabina to the back and was surprised to find a man, woman, and three children huddled in the shadows.

"Is your wife injured?" the woman asked.

"She is not my…" He paused, realizing they had not noticed his slave belt. Otherwise, she would not have made the assumption nor offered them aid. "Yes. Can you help her?"

Dacian laid Sabina down on the cool tile of the shop floor, and the woman bent over her to wipe at the blood on Sabina's face.

He looked at the man.

"Thank you for allowing us to come into your shop."

"Oh, this is not our shop. My children could not go on any longer, so we came in to seek shelter from the falling stones. We will wait here until it is safe again." The man glanced at the gladiator slave belt, visible now that Dacian was no longer holding Sabina in his arms. He looked Dacian in the eye, a silent warning in the father's hard stare. "You and your *wife* are welcome to take shelter with us."

Relief eased Dacian's mind. Though he did not like it, the man likely realized a gladiator with fighting skills might come in handy against the panicked masses in the streets.

Sabina groaned, and Dacian turned to her.

"She will be fine," the woman said. "It is merely a scratch."

He sat down on the floor with his back against the wall and pulled Sabina into his lap, letting her head lay against his chest.

"Rest. We will stay here for a while."

Sabina snuggled closer to him.

"That sounds wise." She placed her small hand in his, entwining their fingers. "Husband."

Dacian squeezed her tight, clutching at the impossible dream of the beautiful girl in his arms ever being his.

ᛈᛟᛗᛈᛖᛁᛁ

They hid in the shop and held each other close as the world fell down around them. Pebbles and ash rained down into the room from the opening in the roof. As each hour passed, the hill of stone and rubble filling the merchant's cistern grew taller and overflowed, forcing them all to climb the ladder to the second story to avoid being buried alive.

There they waited, until outside all suddenly grew quiet.

"Is it over?" The man shifted a child on his lap as his wife held the other two to her side.

"Do you think it is safe to leave?" she asked him.

Dacian listened. Not a sound could be heard from the street. The stones had ceased to fall, and the world seemed to stand still.

"Let us go now," he said, "while we have the chance."

They crawled out an open window near the roof of the building and emerged into a changed world. The ground now rose to meet second story windows and rooftops. It was impossible to tell what time of day it was. The sky was black with smoke, the sun gone from view as if the gods had plucked it from the sky.

Dacian and Sabina looked toward the mountain, unable to see its majestic peak in the distance. Floating soot burned their eyes, and they had to cover their mouths to breathe. They turned and followed the merchant's family, stumbling over the debris filling the streets as they tried to make their way to the city gates.

They had taken no more than a few steps when an enormous blast rent the air, nearly knocking them off their feet. The sound of a thousand chariots roared closer and closer.

Panic seized them all.

"Run!" Dacian shouted.

The heat wave hit them first, the blast of hot air slamming them all to the ground. Dacian covered Sabina's body with his own in a desperate effort to shield her. His large warrior's hand cupped her head, pressing her face into his chest. A rush of searing wind surrounded them, the hot gases sucking the air from his lungs.

Dacian's eyes stung, and Sabina's image blurred before him. He could feel her thrashing beneath him, struggling for a precious breath of air. But there was none.

All too soon, Sabina went still in his arms, her eyes closing as if in peaceful slumber. Dacian took one last look at her beloved face, then laid his head down next to hers.

As they held each other in an eternal embrace, the ashes continued to fall, covering them like a gentle blanket of snow.

Chapter V

"Well, I'd have to say you were right about the sparks."

Smithers clicked the remote control, and the screen disappeared into the clouds.

Marsha gasped. "Oh dear, what was that?"

"It's called an eruption. Volcanoes do that every now and then."

"Well, nobody told me about a scheduled natural disaster." Marsha turned and glared at Hershel. "Did you know anything about this?"

"Me? No, no. Of course not."

Smithers drummed his fingers on his desk. "It was in the memo. Didn't either of you read it?"

Marsha looked at Smithers with wide owl eyes.

"Memo? What memo?"

Smithers sighed deeply and rubbed at his frown-creased forehead.

"The one that came out at the turn of the century. It had all the scheduled natural disasters listed, including this one."

"Oh, pooh. How am I expected to remember back that far?"

"That was only seventy-nine years ago. It was almost yesterday."

Marsha reached over and swatted Hershel on the arm.

"Why didn't you remind me?"

Hershel scooted out of harm's reach before she could bat at him again.

"If you couldn't remember it, how do you think I was supposed to? You're the one who always keeps track of that sort of thing."

Marsha turned to face her boss, pulling her gray knit sweater more tightly around her frail frame. She put on her most business-like demeanor and even had the bravado to look down her nose at him—or at least try to.

"Apparently neither of us received that memo. You know how messed up the deliveries can be around here sometimes. Why, I remember once—"

"It really doesn't matter now, does it?" Smithers picked up a document from his desk and waved it in front of them. "Do you know what this is?"

Marsha squinted at the fluttering paper, trying to read the small print. Hershel nearly fell out of his chair as he tried to lean closer to get a good look at it.

"It's their contract. A contract you both signed back when Male 2028 was conceived and Female 5923 was well into the planning stages."

Smithers pulled a pair of bifocals from his breast pocket and perched them on his hawk-like nose.

"It clearly states here that these two mortals are to join, go forth and multiply, live a long and prosperous life, then report directly to their assignments up here when their time on Earth is over." Smithers removed his glasses and set them and the contract carefully on his desk. "They can't very well do that when they're dead, now, can they?"

"No, I don't suppose they can," Hershel replied.

"So, what do you two propose we do about this little situation?" Smithers looked at them as if the answer should be quite obvious.

"Well, we could... maybe..." Hershel finally shrugged. "I don't know. What's usually done in a situation like this?"

Smithers slapped his hands down on his desk. "Situations like this don't happen. *He* doesn't like it when things don't go according to plan."

Marsha held up her hand, a tiny space showing between her thumb and forefinger. "Perhaps we could get permission for a teenie, weenie miracle?"

"And just what kind of miracle were you thinking of?"

"I don't know." Marsha shrugged. "*He* could raise them from the dead. *He* did it with Lazarus, after all."

"Lazarus was an old man buried in a cool, dark crypt. And his resurrection was planned, I might add. However, your clients have been barbecued from the inside out and buried under fifteen feet of ash, rock, and what's left of that mountain. There's not exactly a great deal left of them to raise, even if *He* was inclined to do so."

"Oh, dear." Marsha cast a worried look Hershel's way. "Whatever shall we do?"

"Don't look at me. I wasn't the one who thought the Mediterranean would be a lovely place for them to fall in love."

"It was a lovely place, until that volcano had to go and spoil everything."

"Enough!" Smithers growled. He glared at them for what seemed like an eternity and then scribbled something down on a piece of paper. "Although this is highly irregular, I'm going to approve for Female 5923 and Male 2028 to have another life. You two find an appropriate place and time for them. And for heaven's sake, don't let anything go wrong this time."

POMPEII

The chamomile tea was exactly the right temperature and flavored with just a hint of lemon. It did wonders to warm old bones. As Marsha raised the dainty china cup decorated with delicate pink flowers for another sip, she spied Hershel reaching for his second piece of pound cake.

A voice whispering in her ear made Marsha nearly spill the tea all over Eleanor Donnelly's prize lace tablecloth.

"Mr. Smithers needs to see you both in his office. Now."

Looking over her shoulder, she spied the messenger angel standing behind her in his crisp white suit, clipboard held firmly in hand. He wore his short black hair slicked back and a pair of half-bifocals perched on the end of his pointy nose.

Marsha glanced at Hershel, who had stopped in mid-chew with cake crumbs poking out of the corner of his mouth. He swallowed with obvious difficulty as her teacup clattered in its matching saucer.

"Whatever could he want to see us for now?" She feigned innocence, even as Hershel stared at the messenger, his eyes bugging out in fish-eyed guilt.

"I believe there has been another problem with your clients."

"Oh, dear." Marsha's shoulders slumped in defeat. "Not again."

"You'd better hurry," the angel prodded. "He doesn't look very pleased."

"Does he ever?" Hershel asked as he scooted his chair back.

"I've never seen him this angry before," the angel said as he motioned for them to speed up. "In fact, I even heard him say something about a permanent reassignment."

"For our clients?" Marsha asked.

"No, for you two."

"Oh my, this does sound serious." She stood up and brushed nonexistent crumbs from her sweater. "Come, Hershel, we'd best hurry."

Hershel took Marsha's arm and, with one last longing look at his half-eaten cake, followed behind the messenger angel like a naughty boy headed for the principal's office.

Ushered by the same overly cheerful secretary into the cloud office they were becoming all too familiar with, Hershel and Marsha took their respective seats.

The statue of Apollo had been replaced with a large and rather colorful painting by an artist named Picasso. The odd placement of the subject's features gave Marsha the willies. One eye appeared to be looking off to the side while the other seemed to be staring directly at her, daring her to deny her guilt.

SGA Smithers entered the office and walked around them to stand at his desk. He threw a handful of papers on the tabletop and sat down without acknowledging their presence. Reaching out his hands, he calmly placed them on either side of the stack of papers.

His quiet demeanor unnerved Marsha. She'd much rather

have him yelling and screaming at her than this calm reserve. She had absolutely no idea what he was thinking.

Finally he looked at them, staring first at her and then at Hershel. Marsha could hear Hershel squirming in his chair without looking at him. It took everything in her not to squirm a little herself.

"Do you mind telling me what the problem is with your two clients?"

"Well, Mr. Smithers, it seems we've run into a few minor glitches with them."

"A few *minor* glitches? I don't call sending these people back not once, not twice, but three times a minor glitch. It's been over eighteen centuries since this whole fiasco started, they've been returned three times, and you two still haven't gotten it right. What is it going to take?"

Marsha cleared her throat.

"Well, to be honest, not all of it was our fault."

"Not your fault?" Smithers's bushy brows rose so high on his forehead that Marsha thought they were going to disappear into his scalp. "How is it not your fault? Please explain it to me."

"Well, first there was the volcano incident."

"I know, I know. You missed the natural disaster memo. We've been over that one." Smithers picked up a paper from the stack in front of him. "It says here that you then sent them back to the fifth century. Ah, I see that Female 5923 did get married."

Marsha nodded in agreement.

"Yes, as a matter of fact she did."

"To Attila the Hun! Exactly how did that mix-up happen?"

Marsha placed her hands on her knees, trying to stop them from shaking beneath her navy wool skirt.

"Well, it was all planned that she was to be betrothed to Attila, but Male 2028 was supposed to save her before the actual wedding took place."

"Yes, I'm listening."

"Apparently there was a typo on the relocation application

for Male 2028."

"Really?"

"You see, he was supposed to return as a Hun on horse-back."

"And he was sent back as…?"

Marsha and Hershel glanced nervously at each other.

"A monk with a hunchback," Hershel mumbled as he sank lower in his chair.

"I see. And did either of you proof the relocation form before it was sent down?"

"I thought Hershel had done it."

Hershel looked at Marsha as if she had just implicated him in a murder.

"Me? I thought you did it."

Smithers held up his hand, effectively halting what could have turned into a full-blown spat. He glanced down at the paper in his hand and then back at the two of them.

"So, Attila died on his wedding night."

Marsha raised her finger in the air. "Now, that was planned."

"Yes, I know. However, he was supposed to die a brutal warrior's death. It was the least he deserved. After all, he wasn't called the Scourge of God for nothing."

"Yes, well, things got a bit out of hand."

"A bit out of hand? The girl clobbered him in the face with a serving tray. She knocked him unconscious, and the man died of a nosebleed in his own marriage bed."

"Could you blame her?" Marsha huffed. "I certainly wouldn't want to see that filthy, drunk barbarian coming at me with lust on his mind."

Smithers closed his eyes and shook his head.

"It doesn't matter now. At least Attila reached *his* final destination on time. So what went wrong with the two of them after that?"

"Well, Male 2028 did rescue her as planned."

Drumming his fingers on the desk, Smithers looked expectantly at each of them.

Marsha and Hershel exchanged wary glances. Finally, Hershel spoke.

"His mule trampled him to death while they were trying to escape."

"How unfortunate. Not altogether surprising, considering you two, but unfortunate nonetheless. So, what became of Female 5923?"

"It seems she spent the rest of her life hiding in the Caspian Mountains from the Huns, who wanted to execute her for killing Attila."

Smithers breathed a heavy sigh.

"I supposed that's understandable, given the circumstances."

He picked up a second piece of paper. If it were possible, Smithers's scowl deepened even further.

"I'm not sure I even want to go into the Middle Ages episode. Why, they didn't even manage to meet each other that time."

Marsha shuddered, the memory of that past life still fresh in her mind.

"Well, they might have if it hadn't been for that nasty Black Death thing going around."

"Yes, sending him back as a rat catcher during the plague wasn't the brightest of ideas, was it?"

Marsha cast her eyes down to her hands clasped tightly in her lap. Hershel tried to look anywhere else but at Smithers.

Scanning further down the page, Smithers read on.

"I see while I was on vacation, you two managed to send them back for a third time."

"Yes, well, it didn't seem like it would hurt."

"No, at this point I suppose it wouldn't have hurt… if they had been sent back so they could have been reasonably close in age."

Marsha glared at her husband. "That was his fault."

Hershel grew pale, small beads of sweat popping out on his shiny bald head.

"Tell him, Hershel."

Hershel cleared his throat and tugged at the edges of his cardigan sweater, trying to regain some composure.

"Well, you see, they were showing a replay of the Thirty Years War at the Cineplex, and I didn't want to miss it."

"Apparently, that was why you were thirty years late getting Male 2028 to the drop off station?"

Marsha jumped to Hershel's defense.

"At least we got them to meet that time."

Smithers rubbed his temples in circles, pressing so hard that Marsha thought he might pop his eyes out of their sockets.

"Having her nearly run over him with her carriage is hardly what I would call 'meeting.' And besides, he was only thirteen, and she was what? Nearly fifty?"

"Forty-three," Marsha corrected him. "And age wouldn't have mattered once he'd grown to manhood."

Smithers stopped rubbing and looked at Marsha.

"Yes, unfortunately she died before that could happen, didn't she?"

"How was I supposed to know that the lead in her cosmetics was lethal?"

"Well, we know that now, don't we?"

Smithers clasped his hands together and laid them on top of the papers on his desk.

"If it were up to me, I'd have you both reassigned to something with less responsibility, such as snowflake design or sand grain inventory. As it is, *He* wants you both to see this thing through to the end."

"*He* does?" Marsha and Hershel said in unison.

"Yes, but there is a condition."

Marsha was afraid to ask. "What's that?"

"You're both to go on location."

"On location?"

"Yes, you will return to Earth and personally supervise Male 2028 and Female 5923 to make sure their contract is fulfilled this time."

"Go down there?" They looked at each other. Why, the very

idea was unheard of. "For how long?"

"For as long as it takes." Smithers pointed his finger at them. "Remember, this is your last chance to get this right. For heaven's sake, these people aren't cats. They're not supposed to have nine lives."

Posterity, posterity, this is your concern...
Be attentive.
Twenty times, since the creation of the sun
has Vesuvius blazed, never without a horrid
destruction of those that hesitate to fly.
This is a warning, that it may never
seize you unapprised.
The womb of this mountain is pregnant with
bitumen, alum, iron, gold, silver, nitre,
and fountains of water.
Sooner or later it kindles, and when the sea
rushes in, will give birth vent...
If you are wise, hear this speaking stone.
Neglect your domestic concerns, neglect your
goods, and chattels, there is no delaying.
Fly.

Anno Domini
in the reign of Philip IV, Emmanuele Fonseca, Viceroy, 1632
From a plaque inscribed in Latin
and erected in the village of Portici,
warning its citizens of the evil of Vesuvius

CHAPTER VI

June, 1943
Pompeii, Italy

Serafina blew softly on the dirt, effectively puffing away nearly two thousand years of dust and ash from the object hidden beneath.

A speck of shiny silver glinted at her in the bright afternoon sun. She held her breath, fighting the urge to dig her hands deep in the dirt and rip the priceless artifact from its earthen tomb.

Years of study and practice had taught her restraint at times like this, even while the excitement of discovery pounded through her veins.

She lay prostrate in the dirt with a small pick in one hand and a soft brush in the other and began the arduous task of unearthing her prize one grain of dirt at a time.

After an hour of backbreaking work, the relic was partially exposed. Serafina inspected what appeared to be a large silver cup still half-buried in the ground. Raised skeletons depicting scenes of celebration covered the exterior. She shifted to allow more sunlight to shine on the cup. Brushing the last layer of dust from its surface revealed an engraved inscription around the rim.

VIVO DUM VOS HABEO CRASTINUS INCERTUS.
Enjoy life while you have it, for tomorrow is uncertain.

The irony of the words struck Serafina as she traced her finger over the intricate carvings. There had been no tomorrow for the unlucky citizens of Pompeii.

"Well, well. What have we found here?"

She didn't have to look up. Giovanni Ragusa's deep voice was all too familiar.

"I should think that would be obvious. It's a pre-Columbian urinal."

She heard him growl behind her. As usual, he did not appreciate her sarcasm.

He squatted beside her and tried to edge her away with his shoulder.

"Very funny. Let me see that."

Serafina fought the urge to cover the object with her arm like a child hiding a test from a cheating classmate.

"No, it's my find. Go dig in your own hole."

He sat back on his heels, a look of disdain marring his handsome features.

"As senior archeologist on this site, this whole damn city is my hole."

"I think Signore Moretti would have to disagree with that," she said, referring to the Director of Excavations.

"Senior archeologist in charge of this region, then." Giovanni brushed at the dust on his pants, dust that was ever-present on anyone digging in the ruins. "Which makes me *your* superior, at least. Now let me see it."

Serafina hated when he was right, especially since he never hesitated to point out each and every occasion to her. She slowly stood and stepped back, giving him access to the silver cup.

Looking down on his dark head, she wondered how she had ever thought he was attractive.

She took that back. He was handsome—a handsome ass. His good looks and smooth talk had fooled her once, years ago. But she had learned her lesson the hard way, and since then he did nothing but irritate her.

She watched as he bent to examine the cup. She allowed him this one liberty, but stopped him when he reached to pull it out of the ground.

"As senior archeologist, you should know procedure by now. The find has to be documented and photographed in place before it's removed."

Giovanni stood, his eyes narrowed to slits as he glared down his hawk-like nose at her.

"You're so right. Well, go on, then. Get the camera, and document your find. What's one small tin cup compared to what I've discovered so far?"

"Only one more that you didn't find."

Serafina turned on her heel and left him standing there.

How did the man have the ability to get under her skin so? Of course, he had more experience, and as a result, more credited finds, which he never stopped reminding her of. But that was going to change. She would eat dirt before she let him think he was a better archeologist just because he was a man.

Hurrying to a previously excavated Roman villa now used as a temporary supply building, she grabbed the Brownie camera and a documentation form.

The excitement of the discovery quickly returned. She had been digging at the Pompeii ruins for three years, and the silver cup was her biggest find so far. Oh, she had done her share of assisting in the excavation of other archeologists' great finds, but this one was hers. All hers.

As she returned to her dig site, she saw Giovanni standing over her find with Alfonso Moretti and his assistant, Heberto.

Apprehension pooled in the pit of her stomach as she approached. The men seemed oblivious to her presence at first. Then Giovanni looked up, an expression of false surprise on his face.

"Ah, I see you finally showed up with the camera."

He snatched the camera from her and prepared to photograph the silver cup.

"As you can see," he said to the men as he looked through the viewfinder on the top of the box camera, "from what I've unearthed so far, the cup seems to be in perfect condition."

Serafina nearly choked.

"What *you've* unearthed?"

Giovanni raised his head and turned to her.

"*Sì*, although I will have to admit that Signorina Pisano did assist a little with the excavation."

"*Maledicali!* That's my find, Giovanni, and you know it."

She lunged at him, wanting to claw out his eyes, but Heberto grabbed her by the arm before she nearly trampled the silver cup.

Giovanni shook his head at her.

"Poor Serafina. I warned Signore Moretti that you might do this." He turned to the director. "She has been upset lately, since she has yet to make a significant find of her own."

She lunged again, nearly breaking free of Heberto's grip. He held her with the strength of a young man, even though he was old enough to be her grandfather.

"You son-of-a—"

"There now." Moretti patted her shoulder as if he were consoling a child. "You will have your chance to make your own discoveries, Serafina. For now, let Giovanni do his work."

"But—"

"You heard the director," Giovanni smiled, but his obvious lack of respect for her showed in his eyes. "Why don't you go find your own little hole to dig in, and leave the serious archeology to men with more experience?"

She reeled, the impact of her own words thrown back in her face felt like a physical slap.

How dare he do this to her?

Heberto turned Serafina and started walking her away.

"Take heart, little one. Everything will work out for the best. There are greater things for you to discover. I am certain of it."

Serafina barely heard the older man's kind words. She looked back over her shoulder, unable to believe what had happened.

Giovanni Ragusa had just stolen her find.

POMPEII

David Corbin walked up to the main entrance of Pompeii, his heart in his throat.

So far, so good.

No one seemed to pay him any attention. With his civilian clothing, black hair, and dark features, he blended in easily with the Italian people on the street. It was one of the reasons he had been hand-picked for this assignment. That, and the fact that he spoke fluent Italian and passable German. They were skills that kept him from the front lines for the time being, much to his war-hero father's disappointment.

The old man might be proud of him, if he knew what David was doing and where he was. But he didn't. No one did, except for David's unit stationed far away on the coast of Africa.

Sent to spy on the Germans encamped near Pompeii, he was to find out if the rumors were true that they were hiding munitions within the ruins. It was simple, really. Hire on at the dig site, observe their movements, and report back to headquarters when he located the hidden munitions.

Simple, as long as he didn't get shot along the way. Unfortunately, if anyone discovered he was an American on enemy soil, that's just what might happen.

His first sight of the ruins surprised him as he walked through the *Porta Marina*. He wasn't sure what he had expected. Maybe a group of old men poking around a bunch of rocks with shovels in their hands. Certainly not a complete city with standing buildings and streets. Granted, the buildings had no roofs, and some were missing a wall or two, but it was a city nonetheless.

Clusters of people milled about, and he picked up bits and pieces of their conversations. Tourists mostly, from what he could tell. A couple from Hungary stood to his right. Off to his left, a large group of Austrians was trying to figure out a map printed in Italian. And, of course, the Germans. Some were civilians, while others were soldiers in uniform strolling among the ruins. Apparently, even a war didn't stop the tourist trade.

Spotting one of the tour guides, David asked him where to go to find out about hiring on at the site. The man pointed toward a long, narrow street. The uneven cobblestones led

David down an ancient road into the heart of the ruins.

The deeper he walked into the city, the fewer tourists he encountered, since this area had hardly been touched by the archaeologists. With the exception of a few scattered buildings, only the street had been excavated, leaving the vacant facades of the empty homes and shops to watch him as he passed by.

Just as he was suspecting he'd taken a wrong turn, he encountered a bustling hub of activity. Men, young and old, were at work everywhere. Some pushed wheelbarrows filled with dirt down the narrow street, while others labored in shallow pits under white canvas tents to shield them from the hot summer sun.

David scanned the workers, then approached the one who looked like he was in charge. The man inspected him from head to toe, then called out to someone down in one of the holes.

Within moments, a man climbed out of the pit and walked up to David.

"*Buon giorno, signore.* Can I help you?"

He looked down on the little old man who took off his sweat-stained canvas hat to wipe at the beads of perspiration on his forehead. The man was a good foot shorter than David, and his balding head was pink and peeling from sunburn.

"*Sì,* I am looking for work."

The old man nodded and replaced his hat.

"Come with me, then. My name is Heberto, and I am assistant to the Director of Excavations. I'm certain he will hire you. With the war, we are in short supply of young, strong backs." The old man grinned and pointed at himself. "As you can see, some of us are not so strong or young anymore."

They walked past several villas and shops, the cracked plaster walls and gaping doorways silent testimony to the bustling city that once was. David thought it odd that none of the buildings had any windows, at least none facing the street.

They entered one of the ruined villas and walked down a short, narrow hallway. Stepping down into what appeared to be a single large room, he noted that the walls were still covered with faded fresco murals, and the mosaic tile floor appeared to be in almost perfect condition. A large square cut out of the center of the roof allowed light to flood the room.

A man of about sixty sat at a large wooden table near the center of the room examining a small silver cup, while all around him lay piles of cracked pottery, pieces of broken columns, and small, limbless statues.

"Signore Moretti, I have a young man here who seeks work. I think we can find a place for him, *si*?"

The man looked up from his work.

Stepping up to the table, David removed his hat, and the lies he had rehearsed for days tumbled easily from his mouth in flawless Italian.

"My name is David Corbelli," he said, pronouncing his first name the Italian way—*Dah-veed*—and modifying his surname to a similar, local one. "I am from Naples."

The professor eyed him suspiciously. "You are a young man. How is it that you are not fighting in the war?"

"Busted ear drum."

Moretti cocked a questioning brow at him.

"I may not be able to hear the enemy coming, but I'm still strong enough to do a hard day's work."

The man seemed to take him at his word.

"Have you ever worked on an archeological dig before?"

"No, but I am a fast learner."

"Very well, send him over to insula four. We could use more diggers there."

Heberto stepped up beside David, the man's small frame making David feel like a giant beside him.

"Perhaps he could be of use at the *thermopolium*. I'm certain there is plenty of work still to be done there."

Moretti glanced down at the cup in his hand.

"Perhaps you are right. Serafina could use some help."

The decision made, Heberto led David out of the villa and down the street. As they walked, Heberto pointed out various buildings, telling David their names and what the archeologists thought they were used for, but David only half listened. He was paying more attention to possible vantage points, trying to determine in which direction the German camp might lie. Soon, they came to a building were only the front room had been excavated, while the rest remained buried under tons of dirt. They climbed the mound of earth surrounding its exterior wall, and Heberto drew David's attention to a small figure in a shallow pit at the top.

Roomy, tan trousers and a full white shirt did little to hide what was undoubtedly a very feminine figure beneath. David watched the woman digging as they approached. Each vicious jab of her shovel stabbed deep into the defenseless earth. She flung the dirt over her shoulder to fall nowhere near the bucket it was intended to land in.

The woman threw the shovel at the ground in an obvious fit of temper, then dropped to her knees and began digging with her bare hands.

"Serafina," Heberto called as they drew near. "I have brought you someone to help with your digging."

With her back to them and a large-brimmed straw hat on her head, he had yet to see her face. She stopped clawing at the ground and placed her dirt-caked hands on her equally filthy thighs, the rapid rise and fall of her shoulders evidence of her recent exertion.

"This is David Corbelli. The professore has assigned him to work with you."

The woman's knuckles turned white as her fingers squeezed her thighs. Long seconds trickled by like the sweat running down David's temples without a movement from her. Finally, she stood and turned to them. David was shocked, to say the least.

Expecting to see the typical straight dark hair, brown eyes, and olive skin so common among the Southern Italians, instead he was met with large blue eyes and a light, tanned complexion with just a smattering of freckles. Wild tendrils of hair escaped the confines of the hat, but the shadow it created prevented him from telling what color it was. Serafina Pisano looked so wholesome and all-American, he could have plucked her straight off any one of a dozen farms in Virginia.

Then, she opened her mouth, and any illusions he had about her disappeared. A stream of colorful Italian curses flowed off her tongue, some aimed at him, but most directed at the male population in general.

Nope, American she was not. Serafina Pisano was all fire-breathing Italian.

Hands on her hips, she inspected him up and down.

"Great. That's all I need—another hot-blooded male." She turned and stalked off, leaving David and Heberto to stand in her dust.

Watching her storm away, David caught sight of Mount Vesuvius rising silently in the distance beyond the ruins. After witnessing Serafina's explosive eruption, he wondered which was more volatile—the mountain or the woman?

POMPEII

Heberto crept silently into Maria Angelico's home and made his way down the hallway. The house was quiet, the only sound the clattering of dishes in the kitchen sink. Most of the tenants who rented rooms in the villa had not yet returned for the evening.

The old woman's back was to him as he entered the kitchen, her attention focused on the dirty dishes. He tiptoed behind her and reached around to sneak a *zeppole* cooling on a tray on the counter. Without turning, Maria slapped at his hand with a soapy wooden spoon.

He jerked the offending appendage back and cradled it against his chest.

"What did you do that for?"

"You'll spoil your dinner. Besides, we're not in heaven, Hershel." Marsha turned from the sink and shook her index finger at him. "You *can* get fat, your arteries *can* clog, and you *can* have a heart attack. Don't you even think about dying on me and leaving me here alone to finish this job."

"Darn it, Marsha." Hershel pouted. "You're taking all the

fun out of being mortal again."

"We're not here to have fun. We're here to see to it that David and Serafina get together." Marsha handed him one of the warm fritters and motioned him to sit at the small linoleum table before taking the chair opposite him. "So, how are things progressing on your end?"

"Fine. I've managed to get David assigned as her assistant. That should give them plenty of time alone together."

"That's wonderful! And so fast." She reached across the table and patted his hand. "I'm very proud of you."

Hershel shrugged, but beamed all the same at his wife's praise.

"It was nothing, really. Just a little suggestion in the Professore Moretti's ear was all it took."

Marsha bounced in her chair, hardly able to contain her excitement. "Oh, I can't wait to meet him. What's he like?"

"Let me see, he's—"

"Is he handsome?"

"Well, I guess he's—"

"Is he tall or short?"

"I'd say —"

"What about his eyes? Are they blue or green?"

"I think they're—"

"Oh, never mind." Marsha waved her hand at him. "You wouldn't describe him right anyway. I'll just have to find out for myself."

Hershel stared at her with a slack-jawed expression, not daring to say another word.

She put her elbow on the table and rested her chin in the palm of her hand. Her face took on a dreamy glow.

"I can't believe he's finally here. Serafina has been living with us so long, it's like she's our own granddaughter. I thought he would never come, and now he's finally here. After so long, I can't believe it's all starting to happen."

He popped the last morsel of the *zeppole* into his mouth.

"Now, maybe we can finally go home."

"We can't do that. We have to stay until they fall in love."

"Might be a while, then. She wasn't too pleased to have him around. Barely spoke a word to him all day except to tell him where to dig." Hershel used the tip of his finger to pick the crumbs from the tabletop and licked them off, one at a time. "And he kept calling her Simon Legree under his breath."

Marsha's attention snapped back to Hershel.

"Oh, that's not good. Not good at all. I wonder why she doesn't like him? They're soul mates. They should have been immediately drawn to each other. Were they attracted to each other at all?"

"I don't know."

"Of course you don't know. You're a man. Men never know about these things." Marsha *tsked* in exasperation and wiped up the remaining crumbs with a napkin, effectively ending his miniature snacks.

He pouted, then leaned back in his chair.

"I don't see what the problem is. The hard part's over. We got them together. Why can't we let nature take its course?"

Marsha shook her head.

"We did that the last four times, and look where that got us. No, we have to stay on top of things and make sure it goes smoothly from here on out. We have to make sure they fall in love."

"How? I mean, we're mortal now. We can't be with them every minute."

"I know." Marsha stood and walked over to the stove. "You just make sure they don't kill each other at the site, and I'll try to soften up Serafina when she's here."

Hershel came up beside her and peered into the simmering pot of stew. She adjusted his collar, then pulled his head down by the ears and kissed him on his balding scalp before shooing him out of the kitchen.

"After all," she called after him as he headed down the hallway, "how can we expect her to fall in love with him if she doesn't even like him?"

CHAPTER VII

What in the world could be taking him so long?

Serafina might have to take on the new worker as an assistant, but she'd be damned if she was going to babysit him all day long. She'd given him the easier job of removing the sterile ash and volcanic debris. All he had to do was shovel the dirt. Any idiot could do that. She wasn't about to trust him with possibly getting near actual artifacts and damaging them because he didn't know what he was doing.

And now he was gone. Again.

Throwing her trowel in the screening bucket, she rose to her feet and arched her back to stretch her aching muscles. Sitting in one position for hours on end was hard work, not to mention that the dust and ash she inhaled every day were probably not doing her lungs any good.

She needed a break, and she needed to find out where her so-called assistant had gone. When she found him, David Corbelli was going to be fired, if she had anything to do with it.

She started toward the main excavation area, but she hadn't gone far before her long-lost worker caught her eye. His wheelbarrow was empty, so he had obviously just dumped his latest load of dirt at the trucks. He should have been on his way back to her dig site to remove another load, but he wasn't. Instead, he walked down the road pushing his empty wheelbarrow, going right past the turn he should have made.

Where on earth was he going?

Curiosity temporarily cooling her ire, Serafina decided to follow him. Sticking close to the buildings, she shadowed him. He turned down a small side street heading toward the east wall. Why was he going there?

As he walked further away, the stones gradually gave way to dirt and grass rising up an incline, evidence of where the excavations had yet to expand. Every now and then, he would glance behind himself. Did he know he was being followed?

She hurried after him, but by the time she jogged the three blocks to the end of the street, he was nowhere in sight. His wheelbarrow sat abandoned at the base of the inner stone wall that surrounded the city ruins. Glancing up, she spied him perched next to one of the crumbling guard towers built into the wall, staring out into the distance.

What was he looking at?

Determined to find out, Serafina walked to the base of the wall and began scaling the jagged stone steps up the side of the tower.

POMPEII

The late afternoon sun beat down on his shoulders. David pulled his hat lower to shadow his eyes and leaned against the rough stone of the tower.

Italy was damn hot, and it was only the beginning of summer.

Being reduced to doing hard, manual labor didn't help. Things might've been easier if he were a convict on a chain gang. He certainly felt like one. All day long, he shoveled load after backbreaking load of dirt into a wheelbarrow. Then he pushed it down the rutted cobblestone street to trucks waiting to haul away the useless volcanic ash and rock. He did this day after day, while Serafina Pisano sat on her trouser-covered ass in the shade of a canvas awning, scraping at the dirt with a pick no bigger than the one his dentist used to clean his teeth.

Unfortunately, a little reconnaissance had revealed that the German camp was located clear on the opposite side of the ruins. Every time he made the long detour to observe what he could from one of the old guard towers built into the city wall, it took him twice as long to return with the empty wheelbarrow.

He gazed out over the Italian landscape, past small stucco houses and fertile green farms to the modern seaside town of Pompei. He couldn't see the Bay of Naples a mile away, but the Mediterranean breeze occasionally brought the smell of the sea to his lofty vantage point.

Returning his attention to the activity just below him, he laughed to himself. The informants had been right. The German encampment sat right under his nose, just on the other side of the crumbling walls of the ruins. In fact, if David had jumped from the wall, he would have landed in the middle of a group of soldiers taking a smoking break behind a large canvas tent.

From what he could tell so far, the place didn't look like much, but looks could be deceiving. The Allies believed the Germans were using the ruins to hide munitions. His job was to find out if it was true.

The crunch of rock beneath stealthy feet instantly put him on guard. He spun and dove on the intruder, slamming the person to the packed earth that filled the space between the two stone walls surrounding the city. He pulled the knife hidden in his boot and instantly pressed it against the intruder's jugular, biting into soft white skin before he registered who the person was.

"Jesus, Pisano. What are you doing sneaking up on someone like that? I could have killed you."

"I noticed." Startled blue eyes met his, and her small, soft body cushioned him from the hard, rocky soil. "Now get off of me."

He shifted, but then experienced a sudden flash, a small speck of a memory—a time when he had seen her look this way before. She on the ground beneath him. And he on top, covering her body protectively. But he couldn't place it, couldn't quite remember it. Then, just as quickly, she looked away, breaking the connection, and the sensation was gone.

David stood and offered his hand to help her up.

Serafina slapped it away and stood by herself, dusting off the back of her dungarees with angry swipes of her hands.

"What are you doing over here? You're supposed to be working for me."

For a moment, he didn't answer. What could he say that would make sense? What excuse could he make that would not jeopardize his mission?

"I thought this might be a good spot to dig?" It came out as a question, but apparently she took it differently.

"You thought..." She appeared to choke on the words. "*What?*"

David glanced around them while he considered the situation. If he could convince her to dig here, he could keep an eye on the enemy all day. It might make his life a little easier, at least where spying on the Germans was concerned. Serafina, on the other hand, was a different issue.

He grappled for an explanation to appease her.

"Well, you haven't found anything so far where you've been digging."

"Not found anything? I'll have you know—" She stopped abruptly, biting off whatever she had been about to say. "Signore Corbelli, you have only been working here for three days. How can you possibly know what I have and haven't found?"

He shrugged. "Okay, so you haven't found anything while I've been here. Maybe you should try digging somewhere else."

"Excavating a site takes time to do properly. Artifacts are not discovered every day. Sometimes it takes weeks, even months before a significant find turns up." She walked up to him and jabbed her index finger into his chest. "All that is beside the point. I'm the archeologist here. You are the laborer. You dig where I tell you to dig."

David crossed his arms over his chest, forcing her to step back. Now that he'd started down this road, he wasn't about to abandon the idea.

"Just what's so wrong with this spot?"

Serafina looked around, then turned her angry attention back on him.

"Nothing is wrong with this spot, but we do things systematically here. We don't just dig wherever we feel like it. Right now excavations are taking place on the *Via dell'Abbondanza*, and that's where we should be working. Now."

"Well, I think this would be a great spot to dig. It's far away from all the noise of the other digging and…" He gestured over the wall. "We have a beautiful view to enjoy while we work."

"I'm not interested in the view. And you shouldn't be, either, if you want to keep your job."

Her words caught his attention. Being fired would certainly throw a monkey wrench into his mission. Could she do that? Would she?

Just then, Heberto called from the base of the wall, drawing the attention of both of them.

David groaned. Spying on the Germans wasn't going to be easy if everyone working at the ruins decided to stick their noses in his business.

Serafina climbed down the wall, and he followed her, surprised at her agility descending the jagged stones. Most of the women he knew would never have climbed that height in the first place.

When they reached the ground, Heberto was still wheezing due to the long walk from the main dig area and was hunched over with his hands planted on his knees. He gasped for breath, and David worried the old geezer might die from a heart attack right there in front of them.

Serafina went to help the elderly man to straighten up.

Heberto regarded them with incredibly sharp eyes.

"What are you two doing here?"

"*We* aren't doing anything." She gestured in David's direction. "Kindly tell him that archeologists don't go around digging holes wherever we feel like."

Heberto looked puzzled.

"What? Why is he digging here?"

David decided to jump to his own defense before she tried burying him in one of those holes.

"I'm not digging here, but I was just telling Signorina

Pisano that I thought it might be a nice place to try."

"And I was just telling him that he was about to be fired."

Heberto looked a bit disconcerted.

"Oh, I don't think we can fire him."

"Why not? He's not doing his work. He's wandering off into areas he shouldn't be. I certainly think that's grounds for dismissal."

"Why don't you try shoveling more than a spoonful of dirt at a time?" David grumbled under his breath. "Then you might find out what real work is."

"Real work? Why you—"

Damn, the woman had keen hearing.

"There now, children. There's no need to argue." Heberto stepped between them, apparently afraid they might actually come to blows. David found the idea tempting, if it would shut her mouth.

"I'm afraid I cannot fire Signore Corbelli. With the war, strong men are hard to come by, as well you know. We need him." Heberto put his arm around her shoulders. "As it happens, I think it would be a good idea for you to try digging away from the others for a while, Serafina."

David couldn't help but notice a wave of hurt flash in her blue eyes. She shook off Heberto's arm and stepped back.

"Why?"

He gave her a knowing look.

"After what happened the other day, perhaps some distance from Giovanni would do you good."

"I can handle Giovanni. Heberto, I've been working on the *thermopolium* excavation for over a year now. You can't take it away from me."

"I'm not taking it away from you. I'm giving you a chance to start new. Trust me. Think of all the wonders that lie here waiting for you to find them."

Serafina crossed her arms and chewed on her lower lip. David wondered if she might start crying. God, he hated it when women cried. Finally, she sighed and nodded.

Heberto beamed.

"*Buon, buon.* I'll go make the arrangements with Moretti. You can both start here in the morning."

David watched as the old man stumbled back down the street, trying to navigate between patches of tall grass and wildflowers growing where Pompeians once walked centuries before.

Could it have really been that easy? Then he spied Serafina's stiff back in front of him and something told him that he may have won a battle, but the war between them was far from over.

She turned to him, and the expression on her face could have frozen water in the hot Italian sun.

"Fine, Signore Archeologist. Since you are such an expert, where should we dig?" She flung her arms out, gesturing all around her. "Pick a spot. Any spot." Then she bent down, scooped up a rock, and shoved it into his hand. "Here. Go ahead, throw it. I'm sure wherever it lands will be as good a place as any."

She turned and stalked away, just as she had done the first time he saw her.

"Wait, Sera. Come back here. Let's talk about this."

"Don't call me that. My name is Serafina. Signorina Pisano to you." She turned and glared at him with her hands fisted on those trouser-covered hips. "And what is there to talk about? It seems to me that you've done plenty of talking for the both of us. I don't know how you did it, but in less than one week you've managed to make your opinion more valuable to my superiors than my own, and I've worked here for over three years." She looked off into the distance for a moment. "For some reason, that seems to be happening a lot lately."

"I beg your pardon?" He didn't have a clue what she was talking about.

"Never mind. Congratulations. You got your way." She started to turn away, but swung back to face him, pointing her dainty little finger at the ground. "Just make sure you stay put. I don't need you wondering off someplace else every day. You might not value my time, but I do. It takes me too long to track you down. Now, go home, Signore Corbelli. Quite frankly, I think I've had about enough of you for today."

"Don't worry, *Sera*." He deliberately drew out the shortening of her name. "Starting tomorrow, you won't be able to get rid of me. In fact, I'll stay so close, I'll be like your second skin."

Her eyes widened, and her mouth dropped open. She looked utterly appalled. Even though most of what she had said was true, it didn't do his male ego any good to realize she would rather be anywhere but where he was.

She regained her composure quickly, and her eyes narrowed to slits filled with contempt.

"Just be here, Signore Corbelli. Unless you'd like to do me a favor and not come back at all, since apparently I can't even get you fired—yet." Serafina turned and began walking away from him again.

If the dressing down she'd just given him hadn't riled him enough, the sight of her angry backside sashaying away from him did. David squeezed the rock she'd shoved in his hand so hard, he thought he might crush it.

He knew it was juvenile. He knew it was stupid. But he did it anyway.

He threw the rock at her, aiming to send it close enough to startle her, but not actually hit her. Of course, that was the precise moment she decided to turn around and yell at him again.

The rock whizzed by her head, missing her cheek by a few inches. Her quick reflexes had her sprawled on the ground, staring at him as if he'd just tried to shoot her.

"*Voi asino!*" You ass.

For the second time in less than ten minutes, he'd managed to knock her to the ground. It was quite obvious that Serafina's already low opinion of him had now hit rock bottom.

David ran to her and dropped down on one knee by her side. He cupped her cheek and examined her face, worried that he might actually have hit her.

"Sera, are you hurt? I didn't mean… I'm sorry…"

She stared up at him, and her expression surprised him. Where he expected pain or anger, he saw startled confusion and a vague awareness. What the hell did that look mean? Then her eyes narrowed, and the odd expression was gone as quickly as it had come. Rage took its place.

He couldn't blame her. Since they'd met, he'd slammed her to the ground, held a knife to her throat, and nearly slugged her with a rock. She had every right to think he was some kind of madman.

"Don't touch me."

He instantly released his hold, but didn't pull away.

"I said I was sorry."

"Get. Away. From. Me." She bit out the words through clenched teeth.

He sat back on his heels, giving her the space she needed.

"I swear it won't happen again."

She sprang to her feet, spun on her heel, and stalked away with the regal bearing of a queen. Only the dust coating her shapely backside diminished the total effect.

Without looking back at him, she shouted over her shoulder, "If it's the last thing I do, Signore Corbelli, I'm getting you thrown off this dig site."

As David watched her walk away, he knew he had his work cut out for him. And that work wouldn't be spying on the Germans or digging in the rock hard dirt.

It would be getting Serafina Pisano to trust him.

POMPEII

The government had placed restrictions on everything since the war began, including the use of gas to heat water. Each apartment in Serafina's building had a specific day when its residents could bathe or do laundry. Tonight was her night to take a bath, and she planned to relish every second of it.

Her building was actually an old town villa converted into small flats, but her landlady hadn't gone so far as to install a bathroom in every apartment, so each floor had to share a common one. She donned her threadbare bathrobe and gathered up shampoo and soap from under the sink in her kitchenette. Throwing a towel over her shoulder, she prepared to indulge herself for a while.

As she headed to the door, an old black-and-white photo on the wall caught her attention. The woman in the portrait was breathtakingly beautiful. Young and carefree, she smiled with a naive girl's innocence and love of life, eager to embrace all that the future held in store for her.

But that had been before she met the man who was to be Serafina's father. After that, everything changed for the girl in the picture.

She adjusted the frame, running her finger over the glass as if she could caress the smooth cheek beneath. She still missed her mother terribly, even after all these years.

Taking in a deep breath, she tried to shake the melancholy feeling that came over her every time she thought of her mother and all that she had sacrificed for her only child. She could do nothing to change the past, and if her mother were still alive, she would tell Serafina that she wouldn't want to, just as she had told her a thousand times while she was alive.

Serafina left her room and made her way to the bathroom at the end of the hall. Walking past the banister overlooking the stairs, she met her landlady as the woman came up from the first floor.

"Ah, Serafina. You're home early. Is anything wrong?" the old lady asked.

Everything. "No. It's just been a very long day, and I could use a bath."

"I can see that." Maria Angelico touched the tight bun secured at the nape of her neck, no doubt making sure not a hair strayed from its rigid confinement. "There are not many young ladies who would enjoy getting as dirty as you."

"I wouldn't say I enjoy it. It's just part of the job."

"How does it go over at the ruins?"

Serafina leaned her back against the wall, settling in for the long chat that inevitably came when speaking with Signora Angelico.

"I've had better weeks."

"Is that so?"

She smiled down at the old woman. Small and frail, Maria was old enough to be her grandmother. Maybe that's why Serafina found it so easy to confide in her. Behind the tiny stature and wrinkled skin hid a giant wall of strength that she had leaned on more than once.

"Giovanni and I had a bit of a disagreement over the dig site we were working on together."

"Really?" The old woman's face lit up, eager to hear any gossip, no matter the source. "What about?"

"He seemed to think he had the right to claim an artifact I found." The incident still had her grinding her teeth.

"Oh, my. That wasn't very nice of him." Maria frowned and cocked her gray head to the side. "What did you do?"

"I argued with him about it in front of Signore Moretti." She groaned inwardly at the memory of the spectacle she'd made of herself.

"Oh, Serafina, you didn't! What did he do?"

"He gave Giovanni the credit, and I got reassigned to another location in the ruins."

"Oh, you poor dear. That doesn't seem fair."

Serafina sighed. Since when had anything in her life been fair? It seemed as if it was always one thing or another, the latest being her banishment to the far regions of the ruins. At least that's how it felt.

"It's not that bad." *Yes, Serafina, say it enough, and you might start believing it.* "The new area I've been assigned has hardly been touched. Who knows what might be discovered there?"

"That sounds exciting." The old woman actually clapped for her.

"I suppose so." She nodded, trying to see Maria's excited view of things. "And since I'm in charge of the new site, there can be no 'misunderstandings' about who discovers any artifacts there."

"Well, it seems like it could be a wonderful opportunity for you."

It could be, if I didn't have David Corbelli there to irritate me constantly.

"They even gave me my own assistant."

"Really? An assistant?" Maria's eyes widened. "Now that sounds impressive."

It did sound impressive, and she knew she should feel a certain amount of pride, since up until now she'd always been someone else's subordinate. She should be happy, because getting her own assistant validated her standing as a serious archeologist, if only just a little. She should be ecstatic that she was put in charge of her own area of the dig.

So why wasn't she?

"He's not an archeologist. He's really just there to help me with the heavy work."

Maria nodded in understanding. "The big, dumb, strong type, eh?"

Serafina thought of David lifting shovel after shovel of dirt, the muscles of his arms and back shifting beneath his sweat-soaked shirt. His deep brown eyes came to her mind. Shadowed under his hat, they seemed to be constantly surveying the area around him. It hadn't taken her long to figure out that he wasn't an average laborer.

"*Sì*, he's strong, but I wouldn't say he's dumb."

Something was definitely different about him. He had an awareness, an intelligence—one that he almost seemed determined to hide. And that made her uneasy. People hid secrets for many different reasons—she should know—and usually those reasons weren't good, and the secrets behind them were even worse.

Maria reached out and patted her on the hand.

"Well, perhaps you will get on better with this new young man than you did with Giovanni."

Serafina thought about how they'd clashed from the moment they'd met. He seemed determined to challenge her at every turn.

"Somehow, I doubt it."

Shoving herself away from the wall, she made her way to the bathroom, wondering if David Corbelli might turn out to be a bigger problem for her than Giovanni ever was.

CHAPTER VIII

David left his rented basement flat at quarter of ten and walked through the dark streets to the heart of modern Pompei.

The *piazza* was an open area bordered by small cafés and shops, usually packed with local farmers selling produce and women shopping for fresh vegetables for the day's meals. But in these times of war, the farmers were seldom there. Most of the produce they grew went to feed the soldiers. Very little was available to the Italian citizens, and what was left was severely rationed. Often times the farmers sold what they could on the black market at outrageous prices. War rations didn't buy much for the honest citizen nowadays.

Though the market stalls had closed up for the evening, the *piazza* was still bustling with activity. Men and women sat in small groups, sharing wine and smoking cigarettes. David wove around clusters of people who'd stopped in the middle of the street to chat with friends and acquaintances. They had no worry about cars careening down the narrow streets. Gas was reserved strictly for military use, and, of course, for the wealthy who could afford to pay the black market price.

He wandered down the street, feigning interest in a shop window here, a war propaganda poster there.

"*Ha ottenuto una luce?*" A deep voice from behind asked if he had a light.

He winced at Frank Sullivan's mangled use of the Italian language. The guy wouldn't last five minutes among true Italians before they realized he was an American.

"Come on," David replied in a low voice, turning Frank away with a nod of his head. "Let's go somewhere where we can talk."

He led Frank to an empty alley where they could speak English without the risk of being overheard. Once safely out of earshot, Frank pulled a rumpled pack of cigarettes from his shirt pocket and offered one to David.

David held up his hand to decline. "No, thanks."

"Take it," Frank prodded. "If there's one thing I've noticed, the Italians smoke like chimneys. It might look better if someone passes by and looks this way. Otherwise, they may think we're up to no good, sneaking down here like this."

"Either that, or they'll think we're two lovers looking for a place to do some hanky-panky."

Frank looked mortified, his whole body physically shivering from his cap-topped head down to his toes.

"Christ, I hope not."

David chuckled and took the cigarette, an Army-issue Lucky Strike. "Heaven forbid there's any doubt of your sexual preferences, even to strangers."

"You better believe it, buddy." Frank lit David's cigarette after firing up his own. He took a long, hard drag and blew the white smoke into the air between them. "So, what have you got for me?"

David took a pull on his own cigarette and had to smother a cough as the burning tobacco seared a trail down his throat. The filterless cig left a bitter taste in his mouth, along with a few stray bits of tobacco, making him wonder why anyone would want to smoke in the first place. He hadn't smoked since he was a teenager, and that brief habit had quickly ended when his father caught him and beat the shit out of him.

"Everything has gone as planned," he answered when he finally caught his breath. "I signed on at the dig site and even got my work location reassigned to an area close to the German encampment."

"That's great. What have you been able to observe?"

"Plenty." David went on to describe the German camp, their movements, and practice sessions.

Frank's Italian might be atrocious, but he had a mind like a steel trap. Anything David told him would be committed to memory and relayed verbatim back to headquarters. He had been assigned as David's counterpart for just that reason. Written notes on the Germans would be an instant death sentence if found on either of them.

Frank was tan, just like David, helping him blend in with the locals. The short cut on what was left of his hair hid the fact that he was once a blond surfer-boy from California. A little boot polish and a dark gray cap covered the rest. If he appeared to be a little better fed around the middle than most Italians, no one seemed to notice.

"… and that's about it," David finished, dropping his half-smoked cigarette with its three inches of ash on the cobblestones and crushing it beneath his heel.

"Any sign of stashed munitions?"

"None that I've seen, but I haven't had a chance to search all the ruins yet. It's a bigger place than I thought, with lots of out-of-the-way places to hide guns and artillery."

"Well, the informant swears they're hiding them in the ruins somewhere. You need to find out where, and soon."

"I know. I know."

A long silence hung between them. Both men had learned early on that a friend made today could be shipped home in a pine box draped with the stars and stripes tomorrow. But that hadn't prevented the two of them from becoming as close as brothers.

"So, what's the problem?" Frank finally asked, taking a last drag on his cigarette before he sent the butt flying down the alley with a flick of his fingers.

"Nothing. Like I said, everything is going as planned. It's been almost too easy."

"Almost?"

Damn Frank, he was always observant, and after their two years in the service together, he knew David too well.

"Well, there might be one small problem."

"What is it?"

"Her name is Serafina Pisano."

Frank's expression changed from one of concern to one of

sly interest. "Oh, a woman. That figures."

"No, no. You got it wrong. She's my partner at the dig site. Well, actually, she's my boss."

Frank's smile crinkled his face in a dozen creases, evidence of his years spent in the sun. "Now, this *is* getting interesting."

"She's one of the archeologists. She's young, but she seems to know her stuff."

"So, what's the problem? I wouldn't mind working next to a beautiful *signorina* every day instead of a bunch of smelly guys who've been wallowing in the trenches."

"I doubt that." He rubbed at his shoulder, the muscles clenched in a constant bunch of knots. "She has me digging holes and hauling dirt from sun up 'til sun down. I haven't done this much hard labor since I spent summers baling hay on my uncle's farm."

"You break my heart," Frank laughed, obviously not believing David's tale of woe. "So, whose side is she on?"

"Definitely not ours."

"Well, that just means you need to stay on your toes."

"You got that right. One slip, and she'll have me trussed up and handed over to the Germans before I know what's hit me."

"Wow, is she that hard-assed?" Frank pulled out another cigarette and lit it.

"You better believe it." He declined Frank's offer of a second cigarette. He still had an incredible urge to brush his teeth after the first one. "She's already tried to have me fired once. I'm just glad there's an old guy working there who seems to have taken a liking to me. He wouldn't let her do it."

"Sounds like he should be your new best friend."

David chuckled. "He is a neat old guy. Sera, on the other hand. One minute she seems to be pissed off at the whole world, and the next she's…"

Frank leaned in and prodded him to continue. "She's what?"

"Nothing." David shook his head. "She's hard to figure out. Sometimes, I think she might suspect me. Every now and then,

I've caught her looking at me in a weird way, like she's trying to figure me out or something."

Frank elbowed him in the ribs and winked. "Maybe she just wants to get to know you a little better, if you know what I mean."

Thinking of Sera, he recalled the strange way she'd looked at him after he nearly hit her with the rock.

"No, I don't think so. It's something else."

It was almost as if she already knew him, in more ways than he wanted her to.

POMPEII

If David Corbelli thought Serafina's mood would improve with a good night's sleep, he had another thing coming.

She hadn't slept much at all as the events of the past two days kept replaying through her mind. First, losing her first significant artifact, then losing her excavation site on the whim of a dirt digger who didn't know the first thing about archeology. The very idea still irritated her.

The rising sun had already warmed the early morning air as she pedaled her bicycle toward the ruins, wondering about him. There was something strange about Corbelli, and she couldn't put her finger on it.

His tendency toward violence unnerved her. She could overlook the incident with the knife —almost. After all, she had intentionally snuck up on him, and in these uncertain times of war, you never knew who was friend or foe. Some people tended to be jumpier than most, some less likely to trust a stranger. Heaven knew, she didn't trust him.

His constant wandering off from the dig site was what bothered her most. Was he lazy and trying to avoid doing the work? Or was there something more nefarious behind his frequent disappearances?

Serafina's imagination began churning out a dire scenario.

Were his forays around the city for criminal reasons? Was he scouting artifacts already unearthed in order to steal them later? She shuddered at the possibility.

Pompeii had been plundered and her treasures stolen for nearly two hundred years since her rediscovery. Precious artifacts were often sold on the black market to unscrupulous collectors for tiny fortunes. Anger at the rape of history made her blood boil. Thieves had no respect for the history of Pompeii. They'd even gone so far as to hack precious frescos off the villa walls on several occasions.

Unfortunately, the Archeological Society had no money to hire guards for the site, and the Italian government had to deal with the small issue of a war. That left the archeologists to protect Pompeii and her artifacts—and her to keep an eye on that scoundrel, David.

By the time she reached the east entrance just after dawn, she had all but convinced herself that he was a thief.

Serafina often came to the site early before the others arrived. Besides being the coolest time of the day to work, it was also the quietest. She liked working alone with just the ancient stones for company. Sometimes she could swear she heard them speak to her, telling her stories of a time long ago.

Feeling better as the familiar ruins surrounded her, she walked quickly to the new dig site, eager to get some work done before she had to deal with David Corbelli again.

And that's where she found him.

David had beaten her to the site. He was already pulling up clumps of grass and tossing rocks and stones into the wheelbarrow. From the sweat stains under his arms and down the V of his shirt, she could tell he'd been working hard for quite some time.

She walked up to him slowly, careful this time to make sufficient noise so that he knew she was coming. He looked up as she neared, resting one arm on the handle of his shovel and wiping the sweat from his brow with the other.

"You're late, Sera."

"No, you're early. And I told you to stop calling me that."

"Why?"

"Because I don't like it."

He sent her a cocky smile. "Well, in that case, consider 'Sera' my pet name for you from now on."

She scowled at him. Was he deliberately trying to make her hate him?

His smile broadened.

"Your dirt piles await. Shall we get to work...*Sera*?"

Yes, apparently, he was.

He nodded in the direction of her tent, folded and leaning against the stone wall.

"I forgot exactly where the rock landed yesterday, so I haven't set up the tent yet."

A vision of her lying on the ground with David hovering above her, his warm brown eyes filled with concern, instantly came to mind. But instead of the rush of anger she felt yesterday, an unsettling feeling pooled in her belly.

Where had that come from? She was supposed to be angry at the man, not harboring intimate fantasies about him. Serafina ducked her head to hide her face behind the wide brim of her straw hat, hopeful it would conceal any hint of the conflicting emotions plaguing her.

Finally, she looked up. Clearing her throat, she pointed to a spot near where they fell yesterday.

"I think it was somewhere around there."

David looked surprised that she was actually going to let him choose the spot. Either that, or he was shocked that she had a sense of humor—enough of one to call him on what had transpired yesterday.

"I was just kidding. I figured you would know the best spot to start."

She nodded at his deferral and walked around, getting a feel for the area. Before, her superiors had always told her where to dig. But she knew the signs and knew what to look for.

Previous excavations in this area had only gone a fraction of the way down through the earth and volcanic ash before the digging stopped. The area had been virtually untouched in over eighty years, ever since serious archeologists had taken over where the treasure hunters left off.

They stood at the end of what had once been a small side street lined with merchant's shops. To the untrained eye, it was probably hard to tell because now only the top portion of the second story walls of the buildings peeked out of the earth. The rest was still buried nearly ten feet down under ash and volcanic stone.

She came back to where the rock had landed yesterday.

"Yes, this is the spot."

"Are you sure?"

"Quite."

David shrugged and went to get the tent poles. She stopped him as he dragged them over to where she stood.

"No, set the tent up over there." She pointed to a flat spot near a three-foot section of wall jutting out of the ground. "A lot of sterile dirt needs to be removed before we reach the artifact levels."

"Sterile?"

"Sterile earth means the ash, lapilli, and pumice from the eruption that contains no artifacts. Over twelve feet of it buried Pompeii, and from the looks of things, probably around nine to ten feet are still left to be removed here."

His mouth dropped open. "You mean we have to dig down ten feet before you can even start?"

"No, *you* have to dig down ten feet before *I* can start." Serafina smiled sweetly at him. "You picked the spot, remember?"

He tossed down the tent poles and stalked back to the supplies. No doubt he was looking for another rock to throw at her.

She bent to examine the ground David had just cleared outside one of the walls. She heard his footfalls behind her as he approached, and she braced herself for whatever smart comment he was about to make. She felt him squat down behind her, and a bunch of wildflowers appeared under her nose.

They were the kind that grew all over Pompeii. Vibrant red petals on tall weedy stalks sprouted in patches all over the ruins, even growing in the cracks and crevices of the stones in the walls.

She glanced over her shoulder at him. What was he doing? "Peace offering?"

He smiled, and for the first time, she really noticed his face. The skin at the corners of his brown eyes crinkled, and two small dimples appeared in his tanned cheeks. His teeth were white and straight, and wisps of black curls jutted out from under his hat.

Her mouth went dry as she looked at him, his face so very close to her own, and her heart began to pound.

How had she not noticed it before? David Corbelli was a very handsome man—and the last thing she needed in her life right now.

She reached out and took the small bouquet from him, the wildflowers already wilting in the heat. She stared at them, not really sure what to say. How dare he do something so sweet when she was all geared up to hate him?

"Gr-grazie."

David stood, putting some much-needed space between them, and shoved his hands deep into his pants pockets.

"So, what is this lapilli and pumice stuff?"

Grateful for the change of subject, she set the flowers down and scooped up a handful of small pebbles. She shifted through the stones and pointed at a few tiny fragments.

"Lapilli are small pieces of glass-like volcanic ash." She picked up a slightly larger stone, not much bigger than a marble and riddled with tiny holes. "And this is pumice. If rock can be like a sponge, this is it. Some pumice is even light enough to float on water. Along with tons of ash, this is what covered everything when Vesuvius erupted."

He peered into her cupped hand.

"They all look like rocks to me."

Dropping the pebbles back to the ground, she dusted her hands off as she stood.

"Well, they're not just rocks, but I guess that's what makes me the archeologist. I know the difference."

She looked at David, expecting him to smile at what she meant to be a humorous remark. He wasn't. Instead, he stared at her with intense chocolate-brown eyes.

"So teach me."

Surprised, Serafina returned his gaze.

"Do you really want to learn?"

"Certainly. Since we're going to be working together every day, I should probably learn the difference between a rock and an artifact so I'm not shoveling away something that might be important to your work."

Her work. The words sounded oddly flattering to her. It was rare that an outsider validated what she did as work. Most women who dabbled in archeology did it only as a hobby—young girls from rich families playing at the excavations until the heat and hard work got to them or something more interesting came along.

She squinted at him in the sun.

"Fine. I… we should probably start by putting up the tent before we both wilt like these poor flowers." She touched the toe of her shoe to one of the pitiful red petals lying on the ground. "After that, I'll show you how to grid off the area we will be excavating."

After setting up the tent, he started removing clumps of overgrown grass from the center of what used to be the road while she sketched on paper a plan of the buildings surrounding the site.

They worked in a silent truce throughout the day. He dug where she told him to and she didn't comment when he took a break now and then to climb the tower and rest, even though she thought it odd that he would do something so strenuous to relax.

Once her anger faded, Serafina had to admit that being in charge of her own dig site was exciting. She chose where to dig, she would document every inch of the excavation, and she would get credit for any artifacts they discovered.

She was almost grateful David had forced her into this situation. Almost.

CHAPTER IX

As the sun sank into the Bay of Naples, David and Sera packed up the supplies under the tent and headed toward the east gate.

On their way out of the ruins, they passed Heberto going in the other direction. He was struggling to push a wheelbarrow down the cobbled road. Inside was a large clay jug nestled in a bed of straw.

"Heberto, you're working late this evening," Sera said. "Maria will be upset if you're not on time for dinner."

"*Sì*, but we just finished unearthing this at the *thermopolium*, and Professore Moretti wants it stored in the *horrea*."

"Let me take it there for you. No need for you to eat cold leftovers because Maria is angry at you again."

Chuckling, the old man eased the wheelbarrow down on its back legs.

"I would be very grateful. The last time I was late for dinner, she made me eat dry toast on the back porch."

"Well, we can't have that. Go on, get home while your supper is still hot."

"*Grazie*." Heberto tipped his cap at them. "I'll see you both in the morning."

Sera adjusted her pack and reached for the wheelbarrow, but David beat her to it.

She stepped back, her brow furrowed.

"I said I'd take it."

Ignoring her affronted look, he tossed her his pack and lifted the wheelbarrow by the handles.

"I'll help. Besides, I'm getting pretty good at pushing one of these things around."

She shrugged and heaved his pack over her other shoulder. "Suit yourself. Do you know where the *horrea* is?"

"Nope."

She huffed out a heavy sigh, then started down the road. "Come on, I'll show you."

David followed behind, intensely aware of her stiff back in direct contradiction to her shapely, round backside. How could a woman who looked so soft on the outside be so cold and standoffish on the inside?

"So, what is this thing?" he asked, glancing at the large vessel to make sure it didn't topple out onto the street. "Some kind of wine jug?"

She glanced over her shoulder at him, but kept walking. "Yes, that's exactly what it is. It's called an amphora. We've found many of them at the *thermopolium*."

"The *thermopolium*?"

She stopped and turned to glare at him.

"The *thermopolium* is where I'd been excavating for the past year, until you came along." She paused, and seemed to reconsider her words. "It was a neighborhood bar."

"A bar?" He wasn't sure if he'd heard her correctly.

"Yes. Well, actually, it was more like a café. It served wine and warm food. No seating, though. You either had to eat standing or take it with you. We've also excavated a brothel a few streets over, complete with numerous frescos depicting all the, um, various services one could purchase from the prostitutes there. I'll have to show it to you sometime."

"Well," he cleared his throat and tried to control the flush racing up his neck. He couldn't tell if she was flirting with him or not. This was not a topic he typically talked about with a woman. "That would definitely be something to see."

She continued walking beside him, a smug smile on her face, and he couldn't help but feel she was finding humor at his expense. That was okay. He would much rather have her laugh at him than be angry.

As they made their way past the empty shops and villas, he sensed the ruins slowly turning into a ghost town. The setting sun created long shadows, reaching out from dark crevices like groping fingers trying to pull him into a vacant alley or doorway. During the day, the city was alive with the sounds and activity of the archeologists, laborers, and tourists moving about. But now, as darkness fell and the ruins where once again left to stand by themselves throughout the lonely night, he could all but feel the dead preparing to come out from the shadows and claim the ruins for their own once more.

He glanced at Sera walking quietly by his side. The creepiness certainly didn't seem to bother her one bit. In fact, she appeared to be almost serene in her surroundings. She looked so at ease in the ruins that he could almost picture her as a young Roman girl from centuries ago on her way to the market or a play. If he wasn't so acutely aware of her being a living, breathing woman, he might think her one of the ghosts of Pompeii, too.

They came to an intersection, then walked along a large open area, the grassy lawn surrounded by tall white columns standing like silent sentinels as they passed.

"What's this place?" he asked with a nonchalance that belied his unease at the silence threatening to envelope him.

"Hmmm?" Pulled from her reverie, she looked to where he pointed. "Oh, that's the Forum. Two thousand years ago, it was the heart of the city. All day long, it would be filled with hundreds of people going about their business, visiting with one another, and politicians giving speeches. Slaves and wealthy alike could be found here side by side. Everyone had to cross though the Forum at one time or another."

Yeah, I can almost see them walking around there right now.

Sera stopped at a sheltered area cut into a long expanse of stone wall.

"This is the *horrea*, or what we lovingly call 'the pottery shed.' It used to be a grain warehouse, but now it's where we store some of the artifacts until they're ready to be shipped to the museum or restored and returned to where they were found."

The so-called pottery shed was actually a large recess built into three stone walls two stories high. It was open on one side and covered with a wooden roof which he didn't doubt let in more rain than it kept out.

Metal scaffolding lined the three walls, its wooden shelves overloaded with a myriad of clay pots and amphorae. He could practically hear each shelf groan as it bowed from the weight of its burden. Between the wall shelves and tall freestanding shelves threatening to tip over at the slightest touch stood makeshift tables created from boards supported on wooden sawhorses. A menagerie of items sat piled on top, with many more objects shoved underneath. Every available space held some artifact or relic, leaving barely enough room to walk among them.

"A fine way to protect priceless artifacts."

It was only after catching her sharp glare that he realized he'd said the words aloud, and for a moment he worried that he may have spoken them in English.

"Yes, well, government funding only goes so far, especially when there's a war going on. We do what we have to do."

David breathed a sigh of relief. All it would take to blow his cover was one slip of the tongue.

"Here, put the amphora on this shelf." She indicated one of many shelves lined with identical clay vessels.

He did as he was told, surprised when the shelf didn't collapse under the added weight. As he turned, he noticed a small statue on one of the tables.

He wedged his way between broken columns and waist-high pottery to take a closer look at a statue of a young child lying on its side. David reached out and ran his hand down the child's leg, its surface bumpy and rough to the touch. Definitely not the smooth marble work of art he had come to expect from the ancient Greeks and Romans.

"I hope whoever carved this didn't quit his day job, because he sucked as a sculptor."

"That isn't a statue."

He glanced up at her. A sad smile tugged at her mouth, but there was no joy in her expression.

Setting down the backpacks, she walked over and delicately touched the top of the figure's tiny head.

"It's a plaster cast of a young boy who died in the eruption."

He snatched his hand back.

"You mean this was a real person? A kid?"

Sera nodded. "Flesh and blood."

He looked at the body cast again, now seeing the delicate features clearly for the first time. The boy appeared to be sleeping peacefully, without a care in the world.

"But, how… ?"

She stroked the child's head, running the back of her hand down the boy's cheek much like a mother would caress her own son.

"When Vesuvius erupted, small stones and ash fell from the sky for several hours. During that time, most of the people of Pompeii had time to escape, but many stayed behind thinking they could wait it out and the danger would pass."

"That was stupid."

She shrugged. "Not to them. At the time, Pompeii was still rebuilding from a major earthquake that occurred ten years earlier. Most of the people fled the city then, too, only to have to return with all their belongings. Much of what they didn't take with them had been damaged or looted by thieves. I'm sure they thought this time would be much the same."

He shook his head at the idiocy of it.

"I find it hard to believe they couldn't tell the difference between an earthquake and a volcano eruption."

"They couldn't see the volcano. In fact, they couldn't see much at all. The first phase of the eruption blocked out the sun, turning day into night. Even with their lamps and torches, they could only see maybe a foot or two in front of themselves because of all the soot and ash in the air. The unfortunate ones who decided to stay sought shelter where they could."

"Bad choice."

"Unfortunately for them, it was." He watched her draw in a

deep breath as if she couldn't get enough air into her lungs. "The pumice rained down for hours, piling up twelve feet high. Some were crushed when the weight built up and the roofs collapsed on top of them."

"Ouch." David glanced up at the flimsy wooden roof over his head, now looking more insubstantial than ever. It wouldn't hold back twelve inches of dust, much less twelve feet of ash and lava rock.

"Others were trapped inside their hiding places as the volcanic debris blocked up the doors and windows, and they couldn't get out."

"So they were buried alive?"

"Basically. Eventually poisonous gases seeped in through cracks and crevices and killed them." He found himself holding his breath. Was that the faint odor of sulfur he smelled? "We usually find their skeletons huddled in the corners of buildings or in the cellars."

"What a horrible way to go."

"There are worse ways. Once the rain of ash and pumice stopped, those who weren't trapped or crushed thought it was safe to leave and tried to escape the city then."

"Do I really want to know what happened to them?"

Sera's eyes took on a distant look, as if she were in another place, another time, and no longer aware that he was there.

"The mountain's sudden silence was deceiving. Vesuvius wasn't done yet. Up until then, she'd only been warming up. As the last of the citizens of Pompeii tried to flee the city, Vesuvius erupted with a vengeance, sending a pyroclastic flow racing down the mountainside."

"A pyro-what?"

She continued on, as if she hadn't heard him. "The hot air and toxic gases hit them first, dropping the people in their tracks, blistering their skin and scorching their lungs, suffocating every living thing in their path."

He tugged at the collar of his shirt, finding it hard to breathe himself as she told the tragic story.

"A shower of ash came next, covering everything in sight.

Rain followed, turning the ash into mud that later hardened like a layer of cement over the victims' bodies."

David could almost feel the hot, wet ash on his skin, weighing down his clothes and clogging his throat.

"As the centuries passed, the flesh decayed, leaving hollow cavities in the ground where the bodies had been. When we find one of these cavities, we pour a plaster compound into it. Once it hardens, we chip the volcanic layer away and are left with a perfect cast of the person at the exact moment of their death."

He looked at the child, a boy who couldn't have been more than three or four. He had hardly begun to live before the volcano had taken his life.

"Poor little guy."

She continued to stroke the plaster face of the child, oddly comforting a small boy who had been dead for nearly two thousand years.

"In the confusion and chaos, he must have been separated from his parents. We found him curled up in the doorway of a villa, all alone, lying there just as you see him now."

He glanced up from the cast in time to see a tiny tear fall, leaving a sad trail down the dirt on Sera's cheek. Reaching across the plaster child, he caught it on the pad of his thumb, startling her back from wherever she had been.

She stared at him, obviously surprised by the gesture. When she began to pull away, he stopped her by cupping his hand against her damp cheek. A wealth of emotions shadowed her face—shock, embarrassment, sorrow. Then she closed her eyes and ever so slightly turned her face into his palm.

David didn't know what to say. What could he say? The reality of the eruption seemed all too real to him now, as if he had just experienced the horror for himself. He sensed she felt the same way.

"I'm sorry," she whispered when she finally did pull away, leaving his empty hand to hang in the air between them. "I don't normally do this."

He let his hand drop to his side, curling his fingers to capture the warmth left by her cheek. The air around them felt too intense. He needed to find a way to lighten things before it became downright awkward.

"What? You don't give ignorant laborers personalized guided tours of the ruins every day?"

His attempt at humor seemed to work. She smiled, swiping at her cheek and smearing the wet tear trail into a muddy streak. He was suddenly struck by how beautiful she was in the fading light, smudged cheek and all.

"Well." She cleared her throat, donning her normal reserve like a protective coat. "I guess that's the end of your history lesson for the day. We should get going if we want to be out of here before it gets too dark."

Disappointed that whatever spark had flashed between them had died, he nodded. "Yeah. I guess so."

They left the pottery shed in silence. After retrieving their bicycles outside the east entrance, they headed down the road toward the modern town of Pompei, built in the shadow of the sleeping giant, Vesuvius, just as the ancient town had been.

Sera confounded him. One minute she seemed made of stone, the next she cried over a child whose only trace of existence was now a plaster cast. He wondered if she ever felt that deeply for a living person, if she ever let her guard down. Or did she only put up the walls when she was with him?

But she had shown him a crack in that wall tonight, and as they went their separate ways, David found himself wondering if he might be able to knock it down, stone by stone.

Then he reminded himself that he didn't plan on being there that long.

POMPEII

Serafina parked her bicycle in the small courtyard behind the Angelicos' villa and slipped in the back door. As she made her way down the center hallway, she tried not to make noise on the black and white tile floor.

Her attempt was in vain. As she passed by the Angelicos' door, Maria stepped out, wiping her hands on her stained apron.

"Serafina? I thought I heard someone. My, aren't you late coming home this evening?"

Serafina continued on, then paused with her hand on the newel post at the base of the stairs.

"Yes, well, I got a little side-tracked tonight with work."

"Oh, any interesting discoveries?"

Yes, about myself. I'm soft-hearted and a sucker for a handsome face.

"No, nothing yet. But then, I've only just begun in the new area. It'll probably be a while before I uncover anything at all."

Maria nodded in understanding. "So, how is it with the new young man?"

How was it that the old woman could come right to the heart of the matter?

"Fine," she lied. If she felt differently, she wouldn't admit it, not even to herself. "I'm really tired, Maria. I'll see you in the morning."

"Good night then." Maria smiled and slipped back into her rooms.

Serafina raced up the stairs and closed herself inside her flat. She should feel safe and comforted there, but she didn't.

She looked around, seeing only a place where she slept and kept her clothes. Just the bare necessities remained from her life before her mother died—a beat-up table with three chairs in the tiny kitchenette, a worn green couch and scarred coffee table in what passed as a sitting area, a quilt-covered iron bed and wooden dresser in the back near the window.

No, this place wasn't her home. The ruins were. They were where she felt the most comfortable. Usually.

She attempted to hold back the sob that threatened to choke her. She did her best to remain detached from the personal tragedy of the disaster, but every now and then something would slip through the cracks.

The child.

She hadn't been the one to discover the body cavity or to pour the plaster into the holes to make the cast. But she had been there when the other archeologists chipped away the hardened shell and lifted what was left of the tiny body from its grave of ashes. Her heart had broken thinking of an innocent child suffering so, all alone with no one to help him.

Just like she felt right now. Alone.

She pushed herself away from the door and dropped her pack on the kitchen table.

She needed to get a hold on herself. What had brought on this upheaval of emotion? Granted, her simple life had been disrupted the past few days, but that shouldn't have her in tears. She'd faced worse hardships and disappointments in her twenty-three years. She was a stronger person than that.

Taking a deep breath to clear her head, Serafina lifted the flap of her pack to take out her empty lunch pail and canteen. As she reached in, her fingers brushed the wilted petals of forgotten wildflowers, and one last tear escaped to fall slowly down her cheek.

CHAPTER X

The *chunk-swoosh-thunk* of his shovel stabbing into the dirt, sliding off the blade, and landing in the wheelbarrow had a hypnotic effect, creating a rhythm to David's labor. He shoveled without conscious thought, the monotony of the movements helping him forget the strain on his back and the blisters on his hands.

Day after day, he and Sera worked in veritable silence as the sun rose high in the Mediterranean sky, baking the exposed dirt until it cracked. This morning, a gentle breeze blew in from the sea, bringing some relief from the heat. It also picked up the fine volcanic ash that coated the ground and swirled it upward to sting his eyes and parch his throat.

Taking a break to get a drink of water, he glanced up from his pit to where Sera worked at the screening table. Using a screen stretched on a wooden rack, she sifted the dirt he shoveled to catch any small artifacts that might be present in the upper levels of debris.

It was becoming a typical scenario. Ever since the evening he comforted her over the plaster child, Sera had kept her distance around him, sticking strictly to the business of excavating. She avoided any of his attempts at pleasant conversation or—heaven forbid—friendship. Apparently that small crack in her carefully structured facade had scared the daylights out of her, and she was doing everything she could to prevent it from happening again. The woman put up walls higher than the crumbling ones surrounding the ruins.

Her back was to him as she bent over the worktable under the tent, and David leaned on his shovel and took a moment to observe her.

She was in her element in the ruins. At times, she seemed to be one with the rocks and dirt. He'd joined the army partly to please his father, but he had never had Sera's level of dedication for her work. He almost envied her commitment. It was a strength that he lacked in his own life.

He also admired her shapely backside. Bent over the table as she was, it was shown to rounded perfection in the khaki trousers she wore. The loose cut of the pants gave no hint of the shape of her legs, but the tight waistline suggested a slim figure. She wore a pale yellow blouse today, with the sleeves rolled up and cuffed over her forearms.

David was so busy studying her attributes, a moment passed before he noticed the music. He didn't have to see her face to know that she was the one singing. The fact that she sang as she worked didn't surprise him, nor was he surprised that she had a pleasant voice. The shock was in what she was singing. The song was unmistakable.

The familiar lyrics floated to him across the ancient stones, causing him to hold his breath so that he wouldn't miss a single note.

Oh, give me something to remember you by
when you are far away from me, dear
Some little something meaning love cannot die
no matter where you chance to be

The song seemed so out of place, and it flooded him with memories of home—America.

Why on earth would Sera be singing an American Big Band tune? And in English, no less?

The singing suddenly stopped. She glanced in his direction, the wide brim of her straw hat shadowing her features. She must have sensed him watching her, since he had yet to make a sound.

A movement caught his eye and he noticed a strange man approaching. He wasn't very tall, his apple-shaped body perched precariously on thin, bird-like legs. A wide-brimmed hat shaded the top half of the man's face, but the sun practically bounced off white teeth barely contained in a wide smile.

"Serafina," the man called out as he came closer, "so this is where they've hidden you."

The timber of the voice was slightly higher than what David would normally consider manly. He watched Sera and the man kiss each other on the cheeks, amazed at how openly affectionate the Italians always were with each other.

At least, most were.

He stabbed his shovel in the ground and tossed the dirt into the wheelbarrow. Sera never greeted *him* with kisses on the cheek or anything more than a curt hello.

Of course, he couldn't say he blamed her. For the most part, he'd been a thorn in her side since they'd met, except when that brief moment of tenderness seemed to pass between them.

He sighed as he stabbed his shovel in the dirt again, wondering if he had imagined the whole thing. It didn't matter. It was probably for the best. No sense starting something he couldn't finish.

David glanced up in time to see the man point in his direction, and Sera brought him over.

"Well, well. I wish I had an assistant who looked like him." The guy placed his hands on his plump hips and actually winked at David.

Oh, great. One of those. All he needed was some pervy bone-digger sniffing after him.

"It figures you'd get tall, dark, and handsome, and I get stuck assisting that snake, Giovanni." The man turned to glare at Sera. "Thank you very much for that."

"It wasn't my idea," she defended herself. "Besides, Giovanni is tall, dark, and handsome." She pointed her thumb at David. "You can have him if you want."

"Hey." Why did he feel like a broken-down car no one wanted?

"Right, and have you back working with Giovanni? I'm a better friend than that." The man looked him up and down and heaved a dramatic sigh. "Even if it does mean I don't get the pleasure of working alongside this one."

Now David really felt like a piece of meat, and as he stepped out of the shallow pit, he mentally apologized to any woman he'd ever demeaned with such talk in his past.

Finally, Sera acknowledged his presence.

"David, I'd like you to meet Olympia Becchetti. Olympia, this is David Corbelli."

Olympia? A woman? He was so stunned, he momentarily forgot to take the woman's offered hand. He quickly closed his mouth and, to make up for the errant path his thoughts had taken, raised her hand and kissed her dirty knuckles.

This drew a blinding smile from Olympia and a scowl from Sera.

"Now, that is what I call a gentleman," Olympia gushed. "Maybe I will take you up on that trade. He's much better than most of the old fossils working around here."

"Fine, do what you like. I couldn't care less." Sera turned and stalked away.

He stared after her. If he wasn't so sure she didn't like him, he would have thought her jealous.

"Does she hate all men, or is it just me?"

"No," Olympia chuckled. "It's pretty much men in general."

"Then is she…? She's not a…" He couldn't seem to shake the first impression he had of Olympia, and now the notion stuck in his head. If Sera truly hated men, could she possibly be…?

The shocked look on Olympia's face indicated that she knew what he was inferring, and she laughed at the suggestion.

"Oh, no, no. Serafina definitely prefers the opposite sex. It's just that…" She eyed him from under the brim of her hat. "Let's just say that she hasn't always had the best experiences with the men in her life."

That bit of insight piqued his interest.

"So, she's had her heart broken?"

"In more ways than one. The two men she cared about

most in her life hurt her deeply. Now she finds it hard to let her guard down. She doesn't trust easily." She elbowed him in the ribs. "But don't take it personally. I like you."

Olympia walked over to where Sera was working at the screening table. The two women spoke to each other in rapid-fire Italian, one sometimes starting before the other was finished.

Despite his first impression, he liked Olympia. She had a jolly, deep-bellied laugh and made him feel instantly at ease. By comparison, Sera was serious and reserved, at least around him.

As he watched them chatting together, he could see they were close friends. Their love for archeology appeared to be a strong bond between two women who seemed so different from each other.

David didn't know why it surprised him to find out Sera had friends. Or at least one friend. Since he'd met her, she seemed only concerned with the excavations. He'd never heard her talk about life outside the walls of the ruins.

Apparently she had one after all.

POMPEII

As evening settled over the ruins, David and Sera rode their bicycles along the narrow road toward town. Unaccustomed as he was to riding on the bumpy cobblestones, the pavers threatened to toss him off his bicycle at every turn. Still, he chanced a look up at the volcano in the distance, its peak shrouded by clouds. Or was that smoke seeping from the sleeping giant, awakening once more? He wasn't sure and didn't dare ask. A true Italian would know the difference.

By the time they reached the town, the sky overhead had eased from a bright Mediterranean blue to the dusky purple of twilight. The blaring of an amplified voice caught his attention. The speaker sounded odd, as if he were talking into a tin can, relaying news of the war on the Axis home front.

David glanced at Sera as she rode her bicycle beside him. "Do you hear that?"

"*Sì*. They must be showing a newsreel in the *piazza*."

His heart began to pound. Days had passed since he had seen Frank and heard news of any kind about the war. The archeologists seemed to live in their own little world. The ruins and the artifacts were the only thing they cared about, as if they stepped back in time once they crossed through the stone gate into the ruins, and to them the war no longer existed.

"Let's go watch it." He tried to keep his voice calm and not sound too eager. Any news, even that from the enemy's perspective, was better than none.

She eyed him, her expression put upon, as if he had just asked her to clean the latrines. Finally, she nodded.

"All right. Come on."

She pedaled down the narrow street toward the center of town, leaving him to struggle to keep up with her.

When they reached the *piazza*, he spied a film projector perched high up on a wooden stand. It cast a grainy black and white image against the cracked plaster wall of a building on the opposite side. The picture jerked occasionally on its makeshift screen, the tattered film riveted with holes and scratches from its constant showing in town to town.

As he watched transfixed, a bird's eye view showed German bombers dropping their lethal arsenal on British targets far below, clouds of destruction rising silently in the air. The next scene showed innocent citizens in the town of Livorno running for cover with black smoke in the background as oil refineries exploded and burned. Then the film cut to young Italian soldiers fighting in muddy trenches, while the newscaster's voice played over it all. He spoke of the Allies' total disregard for innocent citizens as the film showed American planes dropping bombs on the town of Foggia, destroying the Axis airfields located there, along with much of the town.

David shook his head at the biased newscast. He knew some of the guys who had flown that mission. Hours before the air raid, the Allies had dropped leaflets over the populated targets, warning the citizens so they could evacuate the cities in time. The incident was just another example of how Mussolini twisted the truth to suit his needs.

The image switched once more, showing the aftermath of destruction in Livorno. As the townspeople picked through the debris, the crumbling stones and rubble-filled streets reminded him of the ruins.

He sensed Sera stiffening beside him.

"What?"

"How dare they bomb cities full of people? How can they do that, with the centuries of architecture and the museums with their priceless works of art? Don't they realize how irreplaceable it all is?"

He felt her pain, but he also understood the other side.

"This is war, Sera, and unfortunately there is often a high price to pay, both in property and human lives."

"It's not just property. It's history. It's our past. Once it's destroyed, we can never get it back."

She looked ready to climb the scaffolding, tear the projector down, and rip the film from the reel with her bare hands.

"Damn the Allies," she growled under her breath. "Damn the Americans."

Her fierce hatred of the Allies—and apparently the Americans in particular—shocked him. Granted, Italy was fighting against the Allies. But at this point, it was mainly so Germany would not retaliate against the Italian people after Mussolini had pledged their support and gotten them into this mess. Most Italians were tired of the war and would rather not be in it at all. The average citizen was more or less ambivalent to the Allies.

But not Sera. Her hatred was visible in every fiber of her being—in the way she held her shoulders back, the way her jaw clenched, and her fists balled at her sides with the knuckles turned white. She hated the Americans with a passion.

"Perhaps we should go," he said.

"Yes, I've seen enough."

They left the *piazza* and rode down the street together, eventually parting ways. As he continued alone, he couldn't get over how strong her emotions were after seeing the newsreel. Was she such a loyal Fascist that she hated anything that went against the movement, Germany, and Hitler? Somehow he found that hard to believe.

There had to be something else, and David needed to find out what it was. His mission might depend upon it.

ᛈᚮᛗᛈᛖᛁᛁ

A door slammed somewhere in the house for the second time in less than fifteen minutes. Hershel jumped in his overstuffed chair, causing him to rip the week-old newspaper he was reading.

Marsha stalked into their sitting room, shoved Hershel's feet off the ottoman where they'd been resting comfortably, and flopped down on it.

"We have a problem."

Obviously, Hershel thought. "What is it this time?"

"Serafina just came in, and she's madder than a monkey on a fire-ant hill."

Hershel lowered the paper to his lap, scrunching up the edges as he did so.

"Oh, no. What has he done now?"

"Who?" Marsha looked momentarily confused. "David? No, it wasn't something he did. At least, I don't think so. No, she just came from seeing the newsreel in the *piazza*, and it's gotten her all fired up again."

"About what?"

"Well, in case you've forgotten, our little Serafina has an intense dislike of Americans."

"So?" He lifted the paper up again and tried to find where he'd left off.

Marsha swatted it back down into his lap, crumpling it beyond hope, and glared at him.

"So, David is American."

"So?" The light bulb inside Hershel's head finally flashed on. "Oh, no."

"Exactly. We need to make sure that she doesn't find out about him until we're… until she's ready."

"And how are we supposed to do that?"

"I don't know. So far, he's been doing a good job of keeping her in the dark, but she's a smart girl. I'm worried what she'll do when she does find out."

The problem was starting to make Hershel's head hurt. And just when everything was starting to fall into place.

"So, what do you propose we do about it? I mean, as mortals, we can't exactly perform miracles down here. It's not like we can sprinkle angel dust on his head and turn him into a real Italian for her."

"Don't you think I know that?" Marsha propped her elbow on the arm of Hershel's chair and tapped her fingers against her chin. "We need to come up with a plan. Something to speed things up a bit and bring them closer, so that by the time she does find out, it won't matter."

He shrugged. "Why don't we just tell them they're soul mates destined to be together, so they can just go ahead and get on with it?" He smiled at himself. Why, the idea was absolutely brilliant. He didn't know why they hadn't thought of it before. "That should certainly speed things up."

"Hershel." Marsha frowned and shook her head at him. "Even if we could tell them—which we can't, you know it's against policy—do you think they'd actually believe us?"

"No, I suppose not." He slumped back into his seat. Drat, and here he'd thought he'd come up with the perfect answer. "So what more can we do? After all, they're working side by side five days a week as it is."

She stared off into space, and then a wicked gleam brightened her eyes.

"Evidently side by side isn't close enough. I think our young lovers need to have something happen to bring them closer. A lot closer."

Hershel stared at his wife. He didn't like the sound of her voice.

"Marsha, what are you going to do?"

"It's not what *I'm* going to do." She grinned impishly. "It's what *you're* going to do."

CHAPTER XI

David worked in one of the holes they had started excavating in the center of the old road. A tent shaded the shallow pit, its thick canvas tarp bucking gently in the soft breeze that managed to slip over the high stone walls.

He shook his head. It was the third tent they had erected on the site. He was grateful for the shade, but the damn place was starting to look like the county fair back in Bedford. As he dug, Sera begin singing a soft, melodious tune and he recognized the song immediately.

"I'll Be Seeing You."

It was another Big Band hit, and, just as before, memories of America flooded him. Only this time, the longing for home tangled with the Italian-accented lyrics, recalling a more recent memory of a beautiful archeologist weeping over a long-dead child.

How was it that she could make him think of home when he was thousands of miles away in a foreign country surrounded by the enemy?

He looked at her digging in the dirt under her own tent, so engrossed in her work that she seemed oblivious of the world around her, and reminded himself that he stood just a few feet away from one of the people his country was fighting against.

He scraped up another layer of dirt and enjoyed listening to her sing, until an odd sound drew his attention. He could have sworn he heard something hit the top of Sera's canvas. He glanced skyward for any sign of an impending thunderstorm, but as far as he could see, there was only clear blue sky.

Shrugging off the sound, he bent once more to his task. Then he heard it again, the plunk of something hitting the tent, followed by a soft tumbling sound as the object rolled down the slant of the canvas to drop with a clunk on the ground.

A bird? Hail? He glanced around to see where it might have come from, but he and Sera appeared to be completely alone in this area of the ruins.

He shook his head and went back to work. All the non-stop digging had him hearing things now. Or so he thought, until he heard it again.

Plunk... rattle, rattle, rattle... cherchunk.

He looked toward Sera's tent and noticed that she had heard it, too. She'd stopped singing and was softly humming the tune. Her movement was almost imperceptible. She didn't even look up as she set down her trowel and scooped up a handful of small pebbles.

David waited, curious to see what she was going to do.

Plunk... rattle, rattle...

The rock hadn't hit the ground before she bounded out of the trench and started flinging pebbles at a low section of wall on the edge of the dig site. Jumping back into the pit, she flung herself on the ground as a barrage of small stones came flying back in her direction.

In her prone position, Sera was safe from the onslaught, but David felt the sharp stings on his thighs and arms as he was pelted with tiny rocks.

"Hey! What the—?"

Giggles erupted from behind the crumbling wall. Three young boys jumped out from hiding and proceeded to run around the site, whooping like little wild Indians.

Sera hopped out of the hole and grabbed the slowest boy by his dirty shirttail, wrapping her arms around him and imprisoning him in a big hug.

"Got you now!"

"No, Serafina. No kisses." The boy struggled to get away, while the other two stopped to laugh at their comrade's plight.

She tried to kiss him on either cheek, then finally settled for placing one on the top of his ruffled hair and released him.

"What took you so long to find me?"

"We didn't even know you had moved until we saw Olympia working with Giovanni instead of you. He wouldn't tell us where you were, but Heberto did."

Her smile momentarily disappeared, her eyes narrowing as she glanced down the road in the direction of her old dig site. "That's because, hopefully, Giovanni has no idea where I am."

"Oh, he doesn't," the second boy chimed in. "Heberto told us to keep it a secret."

"Good."

"Yeah, Giovanni's a *coglione*," the third boy grumbled as he kicked at a rock with the toe of his worn shoe.

Her good humor returned, and she smiled at the three boys.

"If you say so."

The third boy glanced up and took notice of David.

"Is he a new archeologist?"

She looked over in his direction.

"No, but Signore Corbelli is helping me dig here at the new site."

"Is he nice to you?" the first boy asked.

"Anybody's gotta be nicer than Giovanni," the second boy corrected him.

"He's nice to me," she said, never taking her eyes off David, "most of the time."

"Do you need us to kick his ass?" the third boy asked, his bravado diminished by his thin, lanky stature.

"You could try," David answered, feeling a juvenile urge to defend himself.

The boys laughed at his threat and ran around the tents, taunting David to catch them. He hopped out of his hole and lunged at the boy with the gutter mouth, but the boy was quick as an alley rat and dodged out of arm's reach.

Sera joined in, circling one of the boys around the sifting table. They pivoted and dodged, until the boy darted back out into the open area. She was quick on his heels, and her hat flew off as she chased after him.

David stopped in his tracks, and the boy he was after dashed away out of sight. David had never seen her without that stupid straw hat on. In the bright sun, her brown hair lit up in a thousand shades of gold and bronze. The wavy tresses tumbled down around her shoulders as the breeze tossed the locks about her face. Tucking an errant strand behind her ear, Sera laughed as she bent to retrieve her hat, and he was struck again by how beautiful she was in the rare, unguarded moment.

Still staring, he wasn't prepared when his own hat was slapped off his head from behind. He spun around to grab the miscreant, only to trip over the shovel at his feet. He careened into a tent post, and then slid against the tight rope tethering it to the ground. A streak of fire burned across his back as he went down, until the iron spike gave way and pulled from the earth, collapsing the corner of the canvas tent on top of him.

"David!"

The tarp lifted, and a cloud of swirling dust clogged his throat and burned his eyes.

"Are you all right?" Sera asked.

He lay sprawled in the dirt, staring up into her concerned face, the sun a bright halo around her head.

"I'm fine. Just my pride is hurt."

Her frown transformed into a broad grin. "*Sì*, it's not very *machismo* to be bested by an eleven-year-old boy."

"I wasn't bested, merely caught off guard."

"Sure you were." She offered her hand and helped him to his feet.

"Sorry we wrecked the tent, Serafina," one of the boys said as the three gathered around them.

"It's not me you should apologize to." She nodded her head in David's direction.

"Sorry, Signore Corbelli," the boys said in unison.

"Apology accepted." He tried to look stern, but it was hard when faced with their contrite expressions. "Next time I'll be ready for you."

"You're on," said the one who'd gotten the better of him.

"Go on now." She waved them away. "We've got a tent to repair."

"Bye, Serafina," the boys shouted as they raced down the street, their joyful laughter a stark contrast to the horror of the war going on outside the ancient walls.

"Isn't it a bit dangerous for children to be playing in the ruins?" he asked as he brushed the dust and dirt off his pants.

"Sì, but it's safer than running around the countryside where the Germans might run over them with one of their tanks, or the Allies might shoot them for the fun of it."

His expression must have surprised her, because she raised a challenging brow in his direction.

"Don't look so shocked. I used to play in the ruins myself as a child."

"Now, why am I not surprised?" He shook his head and watched the boys disappear around the corner. "I'm amazed that your father allowed you to do it."

Her good humor instantly vanished.

"My father never gave a damn what I did."

She stepped around him and picked up the fallen tent post. Looking at her profile, with her jaw clenched and her lips pressed into a thin line as she struggled to right the canvas tarp, he could tell she was fighting another kind of battle, one deep within herself. Somehow, he had struck a nerve, and a very sensitive one, at that.

"Here, let me help." He reached for the tarp and guided the grommet onto the tip of the post.

"I don't need any— David, you're hurt."

POMPEII

"What?"

"Your back. There's blood on your shirt."

"There is?" He twisted to look over his shoulder, not that he would be able to see the spots of crimson seeping through the rough gray cotton. "Probably a rope burn from when I fell against the tether line."

"Well, let's take a look at it."

"I'm sure it's fine." He shrugged, then failed to hide his wince.

"With all the dust and dirt around here, no open wound is fine. It could get infected."

"Yeah. You wouldn't want to lose your cheap slave labor," he grumbled as he righted the corner of the tent.

"You're not cheap slave labor. Your work is very helpful and much needed. I couldn't do this without you."

"Thanks." He turned to face her, surprise at her concern evident in his expression. "It's nice to know you care."

Serafina took a step back, flustered by his comment. Did he really think she was cold and heartless enough not to worry over him?

"Here, sit down." She indicated one of the two stools under the shifting tent. "Take your shirt off so I can get a look at the damage."

David unbuttoned his shirt and shrugged it from his broad shoulders, exposing a strong chest and toned stomach. Serafina's breath evaporated from her lungs. Her heart pounded wildly, and her blood pulsed in certain lower areas where it had no right to be pulsing.

Not for David.

She grabbed her canteen and a clean rag, busying herself with the items she might need to clean the cut as he sat on the stool and waited.

She blew a loose strand of hair out of her face. What in the world had come over her?

When she turned back, she nearly tripped over the other stool.

David sat still as stone, looking as only God could make a man. He was beautiful—the only word to describe him at that moment. The sunlight filtering through the tent kissed every curve and muscle, gilding each hollow and ridge on his body with a golden hue.

She sat on the stool behind him before he caught her ogling him. Placing her hand against her thundering heart, she tried to catch her breath. She unscrewed the top of her canteen, wet-ted the rag, and attempted to pull herself together.

Oh, come on, you've seen a man's bare chest before.

Yes, a little voice inside her head chimed in, *but never looking like this.*

She dabbed at the cut, the angry raised welt a vicious stripe across his strong back.

"Ow. Take it easy."

"Sorry." She tried to calm her voice. After all, it wasn't his fault she'd lived the life of a nun for far too long. "There's some dirt ground into it. I need to clean it out."

She gentled her touch and allowed her fingers to graze his skin, the heat of him warm against her fingertips.

She heard his intake of breath, but whether it was from the cool rag on his cut or her fingers on his skin, she couldn't be sure.

As she dabbed at the rope burn, her vision blurred, and the raw mark shifted and grew. Soon, his back was covered with deep, red lash marks, as if he'd been whipped repeatedly. She felt sick, seeing strips of torn flesh and oozing welts where his smooth, tan skin used to be.

Serafina squeezed her eyes shut. But try as she might, the image of David, his back torn and ravaged, was still there.

He shifted and spoke over his shoulder to her.

"Sera, are you all right?"

POMPEII

"Fine. I'm fine," she snapped, swiping her hair out of her face.

She was lying. He could tell. But about what, David couldn't be sure.

Suddenly the question that had been in the back of his mind since they'd seen the newsreel appeared front and center. Why did she hate the Americans so? Common sense told him to leave it alone, that her reasons were none of his business.

But the soldier in him wanted to find out what Sera's secret was. Everyone had one. Lord knew, he was living proof of that. He needed to know if hers might somehow jeopardize his mission. All he had to do was find the right trigger to get her to talk.

The tunes she hummed when she thought no one was listening drifted back into his head.

"So, why do you sing American songs?"

The press of the cool cloth on his back stopped.

"I wasn't singing," she replied, but the telltale force she used when she resumed cleaning his cut told him she was embarrassed that he'd caught her at it.

"Yes, you were. And that's not the first time I've heard you doing it."

Angling to look at her over his shoulder, he planned his next words very carefully.

"What I find interesting is that you seem particularly fond of American Big Band tunes. I thought you hated Americans."

"I do."

"But you like their music?"

Sera's expression shifted to guarded in an instant. She pulled away, putting the relative safety of space between them. Even though she no longer touched him, David could still feel the heat of her fingertips burning a trail down his back.

She tossed the rag on the table and screwed the top on her canteen.

"It's not a crime."

"Ah, but Mussolini might disagree. It's illegal to listen to Allied broadcasts, and that's the only place you could be hearing those songs."

When her eyes met his, he saw alarm in them. Her face grew pale, making tiny brown freckles stand out on her checks. She stood and went back into the pit and resumed digging. The scrape of her trowel in the ash and pumice filled the silence around them.

"Don't worry. You aren't the only one to sneak a listen to the Allied broadcasts. If I had a radio, I'd listen to them myself." That, at least, was no lie. What he wouldn't give to hear daily news on the Allied front.

Sera sat in her little trench and stared at him. He could

almost see the wheels in her head turning as she weighed his words. Could she trust him? Would she?

Finally, she let out a heavy sigh.

"Maria and Heberto listen to the BBC on the radio, and occasionally I listen with them. Sometimes they play the Big Band songs. Besides, it's better than listening to Mussolini talk about the war."

"So, you don't like listening to *Il Duce's* lies?"

"They're not lies." Once more, her defenses came up.

David walked over and squatted down on the edge of the hole.

"Maybe not all of them, but you can't tell me you believe everything he says. That the war is succeeding? That Italy is stronger than ever because of her ties with Hitler?"

The scraping stopped, and she looked at him as if he were stupid.

"Do you expect me to believe the Americans are telling the truth about the war? That they care what happens to us as they trample their way across Italy to Germany?"

He shrugged to mask the tension he was feeling. He had to be careful. He was treading on fragile ground. If he asked too many questions, he risked exposing himself instead of discovering what lay behind Sera's issues with America.

"From what I've heard, the Allies aren't so bad. I've heard they've been dropping supplies for the poor and hungry all over Italy. Their medics treat the wounded and sick with medicines they might never get if it weren't for the U.S."

"That's just Allied propaganda." She turned back to her work, gauging deep chunks of earth in the pit. "They also drop bombs on innocent women and children. Those same bombs destroy centuries of art and history, so don't tell me the Allies care about us."

"And I suppose the Germans have been nothing but courteous to the citizens of Italy?"

"They've been better than the Americans."

"What has America ever done to you?"

David had to know. His mission—his life—might depend

on it.

"They're the enemy."

"So are Britain and France, but you seem to hate Americans in particular. Why?"

Sera's hand gripped her leg, the knuckles turning white as she clutched the muscle of her thigh.

"They have no business being here."

"Only Hitler and Mussolini think that." He rested his chin on his folded arms, prepared to pick at whatever scab he needed to in order to get some answers. "If the Allies can bring about the end of the war, all the better. Most of Italy couldn't care less who wins anymore."

"There are some who still care."

"The Fascists." He eyed her speculatively. "Are you a Fascist, Sera?"

She glared at him, her mouth compressed into a thin, hard line. He knew he was pushing her hard, but it was the only way he could get to her secrets.

"No, of course not."

"Then what is it? You certainly don't strike me as a resistance fighter." The very thought of reserved Sera with a gun in her hand almost made him laugh. Threaten her precious ruins, and she'd fight like a mother lion protecting her cubs, but otherwise she didn't seem to care about anything else.

"Tell me. Why do you hate the Americans so?"

The force she used with the trowel when she resumed digging told him he was getting too close, and she didn't like it. She turned her head away from him, and for a moment he thought he may have pushed her too far. Or maybe he hadn't pushed her far enough.

"Why, Sera?"

She threw her trowel in the dirt and whipped around to look at him, her blue eyes shooting daggers of fire.

"Damn it. Because my father is one."

CHAPTER XII

Serafina stared at David as his tan face paled. Had she shocked him? Was he appalled?

She told herself it didn't matter, that everyone in town knew what she was. It would have been only a matter of time before he found out, too.

But it did matter.

Bastarda. The word still hurt even after all these years. The looks from the women in the marketplace as she shopped with her mother, comments whispered behind cupped hands to protect a child's sensitive ears.

But she'd heard them. The taunting of her classmates when she was a young girl, words hurled at her on the playground like stones thrown at a stray dog. *Bastarda.*

Would David reject her, too?

Could he see her pain? She knew the truth was there, written all over her face. She could feel the strain in every muscle of her body as she tried to hold back the emotions.

He finally closed his gaping mouth, and a look of genuine concern replaced his stunned expression.

"Jesus, Sera. What did he do to you?"

Her shoulders slumped as the fight went out of her. She didn't have the strength to keep the past buried any more. At least, not with David.

"My mother was the prettiest girl in Pompei."

He moved from his squatting position to sit on the edge of the pit. She spoke so softly, he had to lean closer to hear her.

"She had her whole life ahead of her... and then she met a man. It was during the Great War. He was an American soldier stationed in Naples. To a girl from a small, remote town, I supposed he seemed brave, heroic. It wasn't hard for him to sweep her off her feet."

Understanding dawned in David's eyes as he listened to her story.

"Your father?"

"Yes." Her hatred of the man still left a bitter taste in her mouth. But she would not cry over him, not anymore. He wasn't worth it.

"What happened?"

She shrugged, trying to show her indifference over the man who gave her life. But if the simple act didn't fool her, how could she expect it to fool David?

"He did what a lot of American soldiers did then. Promised her the world, took what he wanted, and then left her behind."

"And you? Did he leave you behind, too?"

She ran her fingers through the loose earth in front of her, staring down at the dirt and ashes as they slipped through her fingers.

"He told my mother he'd send for us after the war was over."

"But he never did?"

She turned her head away. The story was all too familiar for many soldiers returning from war. Everyone knew that, but it didn't make the hurt any less. She shook her head.

"No, he sent a few letters and some money in the beginning. But even that small gesture stopped after a year or two."

"So, what happened?"

"My mother was disgraced. Her parents—my grandparents—stood by her, but most of the town shunned her when they found out she carried a bastard. An American bastard."

David sat silent for a long time. What was he thinking? How would he look at her now? She kept her gaze on the dirt in front of her, not daring to look up to see.

Finally he spoke, his voice a soft whisper.

"That must have been tough for her."

"It was."

"Did she ever marry?"

She thought of her beautiful mother's lovely face slowly becoming etched with lines of worry and exhaustion as she struggled year after year to support them both.

"No. This is a small town. People here don't forget that easily."

"What about you? It must have been hard for you growing up without a father."

Serafina recalled the many times she ran home from school, the other children's voices chanting close behind her as she darted down the narrow town streets.

"Children can be very cruel to anyone who's different."

"I'm sorry." There was a long silence between them before he spoke again. "Did you ever meet your father?"

"Once. My mother had me study English after school. I didn't know why at the time, but after she died, I found the few letters he'd sent her, and I knew. She was preparing me to meet him someday. So when I was nineteen, I went to America to find him."

The flapping of the canvas tent over their heads seemed to rip at the silence between them, the sound of the meager breeze tearing large holes in the delicate fabric of her emotions.

"And did you find him?" he finally asked.

She nodded.

"It took a while, but I finally did. In Arizona. I even spent a year studying archeology at the university there, trying to get up the courage to knock on his door and meet him face to face."

She could feel the sob welling up in her chest, threatening to burn a hole in her heart. The memory of his distant, dispassionate eyes when she told him who she was. The sound of the door slowly closing in her face, shutting her out of his life forever.

"He told me that he already had a family. He told me... to go back home."

Before she realized what he was doing, David slid down into the shallow pit and took her into his arms.

"I'm sorry, Sera. I didn't mean to bring up bad memories."

His arms felt so strong and comforting around her, she wanted to sink into his warmth. His smell, of musk and sunshine, surrounded her.

"He didn't want me," she sobbed, the dammed up emotions bursting forth as she clutched at his shoulders. "He didn't… want me."

He rocked her as if she were a child, one arm around her waist while the other cradled her head against his chest. Her tears dropped one by one on his skin, leaving wet streaks down the dust and dirt where his heart hammered beneath her cheek.

He held her for what seemed like an eternity, and then she felt his fingers beneath her chin. Gently, he tilted her head up and looked deep into her eyes.

"How could he not want you?" His gaze flicked to her mouth, then returned to stare at her eyes with a burning intensity. "How could anyone not want you?"

His brown eyes held all the warmth and compassion she'd never received from her father. From any man, for that matter. She felt herself falling into their depths, drowning in the fire blazing within them. She was lost.

He bent his head and kissed her, gently at first. She let him in, clutching at him and pulling him closer. The kiss deepened until his tongue crossed the boundary of her lips to delve inside. She welcomed the invasion, sinking deeper into his hold.

The thumping of the canvas overhead echoed the beating of her heart. Her head swam as he crushed her to him. She had never felt so comfortable, so desirable, so wanted. All were foreign feelings to her, and yet they felt so familiar with him.

David's hand moved from her waist to cup her cheek as the other held her head firmly in place for his kiss. His passion obliterated the painful memories, and, for the moment, they were the only two people on Earth.

Then he pulled away, leaving her bereft of his warmth. She tried to follow his mouth, but his hands on either side of her head would not let her.

She slowly opened her eyes, and the fog of desire quickly evaporated. A strange look had replaced the fire that had burned in his eyes only moments ago—a look that spoke words her mind could not decipher. He traced the curve of her moist lips with his thumb, a wistful expression clouding the passion on his face.

She could have sworn she'd seen that look on his face before, but for the life of her, she couldn't recall when or where.

"I'm sorry. I can't," he said. He gently released her and leaned back, putting a wide gulf between them. "I shouldn't have done that. I don't want it to be like this… not this way."

What did he mean? That he wanted to continue this, at some other time, some other place? Did she want to? Her emotions were in such turmoil, she wasn't sure what she wanted.

But it didn't matter. David took the choice from her.

He stood abruptly and walked away.

POMPEII

Marsha glared at Hershel, her hand fisted on her boney hips.

"You were supposed to get the boys to horse around with them so that Serafina could show her fun, nurturing side, not get David nearly killed."

"He wasn't nearly killed." Hershel crumpled his hat in his hands as he stood in the doorway of their kitchen. "It was a minor rope burn. Not like he lost a leg or anything."

She shook her finger at him.

"Lucky for you. With our record, we can't afford any minor anythings. They have a way of turning into major somethings, like the death of one or the other."

"Nobody died, and he did get to see her caring nature when she tended to the scrape on his back, just like you wanted."

"Well, that's good to know."

Marsha wiped her hands on her apron and took Hershel's lunch bucket and hat from him, setting them on a counter crowded with cheap porcelain bric-a-brac.

Hershel rubbed at the back of his grimy neck as he took a

seat at the kitchen table.

"I'll tell you, Marsha, being mortal again is hard work."

"Oh, stop whining, and tell me what else happened," Marsha said as she joined him.

He hesitated a bit too long, and she gave him the *look*, the one that said she could tell he was hiding something.

"What went wrong?"

"Hmmm?"

"Spit it out, Hershel. I can tell something went wrong. What is it?"

He winced. "Well, it appears David knows about her being half American and all."

She gaped at him like a fish tossed on the beach.

"He knows? How on earth did that happen?"

Hershel shrugged and started picking at the dirt under his fingernails.

"I guess it was when Serafina told him."

"She told him? How do you know?"

"I heard her tell him about it. I went to their area of the dig to check on how our little plan with the boys was progressing." Hershel looked pointedly at Marsha, just to make sure she knew he was doing his part of the job. "And I found them together."

"Together? What do you mean together?" She stepped closer, eager to hear any bit of juicy gossip.

"Well, when I got there, he was holding her, and she was crying about her father."

"Holding her? Holding her how?"

He was confused for a moment. "What do you mean how? His arms were wrapped around her. How else do you hold someone?"

"Think, Hershel. Was he holding her like a friend or like a lover?"

"I don't know. Is there a difference?"

"Of course there's a difference," Marsha grumbled, then shook her head. "And you wonder why we never had any children."

"What's that?"

"Never mind." She turned her attention back to the issue at hand. "What happened after he found out? How did he react?"

"I suppose he looked a little pale to me. Maybe even a bit queasy. Of course, she was really carrying on, sobbing all over him. It's enough to make any man uneasy."

"Of course you'd think that." She frowned at him. "Any time I get the least bit emotional, you run and hide."

"I do not." Hershel stiffened his spine. "At least not always," he conceded as his shoulders resumed their normally stooped posture.

Marsha glared at him, calling him a liar without saying a word.

"Well, can you blame me? Once you get started, you sound like an alley cat with its tail caught in the screen door."

Now it was her turn to get defensive. "I do not sound like a screeching cat."

"Oh, you're right, dear. It must be all the real ones in the neighborhood joining in the chorus who make all that racket."

"Now you're just being silly. Let's get back to David and Serafina. What else happened?"

"I don't know. I left. I didn't want them to catch me spying on them at such a tender moment." Hershel raised his bushy grey brows at Marsha, letting her know that he included the last bit of romantic information for her benefit.

He stood to go change out of his dirty work clothes, but stopped just before he left the kitchen. With his hand resting on the doorsill, he turned back to Marsha.

"Oh, yeah. And he kissed her."

"*What?*" She jumped up, knocking over her chair and sending it clattering on the tile floor. She chased after him down the narrow hallway. "He kissed her?"

"Yes. Almost forgot that part," he said as he entered their bedroom.

"How could you forget that? It's the most important part."

She plopped herself down on her small twin bed and stared across Hershel's matching one as he stood beside it unbuttoning his shirt. He shrugged out of the dirty garment, revealing his thin, boney body in a white undershirt stained yellow under the arms from long, hot days digging at the ruins.

"This is fantastic." Her eyes took on a dreamy glow. "He kissed her... even after he found out about her tainted background. I was so worried it might be a problem."

"Why would it be a problem?" Hershel pulled a clean shirt out of the armoire. "I mean, I can see if she found out about him, it could get ugly. But what's wrong with him knowing about her?"

Marsha pursed her lips, making the thin lines around her mouth more pronounced.

"I would have thought it would have put him on guard around her. After all, if his true identity is discovered, it could jeopardize his mission, even his life. Of all people, he now knows that Serafina might pick up on any Americanisms he may let slip."

Hershel finished buttoning his clean shirt, only to find he'd misaligned the holes and had to start over again.

"He certainly didn't seem too worried about it when I left them."

"Obviously not, if he was kissing her." Marsha stood and smoothed down the wrinkles on the bedspread. "This is just wonderful. At this rate, our mission on Earth might be over sooner than we anticipated."

POMPEII

American?

How could he not have guessed? The American Big Band tunes she liked to sing. The sky blue eyes, highlights of red in her caramel brown hair, and freckles on an otherwise dusky complexion. It seemed so obvious now. It took everything in him not to slap his hand against his forehead at how he could have missed it.

What kind of spy was he? David berated himself as he rode his bicycle through the narrow streets of Pompei.

Then he reminded himself that such physical characteristics in Italy weren't uncommon, especially in northern Italy where the Swiss, Germans, and French had infiltrated the population centuries before. He recalled Sera's fluent Italian and all her mannerisms. She may have been born with some of her American father's looks, but she had certainly gotten her fair share of her mother's Italian character.

Still, he should have known. Should have sensed it somehow.

In a way, he supposed he had suspected something. That's why he'd kept pushing her, trying to get her to open up. For the longest time he hadn't thought she would. Why should she? Why should she confide in him when they hardly knew each other?

But she had. She'd trusted him with her darkest secret.

The hurt when she spoke of her father was undeniable. Apparently, he had reopened deep wounds she kept hidden from the rest of the world. He ached for the lonely child she must have been. No wonder she was so aloof. She'd grown a very hard shell years before.

And he had cracked it wide open with a few well-aimed words.

Thinking back to the previous afternoon, all he had wanted to do at the time was comfort her, to somehow make things right. And so, idiot that he was, he'd slid down beside her in the pit and taken her in his arms.

It had seemed innocent enough and the right thing to do at the time. Something a friend would do. But even as he held her, he'd thought, *Better to keep your distance, Corbin. The closer you get, the more likely she is to find out who you really are.*

Then when she turned her tear-filled eyes up to his, his concern for his mission had gone flying out the window. At that moment, he just worried about her, and he comforted her in the only way he could.

He'd kissed her.

Stupid. Stupid. Stupid.

The word was becoming a mantra in his head as he made

his way to the weekly rendezvous with Frank. This time they were meeting just outside of town, on the main road leading to Naples. There was plenty of tourist traffic, so two men stopping to chat with each other generally went unnoticed.

"Where have you been?"

David hopped off his bicycle and took the offered cigarette without question this time.

"My landlady tried to talk me into going to Mass with her this morning. I had to convince her that my soul wasn't in dire jeopardy of burning eternally in hell."

"That's what you think. She might have a point there." Frank grinned, obviously not feeling the least bit sorry for him. They strolled to the top of a hill, away from traffic.

"Any luck finding out where the Germans are stashing those munitions?"

"Not yet. The ruins are crawling with *krauts*, but they're behaving more like tourists than soldiers. Other than the weapons they carry on them, I haven't seen a single piece of heavy artillery come through the gates."

"Well, they've got to be putting them somewhere." Frank took a drag on his cigarette. "And you need to find out where soon."

"I know. I'm doing as much searching as I can without drawing suspicion. Speaking of which, I've got a big problem to deal with."

Frank's amused demeanor instantly turned serious. "What's up?"

"That woman, the one I work with... for? I just found out she's half American."

Frank blew out a long whistle along with the smoke he'd just inhaled.

"How can that be? Weren't all Americans still in Italy put in detention camps in forty-one?"

"That's what I thought, too."

"So, why isn't she in one? Just how American is she?"

David shrugged, reluctant to rehash Sera's painful childhood with someone who didn't know her.

"She's a World War I by-blow. Apparently, her father was an American G.I. stationed in Naples, but he never married her mother. She's spent some time in the States, but I guess since she considers herself more Italian than not, she's not considered a risk. Plus, she's made her loyalties painfully clear, and it isn't with our side."

Frank pointed two fingers with the cigarette wedged between them at David.

"Yeah, but she's a big risk to you, my friend."

"Don't you think I know that?" *In more ways than one,* he thought as the memory of their kiss flashed through his mind. *Stupid, stupid, stupid* chanted through his head once more.

Frank dropped his cigarette in the grass and crushed it beneath his heel.

"If I were you, buddy, I'd get myself as far away from that lady as I could. One slip from you, and she could blow the whole mission."

David knew that. His mission, his life, might depend on it.

But how could he stay away from her when all he wanted was to kiss her again?

CHAPTER XIII

David parked his bicycle beside the others left outside the entrance to the ruins. Sera's was already there, and his stomach tightened into a knot knowing she was somewhere behind the stone walls.

He couldn't be sure if the feeling was one of apprehension or anticipation at the thought of seeing her again. All weekend, he'd thought of nothing but Sera and the fact that she was part American.

That, and the kiss they'd shared.

Frank was right. He needed to get far away from her as fast as he could before she discovered who he really was. She was simply a risk he couldn't take.

He passed several groups of people standing about and caught fragments of their conversations. The fact that people still found the time and money to travel during times of war amazed him. Each day the ruins literally crawled with tourists eager to look at the tragedy the archeologists were slowly uncovering in the ancient town. He supposed people used to come from all over the world, but for the moment, only the Italians, Germans, and Japanese were welcome. U.S. citizens did not dare travel abroad. He was the only American within a hundred miles.

Except for Sera.

A chorus of giggles filled the air as he made his way down the rutted street. He glanced over at a group of teenaged schoolgirls dressed in matching green plaid skirts and white short-sleeved blouses. They clustered with their teacher around one of the archeologists as he basked in the circle of their admiration. The man spoke Italian in a deep voice, explaining to the girls the rudimentary methods of excavating the ruins.

He held the class in rapt attention, but David couldn't tell if their focus was on the lesson or the lecturer. He would guess women might consider the guy handsome with his dark Mediterranean looks. Of course, he didn't have much competition, given the average age of the other archeologists and laborers at the ruins was fifty.

As David drew closer, he could tell from the smug look on the man's face and his cocky stance that he was aware of that fact and not afraid to exploit it.

One of the young girls laughed at something the man said, and he smiled back at her, revealing a row of perfect white teeth displayed against tanned skin. Christ, the girl couldn't have been more than fifteen.

He paused, struck by the feeling that the man was familiar somehow, that he had seen him somewhere before, but he couldn't quite place him. He shook his head in disgust. He had met the man's kind before and never could understand how women fell for them. Maybe that's what seemed familiar about him.

As he passed the group, David overheard the man describing all his discoveries at the site. By his account, he had single-handedly unearthed the whole city himself.

"*Che palle.*" Bullshit. David coughed into his fist, half-heartedly trying to muffle the derogatory comment.

Mr. Showoff glanced in his direction and narrowed his eyes at David until one of the girls drew his attention away with another question about his famous discoveries.

David shoved his hands in the front pockets of his pants and continued on his way. Let the mother hen of a teacher keep an eye on her chicks while the fox was about. He had his own problems to worry about.

Sera. What was he going to do about her?

Common sense told him to request a transfer to somewhere else on the dig. Maybe he could work with Sera's friend Olympia? She seemed to get along with him well enough. Or better yet, he should just quit and find another job somewhere else outside the ruins, one that would allow him free access to observe the German's movements. But no better place existed. He needed to be on the inside, to find out where they were hiding munitions.

Neither of the choices was good—leave now and possibly sacrifice the mission, or stay and risk being discovered and shot as a spy.

Man, this sucked. So much for thinking this would be a simple mission. Of course, nothing about the mission had been simple since meeting Sera. With a heavy heart, David realized that was the hardest part of all. His greatest reason for leaving was the main reason he wanted to stay.

Sera.

He was so focused on figuring out what he was going to do, he nearly knocked down poor Heberto coming the other way in the street. He reached out and steadied the old man by his thin shoulders.

"Sorry about that. Are you all right?"

"Oh, fine, fine. These old bones aren't as brittle as you think." Heberto brushed some dust off the front of his khaki vest, smiling up at him all the while. "So, how are things going over in your area?"

Here it is, he thought. *Here's my chance to get out of this situation before it's too late.*

"Actually, I need to talk to you about that. I'm afraid I can't work here anymore."

Heberto's smile instantly vanished.

"Oh, dear. Why not?"

"It's just that… well, I don't think I can work here any-more."

"Really?" Heberto's brow creased in confusion. "I thought you and Serafina were getting along."

"We're getting along just fine." *Too fine.* "It's not that."

The old man placed a grandfatherly hand on David's shoulder, and they started walking down the street together.

"Now, I know Serafina can be a bit of a trial. Sometimes she can even get downright bossy."

"No, no. It's nothing Sera has done." *It's who she is that's the problem.*

"Oh, then what is it?"

She's half-American. She speaks English. She could figure out who I am and blow my cover. She could jeopardize the whole mission. All valid reasons to avoid her, but he couldn't give a single one of them to Heberto.

The old man seemed to sense David's hesitation.

"You have to understand some things about Serafina. She hasn't exactly had the easiest life…"

I know, she told me all about it.

"… and it takes her a while to warm up to strangers."

David had to choke back a humorless laugh. *Hardly. She just about burst into flames when I kissed her. Both of us did.*

"But believe me, once she trusts you and lets you get close, you'll have no greater ally."

Sure, until she finds out I've been lying to her all along, and I break that trust into a thousand pieces.

David looked up to find Heberto had walked him all the way to the street leading to their dig site. He could see Sera down the road, working alone under the canvas tent.

Heberto patted him gently on the shoulder, bringing David's attention back to the old man standing beside him. He looked at David with eyes that spoke of wisdom learned through decades of life experiences.

"David, I've known Serafina since she was born. She's been like a granddaughter to us. Whatever it is, you can trust her. Take a chance. You may be surprised at what you receive in return." Heberto smiled and walked away.

David watched him go. Why was it he felt the old man knew something he didn't?

He turned back to find Sera watching him. Well, he was here now. He had no choice but to trust her, at least for another day.

As he walked toward her, he wondered what she would do if she found out he was an American spy. Probably shoot him on the spot.

She stared at him with her fathomless blue eyes. What was she thinking? What was she feeling? She looked unsure, tentative. Was she experiencing the same emotions he was?

The uncomfortable silence seemed to expand in the space between them, until he thought it might explode from the tension.

"You left early on Friday."

Well, at least she was brave enough to face the subject head on. Coward that he was, he'd left the site that day, running like a frightened dog with his tail tucked between his legs. It had been wishful thinking that she might have forgotten that part.

"Yes, well." What could he say? *Your confession scared the hell out of me, but kissing you scared me even more, so I got the hell out of there as fast as I could.* "What happened between us... it was a mistake. It shouldn't have happened."

One thin brow arched at him under the brim of her hat. "A *mistake*?" She bit out the last word through clenched teeth.

"Yes... no. I mean, I can't...we shouldn't... it's probably not a good idea for us to..."

"I see."

No, she didn't. And he wasn't helping things, tripping over his own tongue like a virgin schoolboy.

"Is it because of what I am?"

Yes. "No, it's not that." Jesus, he couldn't think when she looked at him with those big, blue eyes brimming with wariness and vulnerability.

"Then what is it?"

The tone of her voice said she didn't believe him. Who could blame her? He evidently wasn't doing a very good job of lying. What she said was the truth, but he couldn't tell her that.

"Is there..." Sera bit her lower lip, obviously trying to hold back whatever question she was about to ask. She finally asked it anyway. "Is there someone else?"

"Yes." He jumped on the excuse. *And her name is America.*

He regretted his answer as soon as he saw the hurt flash in

her eyes. She turned away and ducked back under her tent. Damn, he hated to lie to her.

David sighed and walked over to pick up his shovel. It was probably better this way, letting her believe there was another woman. Maybe it would be all he needed to keep his distance. And distance was what he needed right now. Like it or not, he had a secret to keep, even if he had to hurt her to do it.

POMPEII

"*Gli uomini sono feccia*." Men are scum.

"Hear! Hear!" Olympia clinked her glass of wine to Sera's, then caught the disconcerted look of the elderly woman sitting across from her. "Well, except for Heberto, of course," she conceded to Maria, their third drinking partner.

The three women sat at a tiny table in a small café. They'd been there for nearly an hour and were on their second bottle of wine. It wasn't an expensive bottle by any means, but it served its purpose.

"Well, of course not Heberto." Maria toasted with her own glass and took a tiny sip. "Although he does have his moments."

"Yes, but even his few moments probably can't compare to the rest of the male race," Sera grumbled.

Maria reached over and patted her hand.

"There now, dear. Don't throw all the grapes out because one has a worm in it. I'm sure there's someone out there who's just perfect for you."

Sera shook her head. "I doubt it. At least I've certainly yet to meet him."

Maria frowned, then smiled hopefully at her. "Well, what about that nice young man you're working with?"

Olympia nearly choked on her wine. "He's the scum she's talking about."

"Really?" Maria looked surprised, glancing back and forth between Sera and Olympia. "Heberto says he seems like such a pleasant young man."

"Yes, a true gentleman. One that kisses me one day and

tells me he has a girlfriend the next."

Now it was Maria's turn to sputter. "But he can't have a girlfriend."

"Why not?" Sera asked. "It's the story of my life. Fall for a guy, then find out there's another woman waiting in the wings."

If the truth be told, she was angrier at herself than David. She'd let her guard down around him. Again. She never should have done that. For heaven's sake, he even had her thinking of herself as Sera now.

What was it about him that got under her skin? How could he get her to forget herself so easily? And why did he seem almost... familiar?

She groaned inwardly, recalling their kiss in the pit. *My God, I practically threw myself at the man. How desperate am I?*

Maria's large eyes opened wider as she stared at Sera, her interest suddenly piqued.

"So you've fallen for him, have you?"

Apparently, Maria was choosing to ignore the "other woman" part of the story.

Sera casually waved her hand in the air, while inside she desperately wished she could take back the words.

"No, that's not what I meant. It's just that, well, I thought he might be different. But apparently, he's not."

The disappointment tasted bitter in her mouth. She took a big sip of wine to wash down the foul taste.

"This just can't be. It has to be a mistake," Maria mumbled, then turned to Sera. "Perhaps you misunderstood him?"

"Oh, I don't think so." She chuckled humorlessly. "I asked him point blank if there was someone else, and he said yes. It doesn't get any clearer than that."

Maria still looked confused. "I just don't understand it. This wasn't supposed to happen."

"What wasn't supposed to happen?" Olympia tore a piece of bread from the loaf they were sharing and popped it in her mouth. "What are you talking about?"

Maria paled and looked guilty at being caught talking to herself. Lowering her eyes, she began tracing the pattern in the white lace tablecloth with her finger.

"Oh, don't mind me. I'm just an old woman rambling on about fate and destiny." She sighed and cast a pitying look in Sera's direction. "It just seems that after all you've been through, it's time for you to have a chance at love, that's all."

Sera picked up her glass of wine and watched as the light from the candle on the table refracted in its burgundy depths.

"Well, Maria, I suppose love just isn't meant for someone like me. It seems that the Fates or Destiny or whatever's out there has screwed up once again."

POMPEII

Hershel paced the floor of the dimly lit living room, glancing at the clock on the mantel as it slowly ticked away each passing minute.

Ten thirty-six.

Where on Earth could Marsha be? She'd sent a boy with a note saying she'd run into Serafina and Olympia and was going to have dinner with them. That had been at half past five. Honestly, how long did it take three women to eat?

As if in answer, he heard the front door to the building open and close. The sound of shuffling feet and muffled giggles echoed down the center hallway. He jerked open the front door to the apartment to find Serafina propping a nearly limp Marsha against the doorframe.

"My stars, what's going on here?"

Marsha's head popped up, bobbing precariously on her thin neck. She squinted at Hershel, finally appearing to focus her bleary eyes on his face.

"None of your business, Signore Man."

The smell of cheap wine wafted to his nose, telling him all he needed to know. She was blind drunk.

"Maria! What has gotten into you?"

Serafina transferred Marsha's weight into Hershel's arms, then looked at him through her own bloodshot eyes.

"Be careful, He-Heberto," she warned him in a slurred voice. "She'sh had a good dose of male bashing tonight. She jus' might turn on you while you sleep."

"Male bashing? What do you mean?"

"It's all Da-*hic*-vid's fault." Marsha punched Hershel in the arm, startling him so badly he nearly dropped her. "Men are pigs."

Her wobbly head plopped on his chest, where she closed her eyes and proceeded to snore softly.

Oh, no. What had David done now? Hershel looked from Marsha to Serafina and back again. And what had the two women done to his poor wife?

"Sorry, Heberto." Serafina turned and wove her way to the base of the stairs, bumping into the wall before she got there. "Olympia and I corrupted her tonight. Be prepared. She's probably going to wake up mad as hell at you in the morning, but won't remember why."

She started up the steps, stumbling on the second one. Gripping the rail tighter, she concentrated on taking the next step carefully, as if her life depended on it.

"Why would she be mad at me?"

Serafina snorted. "Because you're a man."

Hershel watched her stagger up the rest of the stairs and listened as she tumbled into her apartment and slammed the door.

Closing his own door, he shifted Marsha's wilted form in his arms. As tiny as she was, her dead weight felt like a wet sack of cement.

He looked down at her sleeping face, with her mouth sagging open and tiny snores growling from the back of her throat. Why, he hadn't seen Marsha this shnockered in over two thousand years.

"Come, dear. Let's get you to bed."

As he half-dragged his wife to their bedroom, Hershel was already dreading tomorrow. It wasn't going to be pretty.

CHAPTER XIV

The *chunk-thunk, chunk-thunk* of David's shoveling was giving Sera a pounding headache. Of course, the vat of wine she had drunk the night before wasn't helping matters any.

The talk—or what she remembered of it—with Olympia and Maria had eased some of her wounded feelings. But not all of them. The sting of his rejection still hurt.

When she thought back on it, though, she couldn't really blame him for what he'd done. After all, she'd been crying and hanging all over him like a clinging vine. What red-blooded male wouldn't take advantage of the situation? She just wished the red-blooded male in question hadn't already been attached to someone else at the time.

At least she had to give David credit for stopping things before they went too far. If it had been left to her, who knows what might have happened. Sex in the excavation pit? At the time, the prospect had seemed appealing, but now the thought made her ill.

Men. She should have known better. Hadn't she learned anything from her past mistakes?

"So this is where they stuck you."

Speaking of past mistakes. Sera groaned inwardly and looked up into the face of Giovanni Ragusa. Her day just wasn't going to get any better, was it?

"I suppose it was too much to hope you'd never venture over into this area of the ruins."

Giovanni smiled, but the humor never quite reached his piercing dark eyes. He glanced around the site, and she could tell from the way he pursed his lips that he was mentally criticizing how she'd chosen to set it up. His scrutiny passed briefly over the area where David was working and shot back again. Following the direction of his gaze, she turned to see David staring back at the two of them. Both men straightened their spines and stood taller as they appeared to size up each other.

How typically male, she thought.

"You can stop snooping, Giovanni," Sera said, bringing his attention back to her. "We haven't gone deep enough yet to find any artifacts for you to steal."

He actually had the audacity to look offended.

"I don't steal artifacts."

"Steal the credit, then." Damn, but his claiming the silver cup still rankled her.

"Poor, poor Serafina. Still touchy over that little misunderstanding, are we? I would have thought you would be over that by now." He shook his head as if he were talking to a disgruntled child. "Besides, look at what you have now. Just what you've always wanted—your own dig site."

She rose to her feet and climbed out of the hole so he wouldn't be looking down on her quite as much.

"That's right, and anything found here will be credited to me. No more *misunderstandings*."

Standing over six feet tall, he still laughed down at her.

"Yes, but unfortunately this is a poor section of the town. Nothing but small merchants' shops and vendors' stalls. No rich villas or temples. I doubt you will find anything of importance here."

"Then I guess that means you'll be leaving?"

Giovanni might have taken the hint had David not chosen that moment to head to the trucks with another load of debris. He rolled the dirt-filled wheelbarrow up to them, nearly running over Giovanni's right foot.

"Oh, sorry about that," he said to Giovanni, but she could tell by the mock-innocent look on his face and the flip tone of his voice that he really didn't mean it. She had to bite her lip to keep from laughing as Giovanni jumped out of the way at the last minute.

The two men glared at each other, and she could practically smell the testosterone permeating the air.

Ridiculous. Neither of them gave a fig about her, but being the pig-headed men that they were, neither was willing to back down.

Glancing back and forth between them, she was struck by the differences between the two men. Both had black hair, but where Giovanni's was shiny and smooth, David's was soft and wavy. Giovanni had high cheekbones and a strong, prominent jaw line, while David had full lips and a dimple in the middle of his chin.

Both were tall, dark, and handsome—trouble times two and more than she could deal with on top of her morning-after hangover.

With a heavy sigh, she did the inevitable and introduced them.

"Giovanni Ragusa, this is David Corbelli, my assistant. Giovanni is one of the senior archeologists at the ruins."

David wiped his hand on his sweaty shirtfront before offering it to Giovanni.

"I know. I've seen him around."

Giovanni's lip curled slightly as he looked at David's offered hand. Finally, he took it, the muscles of his forearm bunching as he shook it with undue effort. David didn't even flinch, returning the shake with a grip that turned his knuckles white.

Sera couldn't control the roll of her eyes. If she didn't separate them soon, they'd probably start arm wrestling in front of her to prove who was more manly.

"If you don't mind, Giovanni, we have a lot of work to do."

"Yes, I can see that."

He finally released David's hand, staring long and hard at him before turning his attention back to Sera.

Sera should have known by the look in Giovanni's eyes that he was going to do something. She should have known from past experience that he would not leave without getting the upper hand on her—or David.

He reached out and, with the tender touch of a lover, ran the back of his fingers down her cheek.

"*Fino a più successivamente allora, il mio amore.*" Until later then, my love.

He did it so fast, she didn't have time to react. She didn't even draw a breath until after he started walking away.

"*Il mio amore?*" David asked, his brows raised high and an incredulous look on his face.

"Not hardly." Not anymore. She squeezed her eyes shut, willing the sensation of Giovanni's touch to go away.

When she finally opened her eyes, she found David watching her. He was furious, but at whom?

"Why do you put up with that if he's not your boyfriend?"

Why, indeed? The initial shock gave way to anger. Anger at Giovanni for attempting to stake a claim on her in front of David. Anger at herself, because she hadn't seen it coming and stopped him. And anger at life, because she could do nothing about it.

"He has seniority over me, and, like it or not, the archeological world is a male-dominated profession, and a woman who wants to do more than dabble is barely tolerated in it. He could have me fired if I don't follow the rules, and I don't know what I would do if I couldn't work at the ruins."

David turned his attention back to Giovanni's retreating figure as he strutted down the road.

"But is it worth putting up with that?"

Sera tried to swallow the sour taste in her mouth.

"Unfortunately, I don't have a choice."

POMPEII

Hershel crept quietly into the apartment. Early that morning, Marsha had done little more than growl at him when he'd turned on the light to get dressed. He'd beat a hasty exit, leaving her still in her bed. Now, with the house silent and no lights on, he wondered if she'd even gotten out of bed all day.

"Hershel, is that you?" The voice from the living room startled him as he walked past the darkened doorway.

"Yes, dear. It's me." All the shades had been drawn, and he made his way to his favorite chair from memory. "Are you still among the living?"

"Unfortunately," she groaned. After a long pause, she spoke again. "Did you know David has a girlfriend?"

Hershel turned his head, pinpointing Marsha's voice in the vicinity of the couch.

"You mean Serafina?"

"No, not Serafina. There's someone else."

"Someone else? Since when?" As his eyes adjusted to the darkness, he could tell she was lying down, but he couldn't figure out which end was her feet and which was her head.

"I don't know. He just told Serafina about her yesterday."

Yes, he had definitely been talking to her feet. He turned his head slightly so he could speak to where her head should be.

"That can't be. Not after how I saw them together on Friday."

"Well, it is. And we need to find out who she is so we can put a stop to this nonsense. The last thing we need is another woman getting in the middle of things."

Hershel scratched at his forehead. Something just didn't seem right.

"I don't understand it. There was nothing in his contract mentioning another woman. Where did she come from?"

"Who knows?" Marsha grumbled. "With our luck, it was probably in the fine print, and neither of us had our glasses on to read it properly."

"It doesn't make sense." He slumped in his chair, trying to make rhyme or reason of this latest turn of events. "When I talked to David today, he didn't say a thing about having a girlfriend."

"Well, of course he didn't. Why would he mention it to you in passing, when it took him this long to tell Serafina, and he sees her every day?"

"We weren't just chit-chatting." How dare she belittle his efforts. After all, he was the one slaving away at the ruins, doing all the dirty work and making sure David and Serafina bonded, while she stayed at home in ease and comfort. "As a matter of fact, I had to spend a good deal of time trying to talk him out of leaving."

"He was going to leave?" Marsha's dark form struggled to a sitting position. "As in 'quit the job at the site and go away?' He was going to leave our Serafina?"

"That's right. He never came right out and said why he wanted to leave, but you and I both know it's because he found out she's American. I imagine it's got him running scared." Hershel straightened a bit in his easy chair, feeling more important by the moment. "In the end, I convinced him to stay."

"That's good." A heavy sigh came from the shadow on the couch. "Hopefully, he won't change his mind before we have a chance to get this other woman out of the picture."

He hoped so, too. Sitting in the dark silence, Hershel tried to put his finger on what had gone wrong. Another woman? After the lip-lock he'd seen the two of them sharing under the tent, that puzzle piece just didn't fit.

POMPEII

Rain fell in large droplets, splattering mud where it plopped on the water-soaked ground. The rain had been coming down off and on for days, turning the hard, sun-baked earth to brown sludge. Tiny rivers ran down the middle of the stone streets, finding the path of least resistance in the ancient wheel ruts carved by centuries of wagon traffic. It was a miserable time to be working at the ruins, but then, miserable weather suited Sera's mood just fine.

David had barely spoken to her since the infamous kiss. An unspoken understanding seemed to hang between them that they would stay on professional terms and nothing more from now on. That would have suited her fine if their relationship had never progressed beyond that in the first place.

But it had.

She had come to see David as not just a laborer, but as a friend. She missed the way he constantly teased her, always trying to make her open up or to laugh in the moment.

She missed the way he always seemed eager to learn about the history of Pompeii and the methods of excavating the site, how he seemed genuinely interested in her work.

She missed the way he called her Sera, his nickname for her ever since they met. She'd hated it then because it sounded too American, and anything American reminded her too much of her father. But like it or not, from then on, she had been Sera to him.

She shook her head at her thoughts as she dug out another chunk of wet earth with her trowel. Funny how it hadn't taken long for her to start referring to herself as Sera, too. And even funnier still, American-sounding though it was, she really didn't mind anymore.

American. She still wasn't convinced that her being half American didn't have something to do with his change in attitude toward her. She'd had enough experience with others treating her differently once they found out about her tainted blood.

She sighed, feeling the weight of regret deep in her chest. If only she hadn't told him about her father. If only she hadn't broken down and sobbed out her whole sad story to him. If only she hadn't thrown herself in his arms and kissed him. If only there weren't someone else in his life. If only…

Her legs throbbed from kneeling in the wet pit, and her back ached from staying hunched over in the damp air all day. The tent over her head offered some protection, but a fine mist kept seeping its way in under her rain slicker to moisten her clothes underneath.

She looked up as David walked by with his wheelbarrow filled with rocks and wet earth. Day after day, he worked alongside her in the rain and the mud, never complaining. Of course, he'd actually have to speak more than two words to her in order to complain.

Deciding to stop for the day, she packed up her supplies, covered the screening table with a tarp, and followed him down the road. She stayed a short distance behind, giving him the space he obviously wanted, and watched as his broad shoulders bore his heavy burden down the rutted street.

His hips seemed to move in a rhythm all their own, his loose-fitting pants doing little to conceal his muscular thighs. Heat crept up under her slicker, making her skin feel flush against the clammy moisture of the weather.

She squeezed her eyes shut, trying to block out the memory of how his skin felt beneath her fingertips, and another image, hazy at first, replaced it in her mind. It was David, standing with his back bared, vivid red slashes streaking across it as droplets of blood trailed down to his waist.

Her eyes flew open, focusing on where he walked steadily in front of her. His dark green raincoat covered his back where droplets of rain, not blood, ran down the fabric to fall to the ground.

Where had that image come from? The impression chilled her almost enough to make her feel ill.

Sera walked through the gate and went to strap her pack to the back of her bicycle. She couldn't stop herself from watching David as he pushed the wheelbarrow up the ramp to dump it in the back of a waiting truck. White smoke chugged from the truck's tailpipe, its engine running as its driver anticipated the end of the day.

A sharp thud landed in the middle of her back. Turning, she found her favorite three troublemakers grinning at her.

"Very funny. I suppose you didn't think I was dirty enough, so you had to add some more?"

"Yeah," Bruno, the oldest one, chuckled. "It looked like you missed a spot, so we thought we'd help you out."

"Missed a spot, you say?" Sera leaned down to scoop up a handful of mud as she approached the trio. "Seems like you all missed some spots yourselves—like your mouths. How about I make you eat some of this mud?"

The boys laughed in delight, scattering in three different directions. She charged after Carlo, but he suddenly cut to the left, and her feet nearly slid out from under her as she tried to follow after him.

"Ha, Serafina. You're always too slow." She looked up to see Bruno hanging on the side of the dump truck, laughing down at her. "You'll never catch him, trudging about like a fat cow stuck in the mud."

She grinned. "Maybe I can't catch Carlo, but I can still hit you."

She threw the mud clod at him, but he shimmied along the side of the truck to the narrow space between the cab and the load carrier, dodging away just in time. The mud splattered on the side, oozing down the slick metal surface.

The grating sound of metal against metal groaned through the air. Bruno frantically gripped the edge of the truck as the back began to rise. His shocked expression told her everything. He'd accidentally bumped into the control lever, knocking the dumping mechanism into gear.

The boy jumped to the ground, landing on his feet with a large splat in the mud.

Sera breathed a sigh of relief until a movement to the side caught her eye. Little Antonio darted around the back of the truck, just as the hatch started to open under the pressure of the sliding dirt in the tilting bed.

"Antonio, no!" she screamed, charging toward him to shove him out of the way.

The edge of the hatch hit her shoulder as it opened. Dirt, both wet and dry, tumbled out, slamming into her legs and side, knocking her down.

In an instant, everything went dark. She couldn't move her arms or legs. The earth crushed down on her, the weight stealing a little more of each breath she tried to take. Dirt and mud invaded her mouth and nose, filling her airway, coating her tongue, and choking her.

She could feel Antonio's small body under her own. He wasn't moving either. Was he alive? Could he breathe?

Her own air-starved lungs burned, threatening to explode inside her chest. Her eyes watered beneath her lids, the tears mixing with the dirt to make more mud that tried to seep back into her eyes.

She wanted to cry out, but there was no air left to make a sound. Dirt filled her ears. She could hear nothing but the pounding of her own heart as it struggled to continue to beat without oxygen.

Sera!

David? Was he calling to her?

Sera!

His voice seemed so far away, and she desperately reached for it, tried to grab onto it with her mind to keep herself from slipping away. But it was too hard. She couldn't find him.

And then her world went silent.

CHAPTER XV

David clawed at the dirt like a dog.

"Sera!"

One minute he'd been watching her playing with the boys, laughing as she hadn't done all week, thanks to him. The next, she was diving behind the tilting truck bed, trying to shove the smallest of the boys out of the way. In a matter of seconds both were gone, covered by an avalanche of dirt, rocks, and mud.

"Sera!"

He dug with both hands, not daring to use a shovel for fear he might hit her or the boy. Others were all around him on their knees, laborers and archeologists alike, digging at a frantic pace.

With each handful of dirt he shoved away, wet earth and rocks tumbled down from the top of the pile to replace it. It seemed he was getting nowhere, but he couldn't stop. Not when every second counted.

"Hold on, Sera! We'll get you out!"

The drizzle turned the exposed dirt to mud, making it thicker, heavier. He was sure the weight was crushing her and the boy. He tried not to think about it as the sludge oozed through his fingers every time he grabbed for more.

Drops of rain ran down his face, seeping under his collar and dripping off the ends of his hair, mixing with the mud to burn in his eyes. He didn't stop to wipe it out of the way. There was no time.

He dug at the earth with the frenzy of a madman, tossing rocks and stones out of the way, not caring where they landed. Pain ripped up his fingers, through his hands, and along his arms. He was sure he could feel his nails being torn from their beds. But he didn't care. If they didn't get Sera and the boy out soon, both would suffocate. Both would die.

"Damn it, Sera. Don't you die on me."

The image of the plaster child flashed through his mind—a child who suffocated in a rain of ashes. If he didn't hurry, Sera and the boy would die a similar, horrible death.

He threw his back into the effort, tunneling down deeper and deeper in the dirt and mud. God, where were they? He had to reach them in time. He had to.

Finally, after what seemed like an eternity, he scooped away a handful of mud and uncovered Sera's hand, dirty and lifeless.

"Here! She's here!" he shouted. He dug with frenzied motions, working his way toward her head.

The others continued to dig in spots all over the pile. Why wasn't anyone helping him dig here? Hadn't they heard him?

"*Rapidamente! Qui. La abbiamo trovata.*" Quick! Over here. We've found her, he heard Heberto shout.

Only then did the others join David, digging close to him, uncovering her shoulder, her back, her legs, the back of her head. She didn't move at all as they removed the debris from her.

He burrowed his arms underneath her body and pulled her from the dirt. The boy lay beneath her, as still as Sera. Hardly any dirt covered his face and body. Sera had shielded him from most of it with her own body. Still holding her, David wasted precious seconds watching to see if the boy was hurt. Finally, he saw the rise and fall of his small chest. He was breathing. The boy was alive.

There was no time to feel relief. David carried Sera's limp body to a level area of ground, laying her carefully on her back. He wiped at the mud on her face. It was everywhere, in her ears, in the creases of her eyes, packed up her nose.

God, she was so still, so pale, even under all the dirt and mud. He placed his head on her chest. She wasn't breathing.

Somewhere, in the background, he heard the young boy cry out and cheers from the people erupt around him. He wanted to feel happy that the boy was all right, but he couldn't as long as Sera wasn't breathing. God, what should he do?

He did the only thing he could think of. Rolling her onto her stomach, he started pressing on her back, just as he'd been taught to do for a drowning victim. He pushed so hard trying to get her to breathe that he feared he might break her ribs.

"You have to clear her airway."

"What?" David paused, looking to the side to find Heberto kneeling beside him.

"Get the dirt out of her mouth," the old man said. "It's choking her."

Rolling her over, David tilted her head back and put his fingers in her mouth, scooping out the mud that coated her tongue. He placed his head on her chest again.

"She's still not breathing."

He looked at Heberto, feeling absolutely helpless. The old man seemed strangely calm.

"You have to breathe for her."

Breathe for her? What did he mean?

"How?"

"Pinch her nose closed, then breathe into her mouth."

David didn't question how Heberto knew to do this. He just did it. He placed his lips over hers like a lover's kiss, breathing his air into her mouth, praying it would reach her lungs in time.

Heberto moved to kneel across from him and started pressing down on her chest.

"Come on, Sera. Breathe," David urged her.

"Again," Heberto said.

David breathed into her mouth once more and watched her chest rise and fall, then remain still.

Heberto pumped on her chest several more times, then paused.

"Again."

Soon, Heberto didn't have to tell him when to breathe and when to stop. The two men fell into a natural rhythm, ignoring the crowd of onlookers around them.

Over and over again, David breathed for her, trying to stop the ruins she loved so much from taking her life. Finally, she coughed, sputtered, and gagged, gasping for air. He rolled her on her side so that she could vomit up the mud she'd swallowed.

When her spasms subsided, he rolled her back, cradling her in his arms. Sera's eyes fluttered opened briefly. She looked up at him, but he couldn't be sure if she really saw him. Her eyes drifted closed again, her breathing raspy at best, but at least she was breathing.

Only then did relief wash over him.

Somewhere in the distance, he heard the wail of an ambulance siren. Someone must have finally called for help.

He tore his eyes from Sera's face and looked up to see Heberto kneeling across from him, his dirt-covered hands clasped tightly in front of his chest as if in prayer. The old man's lower lip quivered, and his glistening eyes met David's as a single tear trailed down his dirty, weathered cheek.

POMPEII

Marsha dodged through the crowd of people, fear making her clutch at the coat she held draped over her head to protect her hair from the rain. Finally, spying Hershel standing among the other workers, she plowed toward him, grabbed him by the arm, and pulled him to the side.

"I heard there was an accident at the site. What on Earth happened?"

Hershel leaned against the outer wall of the ruins and mopped at his dirty neck with his handkerchief. He breathed heavily, looking like he'd just run a marathon.

"Dump truck... dirt everywhere... little Antonio... Serafina... buried..."

Marsha rested her hands on Hershel's shoulders and tried to calm his nerves.

"Slow down, and tell me what happened."

He finally managed to tell Marsha the story in short, choppy sentences, leading up to the moment they pulled a lifeless

Serafina from the pile of dirt.

Marsha felt her stomach plummet to the ground at the thought.

"Oh, dear. Are they all right? What did you do?"

"I prayed, Marsha. I prayed like I've never prayed before. I even had to use the Emergency Hotline." Hershel straightened and looked at her with wide, owl eyes. "Did you know that it's a direct line to *Him*?"

"What? You mean you didn't get Smithers?"

"No, I was put straight through to the Big Guy."

"No! Really? Oh, Hershel, you know Smithers isn't going to like you going over his head."

"Well, I had to. There was no other way."

Marsha turned to watch as Serafina was lifted onto a stretcher.

"Still, he's not going to be happy about it."

"I'm afraid that's not the only thing he won't be happy about."

"What?" Marsha turned back to him and caught his worried expression. "Hershel, what did you do?"

"She wasn't breathing, Marsha. I had to do something."

Placing her hands on her hips, she glared at him. "What did you do?"

He avoided her penetrating gaze, preferring to fold his dirty handkerchief into a tiny square.

"I told David how to do CPR."

"Hershel! Cardiopulmonary resuscitation won't come into use until 1961. How could you? What if someone saw you two doing it?"

Hershel's head fell back against the stone wall with a clunk.

"I know. But it was either that or Serafina dies, and we're back to where we started."

"This is not going to look good on our final report."

Hershel shook his head, looking older than his twenty-five hundred years.

"That's not all. While we were trying to get her out, David cursed under his breath in English."

"Oh, no." She glanced around at the large crowd that had gathered at the main gate to the ruins. "Did anyone hear him?"

"I don't think so. I added a little bit to the prayer while I was at it, to cover the CPR and David's English. I think because it went straight to the top, it worked. No one seems to recall either."

Marsha breathed a heavy sigh of relief.

"That's good. It could be all over for us if anyone finds out about him. He'll be shot before we can do anything to save him."

"I know." Hershel raked his hand down over his face. "You know, I don't even think he realized he was doing it."

The slamming door of the ambulance brought Marsha's attention back to Serafina.

"I'll go to the hospital to make sure she's all right."

She looked over to where David stood alone, his hands covered with mud to the elbows, watching as the ambulance carried Serafina away.

"Look at him." Marsha reached down and squeezed Hershel's equally dirty hand. "He loves her already, and he doesn't even know it."

POMPEII

She couldn't breathe. The air was so hot, it scorched her lungs. The mud's weight felt as if it was going to crush her.

Sera fought to break free of the earth, but she couldn't move. She felt arms around her, comforting her at the same time they imprisoned her. She experienced an odd sense of relief that at least she wasn't going to die alone.

Prying her eyes open, she couldn't see anything in the black world surrounding her. Then, slowly, the black turned to gray, and she could make out a form beside her. It was David, not little Antonio, in the ground with her.

"David?"

He didn't answer her. Slowly, her vision grew accustomed to the dark. She stared in horror at his handsome face, his eyes frozen open, still, lifeless.

David was dead.

She screamed, but the earthen grave smothered any sound.

Sera's eyes flew open, and she stared up at an unfamiliar ceiling. She felt shaky, disoriented. The room wasn't hers. White curtains were pulled back on both sides of the narrow bed. Similar beds lined both walls, some with people sleeping in them or the curtains drawn, while others appeared flat and freshly made.

Her throat hurt, as if it had been scraped from the inside out.

She heard a noise and glanced to the side of her bed. David sat slumped in a chair, his features softened in sleep.

What was he doing here? Confused, it took a moment for her to remember what had happened. Antonio. The dump truck. She must be in the hospital.

Feeling a weight on her hand, she looked down. David's hand covered hers where it lay on the bed. His long, tan fingers were in stark contrast to the crisp, white sheet. How long had she been there? Had he been with her the whole time?

Sera shifted and winced as an agonizing pain shot through her side. Pulling the sheet up to her chin, she stared up at the ceiling, gulping in shallow breaths of air. Deep breaths weren't possible. They caused too much pain, as if her lungs had been compressed to half their size.

Her breathing slowed. She was safe. She wasn't buried with David deep beneath the ground.

It had been a dream. Nothing more than a horrible dream.

Turning her hand slowly so she wouldn't wake him, she entwined their fingers, needing to hold onto him in the enclosing darkness.

For some reason, even though she knew it hadn't been real, even though David was beside her with his hand warm in hers proving he was alive, she couldn't shake the heart-wrenching feeling that he was dead.

Or going to die.

POMPEII

David arrived at the ruins just before dawn. The ancient streets were empty. The archeologists, laborers, and tourists wouldn't be arriving for another hour or so. As he reached the dig site, the sun crept over the walls of the city to kiss the crumbling stones of the buildings with a warm, golden glow.

At times like this, when the shadows were long and the streets were quiet, he felt most at peace with the ruins. He no longer was unnerved by the tragedy, but, instead, embraced the serenity of the city preserved in its final hour. When he stood alone among the stones, he could almost understand Sera's love for the place, her need to uncover its mysteries.

Sera. Christ, a shiver still ran up his spine every time he thought about how close she'd come to dying in his arms. He'd never been so afraid in his whole life, not even when he'd faced enemy fire as his unit helped push the Germans out of Tunisia.

Three days had passed since the accident, and the site seemed so empty without her here. He'd better get used to it. Heberto told him it might be two weeks before she made it back to work. She was still suffering the effects of aspirating the dirt and mud, combined with several bruised ribs from where the rear door had slammed into her. Neither was conducive to digging in the dirt.

In no hurry to start digging himself, David climbed the crumbling stone tower and sat on his usual perch overlooking the German encampment. Even this early, the Nazis were up and active, preparing themselves to dominate the rest of the world, one country at a time.

Sitting back to watch their movements, David wondered how Sera was doing.

The morning after the accident, he'd left the hospital before she woke up, not sure if she would want him there. Afterwards, he had started to go see her a thousand times, but always stopped himself before he made it out the door. She hadn't wanted to speak to him before the accident. Why would she want to see him now?

Instead, he'd kept close tabs on her through Heberto, who

was working the site with David while Sera was gone. The old guy told him that since she inhaled dirt into her lungs, the hospital had kept her under observation for pneumonia. But that danger had passed, and she had been released, with Maria watching over her like a mother hen.

David banged his head on the side of the stone tower. It hurt, but he felt he deserved the pain. Hell, he deserved a big, swift kick in the ass. If he hadn't kissed her and then turned around and told her that stupid lie about there being someone else, he could go to see her now. But according to Heberto, she hadn't asked for him, hadn't even mentioned his name. Obviously, she didn't want to see him.

Damn, but he hated lying to her. Not that their whole relationship hadn't started out with one big lie about who he really was. But at least they had become friends. She'd opened up, started joking with him, maybe even flirted with him a bit, if he wasn't mistaken. And now they were right back to how they were in the beginning. Her walls were back up, keeping him out, and he was peeking over another one to spy on the Germans every chance he got.

A flash of sunlight off metal caught his attention. A familiar dark head was moving among the Germans in the camp below. He grabbed the binoculars he kept stashed among the rocks and took a closer look.

Giovanni Ragusa. Realization hit David right between the eyes. When he first saw Giovanni in the ruins, he knew that he'd seen him somewhere before, but had never been able to place where. All along, Giovanni had been right under his nose in the Nazi camp.

What the hell was he doing down there?

CHAPTER XVI

David pulled out a ration ticket and handed it to the vendor in the baker's stall. In return, he received two small loaves of hard day-old bread. It wasn't much, but it would be lunch for the day and maybe dinner, too.

Passing a shop window, he stopped to look at the merchandise on display. A new pair of shoes, a record player, and a silver-plated shaving kit were among the items offered—not that many, including himself, could afford such luxuries.

Taking the main road out of town, he turned onto a dirt road leading to one of the vineyards that littered the countryside. He was always amazed at how high the vines grew, a good fifty feet in some places. He'd learned that it was so the farmer could then plant vegetables beneath them, using every available speck of ground.

David sat under one of the many vines, beating Frank to the rendezvous spot, but not by much. Breaking one of the loaves in two, he offered Frank one half before the usual cigarettes could be lit. If David wasn't careful, he might get hooked on the damn things.

Frank took a big bite and scrunched up his face. His Adam's apple bobbed in an effort to swallow it.

"Man, this tastes like shit."

David bit off his own chunk. The bread was hard and dry, its texture like cooked sawdust in his mouth.

"Yeah, with the war rations the way they are, even the bakers can't get good flour to make a decent loaf of bread."

"I know what you mean," Frank continued, chewing around his mouthful. "It's the same all over Italy."

David thought of the meager meals he was eating lately.

161

Combined with the hard work at the ruins, he'd lost a good deal of weight in the month he'd been there. His clothes hung on his lean frame, and his suspenders were the only thing keeping up his pants. If he hadn't blended in with the starving Italians before, he did now.

"I'll tell you, the pasta here is grey, the cheese tastes like rubber, and it's been so long since I had anything with meat in it, I think I've turned vegetarian." David eyed Frank's well-fed physique. "It doesn't look like you've been starving."

"The army feeds me pretty well," he said with a chuckle. "Hey, I could probably sneak you some rations. It'll be the army issue stuff, but at least there's meat, or what used to be meat, in it."

"That's right. You get to go back to camp every week and eat goodies from home, while I'm stuck playing the starving Italian day in and day out."

"Speaking of playing Italian, you haven't run into any more 'problems' have you?"

David knew he was referring to Sera.

"No, she doesn't suspect a thing. I've made sure to keep my distance." *And I had to hurt her to do it.* "She's not around right now, anyway. She got hurt at the site and will be out of commission for at least two weeks."

"Lucky for you."

"Yeah, real lucky." But not in the way Frank thought. Luck was that Sera was still alive.

He gave Frank his report on the German camp's movements. They appeared to be bringing in fresh troops, probably in anticipation of an Allied invasion from the south. He even told Frank about seeing Giovanni in the camp. He still hadn't figured out what he was doing there, but the possibility that he was helping the Germans hide munitions in the ruins had certainly crossed his mind.

David couldn't help thinking about Sera and the way Giovanni treated her. Worse, the way she let him treat her. The guy had sleaze written all over him. Of course, after kissing her and then telling her there was another woman, she probably thought David was just as much of a snake as Giovanni.

Who was he kidding? At least with Giovanni she knew what was coming. David, on the other hand, was lying to her face, and she had no idea, no notion, that it was all an act to protect her, or that the charade was eating him up inside.

As ridiculous as it was, he felt like he needed to make it up to her somehow. As much as he knew he should keep his distance, he wanted to see the smile back on her face and to hear her laughter. He wanted things to go back to how they were before he screwed things up with that kiss.

Frank's offer of rations planted a seed of an idea.

"I think I just might take you up on your offer."

Frank looked momentarily confused. "What offer?"

"I need you to get something for me."

POMPEII

"*Merda.*" Shit.

The soft thud of Sera's hairbrush landing on the rug in front of her dresser sounded almost mocking as she dropped it for the third time. Dropping it wouldn't have been so bad if it hadn't taken her a month to pick it up each time.

Gripping the dresser for balance, she grasped the brush's wooden handle between her toes, raising the brush half way up to meet her outstretched hand. At this point, the maneuver became painful. She winced as a sharp twinge shot through her ribs.

Snatching the offending hair apparatus before it could tumble to the floor again, she straightened slowly and tried to catch her breath.

Under a minute. Not bad. She was getting faster every day at retrieving dropped items with her toes.

She hated feeling this helpless. After three days in the hospital, she was trapped in her apartment, barely able to walk across the room, much less venture outside. She desperately wanted to go back to work, but with her bruised ribs, she was just getting to the point where she could dress herself without

Maria's help.

She missed the ruins. She missed the feel of the dirt running through her fingers. She missed the smell of the ashes mixed with the fertile earth as she dug deeper and deeper in the pit. She missed the excitement that came with each layer she removed, wondering if something priceless might lie just underneath.

She missed David.

It hurt that he hadn't come to see her even once. Didn't he care?

He must, her heart told her. *Otherwise, why would he have stayed by your bedside throughout the first night?*

Yes, her head reminded her, *but then he vanished in the morning, and you haven't seen him since. Maybe he doesn't care that much after all.*

Heberto had told her how David had saved her, digging her out of the dirt like one of her archeological finds. And of how she'd stopped breathing, and he'd forced life back into her.

Looking at her reflection in the mirror, Sera reached up and touched her lips. She didn't remember him doing it, but somehow she could still feel it—the pressure of his mouth on hers, his breath in her lungs. She closed her eyes and licked her lips, almost able to taste him.

A sudden knock at the door startled her out of her fantasy, making her flinch and knock the hairbrush off the dresser and onto the floor again. Not bothering to pick it up this time, she shuffled to the door.

"I'm coming. I'm coming," she grumbled as the pounding continued. She jerked the door open with as much force as her injuries allowed. "What?"

Her irritation was quickly replaced by surprise. David stood in the hall, looking better than a good steak dinner, which she hadn't had in nearly three years. For a moment, she wondered if her wayward thoughts had conjured him to her door.

"So, how's the wounded bone-digger?" he asked, his cocky grin making him look devilishly handsome.

Closing her gaping mouth, she clutched at the neck of her old bathrobe. Damn, she wasn't even dressed, and it was two o'clock on a Sunday afternoon. Most people would expect any decent person to be dressed by now.

David raised his dark brows in question. "Are you going to let me in, or should I just continue this one-sided conversation with myself out here in the hallway?"

"Oh." Sera shook herself and stepped back, running a nervous hand down the side of the hair she hadn't managed to brush yet. "What are you doing here?" *Now, over a week since you snuck out of the hospital on me.*

"I would think that was obvious."

She watched as he glanced around her tiny apartment, and she cringed. The cramped space looked like a bomb had hit it, with piles of clothes strewn about and dirty dishes stacked high in the sink. Normally neat and tidy, she found it just hurt too much to keep it clean right then. She hated to imagine what he was thinking.

His gaze returned to her. "I'm here to see you."

"Why?" *Why didn't you come sooner?*

David shrugged. "I wanted to see how you were doing."

"Fine. Better." Sera winced as she cinched the sash of her robe tighter. "Still a little sore."

"That's good." He shifted his weight from one foot to the other, looking unusually nervous. Did she really make him that uncomfortable? "I was also wondering when you'd be coming back to work."

Sera walked over to the kitchen table, suddenly aware of her bare feet peeking out from beneath her robe.

"The doctor says another week, but I hope it will be sooner."

Pulling out a chair, she eased herself into it. David stepped forward as if he were going to help her, but for some reason stopped himself. Probably because he didn't want to get too close to a woman who looked like she hadn't bathed in a week.

"I'm glad to hear it, because I've been digging holes all over the place and haven't found a damn thing."

"You've been doing *what*?" Her preoccupation with her bedraggled appearance evaporated as a cold chill raced up her spine.

"Digging holes."

Holes. Oh, no. Her site. The carefully laid out excavation plan. The artifacts.

"Oh, God. What have you done? Holes? You can't just go around digging holes. Didn't you learn anything I taught you?"

Sera felt like she was going to be sick. She pushed herself from the table and shuffled to her dresser, her ribs screaming in protest every step of the way.

"Don't worry. It's just a few here and there."

She jerked a pair of trousers from the drawer.

"How many? How deep?"

David shoved his hands in his pockets and shrugged. "Only a couple of dozen or so. Some are only as big as my fist, but there are a few you can stand in."

"Stand in?" Sera felt her stomach plummet to somewhere around her shaking knees. "Please tell me you didn't dig holes that deep."

Panic raced through her. How could he do that to her site? After all the hard work they'd done, he may have ruined everything. Oh, to think of all the priceless artifacts that may have been destroyed forever. She wanted to cry. But there would be time for that later. Right now she had to go to the site and see for herself what damage he'd done. She needed to save what she could.

Struggling with her clothes, she grunted as a sharp pain shot through her ribs. Wrestling to get her foot into her pants leg, she nearly toppled onto the bed.

"Calm down, Sera." David's rich, deep laughter made her pause, balancing precariously on one foot. "I was just kidding. Yes, I have been working at the site, but Heberto has been there to guide me every step of the way. I haven't moved so much as one clod of dirt without his approval."

Relief relaxed her tense muscles until aggravation took its

place.

"That was not funny."

"I know, but watching you hop around like a deranged bunny-rabbit was."

Sera hurled her trousers at David's head, only to be repaid with a sharp jab of pain in her side, making her nearly double over.

"Oh, ouch."

Before she knew it, he was by her side, helping her to sit on the edge of her bed.

"Careful, we don't want you to hurt yourself any worse than you already are."

"Well, you should have thought about that before you started teasing me."

"Sorry, but I couldn't resist." His easy smile slowly faded, and his sparkling eyes softened to a warm, chocolate brown. "You scared the hell out of me, you know."

"I wasn't too thrilled with being buried alive myself." Sera swallowed hard around the lump that suddenly formed in her throat. When had he sat down on the bed next to her? "Thank you… for saving my life."

"I guess that makes us even."

"What?" Distracted by the heat of his body so close, she barely heard what he said.

"When you saved me from smothering under the tent. We're even now, I suppose."

"Yes. Even." She remembered when the tent collapsed on him—and what came after. Was it her imagination, or was he leaning closer? Or maybe she was leaning toward him. Did it matter?

David stared at her mouth, as if he too was recalling their kiss and wanted nothing more than to repeat it. Then he cleared his throat, abruptly making her aware of how close she was to him and how far away she should be.

He stood suddenly, taking a step, then another, away from the bed. Away from her.

"I brought you something."

"You did?"

"Yes. Wait right here. I'll just be a second." He turned and went to her door, stepping briefly out into the hallway.

Sera shook her head to clear the confusing ride his moods were taking her on. One minute he was teasing her, the next he looked ready to eat her alive, and then he acted like he couldn't get far enough away from her.

He returned with a package.

"I thought you might like this."

Smiling, he handed her a thin, brown-wrapped bundle about ten inches square.

"Go ahead. Open it."

Now he was bringing her gifts? What was he trying to do to her?

Ripping at the paper, she tore it open to reveal a record encased in a plain, white sleeve. She looked closely at the black label peeking through the cutout in the center. It showed a drawing of a dog with its head in a gramophone. Underneath the image, gold lettering in English spelled out the title of the song, "Just as Though You Were Here."

"It's Tommy Dorsey and his orchestra," David said. "They play American Big Band music."

"I know."

"Now you can listen to the real thing while you recover."

Stunned, Sera didn't know what to say.

"Where did you get this?"

"You'd be surprised what you can get on the black market."

No, she wasn't surprised. You could buy anything if you had enough money, and the record probably cost him a fortune. Where did he get the money? Certainly not from working at the ruins.

"You… I can get arrested for owning something like this."

He winked at her. "I won't tell if you won't."

Just who wouldn't he be telling?

"What does your girlfriend think about it?"

"What?"

"Your girlfriend? Won't she mind you giving another

woman a gift?"

David averted his gaze, studying the label of the record with intense interest. "She won't have a problem with me giving a get well present to a sick friend."

She didn't believe him. Any woman would have a problem with her boyfriend giving another woman presents.

"Is that what we are? Friends?"

He finally looked back at her.

"I'd like to think so."

The word "friend" hung in the air between them, inadequate and misplaced.

Sera finally tore her gaze away and stroked her hand delicately over the cardboard cover. She couldn't believe he'd done this. Just attempting to buy American records like this on the black market could have gotten him arrested. Both of them could go to jail if the album was discovered in their possession.

But she wouldn't part with it for the world.

"So, do you want to listen to it or not?"

The request took her by surprise, and regret dampened her happiness.

"This is really sweet, but I don't have a player."

He smiled, a wicked gleam lighting his eyes, as he wagged his index finger at her. "Ah, ha. I already thought of that."

He walked once more out into the hallway and returned with a small, portable record player.

"The Angelicos let me borrow theirs. They said you can keep it as long as you like."

He set the player on the beat-up coffee table and plugged it into the wall. Taking the record from her, he placed the disc on the turntable and turned it on.

She heard crackling as the needle touched the spinning record. Violins and horns floated from the speaker, soaring to a powerful crescendo, then softening, followed by the smooth, crooning voice of the singer.

David held out his hand to her. "Dance with me."

Her breath caught in her throat. She had the strangest sense of déjà vu, as if she'd seen him like this before, standing just this way, holding his hand out to her, beckoning her to him. She felt helpless to deny him.

Standing, she walked into his arms. He held her gently as they swayed to the music, the velvety voice of the singer floating on the air around them.

Oh, don't be afraid that distance and time
will finally tear us apart
the farther you go, the longer you stay
the deeper you grow in my heart

Listening to the rhythm of his heart beating under her cheek, the feel of his arms around her, it all seemed so perfect, so right. She wanted to hold onto this moment forever. But as the song came to an end, she knew she couldn't. She wasn't the woman who had that right.

"Your girlfriend might not mind you giving a sick friend a get well present, but I'm pretty certain she wouldn't like this." The words tasted bitter on her tongue.

She felt David's heavy sigh in her hair. She may have imagined it, but he seemed to squeeze her just a little bit tighter, hold her just a little bit longer, before he slowly released her and stepped back. Even though she didn't want to, she let him go.

"No, I don't guess she would."

He walked over to the player and pulled the arm off the record. When he turned the machine off, the soft click sounded like a gunshot in the now silent room.

With his hands firmly on his hips, he stared at the rotating record, the black disc spinning slower and slower until it came to a stop. His mouth was drawn in a tense line. He looked like he was battling for control, struggling with some inner demon. Sera wished she could crawl inside his brain to find out what he was thinking.

"This was probably a bad idea." He spoke without looking at her, as if by meeting her gaze, the fragile grip he held on his restraint would snap. "I should go."

David turned on his heel and walked to the door, sending her heart plummeting to her stomach. His back was stiff as he jerked open the door. He stood in the threshold for what seemed like an eternity, the tension in his shoulders evident through the rough cotton of his shirt. Finally, he turned to face her. The look in his eyes—a mixture of regret, shame, and possibly even longing—was staggering.

Sera gripped the edges of her bathrobe under her chin.

"David, what is it?"

"I…" He hesitated, then smiled, the gesture tight and forced. "I'll see you back at the dig."

He slowly closed the door, and she listened to his footsteps as he headed down the hall.

CHAPTER XVII

"I didn't think you'd be back for another week."

Sera looked up from the excavation pit into David's smiling face. Was it only a few days ago that he'd danced with her in her apartment? It seemed like an eternity. Bruised ribs or not, she couldn't stand being away one moment longer—from the ruins or from David.

"After that fish tale you told me about digging holes, I had to come and see what you've been doing for myself."

"And?"

"And you and Heberto have done a lot of work. I'm very impressed." And she was. They had made a great deal of progress in her absence, clearing a foot or more down on the road between several of the merchants' shops and even up to the wall tower that David seemed so fond of.

David tugged at the brim of his hat and smiled a silly, lopsided grin.

"*Grazie, signorina.*"

Funny, with the odd twang he put in his voice as he spoke the words, he sounded just like one of those cowboys in the American westerns she used to see at the cinema before the war.

Shaking the impression away, Sera stepped out of the pit and brushed at the dust on her pants, feeling oddly nervous around him, like a school girl with her first big crush.

Obviously, he didn't have the same problem. He walked up to her and kissed her gently on the cheek. When he pulled back, he was smiling softly.

"I'm glad you're back."

She could feel the heat rising on the skin of her neck and

knew she was probably blushing like a ripe tomato.

"Me, too."

He pushed back from her and rested his hands on her shoulders, holding her at arm's length.

"So, what do you say about getting back to work, boss?"

"I'd say it's about time."

POMPEII

Sera and David worked side by side for the rest of the week. She mapped out the new area the men had uncovered, and he went back to digging on the perimeter of the pit. Amazingly enough, working seemed to make her ribs feel better, although she always paid for it when she got up the next morning. But it was all worth it to be back digging in the ruins she loved, working beside the man she...

She chased the errant thought away, but it didn't go far.

Each day they worked together, there was always a hungry look or a gentle touch that would pass between them. There was no denying that they were drawn to each other. Though their relationship had escalated somewhere beyond friendship, she knew it couldn't go any further.

But that didn't stop her from wanting him.

Hearing the crunch of rocks behind her, Sera turned to see him pushing his wheelbarrow around the pit.

"Don't miss me too much while I'm gone," he called. He winked at her and was off to drop another load of dirt at the trucks.

She smiled as she watched him leave. It was nice to have the awkward strain gone between them, but in its place was a different kind of tension. The air around them fairly crackled with a longing so strong, she was amazed David didn't lay her down in the dirt and make love to her under the bright Italian sun.

But he never did because there was someone else.

She went back to work, humming the tune to the song they'd danced to that day. If she couldn't have the real thing, she'd relive the memory of what might have been.

It seemed only a few minutes had gone by before she felt strong hands knead her tired shoulders, causing her heart to leap in her chest and a warmth pool in her belly. David?

"I missed you, *carina*," Giovanni's smooth voice whispered in her ear.

She jerked, nearly catching him in the chin with her head as she jumped away.

"Giovanni, what are you doing here?" She hated it when he called her sweetheart.

"When I heard what happened, I could not believe it. I was so worried about you."

Sera batted at his hands as he reached for her again.

"Yes, I could tell from all the flowers you didn't send me."

Giovanni smiled his bone-melting smile.

"Ah, why send flowers that will wilt next to your beauty?"

At one time, the compliment would have sounded genuine. Now she knew better.

"What do you want?"

"You, my sweet Serafina." He looked at her with more sincerity than she thought possible from a man who had once broken her heart. "I want you back."

"What?" After all this time, he couldn't really mean that, could he?

Giovanni stepped closer, but she couldn't find the power to move away from him. His behavior was too surreal.

"When I heard that you nearly died, I realized how much I still love you."

"You can't be serious."

"I've never been more serious in my life. I can't lose you again."

Sera shook her head. "I'm not yours to lose anymore."

"Please, *carina*. Let us put all those bad memories behind us and start again. You and I, we were good together."

Yes, they were. In many ways, they were a lot alike. At one time, she'd thought he was the one for her—a kindred spirit, her soul mate. But not anymore. You have to be able to trust the one you give your heart to, and she didn't trust Giovanni.

Not after she caught him in bed with another woman.

"After what you did to me, how can you even think that I would take you back?"

"I've changed. I learned my lesson. When I thought I'd lost you forever, I realized what you mean to me. There is no other woman for me."

"It won't work. Not this time." She needed to get away from him. Fast, before his charm and smooth talk turned her head the way it always used to.

"But it can work, if we both try. You loved me once. It can happen again."

"No. No, it can't." Why did the air seem suddenly too thin? He was too close. She couldn't breathe.

"Come, *mio caro*. Who else knows you as well as I do? Who understands your passion for the ruins like I do?"

Who indeed?

Giovanni startled her when he cupped her face in his hands.

"And you are a passionate woman, Serafina. No one else knows how to bring it out in you like I do."

Before she could stop him, Giovanni was kissing her, his full lips pressing against her own, his tongue demanding entrance to her mouth.

But the passion he talked about wasn't there anymore. At least not for her. While it was a kiss that used to make her weak in the knees, now all she noticed was that his lips felt chapped from too much time in the sun and that he'd had something with a lot of garlic in it for lunch.

She wedged her hands between them and tried to push him away, but his strong arms held her tight. She closed her eyes and managed to twist her head away. Undeterred, he started trailing sloppy, wet kisses down her neck. Sera groaned, not in passion, but in frustration. When she finally opened her eyes again, she glanced over Giovanni's broad shoulder to find David standing at the edge of the pit.

"Sorry. I didn't mean to interrupt."

His expression was like that of her father the last time she saw him—cold, blank—and it sent a shiver racing through her body.

"David?" Her voice came out in a squeak.

POMPEII

Giovanni turned to smirk at David with a shit-eating grin before Sera pushed the man away, breaking their cozy embrace.

David shifted his gaze to Sera. She looked… could that possibly be guilt in those beautiful blue eyes?

"Don't mind me. I'll just be on my way." He shoved the empty wheelbarrow around the pit, taking the long way around so he didn't have to pass close to the two of them.

What the hell was going on? What was that snake Giovanni doing slithering around Sera? And what was she doing with her arms coiled around him?

He parked the wheelbarrow and picked up his shovel. Squeezing the wooden handle in his grip, he had to mentally slow his breathing, or he risked hitting someone with it. When he finally turned back, Giovanni was walking away down the road. Strutting like a cocky rooster was more like it.

"David, it's not what it looks like."

"Really?" He tried to cover his irritation with indifference. "It looked like two people playing a friendly game of chess to me. What else could it have been?"

"That's not funny. Let me explain."

"There's nothing to explain. It's obvious you have a boyfriend you forgot to tell me about." David laughed humorlessly, thinking of the lie he had told her about his "girlfriend." "I guess that makes us even."

"He's not my boyfriend."

"Well, you could've fooled me. You two looked pretty chummy to me." He stabbed his shovel into the dirt with a bit more force than was necessary. "Funny, from the way you talked about him, I thought you hated the guy's guts. Guess I was wrong."

"You are wrong. I may not hate him, but that doesn't mean I like him, either."

"Well, I'd say that lip-lock you were sharing says you feel different."

"I wasn't kissing him. *He* was kissing *me*."

"Hmm, yeah. You'll pardon me if I appear a little confused on that point."

Sera rested her fists on her hips, defensiveness displayed in every bone in her body.

"Damn it, David. Giovanni probably knew you were close behind and did it on purpose just to irritate you. He's not worth getting jealous over."

Jealous? Was that what he was feeling? If it was, he didn't like it one bit, and the only thing that would make him feel better about the situation would be to pound Giovanni's smug face into the dirt.

Since the schmuck wasn't around, he struck out at the next best thing.

"I'm surprised. I took you for a smart girl. I thought you had more sense than to get mixed up with a smooth talker like that."

"I'm not mixed up with him."

"Tell that to someone who might believe it." He jabbed his shovel into the dirt and leaned on the handle. He stared intently at Sera, making her visibly squirm. "I watched him treat you like trash, and you didn't do a thing about it. Now he makes a pass at you, and you don't stop him. Come on, it's obvious something is going on with you two."

"Nothing is going on between us. Not anymore."

"Not anymore?" His anger began to boil. Now the truth was coming out. "What the hell is that supposed to mean?"

Sera huffed. "Giovanni and I… we were close once."

Close? Close with a guy like that could mean only one thing. David didn't even want to think about the possibility, but that didn't stop the accusing words from spilling out of his mouth.

"Don't tell me he was your lover."

"He was not my lover." Her face glowed beet-red. She looked ready to scream. "If you must know, he's my ex-fiancé."

David felt like he'd been hit in the stomach with a sledge-hammer. Her fiancé? The "ex" part didn't factor in with his suddenly dazed mind. She and that scum had been close. They had obviously been lovers. He couldn't believe it. She'd actually been in love with that snake. She'd almost married him. The thought made him angry as a newly gelded bull.

He spun around and kicked at a rock, realizing too late that it was deeply imbedded in the soil and a good deal less fragile than the bones in his foot. As pain shot up his leg, he was sure he heard a crunch or two. He danced around on one foot, certain that he had broken his big toe.

"Son of a bitch!"

Heaving the shovel through the air like a javelin, he let go with a continuous string of red, white, and blue curses. When he finally calmed down enough to let the throbbing subside, he looked up and saw Sera's stunned expression.

The look on her face had nothing to do with shock over his colorful choice of words.

It was how he had shouted them. In English.

With a sinking feeling, he realized Sera now knew his secret.

David was an American.

POMPEII

Sera felt all the blood drain from her body. Her hands tingled and her heart thundered in her chest. At first, she couldn't believe what she was hearing. If David hadn't kept carrying on like a raving lunatic, she might have thought it all her imagination.

But there it was. She had spent enough time in America to know those words, and the truth slapped her in the face.

David wasn't Italian at all.

She always thought there was something different about him, something she could never quite put her finger on. Now she knew what it was. All the pieces fit together. For someone supposedly from Italy, he knew very little about the history of

Pompeii. His frequent questioning about her loyalty, or lack thereof, to the Fascist Regime. His ability to acquire an American record no one in Italy should own.

But the most damning of all was his persistent need to be in this area of the ruins, and his constant sitting on the wall tower just above the German camp.

The implications exploded like a ticking bomb in her brain. He was not just an American on enemy soil.

David was a spy.

As she stared at him, the dark tan of his face paled to the color of the sun-washed stones. He knew she'd heard him. Staring at her with those dark brown eyes, she could tell he was waiting to see what she would do.

Sera did the only thing a good Italian girl could do when faced with the enemy.

She ran.

She didn't dare look back. She could hear his footfalls behind her, coming faster, getting closer. She was almost to the end of the road. Just a bit farther, and she'd be close to where the tourists were. She could yell. She could scream. She would be safe.

Suddenly he grabbed her from behind, squeezing her bruised ribs, and she cried out in pain. David covered her mouth with his hand and dragged her into one of the empty ruins. She fought him every step of the way, but he was too big, too strong, and it hurt too much to struggle. Setting her on her feet, he spun her around and shoved her up against the smooth plaster wall. With his hand still covering her mouth, she could do little but glare at him.

"If you promise not to scream, I'll let you go."

Reluctantly, she nodded her head. He slowly removed his hand, but she could still feel the pressure of it on her jaw. He eased his hold on her and, given that one bit of freedom, her arm shot out and her hand cracked against his cheek, echoing off the walls in the empty room as his head snapped to the side from the impact.

"Don't." He turned his head slowly back around to face

179

her. Was that remorse she saw in his eyes? She doubted it. Spies weren't supposed to feel guilty for the things they did in the name of their country.

"I never promised not to smack the shit out of you."

"Sera, I can explain."

"Explain what? That everything you've told me is a lie? That you've risked my career and my life spying on my country?" She used what space there was between them to cross her arms over her chest, trying to put up some kind of barrier. David didn't step back an inch, forcing her forearms to wedge against his hard wall of a chest. Fine, she wasn't going to back down either. "Go ahead. Explain it to me."

"I wasn't spying on your county. I was spying on the Germans."

"Last time I checked, Italy was on Germany's side."

"Last time I checked, you were half-American."

Sera felt like she'd been slapped herself. How dare he? She had trusted him, confided in him. After everything she had told him about her father…how dare he be who he was?

She struggled to understand what was happening. In a matter of a few moments, everything she believed about David had changed. Was everything he'd done and said to her just an act so he could be in a good position to spy on the Germans? Had he meant any of it, or had he just used her? When she thought of how he'd held her, kissed her, of how they'd almost…

The hurt was unbearable. She could feel the anger and betrayal threatening to bubble over in the hot, scalding tears she tried in vain to hold back.

He placed his hands on her head, forcing her to look at him. He looked desperate, almost panicked, like a hunted animal.

"Sera, listen to me. You realize what will happen if anyone finds out who I am?"

She nodded her head. Yes, she knew. He would be shot. Could she really turn him in, knowing it would probably mean his death?

No, she could never do that. But it didn't make the sting

any less. She pushed his hands away from her face.

"How could you do this to me? How could you hide this from me, knowing how I feel about America?"

"It's because I *did* know how you felt that I couldn't tell you."

"Then why did you try to be my... friend, even though you knew what it would do to me when I found out the truth?"

"Damn it, you were never supposed to find out." He sighed heavily, but he never took his eyes off her face. "I'm sorry, but I can't change who I am, any more than you can change who you are."

Oh, he was good. Why not add a punch in the stomach to the slap in the face? All these years, she had tried to deny her American heritage, and here he was throwing it in her face.

"What am I supposed to do? It's my duty to turn you in."

"Your duty? Just whose side are you on, Sera? You're half-American, too." If it were possible, he leaned in even closer. "Do you even care about the war? Most of Italy doesn't. They just want it to be over and the Germans to go home. Mussolini has bled this country dry and fed it to Hitler on a silver platter. Can you truly believe being on Germany's side is the right thing?"

"That's not the point." How was it that he could make her feel defensive when he was the one who was breaking the law? "It's all so clear now, what you've been doing up there on that wall. You haven't been looking at the scenery. All this time, you've been spying on the Germans."

"And the information I've learned sitting up on that wall will probably save thousands of lives. American and Italian."

Sera felt like she was caught in some bizarre dream. She rubbed at her throbbing temples, wishing it would all go away, wishing things could go back to the way they were before David ever walked into her life.

"I can't believe this is happening. Do you realize the position you've put me in? You've not only risked my career by having my dig site moved, now you've risked my life by my association with you."

She laughed bleakly as the reality of the situation settled in.

"Everyone in Pompei knows I'm half-American, and if they find out you're an American spy, they're going to assume I've sympathized with you. The Italian authorities aren't going to believe me. I'll be put in a detention camp, and my life will be over... if I'm not shot standing beside you."

David lowered his eyes, a war of his own waging across his handsome face. Finally, he looked back up at her, regret and a plea for understanding where determination and loyalty had once been.

"Is it worth my life?"

Sera stopped. Was it? If his true identity were ever discovered, he would be shot. Did she want that? Could she bear that?

Like a deflating balloon, she felt the fight go out of her.

"No. It's not."

With the calmness came a new awareness of her surroundings. She could feel every inch of him pressed up against her, the heat of his body penetrating her clothes. With every breath she took, her breasts crushed against his chest. His strong arms imprisoned her face on either side against the wall, and one of his thighs had managed to wedge in between her own.

She was surprised that the position did not feel threatening—or rather, it did, but in an altogether different way. It was too intimate. He was much too close. She glanced up, his lips only inches from hers, his eyes boring into her soul.

He seemed to realize the position they were in, too, and something in his expression changed, as if a shade had been drawn down over a lighted window. He stepped back, and she felt as if she might slide down the wall without his support. But she held her back stiff and straight.

"Your secret is safe with me. For now." She shoved herself away from the wall and walked to the door, praying he didn't notice how much she shook with every step. This time, he didn't try to stop her.

Pausing in the doorway, she looked back over her shoulder.

"I won't turn you in. But if they come looking for you, I

won't protect you, either."

She stepped out into the street, the bright sunlight blinding her, and started walking in a daze, not sure where she was going.

It wasn't until Sera had reached the main area of the ruins and stood in the middle of all the tourists that she even realized their entire conversation had been spoken in English.

CHAPTER XVIII

"Heberto!"

Hershel almost cried as he watched his wooden ball bounce across the ground, stopping a mile from the jack. Why did the woman have to shout just as he was about to win his match?

"Yes, my love?" He didn't even try to hide the sarcasm in his voice.

"How can you be playing *bocce* at a time like this?"

Hershel turned and eyed his extremely agitated wife.

"It's simple, really. I took the day off to play a few games of lawn bowling with my friends. Is that a crime?"

Marsha grabbed him by his elbow and pulled him out of hearing distance from his old cronies.

"It is when you miss an opportunity to prevent a disaster."

"Disaster? Serafina hasn't gone and gotten herself buried again, has she?"

"No. It's worse."

Worse? How could anything be worse than being buried alive? "Oh, dear. What's happened?"

"I just received a call from Smithers's secretary. Serafina found out David is American."

Hershel shook his head. Leave it to Marsha to overreact and ruin his *bocce* game at the same time.

"So?"

"*So?*" Her voice was getting dangerously high. "How could you let her find out? It could ruin everything."

"How is this my fault?"

Marsha glared down her superior nose at him.

"You should have been at work where you were supposed to be so you could stop it."

"For heaven's sake, I'm not their babysitter. They're adults. I can't be with them every minute."

"You could if you weren't taking time off to play games."

"Marsha, really." The woman was being unrealistic. "Even if I were working today, I wouldn't be with them in their area of the site. Anything could happen, and I wouldn't be able to stop it. We're not angels anymore, you know."

That took the wind out of Marsha's sails.

"I know. I know. It's just so unfortunate that she found out."

"Well, you know we weren't going to be able to keep it from her forever. She was going to find out sooner or later." Hershel glanced over at his friends to make sure no one was moving his balls while he was gone. "After all, if we succeed, they're going to live together for the rest of their lives. I think she'll notice something when he takes her back to Virginia."

"Virginia?" Marsha's fair skin paled a shade whiter. "My stars, he can't take her to Virginia. What about the ruins? She'll die without the ruins."

"Hmmm. Seems like we have another kink to work out."

"Well, I can't worry about that right now, can I?" Marsha shooed Hershel back to his game. "At the moment, I have to find a way to fix this problem you've gotten us into."

POMPEII

Sera entered the back courtyard of the Angelicos' quiet villa, parking her bicycle in the area reserved for tenants.

Her arrival did not go unnoticed.

Maria knelt on a green and white checkered blanket, weeding the vegetable garden that now consumed a majority of the courtyard. The scene was a common one throughout Pompei. Every available plot of ground in town was used to grow food, yet people were considered lucky if they were able to keep half of what they grew. The Italian and German armies tended to confiscate the majority of produce in the name of national support.

Maria straightened up from her hunched-over position and

rubbed at the small of her back.

"Serafina? You're home early. What's wrong, my dear?"

"Nothing." Sera found it hard to look directly at her. "My ribs were starting to bother me, so I thought I would come home to rest." She felt ashamed. It was like lying to her own grandmother.

"Nonsense. You've been back at work for a week now, and your ribs haven't slowed you down one bit. Something else is bothering you, I can tell."

"There's nothing wrong. I just…"

Maria patted the space on the blanket beside her.

"Then come and sit with me for a while. Keep an old woman company."

Sera could hardly refuse. She sat beside the elderly lady, and Maria set a basket between them. The two women worked side-by-side, pulling stubborn weeds from the earth.

Sera tugged at a particularly strong one that seemed determined to remain imbedded in the dirt. It reminded her of David. Somehow, he had managed to weed his way into her life, and now he refused to go, even though by staying he threatened everything dear to her.

"So, how are things at the ruins now that you're back?"

"We're making some progress."

"Ah yes, *we*. How are you and that handsome young assistant getting along?"

Sera stopped tugging at the weed. What was Maria, a mind reader?

"We're doing fine." *Liar.*

Evidently her conscience wasn't the only one who could perceive the truth.

"Come now, your face is scrunched up so tight, it looks like you just swallowed a bad olive. What's going on between you two?"

Sera felt the burden of David's identity weigh heavily on her conscience. She knew she should never tell—for heaven's sake, she promised him she wouldn't only an hour ago—but the newfound knowledge was practically choking her.

But of all the people she knew, Maria was the one she felt she could trust the most.

"If I tell you something, will you promise not to tell a soul, not even Heberto?"

Maria paused in her weeding and looked at Sera with warm, compassionate eyes.

"This sounds serious. Of course."

"I just found out David is an American."

"Oh, really? My, isn't that interesting." Maria shrugged her thin shoulders and went back to her work.

"Interesting? That's all? You think it's *interesting*?"

"Well, yes," she commented, without even looking up from her chore. "What else am I supposed to think?"

Was Maria getting senile in her old age? Didn't she realize what this meant?

"That makes him a spy."

"A spy," the old woman whispered. She looked up and grinned at Sera, her eyes like two hard-boiled eggs with big blue yokes. "Now that does sound exciting."

"It's not exciting. He's the enemy. What if someone finds out?"

Maria's fascinated look turned to one of censure as she cocked a white eyebrow at Sera.

"No one will find out if you don't tell them."

Sera ducked her head. She already felt guilty enough telling Maria. The woman didn't have to rub it in.

"He didn't tell me. I managed to find out when he spoke English without realizing it. How long do you think it will be before someone else discovers the truth?"

"Well, you'll just have to make sure no one figures it out when he's with you."

What was she suggesting? "You think I should protect him? If I do and it's discovered, I could be arrested for harboring a spy."

Maria tossed a handful of weeds into the basket and crawled on her knees to the next section of the garden.

"You'll do it because you know in your heart it is the right thing to do."

"No, I don't."

"Come now, Serafina. You don't care about the war any more than I do. Why is this really upsetting you?"

Why? Because the David she had come to care about was now the epitome of everything she hated.

"You know, not every American is your father."

Sera felt a shiver race down her spine. How did Maria always have the ability to know what she was thinking? She'd been doing it since Sera was a child, and at times like this, it completely unnerved her.

"I know that."

"Then why are you blaming David for your father's sins?"

"I'm not." *Liar*, her conscience screamed again.

"Yes, you are."

Would her conscience and Maria please stop ganging up on her?

"It's just that… he lied to me."

"No, not really. It sounds to me like he just didn't tell you."

"It's the same thing. He led me, and everyone else, to believe he was Italian."

"But only because he had to." Maria wiped her dirty hands on the blanket, lines of contemplation adding to the wrinkles on her face. "What would you have done if he had told you the truth when you first met him?"

"I don't know."

Both women stood, and Sera helped Maria fold the blanket.

"Yes, you do. You, my hot-headed Serafina, would have turned him in on the spot. Then he would have been shot at dawn, and you would not have the pleasure of knowing him as you do now."

"But that's just it. I don't know him. Not anymore."

"Really?" Maria handed Sera the folded blanket and picked up the weed basket. "It seems to me that the only thing that has changed is the young man's nationality. He's still the same person he was yesterday."

"How do I know that? He's been lying to me all this time.

Maybe he's not at all who he seems to be."

"Then again, maybe he is. You do like him, don't you?"

Sera hugged the grass-covered blanket to her chest like a shield, trying desperately to hold her emotions inside.

"Yes."

"Then trust your heart, and it will show you what to do."

POMPEII

Sera arrived late at the ruins. She knew it was cowardly of her, but she was avoiding David.

Funny how easy it was to refer to him as American David as opposed to the Italian *Dah-veed*. If that was even his real name. He probably lied about that, too. The hard part now was forgiving him for deceiving her, for risking her career and her life for his own cause.

But Maria was right. Had the situation been reversed, what would David do? After all, he never had to become her friend. He could have gone about his business, done his work at the site, and she probably never would have known.

But he had gone out of his way to be nice to her, even when she didn't always deserve it. Maybe that's why the betrayal felt deeper than it should.

As she approached the dig site, her steps faltered. What was she going to say to him? How was she supposed to act?

When she got there, David was standing up on the old stone tower, looking out in the distance as he did several times every day. Only now she knew exactly what he was looking at—the German camp just a hundred yards away.

Her stomach twisted. Maybe Maria was wrong. Maybe she should turn him in. She risked everything if she didn't. Allied sympathizers didn't usually live to see a trial.

David must have sensed her presence. Turning, he leaned a broad shoulder against the crumbling wall and gazed down on her from his high perch, casually sticking a blade of dry grass in the corner of his mouth.

"I wasn't sure if I'd be welcome here this morning."

She was struck by how fluent his Italian was. His voice

sounded so calm, so relaxed. Did he feel half as uneasy as she did? If he did, he hid it well.

"And I wasn't sure if you'd be here at all," she replied.

He shrugged and rolled the piece of grass from one side of his mouth to the other.

"I almost didn't come. I figured instead of you, I'd have the Italian guard waiting with a complimentary blindfold and cigarette."

"Don't think I didn't consider turning you in a half a dozen times last night."

David jumped down from the wall, startling her, and she took an involuntary step back. Just how dedicated was he to this mission? Did he see her as the threat she saw him? Would he kill her if she got in the way? Was he even now planning a way to silence her forever?

Closing the gap between them in four quick strides, he stood so close she swore she could feel her heart pounding even though he wasn't touching a single inch of her.

"So, why didn't you?"

Why did he have to stand so close? She glanced down at his hands hanging loose at his sides. Strong hands that could easily wrap around her neck and squeeze the life out of her before she could utter a sound.

"I promised you I wouldn't."

"People break promises all the time."

Her eyes shot back to his face. Whether he knew it or not, he'd hit a nerve. She tried to pretend telling Maria didn't count.

"Not me."

For a long time he just stared at her. She wondered what secrets he saw, what vulnerability he might sense deep inside and use against her. Regardless, Sera refused to retreat.

"I know." He spoke in English, his voice so low it was almost a whisper. "That's why I trusted you enough to come back."

Now it was her turn to look into his face and search for the truth. His soft brown eyes showed nothing but trust, full and complete. But then again, she'd been wrong about men before.

He tilted his head to the side, and the slight movement blocked out the morning sun in the sky behind him, creating the effect of a glowing halo around his handsome face. But she reminded herself that he was no angel. He was a spy.

She stepped back, needing to put some space between them, and tripped over the forgotten shovel David had thrown in anger yesterday. Her arms spun around, grasping for balance in the air as she felt herself falling. He reached out to grab her, but her feet tangled with his, and they both crashed to the ground.

David raised himself up on his arms above her, concern evident as his eyes flicked over her face.

"Are you okay?"

"I'm fine, except for the fact that I have a shovel digging into my back, and you weigh a ton on top of me."

A slow grin crept across his face, the boyish charm he flashed sending her heartbeat into double-time. He reached beneath her and eased the shovel handle out from under the small of her back. After tossing it to the side, he looked back down at her, his upper body hovering over her with his arms braced on either side of her face.

"Better?"

"You're still on top of me."

The grin slowly faded. "So I noticed."

His eyes mesmerized her as they darkened, the pupils dilating to nearly engulf the brown ring encircling them. She couldn't find the will to look away. He bent his arms, lowering the upper part of his body down onto hers, pressing her into the dirt. He dipped his head, and it took everything in Sera not to lick her lips in anticipation.

Oh, God. He couldn't possibly want to kiss me. Not here. Not now. Not after everything that's happened.

"David, no. You shouldn't. We can't."

"I know." He touched his forehead to hers, his breath falling across her lips like a lover's kiss. "God, Sera. I tried. I tried so hard to stay away from you. To keep my distance. To not get involved. But I couldn't. Something always kept drawing me to you. It still does."

Sera stilled beneath him. What could she say to something like that? How was she supposed to respond?

"I have another confession to make," he said, his forehead still touching hers. "I lied."

"What? When?" Now she was more confused than ever. What was he talking about?

"There is no one else. There never was."

She tried to ignore the hopeful flip of her heart.

"Why did you tell me there was?"

He raised his head and looked her in the eye, his expression full of regret.

"Because I don't know how long I'm going to be here. My mission will be over soon, and I didn't want to start something between us that I couldn't finish. I didn't want to hurt you."

"So you lied to me?" Was that supposed to make it easier for her? As if finding herself attracted to a man she couldn't have—or thought she couldn't have—was easy.

He squeezed his eyes shut, as if by doing so, it made the truth easier to speak.

"It was stupid, I know. But at the time, it was the only way I could think of to keep some distance between us. To keep me from hurting you." He sighed heavily and opened his eyes to look at her. "I didn't want to be like your father."

Sera's heart shattered into a thousand pieces and then re-formed again. She didn't think she'd ever seen David so open, so vulnerable.

"Why didn't you just tell me the truth... about everything?"

His dark eyes pinned her with an intensity that nearly set her on fire.

"Because the truth wouldn't have stopped me from wanting you. I needed you to not want me."

She reached up and touched his cheek, feeling the soft stubble beneath her fingertips.

"Oh, David." Then she repeated the words he spoke to her

when he first kissed her in the pit. "How could I not want you?"

Surprise lit his eyes, and then he lowered his head, inch by slow inch, giving her all the time in the world to stop him. She didn't.

He kissed her, softly at first, just a tender brush of his lips against hers. Her head swam with the feel of him. His unique scent of soap and sun-warmed skin surrounded her. Everything felt so natural, so right.

Her other hand came up, cupping his face and drawing him to her. She returned his kiss, feathering her lips against his. He seemed to hold back until she ran her tongue along his full bottom lip, ripping a primal groan from deep within him. Whatever control he'd had snapped.

He tunneled his arms underneath her and crushed her beneath him, deepening the kiss and taking possession of her mouth with his tongue. It was all-consuming, powerful, and sent her senses into a spinning whirlwind.

His lips left hers to trail down the curve of her neck, and her body warmed to his touch. She heard him inhale deeply, breathing in the scent of her. In that moment, she felt beautiful, cherished, wanted.

His mouth resumed its relentless assault on the tender skin just below her ear, sending tingles shooting through her entire body. She felt the heat of his hand on her waist through the thin cotton of her shirt. His hand rose, burning a gentle trail up her bruised ribs until it cupped her breast. He squeezed her gently, and she arched into his hand.

She heard a strange sound. Did it come from her? Was she actually purring?

His thumb flicked her taut nipple through the fabric, sending a lightning bolt straight to her core, and her hips jerked up off the ground.

"Oh, God! David!"

He moved over her, wedging his knee between her thighs and pressing her down into the dirt with his full weight.

But the fact that he was an American spy came creeping

back from the recesses of her mind. With a groan of regret, she turned her head away.

"David, please…"

He didn't stop. His lips continued to kiss her neck, his warm breath hot on her skin. She couldn't contain the moan that escaped from deep inside. She couldn't stop herself from cupping his head in her hands and running her fingers through his hair.

What was she doing? He was a spy—the enemy—and here she was rolling on the ground with him like some wild animal in the field.

She pried open her heavy-lidded eyes, the only part of her that seemed to obey her. For a moment, her vision seemed blurred, then the ground came into focus, and she saw a small hole gouged in the earth where David's shovel had been.

Sera's body stiffened, her mind trying to grasp the significance of what she saw.

"Get off me."

"Hmmm?" David nestled deeper into the curve of her neck, pressing his leg higher between her thighs.

Finding a sudden burst of strength, she pushed against his shoulders, trying to force him from her.

"I said get off."

He didn't seem to hear. She wiggled, trying to get out from under him, but all that accomplished was to elicit a masculine groan of pleasure.

"Get off!"

He finally seemed to hear her and rolled to the side.

"Sera, what…?"

She didn't have time to explain. She scrambled out from under him and crawled on her hands and knees to the place where his shovel had pierced the ground. She used her fingers to gently brush away the loose dirt around the hole, revealing a hardened layer of volcanic matter surrounding it.

"Oh, my God."

David knelt at her side, looking from her to the hole and back again.

"What is it?"

She could feel herself trembling.

"I'm not sure, but it could be something incredible."

He glanced again to where her hands framed the small crack in the ground. "What's so incredible about a hole?"

"Oh, it's not just any hole. Look." She stuck her fingers inside. "It's hollow."

"So?"

"It might be a body cavity."

He looked at the dark hole in the ground and swallowed hard. "Do you mean to tell me there's a body in there?"

"Not anymore. Bones would be the only thing left now."

She felt breathless. Her whole body shook with the enormity of what may lay just inches away under her fingertips.

"But, if I'm right and this is a body cavity, we can pour plaster into it. Then, once it hardens, we'll chip the volcanic layer away, and we should be left with a perfect cast of the person at the exact moment of their death."

David looked at her, understanding dawning in his eyes, but his reaction over the discovery did not match her own.

"Like the plaster child?"

As he recalled the reality of what could lie just below them, Sera's excitement sobered a bit.

"Exactly."

He seemed a little pale, and she wondered briefly if the big, brave American spy might faint on her.

She turned her attention to the tiny crack in the ground, and everything else seemed to slip away. Nothing mattered now except this. She felt her spirits soar, as if her soul were trying to float out of her body.

Looking back at David, her heart threatened to beat its way out of her chest.

"Have you ever had one of those days when you know, just as it's happening, that it's going to be one of the days you will remember for the rest of your life?"

"Yes."

"This is one of those days."

CHAPTER XIX

"Let me see it! Let me see it!"

David looked up in time to see Olympia's apple-shaped body and pencil thin legs trotting down the ancient road, her beaming smile reaching them long before she did.

"Where is it?" she huffed, coming to a halt in front of Sera.

Sera hugged her friend and led her over to the now-famous hole with pride.

"There it is."

"Is it really a body cavity?" Olympia asked.

David chuckled to himself. He couldn't get over the awestruck expression on her round face.

"We think so. Professor Moretti examined it this morning, but we won't know for sure until the cast is made."

He turned his attention away from Olympia, following the cheerful tone of Sera's voice. Her friend's excitement about the discovery didn't come close to Sera's obvious joy. She was practically glowing, and it made her more beautiful than ever.

He wished she'd send a little of that joy his way, but after the discovery, she'd pulled away. He wanted to think that, in her excitement, she was too busy to pay him much attention, but he knew that wasn't the case.

She was pushing him away on purpose, embracing the awkward tension filling the void between them. He couldn't say he blamed her. She was the smart one, keeping her distance from him now that she knew who he was.

And he was the idiot, trying to kiss her when common sense told him he should do everything in his power to stay on her good side. Making passes at the enemy wasn't a smart way to accomplish that, but at the time, with her body soft and warm beneath his, he'd been powerless to stop himself.

"That's what I heard," Olympia gushed, bringing his attention back to the two women. "Everyone on the site is talking about it. I'm so happy for you."

The women squealed and hugged each other as if one of them had just announced she was getting married.

Even though he knew that wasn't what they were celebrating, the wayward thought tickled at his brain. Just how long ago had she broken off the engagement with Giovanni? Had it been years or only weeks? Was she still in love with him?

"This is so wonderful," Olympia said when the two women finally peeled themselves apart. "I can't wait to see the look on Giovanni's face when he finds out. He's going to swallow a toad."

Speak of the devil.

The smile faded from Sera's face. She looked confused. Or was that concern creasing her brow?

"He doesn't know yet? I thought you said everyone was talking about it."

David stabbed his shovel into the dirt. Why the hell did she care if Giovanni knew or not?

"He couldn't have heard yet," Olympia remarked as she leaned down to get a closer look at the crack in the ground. "He hasn't shown up for work this morning."

"Oh? That's strange. He's usually on time."

Definitely concern, he thought. If she didn't like the guy anymore, why was she worried about him?

Olympia snorted as she straightened back up.

"Not really. He's been late several times this month. His Highness comes and goes like he owns the damn place."

"He better watch out. Moretti isn't going to like it."

"So far, I don't think the Professor has noticed, but if Giovanni keeps it up, he's going to get himself fired, senior archeologist or not."

David watched Sera's expression closely. Just how upset would she be if her ex got the ax?

Sera frowned and shook her head. What was that supposed

to mean? Apathy? If so, it was better than caring about the snake. David would take what he could get.

The two women resumed talking about the significance of the find and the procedure Sera would take to excavate it. She had been thrilled when Moretti told her she could do the excavation herself, with some supervision during the critical casting process. David didn't have to be a mind reader to know how much the show of confidence from the Professor meant to her.

Once Olympia left, they got down to work. The first part of the delicate job was to carefully remove all the loose earth from around the hard volcanic deposit. In short, direct words, she told David that it would be a very time-consuming process. One wrong move, too much weight on a particularly weak area, and the cavity could collapse. He didn't have to be told twice to watch where he stepped.

The task required them to work side-by-side, using hand trowels to scrape the dirt and loose pumice into buckets. As usual, Sera became so lost in her work she started singing. It took only the first few words before he recognized the tune. It was "Just as Though You Were Here," the song they had danced to in her apartment.

Her happiness was contagious, and he started singing the words along with her in his deep baritone voice. Not generally known for his musical abilities, he would be the first to admit that that young Sinatra guy didn't have a thing to worry about from him. But he didn't think he was that bad until he noticed Sera's singing had stopped.

He looked at her. Censure was written on every inch of her face.

"What?" he shrugged, trying to ease the tension between them. "You're not the only one who likes to whistle while they work."

She stared at him with a blank expression, evidently not appreciating his attempt at humor. Obviously, not all was forgiven or forgotten as far as she was concerned.

God, he missed the sound of her laughter, her smile when

he teased her. Why did he have to go and screw everything up? He resumed singing in the hopes that she would lighten up and join in, but she continued to work silently beside him.

Fine, if she wanted to be that way. As much as he wanted to, he couldn't change what happened yesterday. He couldn't take back the words he spoke or make her forget who he was. All he could do was try to make things as neutral between them as possible and hope that they could somehow find their way back to the way things had been before.

David continued singing as if her condemning silence meant nothing to him. He would wear her down and get her to relax if he had to sing Big Band tunes until the sun went down.

He was on his third chorus of "It's Been a Long, Long Time," when a familiar voice sneered from behind them.

"Well, well. Isn't this sweet? Is my little *mezzosangue* feeling homesick?"

They both turned at the same time to find Giovanni standing on the edge of the pit. Glancing quickly at Sera, David watched her face pale, and he knew it wasn't only because of Giovanni's unkind reference to her mixed heritage.

Stupid. He was so stupid to be singing a song in English. Even though they were far enough away from the rest of the workers, people had been coming and going all morning with the news of the discovery. Anyone could happen by the site and overhear them, just as Giovanni had. David knew better than to take such a risk.

Sera stood slowly, dusting her hands off on her trousers, and squinted through the sun at Giovanni.

"What do you want?"

"Interesting," he continued, choosing to ignore her question. "I know you like the American music, but I wonder where he learned to sing it."

David braced himself. Was this it? Would this be the moment she would reveal his identity?

He watched as a cool mask washed over Sera's face, her original panic quickly replaced by the usual serious façade she always wore. She didn't even miss a beat.

"I taught him."

"Really?" Giovanni's dark brows rose under the black hair falling roguishly over his forehead, doubt etched in his features.

"Yes, really." She shook her head at him. "Don't look so suspicious. He doesn't even know what the words mean."

Giovanni stared down his nose at David.

"How quaint of you to teach him. Does he realize how it is you know the words so well?"

David rose to his feet, standing straight next to Sera to get every inch out of his six foot height. It didn't help. Giovanni could still look down on him, since David was three feet lower in the pit.

"He knows about my father." She crossed her arms defensively in front of her. Was she uneasy because he'd brought up the subject of her father, or was she worried Giovanni might discover his identity? David would like to think it was the latter.

Giovanni looked surprised. "You told him?"

David couldn't get over it. They were talking as if he were an idiot and couldn't understand what they were saying. Maybe he wasn't supposed to know English, but both of them were aware he understood every bit of the Italian words they were flinging back and forth at each other.

"Some people aren't as bothered by it as you are."

Giovanni chuckled.

"It never bothered me. Amused me, perhaps, but it never bothered me."

"Well, it certainly didn't amuse me to find out you were sleeping with another woman while I was in America."

That certainly got David's attention. This was getting interesting. Maybe being ignored wasn't so bad after all.

Giovanni's face grew rigid, the chiseled angles of his jaw turning hard as stone.

"You should not have gone. You postponed our wedding to take your little trip."

"Well, it was a good thing I did put it off, now wasn't it?"

"You should've stayed here where you belong. If you hadn't gone to America, I wouldn't have been tempted to stray. A year is a long time to wait. I was lonely."

David's humor at the situation faded. How could he do that to Sera when he supposedly loved her? If it had been David, he would have waited for her forever.

Sera looked ready to blow, like the proverbial Mount Vesuvius. He braced himself in case he might have to stop her from clawing Giovanni's eyes out. Then again, he might just enjoy watching her do it.

"You weren't just tempted. You did stray, and I don't even want to know how many times. My plane probably wasn't even half way across the ocean before you started looking for someone to keep you 'company' while I was gone."

"Serafina, please. I didn't come here to argue with you about the past."

"Then what did you come here for?"

"I heard about the cavity. I wanted to see it."

She stepped to the side and pointed at the hole in the side of the pit.

"There it is. You've seen it. Now go."

Giovanni's face took on the look of a hungry tiger spying its next meal. David half expected him to lick his lips and drool.

"Let's work together on it, you and I."

"What?" Sera appeared so surprised by his suggestion that her arms fell limp at her sides. A second later, her back stiffened, and she shook her head at him. "No. David and I will manage the excavation just fine."

"Him?" Giovanni sneered, jerking his head in David's direction, barely bothering to acknowledge a mere laborer. "He's not trained for such a delicate excavation. I know what I'm doing. Let me help you."

"You mean let you take the credit for it."

David glanced between the two. Something deeper was going on here beyond the typical lovers—or ex-lovers—spat, but he wasn't sure what it was.

"I would never do that." Giovanni looked hurt by her accusation, but even David could tell the emotion was insincere.

"Don't lie to me. It's the only reason you're here. I don't need your help, and I don't want it."

"Fine." Giovanni's face hardened once more. He stared down at them for a moment, and then an unsettling light flared in his eyes. His mouth drew into a slow, menacing smile.

"You should be careful, then, Serafina." He started walking around the edge of the pit, making his way slowly toward the cavity area. "You know how easy it is for thieves and vandals to get into the ruins at night. It would certainly be a shame if something should happen to your new discovery."

The unspoken threat hung in the air all around them. *Let me excavate it with you, or risk losing it altogether.*

If he took one more step, Giovanni would be right on top of the cavity. David's hand shot out and grabbed his ankle. He yanked it hard, jerking him off his feet and landing him flat on his back in the dirt.

Giovanni was back on his feet faster than a cat. "How dare you?"

"Oh, sorry about that. You should watch your step. It can get pretty dangerous around here."

Threat thrown right back at you, asshole.

Giovanni obviously heard the implied warning behind David's words.

"I'll have you fired for that."

"No, you won't." Sera stepped between them. "He's my worker. I say whether he stays or goes."

Giovanni looked back and forth between them, the unspoken assumption that they were more than coworkers dawning on his face.

"So it's like that, is it?" he sneered, piercing Sera with a condemning look. "My, my. Haven't you changed? Tell me, are you spreading your legs for all the laborers now, or is it just this one?"

The last thing David heard was Sera's sharp intake of

breath beside him. A vacuum seemed to suck all other sound from the world around him, leaving only the rush of his own blood whirling inside his head.

Leaping from the pit, his fist slammed into Giovanni's hawk-like nose, and a sickening crunch filled the air. The force of the blow sent Giovanni sprawling in the dirt once more. He rose slowly, clutching his face. Pulling his hand away, Giovanni stared down at his palm, the blood seeping through his fingers to drip like raindrops on the dusty ground. David hoped his nose was broken.

"*Bastardo!*" Giovanni growled then lunged, diving on David and knocking them both down into the pit. David saw Sera scrambling out of the way, but the rage roaring in his ears blocked out everything else.

Both men tried to land blows to the other, their arms and legs tangled in a mass of dust and fury. Drawing his knees up between them, David wedged his feet against Giovanni's stomach and shoved with all his might, sending Giovanni flying through the air. Giovanni slammed into the edge of the pit, but bounced back, swinging, catching David in the jaw as he struggled to his feet.

A starburst of pain blinded David, barely giving him time to block the next blow with his forearm. He swung with his other fist, landing a jab in Giovanni's exposed midsection. As Giovanni doubled over in pain, David brought his knee up, catching him in the chin and sending him on his back. David jumped on him, straddling Giovanni's hips, and grabbed him by the collar.

His world faded around him, David's anger tunneling in on nothing but Giovanni's bloody face as he slammed his fist into it over and over again. He heard the impacts, like a wooden board smacking against a side of beef hanging in a slaughter-house, but he didn't see himself doing it. All that existed at that moment for David was Sera's crushed look, washed in a raging sea of red hate. He felt detached from the violence, separated from the hostile man who was within minutes of possibly killing another with his bare hands. He couldn't stop the fury, the desire to hurt, the need to protect.

Somewhere in the distance, through the waves of bloodlust, he heard Sera begging him to stop. He felt her tugging on his arm, but the limb seemed to have a mind of its own.

"What's going on here?"

Where all of Sera's shouting couldn't break through the fog of rage, Heberto's gentle words stopped David cold.

The sun seemed to burst from behind the clouds, casting a bright light on the carnage below. David released his grip on Giovanni's shirt, letting the dazed man's upper body fall to the ground. He stood and stepped away, sickened by what he had just done to another human being.

Giovanni struggled to his feet, blood running down his face to drip off his chin, leaving bright red spots splattered down the white linen of his shirt. David turned to see Heberto standing on the edge of the pit, staring down on them like an angry grand-father.

"Will someone please tell me what's going on?"

David looked at Giovanni. The man's breathing was labored, and his eyes glared a hatred David was sure reflected in his own.

As his own pain started to replace the blinding anger, David swiped at his lip, blood streaking the bruised knuckles on the back of his hand. His right cheek throbbed, and he knew he'd be sporting a handsome shiner by tomorrow.

"There was a disagreement," Sera answered for them. It was a good thing. David didn't trust himself to speak at the moment.

"I can see that. May I ask what it was about?"

"It was—" she began to say.

"Nothing important," Giovanni interrupted. He wasn't smiling anymore. David could only hope he'd knocked out some of those perfect teeth.

"I beg to differ." David glared at Giovanni. The man might want to avoid a scene, but calling Sera a whore was no small infraction in David's book.

"Obviously," Heberto commented, then turned his attention to Sera. "Why don't you two take a little walk? Let David cool off. I'll escort Giovanni back to the main area and send for a doctor. He looks like he could use one."

POMPEII

Sera couldn't believe what Heberto was asking. He was leaving her alone with David after witnessing that violent outburst? What if he turned on her next?

Of course, Heberto didn't know that she had a reason to fear David.

Tentatively, she reached out to take David's arm, but he shook her off. Fine. She'd rather not be within arm's reach of him anyway.

David jumped out of the pit and started walking, leaving her to follow if she wished. She trailed him down the path running along the city wall. He continued on past the Palaestra and the main entrance, weaving in and out of the tourists milling about, until the pathway ended and he could go no further. Not bothering to slow his pace, he turned left and disappeared into the large archway in the side of the Amphitheatre, disappearing into the cool darkness of the tunnel.

Sera stopped. Should she follow him? Was it even safe to be around him right now? Buried behind her fear and apprehension was concern for him. Was he hurt? Did he need her help? Did he even want it?

She swallowed her trepidation and entered the tunnel, hurrying to reach the light at the other end. Stepping out into the bright sunlight, she was temporarily blinded. When her eyes adjusted, she spied several groups of tourists mingling about, taking pictures of the ruins and talking amongst themselves, completely oblivious to the danger in their midst.

David stood in the middle of the arena, the vast openness of the place making him appear small and harmless.

But she knew differently. She'd just witnessed for herself the caged beast within him.

Sera walked slowly up behind him, afraid that one wrong move, one wrong word from her, would send him over the edge once more.

He must have heard her approach, because he spoke without looking at her.

"It's too dangerous for me to be here anymore."

Dangerous? For him or for her?

CHAPTER XX

David glanced around, feeling like he was coming out of a mad magician's trance and not quite sure how he got where he was.

"What is this place?"

"It's the Amphitheatre." Sera's voice sounded soft and shaky behind him. Was she afraid of him? She should be. He scared himself right now.

"It looks like a small replica of the Coliseum."

"Yes, but this one is older. The oldest one ever built, as a matter of fact." She stepped up to stand even with him, but kept him at arm's length. He watched her look around the arena herself, as if seeing it for the first time.

It felt odd to be carrying on a casual conversation with her after all that had just happened. But he needed to talk about mundane things, anything to calm his rampaging emotions.

She seemed to sense this and continued on.

"When the games were held, twenty thousand Pompeians would gather here to watch hundreds of gladiators fight each other to the death."

David looked at the stone seats surrounding them, most now overgrown with green grass like a soft carpet of moss on river rocks. Rising four levels high, this was where bloodthirsty spectators once sat and watched men kill each other in the name of entertainment.

His body grew cold in the warm air, his stomach tightening like a vise.

"My God, how could men do that to each other?"

Glancing down at his own bloodstained hands, he balled them into fists. Maybe he wasn't so far removed from the violence after all.

"Back then, they didn't think it was wrong. They saw it as a way to rid themselves of the unwanted in society—their criminals, prisoners of war. There were professional gladiators who were paid to compete and made careers of it. I'm sure you've seen the graffiti on the walls—some gladiators were close to movie star status for their time."

"It still doesn't make it right."

"No, but who's to say two thousand years from now what people will say about what we're doing to each other now in the name of war?"

"You're right about that." He pried his eyes away from the empty stands surrounding them. The echoes of a cheering crowd from long ago seemed to howl in his ears. "My father would have loved it."

"What?"

"The gladiator games. He would have loved them. I can just imagine him being in the thick of it, fighting in the arena for the glory of the win."

"What kind of man was your father?"

He didn't want to talk about his father, but that didn't stop the memories from swamping him.

"He was a full-fledged World War I hero. My old man blasted his way through Europe with a machine-gun and a take-no-prisoners attitude. It earned him a chest full of medals and what he thought was the right to demand his only son follow in his footsteps."

"And did you?"

"Oh, I tried. I joined the army like he wanted, but that wasn't good enough for him. Turned out, I wasn't considered 'leader material,' so there seemed little hope of me ever being the man my father was." David finally looked her in the eye, begging her to understand. "Until now."

"What do you mean?"

"World War II came knocking at my door, and, like a dutiful son, I answered the call. I may not be good at the usual army stuff, but when it comes to languages, I'm one of the best there is. They needed someone who could speak Italian and pass as one for a special mission, so I volunteered."

Sera's eyes flared, the old fight coming back into them at the mention of his mission. He watched her bite back whatever comment she thought to make about it. Instead, she took a deep breath.

"That's very brave. Your father must be proud."

An unpleasant feeling crept up on him, something close to shame.

"No, he wouldn't be. Not if he knew the truth."

She took a step closer, a question furrowing her brow.

"What is the truth?"

"I didn't do it to be brave, to be a hero like him. Christ, I did it so I wouldn't have to be on the front lines. So I wouldn't have to kill anybody." He could almost feel the dishonor smothering him. "I did it so I wouldn't have to die."

Sera didn't respond, not that he expected her to.

He snorted, and a half-laugh cracked like a whip in the silence around them, but there was no humor in it.

"Not very brave when it's painted like that, is it?"

David didn't wait for her answer. He turned and walked out of the arena without looking back.

POMPEII

Sera stood alone in the middle of the Amphitheatre long after David's retreating form had disappeared into the darkness of the tunnel. Strange. She'd stood in this very spot many times before, and yet she'd never felt the ghosts of its tragic past as acutely as she did now. Today they practically battled around her in the dust of the arena.

She didn't know what to make of his confession. As strange as it seemed, he saw himself as a disappointment to his father. Here he was, risking his life each day just by being here, and he thought he was taking the easy way out. At any moment, David could be discovered and shot, and he thought he was a coward.

Sera walked back through the empty streets of the ruins. The hollow shops and empty villas that once welcomed her in a calming embrace were of little comfort to her now. The dead whispered from the open doorways, telling her secrets she didn't want to know. There had been enough secrets revealed today.

When she got back to the dig site, it was empty. David was nowhere to be found, and his pack was gone. The site felt lonely without him. Then she looked at the small hole in the earth, and her spirits lifted a bit.

It wasn't just any hole. Somewhere under the dirt and ashes lay the remains of an unlucky Pompeian. If she were careful, she could coax his or her story from the ashes.

But first, the find would have to be thoroughly documented. She couldn't take the chance that Giovanni might try something underhanded again.

Leaving the site, Sera headed toward the main area of the excavations. As she approached, she noticed a crowd of archeologists standing outside the villa Professor Moretti used to catalogue the artifacts. Curiosity got the better of her, and she went to see what was going on.

Alfonso Moretti stood in the doorway, his arms gesturing about his body like an angry octopus. The veins at his temples bulged, and his neck flushed red, a color that was quickly invading the skin of his tan cheeks.

"What's happened?" Sera asked Heberto, who stood in the crowd.

"There's been a robbery."

"What?"

Heberto shook his head ruefully. "Some of the artifacts are missing."

Sera was stunned. She felt violated, as if someone had stolen something from her personally.

"Well, isn't that a coincidence?" Giovanni stepped out of the crowd, drawing everyone's attention, his usual smug smile twisted grotesquely by his swollen lip. "So is David."

POMPEII

"What are you doing?"

David left Sera standing in the door of his basement flat and went back to stuffing his clothes in the beat-up, brown leather suitcase lying on his bed.

"I'm leaving. You were right. My just being here is dangerous for you."

"What about your *mission*?" The harsh emphasis she put on the word dripped with disdain.

He chose to ignore it.

"I'll find another way to do it, but it won't be by working at the ruins and risking your life."

"How considerate of you." There was a long pause while he searched under the bed for any stray socks. "So, are you taking any souvenirs back to the States with you when you go?"

He turned to look at her. She remained in the doorway, her arms crossed in front of her like some prison guard barring the exit.

"What the hell is that supposed to mean?"

"Oh, just that it's interesting you've decided to leave now, when artifacts have suddenly started disappearing from the site. You wouldn't know anything about that, would you?"

"Someone has stolen some of the artifacts?" His momentary confusion at the sudden change in topic quickly faded.

He shook his head. Somehow, it didn't surprise him. After all, it wasn't as if the ruins were kept under lock and key. Anyone who wanted to could probably walk right in and take whatever they wanted.

"Yes, apparently some gold coins and jewelry, a small statue, and a silver cup went walking about the same time you did. If you leave Pompei now, you'll look guilty." Sera glared at him, the unspoken accusation blaring from her blue eyes. "I know for a fact you're always wandering off into areas of the ruins you have no business being in. And I'm not the only one who's noticed. Giovanni has already pointed out to the authorities that you left early today, just before the artifacts were discovered missing."

"Don't look at me like that. I didn't take them. Why would I?"

"You tell me. When you gave me that American record, I wondered how you got the money. I know it cost you a small fortune. Maybe buying contraband on the black market isn't the only illegal thing you've been doing."

David stood stunned. He couldn't believe she actually thought he might steal priceless artifacts. Here he was, risking his mission by leaving to spare her any more trouble, and she was accusing him of theft. The irony of it really pissed him off.

"You know I wouldn't do something like that."

Sera snorted in disbelief. "Well, until yesterday, I wouldn't have thought you'd turn out to be an American spy. Funny how things aren't always what they seem."

No, he didn't think it was funny. Nothing about this whole damn day had been funny.

Out of the blue, a thought weeded its way into his brain. Maybe it was because she'd just mentioned his name, or perhaps the pieces finally fell into place in his own throbbing head, but suddenly an image of Giovanni in the German camp flashed through David's mind.

"Yeah, I know what you mean. You might want to ask the same thing of your ex-lover."

"What?" Her brow furrowed in confusion.

"Giovanni? The high and mighty senior archeologist? The one who is so quick to point the finger at me? You may find it interesting that I've seen him several times in the German camp. It's fascinating what you can see from on top of that wall."

David took a few steps toward her. He didn't miss the fear that flashed across her lovely face or her involuntary step back. Good, she should be scared.

"You might want to try it sometime. Once in a while, you should leave your safe little hiding place behind the ruins and climb up on that wall. Seeing more of the outside world might open your eyes to a lot of what's going on around you."

He took two more steps toward her, bringing him so close he could hear her rapid breathing. This time she didn't move away. Her eyes just flicked back and forth, staring into his.

"And while you're at it, you might want to ask Giovanni what he was doing in the camp the other day showing something shiny and silver to the Krauts. That wouldn't have been your missing silver cup by chance, would it?"

Her nostrils flared, but he could tell doubt was starting to seep into the fabric of her thinking.

"He wouldn't do that. He's too much of a professional for that. He loves the ruins and the artifacts as much as I do."

"Oh, I can tell. He was the consummate professional this morning when he tried to flatten the cavity. No, you're absolutely right. He's not at all likely to do something like steal artifacts. He just threatens to destroy them."

"Why are you trying to place blame on him?"

David mimicked Sera's stance with his arms crossed in front of him.

"Why are you defending him?"

Seconds ticked by before she answered.

"The way I see it, Giovanni doesn't have a reason to be worried. You do. He's not the spy here. He's not the one who's done something wrong."

"You want to know something? One of the first things they taught us in 'spy school' was how to throw up smoke screens."

"What do you mean?"

"When you're in danger of being found out, you point the finger in the other direction, send them on a goose chase. That way, if they're busy looking at someone else, they can't look too closely at you. You might want to try taking a closer look at your ex-boyfriend."

"I've known Giovanni most of my life. He loves the ruins as much as I do. Maybe he isn't above stealing credit for discovering artifacts, but he would never sell Pompeii's treasures to the Germans or anyone else."

"Are you sure, Sera? It seems to me you thought you knew him well enough to marry him and then found out you were wrong. Can you really trust his word now?"

Whatever she had been about to say became lost in the echo of footsteps down the hallway. They both turned to see two Italian police officers standing in the open doorway of David's flat.

"Are you David Corbelli?"

"*Sì.*"

"You need to come with us. You are wanted for questioning in regards to some stolen artifacts."

David laughed humorlessly. "Surprise, surprise." He turned his own accusing look on Sera. "Guess you knew this was coming."

"I haven't told anyone anything."

"*Perdono?*" one of the officers asked.

"Am I being arrested?" David broke in before they could question her further. He was in enough trouble as it was. He didn't need her accidentally revealing his secret in front of the Italian police.

"No, signore. You are just wanted for a few questions, for now."

David nodded and walked past Sera, heading for the door.

The other officer glanced behind him, taking a good look inside his apartment, with the half-packed suitcase lying open on the bed.

"Are you going somewhere, signore?"

Standing in the hallway, David made his expression go blank. He couldn't risk them seeing anything that might be construed as guilt.

"*Sì.* After my argument with Signore Ragusa, which I have no doubt you already know about or you wouldn't be here, I assumed my job at the ruins was over. I figured I'd go ahead and leave before they had the chance to fire me."

The second officer's eyes narrowed, suspicion obvious in his wary features.

"Then you will not mind if we take a look around your apartment before we leave?"

He watched Sera stiffen as she stood behind the two officers. He knew what she was thinking. What if they found something that revealed who he really was?

"Of course," he told the officers. He wasn't worried. There

was nothing to find. He was too careful for that.

But Sera didn't know it, and the thought sent a visible tremor through her body. The officers didn't see it, but he did. He found it almost funny that she could accuse him of being a thief one minute and worry about his safety the next.

They forced David and Sera to stay in the hallway while they ransacked what there was of his small flat. None too tidy when they first arrived, it looked like an earthquake had hit it when they were done. Of course, they found nothing, just as he knew they would.

But that didn't stop them from taking him in.

POMPEII

"Which is it, Serafina? Who do you believe is telling the truth?"

Giovanni and David stood in middle of the atrium of the villa the artifacts were stolen from. Sunlight spilled in from the opening in the roof, casting the men in bright light as they stood before the artifact table like criminals before a judge.

"You have worked with both of these men. Each is saying the other is responsible for the missing artifacts." Professor Moretti looked back and forth between the two men and pushed his dark-rimmed glasses up on his nose. He would have to be blind not to notice they hated each other. Even Sera could feel their barely contained animosity reverberating off the plaster walls.

"Who do *you* believe?" the professor repeated, looking pointedly at her.

Sera looked at Giovanni. She'd known him all her life. They'd grown up together, worked side-by-side in the ruins for years.

Then she looked at David. He had only been here a few weeks. She hardly knew him.

She looked to Heberto, who stood off to the side. Seeing him reminded her of Maria, and the old woman's voice whispered to her, *trust your heart.*

Giovanni had already stolen credit for one of her finds. That in itself no longer surprised her. But would he really steal

215

artifacts and sell them to the highest bidder? He loved the ruins as much as she did. Or at least he used to.

David was an American spy. Everything he'd told her before was a lie. What if he was lying to protect himself now?

Trust your heart.

Giovanni had threatened to destroy the body cavity, although he'd vehemently denied it in front of Moretti when questioned about the fight, claiming he hadn't realized where he was stepping. But she knew differently.

David had fought with Giovanni to protect the cavity and, to her surprise, to defend her honor. No one had ever done that for her before.

Trust your heart.

She'd loved Giovanni, once. And then he'd broken her heart.

David lied to her about who he was, destroying any chance of trust between them.

Trust your heart.

Sera wanted to, but she couldn't understand what her heart was telling her. At the moment, she was so confused, she didn't know what to think.

"I don't know."

"Very well," the Professor sighed. "Since we don't seem to be getting any answers here, we'll have to hand the investigation over to the authorities."

The head officer stepped up to stand between Giovanni and David.

"We have already searched Signore Corbelli's apartment and found nothing." He turned to look at Giovanni. "Since you are also a possible suspect, I must ask you to accompany us to your home so that we may search it also."

What skin on Giovanni's face that wasn't already discolored by bruising flamed red in indignation.

"This is an outrage. I am a senior archeologist here, highly respected in my field. To even insinuate that I—"

"Be that as it may," the officer interrupted, looking back and forth between David and Giovanni, "until this issue is resolved, I strongly suggest neither of you leave the city."

The order hung in the air like a hangman's noose waiting for the next neck to stretch.

"Now, if you will accompany me, Signore Ragusa?"

The officer indicated the open doorway with a flamboyant wave of his hand and followed a fuming Giovanni out of the villa.

The raspy shuffling of feet on the tile floor echoed off the walls as the throng of onlookers who had come to watch the interrogation exited behind them, many of them speculating on who was guilty. Some were even placing bets, and David wasn't the favorite by a long shot.

Sera looked at him, but he stood rooted in the same spot, staring straight ahead. At that moment, she recognized the soldier in him, standing at attention before an unseen commanding officer. She wondered if anyone else picked up on the mannerism.

Finally, he seemed to dismiss himself and turned to leave. As he walked by her, she reached out and lightly touched his arm. He stopped, looking first at her hand and then at her face, but for the life of her, she couldn't fathom what he was thinking.

"So, you're staying?"

"I guess I don't have a choice now, do I?"

CHAPTER XXI

"She *knows*?"

David watched as Frank spun around and strode several paces away, all the while cursing under his breath every expletive known to man. He turned and marched back to where David stood near a drainage ditch beside an olive grove.

Frank's normally jolly disposition was tempered with concern.

"Damn it. I knew I shouldn't have gotten that record for you. You gave it to her, didn't you? Is that how she found out?"

"No, it wasn't." Although now that David thought about it, giving the record to her probably wasn't one of his brightest ideas. He might as well have hung a sign around his neck that read, *Look at me. I'm an American*. But at the time, all he'd wanted was to make her happy, to see her smile again.

"Well, then how the hell did she find out?"

"I think it was when I made the mistake of using one or two of those choice words that just spewed out of that sewer you call a mouth."

"You spoke English in front of her?" Frank's look was almost comical, with his big eyes bulging and his mouth gaping as if he'd just swallowed a bug.

"It's not like I did it on purpose. There were extenuating circumstances." Like a painful, self-inflicted toe injury and a wicked temper that seemed to flare fast and hot whenever Giovanni came sniffing around Sera.

"I'll just bet there were. This is not good, David. Not good at all."

"She promised not to tell anyone."

"Oh, she promised, did she?" Frank nodded his head in mocking acknowledgement. "Well, that makes all the difference in the world. Your American-hating, Nazi-sympathizing boss promised she wouldn't tell." Frank slapped David in the forehead with the flat of his palm. "And you *believed* her?"

David rubbed at his stinging brow. The bruises from the punches Giovanni had managed to land on him had only just started to fade. He didn't need any more.

"Damn, Frank. That hurt."

"It was supposed to hurt, dumbass."

Frank placed his fists on his hips and looked for all the world like a father disappointed with his son's performance. The uneasy emotions it recalled in David were all too familiar. He swallowed the feelings just as he had as a kid.

"How could you screw up like this?" Frank continued. "The Colonel is going to snap his cap. It could jeopardize the whole mission."

Realizing what Frank might do with what he'd just told him put David on edge.

"Look, this is just between you and me. You can just store this tidbit of information away in that sponge of a brain of yours. The Colonel doesn't need to know about it. The Army doesn't need to know about it. Sera's not going to tell anyone."

"Yeah, right," Frank snorted, skepticism etched across his face. "How can you be so sure of that?"

David thought about the many chances Sera had already had to blow his cover—when Giovanni overheard him singing, when the Italian police showed up at his apartment, when they questioned him about the stolen artifacts.

She'd had every opportunity to turn him in, and she hadn't.

"I trust her, Frank."

"How much?"

David stared at the olive trees, their thick, gnarled trunks twisted into contorted shapes on the hillside. He didn't understand it, but Sera's reluctance to reveal who he was gave him a confidence he couldn't begin to explain to his friend.

"With my life."

POMPEII

Sera carefully guided a small spoon with a long, thin handle into the hole and pulled out a scoop of loose pumice.

Tedious couldn't even begin to describe the backbreaking work of removing debris from the cavity. If David thought shoveling dirt was hard work, then sitting in one position, hour after hour, scooping out ash and dirt one spoonful at a time must seem like pure torture for him. He was now getting a taste of, and hopefully a new respect for, the delicate work she did every day. Nothing about it was easy.

But he never complained. Not once did he question why the process was so painstakingly slow. He wasn't even shocked anymore whenever one of them would pull out a bone, the flesh and muscle having decayed centuries before.

She looked over the mound at David, his forehead creased in concentration as he worked on another section of the cavity. Neither of them sang anymore as they worked. The unspoken knowledge that it was too dangerous for them both hovered in the air around them.

She inserted the probe once more, scraping carefully inside the dark hole.

Over a week had passed since the fight with Giovanni and the break-in at the artifact villa. She, along with the entire archeology community, had been shocked when Giovanni ditched the police after leaving the ruins that day. When they searched his apartment later, the police found some, but not all, of the missing artifacts.

It hadn't surprised David.

He didn't say it, but she knew he suspected the missing treasures were probably well on their way to Hitler's private collection by now. The thought made her want to pummel Giovanni. Or hold him down and let David do it again.

He stood and arched his back, stretching stiff muscles, then walked over to his pack near the sifting table.

Sera stopped poking in her hole and watched his every movement.

"Where are you going?"

He glanced at her, not bothering to hide his irritation. She had become his self-appointed guardian. For the past week, she'd made it her business to know where he was at all times, at least while they were working. Even though he was off the hook for the thefts, she still didn't completely trust him.

"Taking a break." Then David boldly added, "I need to check on my second job again."

At least he no longer had to hide what he was doing around her. She bristled, but didn't comment and returned to the tedium of her work.

"Come up there with me."

She almost dropped the probe into the cavity. "What?"

"Take a break, and come have lunch with me on the wall. It's beautiful up there."

Sera shook her head. "You forget. I've lived here all my life. There's nothing in Pompei I haven't seen."

"I'll wager you haven't seen the German camp."

She gritted her teeth and gripped the tool tighter.

"I don't want to. What the Germans do is none of my business."

"Ah," he nodded his head. "The 'ignorance is bliss' approach. Aren't you even a little bit curious about them since they're camped in your own backyard?"

"Quite frankly, no. That's your job."

"Right." David didn't bother to hide the disappointment in his voice. "Well, suit yourself."

Sera watched him walk to the base of the tower and scale the wall like a squirrel up a tree. Or rather, like a sleek panther in the jungle, all power and hidden danger.

She shivered at the memory of that strength unleashed on Giovanni. He'd hardly had a chance against David. She looked up to where he sat in the shadows of the tower with his broad back to her. She trembled again, only this time it came from the unwelcome image of that power unleashed on her in a totally different and very intimate way.

She felt a traitorous pang of regret. He no longer made

those kinds of advances toward her, and only occasionally did he even make an overture of friendship like he just had.

But every now and then, she would catch him looking at her when he thought she wasn't aware. Sometimes, she didn't even have to see him to know he was watching her. She could feel his gaze like a touch on her shoulder, a caress on her cheek.

David turned just then and looked down on her. Was he experiencing the same thing? Had he felt the touch of her eyes on him just then?

Unbidden, his angry words came back to whisper to her. *Once in a while, you should leave your safe little hiding place behind the ruins and climb up on that wall. Seeing more of the outside world might open your eyes to a lot of what's going on around you.*

He hadn't been talking about the actual wall then, and the meaning of his words taunted her now more than ever. Here, inside the ruins, she was safe, comfortable, sure of herself and her place in the world. But once she stepped outside the wall, the old insecurities always closed in. She'd taken the risk once by going to America and lost too much—the fantasy of a father to love her and a fiancé when she returned home. She was content to stay right where she was, thank you very much. Safe, secure… and alone.

Her gaze wandered back up to David, where he once again looked out over the wall. He represented everything she was not. Risk, danger, excitement.

She felt a pang somewhere inside her, a tiny pinprick of sorrow that she had lost something she never had to begin with.

What would it hurt to climb that wall, just once, and see what was on the other side? She told herself that she didn't have to go over the wall. She could always turn around and come back down if she didn't like what she saw.

Sera stood, her knees stiff from sitting with them tucked under her for hours at a time. Dusting off her hands, she took a deep breath. Climbing the wall to where David stood watch went against all the promises she'd made to herself to keep her distance.

She grabbed her lunch from her pack and walked to the base of the wall. Stepping carefully on the stones, she used the strongest ones as steps up the side of the tower.

As she ascended, she recalled the last time she climbed this same wall after David. That time, he'd thrown her to the ground and put a knife to her throat. This time, she felt an altogether different danger waiting for her at the top, but she couldn't stop herself from climbing to it.

"I'm coming up," she called in warning as she neared the top, not willing to make the same mistake twice.

David's surprised smile greeted her as he offered his hand to help her up.

"What changed your mind?"

"Nothing." *Except the meddlesome little voices in my head that won't leave me alone.* She wasn't going to give him the satisfaction of knowing he got to her even a little bit, but the smug smile on his handsome face told her he already knew.

He pulled her up to stand on the dirt-filled space between the inner and outer walls. The ancient Pompeians had built a strong barrier around their city, but it didn't compare to the solid wall of David's body as he steadied her.

"You're not afraid of heights, are you?"

"Of course not." She shook him off. Standing beside him was one thing. Having him touch her was another. It sent a tingling warmth through her body that she didn't want to acknowledge, but craved to feel again. Turning, she looked out over the valley beyond the wall and gasped. "My God, there are so many of them."

"Yes, the camp has tripled in size since I got here."

For one brief moment, Sera had forgotten she stood next to an American spy, but his simple statement served to remind her that he'd been spying on the Germans from this very spot every day for over a month now.

"I had no idea it was that big. Why would they possibly need an army that size here in Pompei?"

He looked surprised. "Do you really want to know?"

Frankly, she surprised herself, suddenly interested in a war she used to care nothing about. "Yes."

"Things are heating up in Africa. It's no secret that it's only a matter of time before the Allies attempt to cross the Mediterranean and invade Italy. Hitler needs to keep her in his power at all costs. To lose Italy would be to expose the soft underbelly of the Axis realm and allow the Allied forces a doorway in through Switzerland to Germany."

Sera was confused.

"But why so many here? I mean, Pompei is not a port city like Naples or a strategic location. Why so many soldiers?"

David looked at her, and she could tell he was gauging her reasons for asking. Did he wonder if she was just curious and really wanted to know? Or was he deciding whether he could trust her with the information if he told her?

A shield fell down over his eyes. He crossed his arms and leaned one broad shoulder against the tower as he looked out over the encampment.

"We aren't sure. That's why I'm here."

She followed his gaze again out over the Nazi army, trying to ignore the hurt his lack of trust stirred in her. He wasn't telling her everything. Then again, why should he trust her? She'd been all but ready to turn him over to the Germans just a few days ago.

"It seems like everything is in chaos down there," she said. "They look like an army of ants, running around all over the place."

"Yes, they do. But don't be fooled. They aren't chaotic. They're extremely organized. And their bite is a lot worse than any fire ant's I know."

The amount of German forces boggled her mind. She'd had no idea there were so many. She glanced at David, leaning casually against the tower as if he didn't have a care in the world. Until this moment, she hadn't realized what he was up against. Looking back out over the valley, she couldn't shake the feeling that he was one man standing against a whole army.

Sera felt a tiny piece of the wall she'd so carefully built around herself crumble. Somehow, without even realizing it was happening, a truce had been drawn between them.

ᛈᛟᛗᛈᛖᛁᛁ

A pounding on the bathroom door startled Hershel so much, he almost fell off the toilet.

"Hershel, what on Earth are you doing in there? The show's about to come on."

He finished as quickly as he could and opened the door to an irate Marsha, her hands fisted on her bathrobe-clad hips and the long white braid of her hair slung over her shoulder.

"Hurry up. It's the last episode, and I don't want to miss it. Nora is about to solve the case."

Hershel grumbled and followed his wife as they shuffled into their dark living room and assumed their usual places—he in his favorite chair, and Marsha on the footstool pulled up close to the radio.

Marsha turned on the power on the small, laminated wood control panel and moved the dial to pick up the BBC on the shortwave, where the show was relayed from America. She kept the volume low. Even though it was ten at night and the rest of the world was probably asleep, they didn't want to risk someone hearing them listening to the illegal broadcast. The sponsor's commercial came on, and in a deep voice, the announcer began lauding the new, improved taste of Lucky Strike cigarettes.

"Good, it hasn't started yet." Marsha wiggled so much on her seat, he worried she might fall off.

The front door squeaked open and shut, and she quickly switched off the radio. Watching the arched opening leading to the hallway, they both knew who their late-night visitor was, but, as usual, they wanted to be sure.

Serafina stepped into the opening on slippered feet, her blue bathrobe cinched tight at her waist.

"Did I miss anything?"

"No." Marsha smiled and waved her in before clicking the radio back on. "It's just about to start."

Serafina walked over and sat in her usual spot on the floor beside Marsha.

As "The Adventures of the Thin Man" started, Hershel looked down at Serafina. Her head rested on Marsha's lap, and his wife absently ran her fingers through the girl's wavy, brown hair highlighted gold in the orange glow from the radio dial. Every Saturday night was the same. The three of them would gather around the radio at ten o'clock and listen in the dark to Nick and Nora Charles as they solved daring crimes.

He shook his head. It was such a shame. She was so young and pretty. She should be with someone her own age, instead of sitting here with two old fogies like him and Marsha. She should be with David. What was taking the two of them so long to figure it out?

Hershel's attention came back to the radio show just as Nick was about to solve the case.

"… and with this evidence, we can prove that—"

"We interrupt this broadcast for a special bulletin…"

"Nooo!" Marsha shrieked, nearly giving him a heart attack and startling Serafina's head from her lap. "They were going to reveal the killer. How could they do this?" she wailed at the small wooden box on the table. She actually reached out and shook the radio.

Hershel leaned forward and placed a calming hand on her shoulder before she could pick up and dash the transmitter to pieces in the cold fireplace.

"There now, dear. I'm sure we'll find out who the killer is tomorrow."

Marsha's face took on a wild, desperate look.

"Tomorrow? But I don't want to wait until tomorrow. How am I supposed to sleep tonight not knowing who the murderer is?"

"Come now, the world isn't ending. It's just a show."

"Not to me!"

"Listen," Serafina interrupted, reaching out to turn up the volume. The reporter's voice crackled over the airwaves, reaching out from London to anyone in Europe who might be listening at this hour.

"British, Canadian, and American Allies have landed on Sicily. Parachutists began dropping from the dark, stormy sky over the island around ten o'clock Friday night. Under the cover of a sudden, harsh gale, eighty thousand Allied troops invaded the island's southern and eastern coasts. They were eventually met with extreme Axis resistance..."

They all sat in rapt attention as the reporter relayed the details of the invasion of Sicily. When the newscast was over, the regular announcer came back on.

"And now, back to the show in progress..."

As Jo Stafford's rendition of "Long Ago (And Far Away)" filled the quiet of the room, Marsha switched off the radio, and they sat in stunned silence. Finally, she turned wide eyes to Hershel.

"What does this mean?"

He shook his head, an uneasy feeling gnawing at his gut.

"If the Allies take Sicily, it's only a matter of time before they invade all of Italy."

He watched as Serafina pulled her legs up to her chest and wrapped her arms around them, resting her chin on her knees.

"What does that mean for us?" she asked, a war of emotions waging in her troubled eyes.

"It means things are going to start getting very ugly around here."

CHAPTER XXII

David walked down the alley between the centuries-old buildings. It wasn't the same alley he had met Frank in the first time, but it certainly could have been. They looked the same all over town with their open apartment windows and tiny balconies. The day's wash hung on drooping lines strung between them, white sheets flapping in the breeze over his head like flags of surrender.

Frank was already there and, judging by the multitude of cigarette butts already on the ground, had been for a while.

"You're late."

David took the offered cigarette out of habit.

"No, I'm on time. You're early." He couldn't help but notice that Frank appeared a little on edge. "What's wrong?"

"Hmmm?" Frank tapped his cigarette with his finger, watching its hanging tower of ash fall to the ground, never once looking up at David. He seemed fascinated by the dancing white specks as they floated on the breeze down the alleyway. "Nothing. You got anything to report?"

David relayed what he had observed of the German's actions during the week. Activity had picked up in the camp ever since the Allies had invaded Sicily. While the Italians on the island had given up quickly and quietly, the Germans stationed there were hell-bent on keeping the island under Axis control at all costs. The Krauts stationed outside the ruins reflected that same determination. They looked just as Sera had described them—like a nest of angry fire ants trying to defend a disturbed anthill.

As he finished reciting his report, the normally attentive Frank still appeared distracted.

"All right, Frank, spill it. I can tell something's bothering you. What is it?"

For the first time since he got there, Frank looked him in the eye. The usual humor was not there. No joke, no sarcastic comment was waiting to shoot from his laughing mouth.

"It's not good, man."

"What?" David had the sickening feeling he was about to get some bad news. And bad news during wartime usually meant someone was dead. Was it one of their buddies from the unit? Most likely. His father? He doubted it. The old cuss was too stubborn to die. "What's happened?"

"You're not going to like this."

"What?"

"I told the Colonel about the girl. About her finding out who you are."

"*What?* Jesus, Frank. Why?" David felt like he'd just been punched in the gut. "I trusted you to keep that to yourself. What the hell did you go and do that for?"

Frank winced, guilt oozing out in the beads of sweat on his forehead. "I had to. Whether you like it or not, her knowing about you could jeopardize the entire mission."

"I told you I'd make sure she kept quiet. It's none of the Army's goddamn business."

"Unfortunately, they think it is. Things are getting hot right now in the south, and every second she's not around you is an opportunity for her to tell someone or let it slip out by accident. They consider her too high of a risk."

David barely felt his unsmoked cigarette drop from his fingers. He swallowed hard, trying to hold back the bile creeping up his throat to choke him, deathly afraid he knew what was coming. The ground under his feet seemed to shift as if his world was being pulled out from under him and he was powerless to stop it.

Frank looked at him with world-weary eyes and placed his hand on David's shoulder in a vain attempt at brotherly comfort.

"I'm sorry, David. They want to make sure she stays quiet.

Permanently."

POMPEII

As the sun rose in the morning sky, David walked to the dig site on the legs of a condemned man heading to the gallows. How could he face Sera knowing what the Army expected him to do?

Silence her. Permanently.

He'd lain awake all night listening to those damned words booming through his head like a ticking bomb.

As he rounded the corner to the narrow street leading to their site, he could see her in the distance, already working.

Alone.

David tried to swallow past the knot wedged in his throat. She was the condemned one, and she didn't even know it. In war, one life was a small price to pay if it saved hundreds, maybe thousands, of others.

But he didn't consider Sera's life a small price. How could they ask him to do this?

He knew the answer. She was just an obstacle to them. A faceless, nameless bump in the road to victory over the Nazis. But to David she was real. A living, breathing human being. One he cared about. A lot.

As he approached the pit, he looked down on her. She seemed so small and defenseless. It would be so easy to sneak up behind her and crush her skull with a rock. He pictured himself dragging her limp body up on the wall and throwing it back down on the stones below like a pile of garbage in the street. No one would ever know. It would look like an accident. Hell, after the incident with the dump truck, she was living proof that accidents on the site could be deadly.

She must have sensed him behind her. Sera stood and turned, smiling tentatively at him. David clenched his fists at his sides. He was so close he could reach out now and snap her thin neck with his bare hands. But could he bear to look into those beautiful blue eyes as he choked the life out of her?

"*Buon giorno,*" a familiar voice called out from behind him.

Sera glanced around David and waved, returning the greeting. "*Buon giorno.*"

He turned to see Heberto walking down the road toward them.

"Serafina," the old man said as he drew closer. "Professor Moretti wants to talk with you about the casting. He needs you to fill out an order for the amount of plaster you'll need so it will be here when you're done excavating the cavity."

Sera looked puzzled. "Don't we have any plaster here?"

"No, it's been a while since the last cast was made, and we're out."

David watched Sera look wistfully at the mound. He knew her expressions so well that he could almost read her mind. *So much has been done, but there's still so much work to do.*

Heberto gave her a friendly shove.

"Go on. It'll still be here when you get back."

As he watched her walk away, David released the breath he hadn't realized he'd been holding. He had to pry his fingers open, stiff from where he'd gripped them so hard.

Sera's cavalry had arrived just in time. The opportunity had been taken away from him for the moment. But, given another chance, could he follow through with what he was supposed to do?

POMPEII

When Sera reached the artifact villa, the Professor was nowhere in sight. After a few inquiries, one of the workers told her he'd been called away and would be back soon.

Reentering the villa, she went to the mismatched file cabinets lining one wall and began shuffling through the papers for the supply order form. Not that it would do her any good. She knew the measurements of the mound by heart, but the Professor would have to help her figure out the volume of plaster needed. Math had never been her strongest subject.

Glancing over her shoulder at the bright sunlight coming through the open doorway, she huffed impatiently. The time this errand was wasting irritated her. She wanted to be back at the site, working on the cavity, not doing damn paperwork.

Grumbling a litany of muffled curses with each wrong form she pulled out, Sera overheard loud voices from just outside the doorway. German-accented voices.

Nothing unusual there. German tourists crawled all over the ruins every day. Although she didn't understand much of the language, her hearing did pick up on two words that made her blood run cold.

"*Wo ist David Corbelli?*"

They were looking for David.

She froze, and her heart nearly stopped. Careful to keep herself hidden in the shadows, she crept closer to the doorway.

"Where is Signore Corbelli?" another asked in German-accented Italian.

"What is this about?" she heard Heberto reply. How had the old man gotten here so fast from where she'd left him at the dig site?

"We have reason to believe that Signore Corbelli is not who he says he is. We have it on good authority that he may be an American spy."

No! No! No! Panic seized her. How had they found out?

"What? It cannot be," she heard Heberto answer. "Why, David is as Italian as I am."

"An Italian who has a fondness for American cigarettes, it would seem." Sera recognized Giovanni's smug voice immediately. What was he doing here? It would figure he had something to do with this. "Or perhaps he's an American smoking his own?" The unspoken allegation hung in the air like a death knell.

"What are you doing here?" Heberto echoed her unspoken question. "I'll have you arrested for stealing those artifacts."

"Not so fast, Signore," a German officer spoke. "A few missing pots don't concern us right now. Espionage against the Motherland is of greater interest to us at the moment."

"You see, Heberto. I'm here under the protection of the German Army, so you can't touch me."

Sera didn't have to see Giovanni's arrogant face to know he

spoke down to Heberto. He'd used that haughty tone of superiority with her enough in the past.

"I'm just doing my duty as a loyal Fascist in helping my comrades flush out the American spy among us. I always knew there was something strange about Corbelli, so when I caught him sneaking down an alley, I followed him. I saw him talking to a man I've never seen in Pompei, and they left behind a trail of American cigarettes."

"Oh, for heaven's sake," Heberto huffed. "Anyone can get them on the black market. Half of Italy trades for them whenever they can. Why, I've smoked a few myself, and they aren't half bad."

"We'll find out the truth soon enough," the German officer said. "We only want to ask him a few questions. If he is who he says he is, no harm will come to him."

Sera didn't believe the officer for one minute. There were too many people who had been taken away to be "questioned" and were never seen or heard from again. And since Giovanni seemed to be behind it all, she had no doubt that David would not fare well in the hands of the Germans, especially since what they suspected was true.

She dropped the papers and crept to the rear door leading to the courtyard of the villa. For once, she was thankful that the building was in ruins. She was able to escape through a hole in the wall that normally wouldn't have been there.

Sera ran down the road, dodging clusters of tourists, trying to beat the Germans to the dig site. Heberto seemed to be trying to stall them, but she didn't know how long the old man would be able to keep them at bay.

She had to find David. She had to get him away before they found him.

She cut over to the empty street that ran along the city wall. Not normally open to tourists, it was the path David used to take the debris to the waiting trucks. Rounding a corner, she nearly ran into him. The edge of his wheelbarrow cut into her thighs, his load of rocks and dirt spilling all over the ground at their feet.

He dropped the wheelbarrow and tried to steady her.

"Sera, are you all right?"

"Hurry. Follow me."

She grabbed his hand and pulled him down a narrow street past villas and shops. She tried to get him to the nearest gate so that he could blend in with the tourists and get out of the ruins. But as they came around the building, she saw Giovanni and the German officers headed their way. They had not taken the main street, but had cut down the alleyways, probably trying to sneak up on David at their dig site.

"Quick, this way."

"What's wrong?" he asked as he let her drag him along.

"No time to explain."

They backtracked down the street and passed through an arched tunnel into the theatre section of the ruins, going past first the small theatre and then cutting across the large one. Just as they reached the tunnel leading back to the main road, she spied several members of the Italian Militia, obviously looking for someone. Extreme fascists, they were as close to a Nazi as an Italian could get and just as dangerous for someone like David.

Sera stopped abruptly, and David ran into her back, nearly shoving her out of the shadows into the street.

"Would you please tell me what's going on?"

"The Germans. Giovanni... somehow he found out about you. He's brought the Nazis here to take you."

"Damn it! How?"

"Something about seeing you smoking American cigarettes in an alley with someone. But how he found out is not important. What does matter is that we've got to get you out of here. Now."

Too late, they heard more angry voices. The Germans had joined up with the Italian Militia and were getting closer.

Turning back, they returned to the large theatre and climbed across the scaffolding erected where the old stage once had been. Dodging around broken columns and a crumbling wall, she led him across an open, grassy courtyard. Running down a colonnade, they ducked into one of the empty rooms. The wooden door was long gone, leaving only the stone walls and restored tile roof over their heads to hide them. She urged him back, pressing his body against the wall.

"Where are we?" he asked.

"In the gladiator barracks," she whispered. "It's where they trained between the games."

"It looks more like a prison cell to me."

Sera glanced around at the small, cramped room.

"This one was."

ᛈᛟᛗᛈᛖᛁᛁ

Panic gripped David's stomach. He felt like a hunted animal, trapped in this small, stone room. But there was something more. He couldn't shake the sense that he'd been in a place like this before, and he had to fight back an unnatural urge to claw his way out, even though the real danger stood somewhere right outside the doorway.

Hearing approaching footsteps, he put a finger to his lips, and they shifted deeper into the shadows. He held his breath as the German soldiers walked past the doorway. They'd made a mistake by hiding in here. If the Germans found them, they'd be trapped. There was no way out of the cell.

"I know I saw them head down this way," he heard Giovanni say.

Sera shook in his arms, and he wrapped them protectively around her. Her head pressed against his shoulder, and he could feel her warm, moist breath against his neck, felt her heart pounding in rhythm to his. He cursed himself for getting her mixed up in this. If they were found together, she would be considered as guilty as he was. She could be shot as a traitor.

He would not get her killed because of him.

He was ready to leave her there in the shadows and reveal himself when he heard Heberto's familiar voice.

"Gentlemen, I haven't been able to locate Signore Corbelli, but here are his papers. I found them in his pack at the site. I am no expert, but it appears that everything is in order."

David was shocked. How had Heberto known where to find his papers? And would the forged documents be good enough to fool the Nazis?

"These must be fakes," he heard Giovanni protest. David had to suppress a feral growl. He wanted nothing more than to tear Ragusa limb from limb. "Corbelli is an American, or at least spying for them. I'm sure of it."

"Since when did you become an expert on official documents?" Heberto asked briskly.

"*Chiudere su, il vecchio.*" Shut up, old man.

The Germans' voices were muffled, and papers rustled as they examined the documents.

"The papers seem to be in order, but we will return later to question Signore Corbelli. Just as a formality. We are very eager to know just where he got those American cigarettes."

David heard them walk away, their voices fading in the distance. Hours seemed to pass before their heartbeats slowed, but he didn't let Sera go. Finally, he felt her relax in his arms. He looked down, and her face was still pressed against his shoulder. He tilted her head up so that he could look into her eyes.

"It's all right. They're gone."

Her pale face still showed alarm.

"For now. But you heard them. They'll be back. What if they take you away?"

He smiled at the concern in her voice, and he repeated the words she'd spoken to him just days before.

"I thought you weren't going to protect me if they came looking for me?"

She reached up and cupped his cheek, a touch so tender it took his breath away.

"I had to. I couldn't bear it if something happened to you. If they found out about you, you would be shot. I…" She faltered, lowering her gaze to his chest. "I couldn't let you die."

Her admission stunned him. He wondered if she realized what she had just risked for him. Only this morning, he was contemplating the Army's order to kill her, and now she was in his arms and telling him she couldn't let him die.

The dutiful soldier and the honorable man waged a fierce battle inside him, tearing his emotions into tiny pieces.

The honorable man won easily. The mission be damned. He wanted the woman he held in his arms, and it would take the German and American forces combined to stop him from having her.

David crushed Sera to him, his lips crashing down on hers, kissing her with a force akin to the new determination inside him. He would keep her safe at any cost.

He felt her initial resistance to his forceful onslaught as she pushed feebly against his shoulders. With one arm still around her waist, he moved his other hand to the back of her head, refusing to let her go.

As he gentled the kiss, she opened to him, tentatively exploring the interior of his mouth, finally matching his passion with her own. He heard her moan, felt it leave the back of her throat and fill his mouth. She relaxed in his hold, wrapping her arms around his neck, pulling him closer, drawing him into her.

David shifted their bodies so that her back was against the wall. Cupping her soft, round buttocks, he lifted her so that her head was level with his own, pressing her up against the stones, pinning her against the wall with his own body and kissing her with all that he had.

Sera wrapped her legs tightly around his hips, the center of her pressing against the hard erection straining between them. Now it was his turn to groan. He thought he might explode if he didn't have her then and there.

Glancing to the side, he noticed a narrow stone slab along the far wall. It looked like it might have once been used as a bed for some poor soul. The thought occurred to him to lay her down on the slab and take her right there.

As much as he wanted to, the notion of making love to her in a filthy place used to hold trained killers was wrong. He couldn't do that to her. She deserved more than that.

But that didn't stop him from wanting a taste of paradise.

Reaching a hand between them, he pulled her shirt from the waistband of her pants. His hand skimmed the soft skin over her ribcage, inching higher and higher until he cupped her breast. He squeezed the soft mound through her bra, drawing a feline purr from her as she tore her lips away from his kiss.

"David," she sighed, running her fingers through his hair and arching her back to press herself into his palm.

He trailed warm kisses down her neck, feeling the pulse of her heart in her throat. Working two fingers over the edge of her bra, he delved inside, finding the ridged tip of her nipple and rolling it between his fingers.

Sera jerked in his hold, but he only gripped her buttocks tighter with his other arm, continuing the relentless teasing of her body. He pumped his hips against her, grinding his shaft against her through their clothes. The air felt electric around them, charged with the heat of passion, the excitement of being alive, and something more that David couldn't name.

Suddenly, there was a flash of light, like lightning from the sky, startling them both. A high, feminine giggle came from the doorway, and David instinctively spun their bodies around, setting Sera gently on her feet and shielding her body with his.

"*Pardoné.* I didn't mean to interrupt," a large woman said in broken Italian laced heavily with a Hungarian accent. She stood in the open doorway grinning at them, her camera with its cooling flashbulb held in front of her like a trophy.

She spoke in her native language to a tall, thin man standing behind her.

"Look, *drága.* I guess the Italians are great lovers. Now I have the picture to prove it." She chuckled at her own joke, the large white polka dots of her pink dress bouncing as she laughed, like marshmallows on a bowl of strawberry Jell-o.

Her husband looked terribly embarrassed, his face flaming crimson as he pulled her away by her pudgy elbow.

"Stop staring, Ilka, and leave the young people alone."

David watched the tourist couple leave, then turned to find Sera quietly tucking her shirt back into her trousers. She had an adorable, rumpled look about her.

"Are you all right?"

She nodded. Her lips had a swollen, just-been-kissed redness to them, and he felt a certain amount of male pride that he'd been the one to do that to her. He reached for her, eager to pick up where they'd left off before being so rudely interrupted.

Sera held up her hands and shook her head. "David, we can't."

Her words felt like a bucket of cold water had just been thrown on him. He dropped his arms to his sides, but made no effort to hide his disappointment.

She took a step forward, then stopped herself. "Things are too unpredictable right now. We don't know which way this is going to go, how the war is going to end. If anything should happen..."

She covered her mouth with her fingers as if trying to hold back words too difficult to say. Turning away, she looked past him, out the door into the distance. The long silence between them stretched his patience to the breaking point. Finally, she looked back at him, a wealth of regret in her eyes.

"You and I, we're a war apart. When this is all over, you're going to go back to America, and my home is here. I just don't want to be hurt again. I'm sorry."

She walked away and, fool that he was, he let her go.

David leaned back against the cool stones of the wall and looked around the cell. Even though it was a very small space, it felt incredibly empty now that she was gone. A lonely melancholy invaded his senses, and the musty, damp odor of the place threatened to smother him. Feeling a panicked need to get out of the cell, he stepped out into the bright sunlight and breathed deeply in the fresh, clear air.

Sera was nowhere in sight, but he wasn't surprised. She was right. As much as they might want it, now was not the time for them. But no matter which way the wind blew in this war, he was determined to do everything in his power to keep her safe.

Even if it meant from himself.

CHAPTER XXIII

The minute Hershel walked into the house he smelled smoke.

"Marsha!"

Panic filled him when he heard no answer. They weren't angels anymore. Fire was not a good thing.

He raced to the back of the apartment, following the choking smell into the kitchen. Black smoke billowed from the cracks around the oven door. Grabbing the first thing he could find, he jerked open the door and pulled out a pan covered with small, blackened mounds. The hot metal pan burned through the thin dishrag, and he spun back and forth looking for a good place to drop it before it blistered his fingers.

Just then, Marsha walked in from the back courtyard with a load of laundry in her arms.

"Oh, heavens! My buns!"

She dropped the basket, spilling the freshly washed sheets on the floor as she rushed to the stove. Grabbing a potholder from a peg on the wall, she took the pan from Hershel before the charred bread ended up flung all over her clean floor.

"Give me that."

Dumping the pan and the buns into the sink, Marsha tossed the potholder on the counter in disgust.

"Well, there goes the last of the flour. We'll have to wait until next week before I can use our ration tickets to make more bread."

Hershel eased himself into a kitchen chair before his shaking legs gave out from under him.

Marsha turned, her anger-pursed lips softening into a perplexed frown as she regarded him.

"What's wrong with you?"

"What's *wrong* with me? You nearly took a hundred years off my life, that's what's wrong. Great Saint Agatha, I thought the house was burning down." Hershel dug in his pocket for a handkerchief and mopped at his sweating brow. "After the day I just had, I don't need that kind of excitement when I first walk in the door."

Comprehension dawned on Marsha's face, and she sat down at the table across from him, the burned rolls already forgotten.

"That's right. Today was the big test. How did it go?"

"Fine, fine." Hershel nodded, folding his handkerchief into a tiny square and shoving it back in his pocket. "It was a little hairy there for a while, until I found David's I.D. papers in his pack, but then everything went smoothly. I think the German officers believed they were real. But I'll tell you, Giovanni was none too happy about it."

Marsha scowled at the mention of his name.

"Drat that man. Why can't he mind his own business? It was bad enough he broke Serafina's heart when she was younger. Why does he have to meddle in her love life now?"

"I don't know. Maybe it's another part of the test."

"Hmmph," Marsha grumbled. "I don't see why Smithers is putting Serafina and David through these tests, anyway. Haven't they been through enough in all their lives together? Couldn't they just once have it go easy for them?"

Hershel rubbed at his throbbing temples. He felt a headache coming on. A big one.

"You know how they work up there. Nothing good ever comes easy. Thank heavens Smithers gave us a little warning about this one so we were ready. I'd hate to think what could have happened." He dropped his hands to the table and looked at Marsha. "You know, I think Smithers wants it to work out this time as much as we do."

"I'm sure he does. After all, he has a boss to answer to, too." Marsha leaned in toward Hershel. "So, how did Serafina do?"

"She did wonderfully. You would have been so proud. I made sure she was in the artifact villa at just the right time so

241

she would be around when the Germans showed up. As soon as she heard they were looking for David, she rushed to get him out of the ruins. I don't think I've ever seen the girl run that fast." A tiny detail tickled at Hershel's brain, and he rubbed at his chin as he pondered the meaning of it. "Lost track of them for a while there. I'm not really sure where they ended up, but they finally showed back up at the site."

"I wonder where they went?"

"Who knows?" Hershel shrugged, then he leaned across the small table toward Marsha until they almost touched foreheads. "But I'll tell you one thing. Something definitely happened between those two while they were hiding. I could see it in their eyes."

"Really? I wonder what."

"I don't know." Hershel winked at his wife, and she blinked in surprise. "But I think they both thoroughly enjoyed it."

ᛈᛟᛗᛈᛖᛁᛁ

"I can't do it, Frank."

"You mean you can't or you won't?"

David paced up and down the small dirt path cutting through a field of tall grasses. He'd dreaded this meeting with Frank all week, knowing he was going to have to tell him he hadn't followed through with the order to eliminate Sera.

"Look, even if I wanted to take her out, I can't do it now. We aren't alone in our area anymore. There's always another archeologist or two coming by since we discovered the body cavity. Hell, it's hard enough for me to sneak away to spy on the Germans. I can't very well arrange an 'accident' when there are other people around." The words sounded so casual to his ears, like they were talking about a car or the weather, instead of taking Sera's life.

"Body? What body?" Frank picked up on that one stray word out of everything David had just said.

"Don't panic. It's a two-thousand-year-old body." At Frank's perplexed look, David spoke slowly, as if to a child. "Remember? My cover? I'm supposed to be digging up artifacts and bones and shit? The body has nothing to do with the mission."

"Oh, right." Frank nodded and took another drag off his cigarette.

Watching the smoke curl like small white snakes out of Frank's nostrils, David held his breath against the sharp smell of tobacco lingering in the air. He'd decided to forgo the smokes today, the memory of how Giovanni had placed that small piece in the puzzle still fresh in his mind. He looked down at their feet where several of Frank's crushed cigarettes littered the path.

"Don't forget to pick up those butts. No sense leaving a calling card around."

Frank glanced down and shrugged. "Sure, whatever."

When his gaze returned to David, he brought the conversation back on track. "But Sera does affect the mission. You can't just pretend you didn't get the order."

"Damn it, Frank. Whose side are you on?"

Concern for David showed in Frank's heavy-lidded eyes.

"I'm on your side. But you can't disobey a direct order. You could get court-martialed."

He stabbed his fingers through his hair and stomped up the path away from Frank. Stopping, he spun around and faced his friend.

"What do they expect me to do? I'm not an assassin."

"No, but you are a soldier. It's your job to protect the mission and see that it's carried out."

"By murdering an innocent woman?"

"She's not innocent. Not now that she knows you're an American."

"Look, Sera is not a risk to the mission."

"How can you be so sure?"

David looked out over the field, the tall grasses waving in the breeze like an exotic harem dancer. The memory of Sera hiding him in the gladiator barracks passed through his mind, followed closely by the feel of her, passionate and willing in his arms, the taste of her kissing him in the dark shadows of the cell. The memory was enough to get him heated up all over again.

Clearing his throat, he couldn't quite look Frank in the eye.

"Let's just say she had the perfect opportunity to turn me in, and she didn't. In fact, she went out of her way, and possibly risked her own life, to protect my identity from the Germans."

David wasn't about to let Frank in on how close he'd actually come to getting caught because of Giovanni. If anyone needed to be taken out, it was that bastard.

Frank stared at him for a moment, studying David with an intense scrutiny that made him uneasy. Slowly, a sly, perceptive grin spread across his pudgy face.

"You're sleeping with her, aren't you?"

The question took David by surprise.

"No!" he denied, probably a little too harshly. *But I wish I was*.

Frank's grin disappeared, and his eyes widened as he blurted out another wayward thought.

"Christ, you're not in love with her, are you?"

The accusation sent a jolt through David, stealing all power from his brain. He found it difficult to form a controlled response, much less get his mouth to speak coherent words.

"We're friends, nothing more."

"Yeah, right." Frank cocked a disbelieving look at him. Obviously, he had taken too long to answer to Frank's satisfaction.

David bent down to pick up the cigarette butts and regain what he could of his composure. Damn Frank. He was too observant by far.

"Listen." David spoke quickly in an effort to steer Frank away from a topic he didn't want to examine too closely himself. "Just tell the Colonel that I'll do what I have to do, if and when the need arises. But right now, I don't have the means or the opportunity to take care of the 'problem' without drawing attention to myself or the mission, which is the truth."

"All right." Frank took the butts from David and shoved

them in his pocket. "If she means that much to you, I'll cover for you. It's your neck."

"Right." But as David turned to go, he realized his heart just might have a small stake in it, too.

POMPEII

Never one for an audience, Sera certainly had one now. It was as if all the archeologists at the ruins had shown up at the site this morning to witness the most critical stage of the excavation.

After another week of painstaking work, they'd finally finished removing all the ash, dirt, and bones that they could reach inside the mound, and today they were going to pump liquid plaster into the hollow cavity to make the cast.

The week had been pure torture. For the first time in her life, she found it hard to concentrate on her work. After what happened between her and David in the gladiator barracks, she found it difficult to remain the detached professional and not jump over the mound and ravish him in front of the other workers.

But he'd accepted her decision not to get romantically involved. Still, a tiny part of her wished he had come after her that day—that he had grabbed her, dragged her back into the barracks, and made mad, passionate love to her. Now all they did was exchange furtive glances over the mound when no one was looking, telling each other without words that in another time, another place, things might have been different between them.

The strain of not knowing if the Germans would come looking for him again was also taking its toll. They hadn't been back. But Sera was still a nervous wreck, glancing over her shoulder every time someone approached, wondering if they were coming for him.

But the Nazis were busy elsewhere, still fighting vigorously to hold Sicily against the Allies, especially since the Italian forces on the island had pretty much surrendered without a fight. Without their help, the Germans didn't have time to bother with David right now. But that didn't mean they wouldn't be back eventually.

Looking at him standing among the Italian archeologists and workers who came to witness the event, no one would know he was a man living on borrowed time. But she did. And she wanted to spend as much of that time with him as she could before he had to go.

At some point, he'd left her and moved to stand on the side with the other spectators to watch. With Professor Moretti, Heberto, Olympia, and several others there to help her, she guessed he assumed she didn't need him. But she did want him there.

"David, come here. I'm going to need your help," she called to him.

He left the crowd and came over to her.

"Are you sure? This is your big moment. I don't want to be in the way."

"This is *our* big moment. If it wasn't for you, it wouldn't be happening."

He grinned at her. "That's not true. You would have found the cavity eventually. My bad temper just sped things up a little."

The mention of the fight they'd had that day brought Giovanni to mind. He hadn't been seen again since he brought the Germans to the ruins looking for David. But he was still around. Sera could sense it, like the ever-present stale odor of sweat that permeated her clothes even after they'd been washed.

Sera grabbed David's hand and pulled him down to kneel on the ground beside her.

"You've done all the hard work with me up until now. You should be a part of this, too."

She didn't miss the look of understanding shining in his warm, brown eyes. Though they might still be wartime enemies, she was making David her equal today.

"Let's get started, shall we?" Moretti announced to the group. The archeologists assigned to help with the casting process went to work, while the onlookers closed in to watch.

A trough of wet plaster sat on the ground between David and Sera. Grabbing a large plastic funnel, she attached a thick hose to it and threaded the tube into one of the holes in the mound as far as it would go.

"Here, hold this."

David grabbed the funnel with one hand and the hose with the other. Sera scooped up a glob of plaster with a small bucket and poured it into the funnel. The white, pasty mixture was just runny enough to slide through the tube with the help of a plunger-type instrument.

Working the hose at different angles to get the plaster into every hollow and crevice inside, they continued the delicate process in tandem as Moretti and the others worked on other sections. As one hole would fill, they'd move on to the next, working their way from the bottom up. When the plaster ran low, the workers behind them would refill the troughs with more. On and on it went, until the cavity was completely filled and the plaster overflowed.

"It is done. Good work, Serafina." Moretti patted her on the shoulder before he left. Watching him go, she felt like a schoolgirl who'd just gotten a gold star from her teacher.

"Thank you," David's soft voice whispered in her ear.

She turned, a thrill running through her body as it did every time he stood this close to her.

"For what?"

"For letting me share this with you."

"I wouldn't have had it any other way."

Slowly, the crowd around them began to disperse, each person congratulating Sera on her find before they left. When everyone was gone and they were completely alone, David and Sera stood side by side, looking at the filled cavity as the sun started to set over the ruins, casting a shadow over the mound like a blanket over a child put to bed.

"So, how long does it take to set?" he asked.

"With the amount of plaster we put in? About a week."

They stood as they were for a few more moments, staring at

the dirt mound now covered with white dots of gooey plaster where the holes used to be.

"Kind of like watching paint dry, isn't it?"

Sera laughed. "Yes, I guess it is."

"So, now what do we do?"

She sighed, the exhaustion of the day finally catching up to her.

"We wait."

"And what do we do while we wait?"

"We go back to what we were doing before we found the cavity."

"Can we?" he asked, a mixture of hope and doubt in his voice.

She knew what he was asking. Unfortunately, she didn't have the answer. Before they found the cavity, she thought he was Italian. Before, they were close to becoming friends. Now, everything was too complicated.

"I don't know."

David nodded and returned his attention to the body mound. He was so close, she could feel the heat of his body warming her side like the setting sun on her face. She ached to touch him, to hold him and celebrate this special day.

Slowly, he reached out and took her hand. Holding it casually between them, he gave it a gentle squeeze. She glanced up at him, and he smiled down at her, the look in his eyes so tender, it nearly took her breath away.

It wasn't the look of friendship or passion that she'd come to expect to see in them. It was a look of intense pride for her and what they had accomplished today.

Right now, that meant more to her than anything.

CHAPTER XXIV

After the excitement of making the plaster cast, Sera was find-ing it very hard to sleep.

The July night was so hot, she'd kicked her worn cotton sheets into a wadded pile at her feet hours ago. The window beside her bed was open to catch any hint of a breeze that might make its way in, but the lace curtains barely stirred, and only voices from the street below carried on the still night air to keep her company as she willed sleep to come.

Although she blamed the heat, her thoughts were what kept her awake.

Thoughts of David.

The memory of his warm look of pride when they'd fin-ished filling the cavity with plaster together. The heat of his touch in the darkness of the gladiator barracks. The fire in his kiss that nearly burned her alive each time she relived it. Why couldn't things be different for them?

Shouts from the street below jarred her from her thoughts, David's image vanishing from her mind's eye like a wisp of smoke in the breeze. The voices grew louder, the entire town seeming to come awake at once.

Glancing at the clock on her bedside table, she saw that it was nearly eleven o'clock. She rose and looked out her win-dow. People were everywhere in the street below, shouting and running about.

Was an air raid coming? The sirens had not sounded.

A fierce pounding on her door had her clutching the win-dow sill in alarm.

"Serafina! You will not believe what has happened."

Grabbing her robe to throw on over her thin nightgown,

she opened the door to Maria's urgent pounding.

"What is it?"

"Come quickly, and you'll see." Maria grabbed her by the arm and pulled her down the hall. For a little old lady, excitement lent her a great deal of strength as she nearly dragged Sera down the stairs.

Maria guided her into the front room of the Angelicos' apartment, where all the other tenants stood gathered around the only radio in the house. Apparently most had been pulled from their beds just as she had.

Ushered to a spot near the others, Sera bent to listen to the broadcast.

"... as was stated earlier, the Grand Council convened yesterday and voted to strip Benito Mussolini of his authority and remove him as Commander in Chief of the Armed Forces. Today, King Victor followed up the Grand Council decision by accepting Mussolini's resignation and placing him immediately under arrest. Mussolini was escorted by armed guards..."

"What does this mean?" Sera asked as Heberto wrapped her in a giant bear hug.

"What else could it mean?" Maria answered. "Mussolini is gone. Italy is out of the war!"

Italy out of the war? Could it be true?

If Italy was out of the war, then wouldn't that mean the Americans were no longer an enemy of the Italians?

Suddenly an impossible future with David now seemed possible.

David. She had to see him.

Sera turned on her heel and ran out the front door.

As she raced into the night, people danced and cheered in the street, many still in their nightclothes and with no shoes on their feet, just as she was.

She wove in and out of the undulating crowd of people. Men and women bumped into her from all sides, some almost knocking her down in their jubilation.

She had to step over broken glass from framed photographs of Mussolini tossed into the street from the apartment windows above. A flash of white fell in front of her, crashing into a dozen broken pieces at her bare feet. She glanced down at a shattered bust of Mussolini, his blank eyes staring at her in stunned silence.

Stepping over the debris, she could not believe what was going on around her. Several fires blazed in the street, their flames fed with Fascist signs and banners torn down from buildings and lampposts. She watched in bewildered silence as remnants of Mussolini's reign floated up with the cinders to dance in the dark night sky.

Sera ran on, finding herself near David's street without knowing how she'd gotten there. She fought through the mob blocking her way.

Then the crowd seemed to part, and David was there, only a few yards away. He still wore his dusty work pants, but his shirt hung open as if he'd hastily thrown it on without bothering to button it.

They stood and stared at each other for what seemed like an eternity. Finally, she rushed into his arms, and he wrapped himself around her.

No words needed to be said. They both knew what the news meant for them.

He held her tightly and kissed her hair, her cheek, the side of her neck. Then he was kissing her mouth with a passion that stole her breath away. He pulled back, and they looked at each other, both breathing heavily, their arms locked around the other as all of Italy rejoiced around them.

The shouts and cheers seemed to fade into the distance as her whole world centered on his face. David looked at her with a hunger that nearly consumed her, and she read the unspoken question in his eyes.

She nodded her answer, not daring to break the magic of the moment with even one word.

POMPEII

David took her hand and led her through the crowd, plowing through the revelers with single-minded determination. He entered his building and pulled her down the stairs to his rented basement flat, jerking open the door, then slamming it shut behind them.

The cramped apartment was dark, and David thanked heaven for small favors. He hadn't cleaned it in days. Christ, he hadn't even made the bed, but that wouldn't matter in about ten seconds.

When he'd heard the news broadcast on the radio, his first thought had been of Sera. He had to see her. And like everyone else, he had rushed out into the streets in the middle of the night.

It seemed as if she'd been summoned by his very thoughts because suddenly she was there, more beautiful than he ever could have imagined. Her white nightgown and bare feet made her look like an angel. One sleeve of her robe had fallen down her arm to reveal a creamy white shoulder. Her wind-tossed hair fell in amber waves about her face, and she glowed like a fiery seductress in the bonfire's firelight.

Now here she was, his angel-siren, warm and willing in his arms. The meager light from the street lit her profile, and he reached up to trace the line of her cheek. She turned her face into his hand and kissed his palm, then looked up at him, a wealth of emotion vivid in blue eyes gone dark in the dim light.

His hand moved to her shoulder, peeling away the remaining sleeve of her robe and letting the garment drop on the floor to pool at her feet. David bent and swung Sera up in his arms and for a moment just held her. She wrapped her arms around his neck and laid her head on his shoulder.

He gently laid her on the rumpled sheets, the moonlight coming through the window casting a patchwork of light and shadow across her luscious body.

David jerked off his shirt, thankful it wasn't buttoned or they would have ricocheted all over the room like bullets. He followed her down on the bed and pressed her body into the thin mattress, causing the springs to groan beneath their weight. The twin-sized iron bed had always seemed small when he slept in it alone. Now, with the two of them in it, it felt incredibly tiny.

He kissed her, and she returned his passion with her own. Then he trailed his lips along her jaw to her neck, moving slowly across her collarbone to her shoulder. He kissed the thin strap of her nightgown, then ever so slowly slipped it off her shoulder and drew it down her arm. The dark nipple on the soft curve of her breast rose and fell with every breath she took, begging him to take it in his mouth.

He trailed his lips down the swell of her breast to lick at the quivering nipple, and it hardened with a single touch of his tongue. He circled the areola with his tongue, closing in on his prize in ever smaller circles.

Sera arched off the bed, digging her hands into his hair and offering more of herself to him. And he took it, sucking the nipple into his mouth and swirling the rigid tip with his tongue. He tugged it gently between his teeth, drawing a low, throaty moan from deep within her.

He moved to kiss the underside of her breast while his hand skimmed down her ribs and over the curve of her hip. She raised her knee, rubbing her bare foot up and down his trouser-covered calf.

Trailing his touch down her leg, he lifted the hem of her nightgown and slowly slid it up her leg to bunch at her hips. His hand moved to cup her between her legs, where her cotton panties proved to be a thin barrier to the secrets hidden inside.

His fingers rubbed in small circles, pulling the moisture from within her to wet the material with a warm, musky scent. Sera arched her hips into him, pinning his hand between their bodies.

David looked down at her. Her head was thrown back and her hair fanned out on his pillow in a tangled mass. The moonlight from the window showered down on her, illuminating her in a soft, ethereal glow. She literally took his breath away.

"God, you are beautiful."

She looked at him and licked her lips, leaving a trail of moisture to glisten like tiny specks of glass. He kissed her again, their tongues dancing and twining about each other.

Breaking away from his lips, she trailed kisses along his jaw to his ear, taking the soft lobe between her teeth and panting softly.

"Please, David," she whispered. "Touch me more."

He grabbed the edge of her panties and tugged them down her hips and over her thighs. He eased them down her long, slim legs and tossed them somewhere over his shoulder.

His hand returned to find her, delving between soft curls to find the warm folds beneath. He inserted first one, then two fingers inside her, touching the moist inner walls. Her muscles clamped around his fingers, squeezing them so tightly, his straining erection felt it at the same time. David reached down and started to undo the buttons on his trousers, his fingers trembling in his haste.

Shots rang out from the street as his hand paused on the last button. They both went still, the sound of their heavy breathing loud in the sudden silence around them.

The cheering outside had stopped. The thunder of stampeding footsteps sounded through the open window above their heads. Voices that had been shouting in celebration were now crying out in alarm.

"What's happening?" Sera asked.

"I don't know." David stood on the bed and peered out the window, but couldn't see a thing in the dark alley on his side of the house.

Jumping off the bed, he threw his shirt back on, buttoning it as he headed for the door. He stopped short of opening it when he heard Sera's soft footsteps behind him. He turned to her just as she was pulling her robe over her wrinkled nightgown.

"Stay here until I find out what's happening."

Even in the dim light, he could tell she was glaring at him. It didn't matter—she could get as angry as she liked. Her safety was important, and she'd be safest if she remained where she was.

"Stay here. I'll be right back." David kissed her and closed the door before she had a chance to respond.

Caution slowed his steps as he made his way down the darkened hallway and up the stairs to the first floor. He cracked opened the front door to the building just enough to look down the street.

People were still on the street, but not nearly as many as before. Those who remained were mostly young men standing back in the shadows. Several bonfires still blazed in the street, their flames left unattended.

"What's happening?" Sera's voice whispered from the dark behind him.

David groaned. Had he really thought she would listen to him?

"I'm not sure yet." He held his hand out to her and drew her to his side, opening the door a little further so she could see out, too.

Two men raced from the shadows out into the street. They were young—barely more than boys—and yet they alone braved whatever it was that the others apparently now feared.

When they reached the lamppost at the corner, one braced himself against it while the other climbed his shoulders. The latter reached up and grabbed the Fascist banner that hung from the pole, ripping it down with the weight of his body.

As the two ran toward one of the fires with the banner, shots rang out from the street. David pressed his back to the wall, pulling Sera closer to his side. When he looked through the narrow gap in the door again, the boy who had torn down the flag lay sprawled on the street, his young body gone deathly still. The other boy ran in their direction, obviously hoping to find refuge in the darkened alley. The rattle of gunfire ripped through the night, and the young man crumpled on the sidewalk before he could reach the shadows.

Sera covered her mouth with her hand and pressed her face into David's chest, muffling her cry of anguish. His arm tightened around her shoulders, drawing her closer to the safety of his body.

The sound of truck engines warned of approaching vehicles. Several armored trucks bearing the Fascist emblem on their sides rolled down the now silent street. As the convoy passed the body of the fallen boy, a loudspeaker mounted on one of the trucks blared an announcement to the citizens of the town.

"The war is continuing. Italy, the jealous guardian of her age-old traditions, remains loyal to her pledged word. Any sign of rebellion against the new Badoglio government will be considered an act of treason against the Fascist regime, and offenders will be shot on sight."

The procession continued past them and down the street, blaring the announcement over and over again in German as well as Italian. It was obvious the new government wanted any Germans within hearing distance to know that the Italians were still loyal Fascists under Hitler's thumb, even though Mussolini was gone.

David glanced down at Sera. He was certain the same despair that he saw in her eyes shone in his own.

Whether the announcement was true or not didn't matter. What did matter was that, as far as Italy was concerned, David and Sera were still enemies.

CHAPTER XXV

Walking Sera home that night was the hardest thing David had ever done.

They didn't speak. They didn't touch. They didn't even say goodnight as she slipped in the back door of the Angelicos' dark villa.

Having her stay at his apartment until dawn would have been the safest thing to do, but he didn't know if he would have been able to keep his hands off her. But, given the circumstances, that's what he needed to do. Watching two young men gunned down in front of them brought the war—and the realization that they were still enemies—into harsh reality.

Once again, the day dawned bright and new. And like any other Monday, he got up and went to work just as everyone in town was doing. On the outside, everything appeared nearly the same. After the chaos of two nights ago, the town seemed to slip back into its normal routine, the only difference being that people had to walk around long-dead bonfires and piles of debris, choosing to ignore them as if they weren't there. But David *felt* different and, just as everyone else was probably doing, he kept it hidden as he made his way to the ruins.

Approaching the site, he could see Sera getting the equipment ready for the day. She was graceful and fluid as she moved about the tables under the tent, and even under her mannish work clothes, she looked beautiful to him.

He closed his eyes, unable to shake the vision of her standing in the firelight in the middle of the street. Every time he thought of her lying on his bed, ready to welcome him into her arms, he had to fight back the fire inside threatening to consume him.

When he opened his eyes and looked at her again, he wanted nothing more than to walk up to her, pull her into his arms, and kiss the daylights out of her. He wanted to lay her down under the canvas tent and unbutton her shirt to see those glorious breasts in the bright light of day. He wanted to kiss them, taste them, and lose himself inside her until the war went away and nothing but the two of them existed.

But he couldn't. Not now.

At any moment, their lives could be completely torn apart. Neither of them knew what tomorrow might bring, and until this damned war was over, it wouldn't be fair to her. To either of them. But that didn't stop him from wanting it just the same.

Sera turned as he approached. Dark circles weighed heavily under her eyes. Her expression as he drew closer was one of apprehension and regret. Evidently, he wasn't the only one who hadn't gotten much sleep. He wondered if it was for the same reasons.

"Are you all right?" he asked, stopping a few steps away from her, afraid if he got too close, he might act on the fantasy that had rampaged through his head.

"I don't know."

God, her eyes were haunted. Had he put that look there?

"Talk to me. Tell me what's going on in that head of yours."

Her face grew pinched, and she looked away.

"I'm not sure." Then she closed her eyes and shook her head, as if correcting herself. "I'm feeling things I shouldn't feel. Wanting things I can't have."

He nodded, understanding exactly how she felt.

"I know. Right now I want nothing more than to take you in my arms and forget that we're enemies in this damned war."

Her eyes flew open, hope and desire flickering in them before her stubbornness smothered them out.

"But as far as Italy and America are concerned, we are enemies."

"No. No, we're not." He shook his head in denial. "Our countries may say we are, but I know we're no longer enemies. Not after what happened between us."

A telling blush crept up her cheeks, and he watched her swallow hard. Was she regretting what had almost happened?

"Then, what are we? After the other night, I don't think we can call ourselves just friends anymore."

David took a step forward. He stood so close, all he had to do was reach out and she would be in his arms. But he didn't.

"No. I think both you and I know we're more than that now. We can't ever go back to how it used to be."

"Then what are we going to do?" She looked so lost, as if she wanted him to give her a simple answer when there was none.

"I know what I want to do." He stepped even closer, until their bodies nearly touched, forcing her to look up at him. He didn't miss the flaring of her nostrils or the darkening of her blue eyes. But she didn't retreat, as she always had before. She just stood there, looking at him, making him want her more with each breath she took.

"What do you want to do?" she asked, her voice husky and low. She almost whispered, as if she were afraid of what his answer might be, but wanted to hear it all the same.

An ache of longing shot through him, so real he thought he might double over from the pain.

"For starters, I want to rip that damned straw hat off your head and run my fingers through your hair like I've ached to do a thousand times." The force of holding back from doing just that nearly killed him.

Sera's eyes danced back and forth with his own, gauging, probing, wanting. Time seemed to stretch on forever, a million questions flying through the air between them without either uttering a single word. Finally, she reached up and slowly peeled the hat from her head, letting it tumble to the ground. It was all the invitation he needed.

Contrary to the heat of his words, he reached up with one hand and gently touched his fingers to her temple, tunneling them along her sensitive scalp through the silky, brown waves. She closed her eyes and groaned, turning her face into the palm of his hand.

He brought his other hand forward to cup her cheek and brushed the pad of his thumb across her lush lips.

"And I want to kiss you, here, now, in the bright light of day, until we're both breathless and wanting more."

"Oh, David." Her hands caught his wrists, but she didn't pull his hands away. Instead, she moved hers up to cover his and hold them in place. Her eyes opened then, looking at him with the same smoldering passion he'd barely been able to make out in the moonlit darkness of his room.

Drawing her closer, he stared deep into her eyes, trying to bore himself into her soul.

"I want to lay you down and crawl inside you until I don't know where you begin and I end."

All thoughts of what they could and couldn't have didn't matter in that moment. All that mattered was Sera and the way she was looking at him right now. The trust and longing in her eyes broke down any walls that might still be standing between them. He leaned in, eager to take what she offered and make his words come true.

Then, somewhere close behind him, he heard the unmistakable click of a gun being cocked.

Pulling back slowly, he dropped his arms and turned to find Giovanni standing behind them, a Luger pointed straight at David's heart.

"Sorry," Giovanni said in mock apology. "Did I interrupt something?"

David heard Sera's gasp from behind him. "What are you doing here?"

"What does it look like? I'm making a citizen's arrest. Did you know the Germans offer quite a sizeable reward for turning in spies?"

"But he's not a spy," she snapped.

"Like hell he's not." Giovanni's hate-filled eyes never wavered from David, and neither did the aim of his gun. "I'm not stupid. I saw him sneaking down an alley to meet his friend. I found the American cigarettes they so carelessly left behind. It's not a huge leap to figure out they were up to no good."

"Just because he stops to talk to a friend and smokes a few contraband cigarettes doesn't make him a spy."

"No, maybe not." He turned his gaze briefly to Sera, acknowledging her reasoning with a slight tilt of his head. "But the fact that he noticed me in the German camp on several occasions does. The only way he would have seen me there is if he'd been watching them on a regular basis. No one does that out of mere curiosity. Only a spy would." Giovanni turned his cold stare back to David. "And thanks to him, I'm a wanted man. My reputation as an archeologist is ruined. I can never work on a site again."

"You did that to yourself by selling priceless artifacts," Sera pointed out. "How could you? I thought you loved the ruins."

Giovanni's sharp laugh cracked in the air. "Serafina, you are so naive. Selling artifacts to the Germans is far easier and much more lucrative than just digging them up." He smiled at her, his soulless eyes reminding David of the lazy crocodiles that sunned themselves on the riverbank near the base camp in Africa, deadly predators that looked deceptively calm, but were constantly on guard for an easy meal from an unwary victim. "They really liked the silver cup, by the way. Thanks for finding it for me."

"*Bastardo!*" She lunged at him, and Giovanni quickly swung the gun in her direction.

"Sera, no!" David grabbed her before she could take another step and shoved her behind him.

"Smart man." Giovanni's look was cold and hard. "We're going to take a little walk now. All three of us."

"Where?" David asked, although he could guess the answer.

"To the German camp. I'm sure they'll be very eager to talk to you about what you've been doing." A sadistic glint came into Giovanni's eyes. "I can only imagine the inventive methods the Nazis have for getting information out of a spy. Before they execute you, of course."

"Giovanni, don't do this," Sera pleaded. "If you ever cared about me at all, please don't do this."

"This isn't about you," he spat. "I need the reward money now that I have a price on my own head, thanks to your lover."

"Money? Is that all you care about?"

"Hardly, although it is an added bonus." His face took on a determined look. "No, when the Germans win this war—and they will—I intend to have my place firmly established with them. Who knows, I may even be made Director of Excavations once it's all over."

"You're insane."

"No, my dear," Giovanni chuckled. "I'm a realist. And right now I'm just ensuring my future by turning an Allied spy over to the Nazis."

"But he's not—"

"Don't you dare defend him, you little whore," he snarled, and then his face hardened against her. "I can just as easily turn you over to the Germans, too. I wonder what the going rate for an Allied sympathizer is, especially one who's half-American?"

Sera's fists clenched the shirt against David's back and he felt her fear, as physical as his own. It was not an idle threat. He had to protect her, at any cost.

"I'll go with you. Just leave her out of this."

"No!" she cried over his shoulder. She attempted to move, but David reached his arm back to hold her in place and shield her behind him.

"Don't do it, David," she pleaded. He felt the warmth of her words seep through the weave of his shirt, mixing with the sweat trickling down his back. He felt her whole body shake as she trembled in fear for him. "You'll be shot."

"It's going to be all right. Trust me." But even as he spoke them, he had trouble believing his own words.

"So touching." Giovanni waved the nose of his gun in the direction of the old road. "Let's get moving. We shouldn't keep my comrades waiting."

He forced them to walk down the dirt path along the city wall, heading in the opposite direction of the main entrance. It was too early for the tour groups to be this deep in the ruins, so help in the form of a crowd of witnesses would not be likely.

Giovanni took them down the same route David had taken after their fight over Sera. That time, he hadn't paid much attention to where he was going, but now he scoured the area, looking for a chance to escape, waiting for that brief moment when Giovanni might let down his guard.

He was careful to keep himself between Sera and the gun. Giovanni walked several steps behind them, close enough to shoot, but not near enough for David to make a move.

He had to do something. He didn't trust Giovanni not to turn Sera over to the Germans just as he threatened to do. David had gotten her into this. He'd be damned if she was going to die because of him.

His only hope would be to distract Giovanni until an opportunity presented itself.

"So, why didn't your comrades come with you this time?"

Giovanni took a moment before he answered. "They were busy."

Sure, they were. "You mean they didn't believe you after you were proved wrong the last time you dragged them here?"

"I was not wrong!" Giovanni shouted behind them.

David cautioned himself. Distracting Giovanni was one thing. Getting a bullet in the back of the head for pissing him off was another.

"Are you so certain? A few cigarette butts and suspicion from a disgruntled ex-archeologist aren't a lot to go on. What if they don't believe you this time?"

"David, be careful," Sera whispered over her shoulder.

"Trust me," he whispered back. "Be ready, and do as I say."

David slowed his steps, and Sera matched his pace. As he'd hoped, he heard Giovanni's footsteps draw closer behind them.

"Oh, they'll believe me this time."

"How so?"

"Simple, really." Giovanni spoke as if the answer should be obvious. "You're going to tell them exactly who and what you are."

David had to laugh.

"Now, why would I go and do a stupid thing like that?"

Giovanni's voice came from only a few feet behind them, his words uttered with an assurance that he was in control.

"Because if you don't, I'm going to put a bullet in Serafina's pretty little head."

The deadly determination in his voice put David on guard. He wasn't about to see if Giovanni would really go that far.

They were nearing the Amphitheatre entrance. Once outside, there would be little between them and the German camp. If David was going to act, he had to do it now. Without breaking his stride, he stuck his foot out in front of Sera, just enough to catch her ankle and trip her.

"Oh!" she cried as she went down.

David's left arm shot out around her waist to grab her. As they stumbled together, his other hand scooped up a handful of dirt from the ground.

"What are you—"

He spun, tossing the dirt into Giovanni's eyes.

"*Accidenti a te!*" Damn you!

"Run!" David grabbed Sera's arm and tugged her toward the Palaestra. A bullet ricocheted off the stone walls behind them, followed by another. Two shots, six more to go.

The sound of gunfire would no doubt bring anyone within earshot in this direction. If he could get Giovanni to waste all the bullets, they might have a fighting chance, providing he didn't have another magazine on him.

Entering the large enclosure, they kept to the shadows of the colonnade. A quick glance revealed that Giovanni was close behind. He fired, hitting the column next to Sera and showering them with a rain of tiny bits of plaster. Three down, five to go.

David shoved Sera behind the next column, using it to shield them. He saw a shadow at the end of the row of pillars duck into an opening. This was their chance to make a run for it.

Grabbing Sera's hand, he pulled her further down the walkway, ducking behind each column along the way, always watching the end to see if Giovanni reappeared. The main entrance to the Palaestra was just ahead. Once they reached it, they would be one block away from the *Via dell'Abbondanza*, the main thoroughfare through the town. Hopefully, some tourists would be there by then.

David stopped at the archway and peered down the street. It was empty. Bad in that there were no crowds of tourists to disappear in. Good because there was also no sign of Giovanni.

"It's clear. Come on." Just as he stepped out into the sunlight, a shot rang out, hitting the wall beside his head.

"Damn!" David shoved Sera back in the archway. "He must have gone around. He cut us off."

"We have to use the Amphitheatre entrance. It's the only way out of this side of the ruins."

David didn't like it. It was too close to where Giovanni wanted them to be. Too close to the German camp. But they had no choice. Giovanni still had four shots left.

They ran back down the colonnade. David glanced over his shoulder as they reached the end and saw Giovanni's dark form appear in the archway where they'd been standing only seconds before. He charged after them with fury in his eyes, the gun pointed straight at them.

"Hurry!" David shoved Sera ahead of him. "He's right behind us."

Another shot whizzed past as they sprinted down the old road. David thanked God that Giovanni was such a lousy shot. But even lousy shots got lucky sometimes.

As if on cue, a second bullet pinged off the wall to their right, barely missing Sera. Instinct made David pull her to the left, out of danger, but also away from their only way out of the ruins. Taking the only available cover, he yanked her into the darkness of the tunnel leading into the Amphitheatre just as another shot fired behind them. Seven. Only one bullet left.

He practically dragged her through the tunnel, panic making the light at the end look like a beacon of safety. Charging out into the sunlight, they took several strides before the momentum of their flight slowed down.

David looked around them with a sickening feeling. Bad idea. The place offered no protection. Unlike the last time they stood there, not a single tourist was in sight. They were alone in the arena. The entire area was open, with nowhere to hide. They'd never make it to the opposite side and the safety of the other tunnel in time.

David heard the muted sound of Giovanni's footfalls on the stone-paved floor of the passageway and turned in time to see him charge out into the sunlight from the darkness of the tunnel. Giovanni's steps slowed to a walk when he saw them standing there. He grinned as he stopped and took careful aim.

Spinning them around, David tried to shield Sera with his body. The last bullet whizzed by them, imbedding itself in the arena floor with a dull thud. His muscles relaxed as reality settled in. They were either very lucky, or Giovanni really was a crappy shot. Either way, somebody up above must have been looking out for them.

Easing his hold on Sera, David turned slowly to face Giovanni.

"That was eight. You're out of bullets."

Giovanni pulled the trigger again, and the echo of the empty click made Sera jump at his side. With an angry bellow, he heaved the gun through the air. David turned and ducked, covering Sera's head with his arm as the heavy metal gun hit him in the back. Maybe he couldn't shoot worth a damn, but Giovanni sure could throw with a wallop.

When David straightened and turned, the sun was glinting off the blade of a knife in Giovanni's hand. The guy just wasn't going to stop until one of them was hurt.

Or dead.

David slowly bent and pulled his own knife from his boot. Now they stood on equal ground. The two men began circling each other, like wolves closing in on their prey.

"Giovanni, it doesn't have to be this way," Sera pleaded from somewhere behind them.

Christ, he hoped she stayed out of the way. Hell, he wished she had the sense to run.

"Yes, it does," Giovanni growled.

"Why? Why are you so intent on turning David in? Besides the money, what good will it do you?"

"I have to." Giovanni lunged at David, slashing out with his knife.

David jumped back, and the blade sliced through the air.

"I have no choice," Giovanni growled. "I have to prove my loyalty to them."

"Why? You're not German, and you've never been a Fascist."

Giovanni spoke to Sera without ever taking his eyes off David. "You of all people should understand why."

"No, I don't understand. None of this makes any sense."

"Because my grandmother was a Polish Jew." Giovanni spat out the words, as if they tasted bitter and vile on his tongue.

David almost dropped his knife. Giovanni constantly taunted Sera about her mixed heritage, and the irony of that fact hung heavy in the air around them. Giovanni wasn't a full-blooded Italian either.

However, Sera's tainted blood wouldn't send her to a concentration camp or the gas chamber if the Germans found out. Giovanni's could very well be a death sentence if the wrong people discovered the truth. David always felt the man had an air of desperation about him, but he had never considered this possibility.

"That's ridiculous," Sera said. "That's two generations back. The Germans won't care."

"I'm not going to take that chance. One drop of Jew blood is too much. I need a guarantee so they'll know I'm loyal to the Reich." Giovanni pointed his knife at David. "And he's it."

"Handing David over to the Germans won't solve anything.

You'll still be who you are." Sera's pleading voice softened somewhere behind David. "I should know. It took me a long time to accept who I am."

"I won't go to a concentration camp. I can't take that risk. He's coming with me."

"Over my dead body," David said.

Giovanni's eyes took on a crazed look, the black orbs losing any semblance of sanity.

"Well, if that's the way it has to be…"

He charged at David, slashing his knife across David's mid-section. David hunched back, but the sharp edge still managed to slice through his shirt, grazing his stomach.

The roar of a distant crowd carried on the wind. David glanced at the stands, but they stood empty and barren.

He hardly had time to realize he'd been cut before Giovanni came at him again. David fought back out of reflex and self-preservation. Christ, he didn't want to have to kill the man, especially not in front of Sera.

Giovanni changed tactics and thrust his knife down in a stabbing motion. David brought his knife up, blocking the strike. The daggers came together, and the hilts caught like fencing foils. But though the blades were shorter, they were no less deadly.

Cheers echoed behind him, but he didn't dare look to see where they were coming from.

Giovanni twisted the joined knives in a wide arc, breaking the hold and sending David's blade flying through the air.

They separated and circled once more. Giovanni came at him again, growling like an enraged bear, his knife raised.

David blocked the attack with one arm while he reached for the knife with the other, grabbing Giovanni's hand in both of his. They wrestled, the weapon caught between them in a fierce tug of war. David refused to let go. If he did, he was a dead man.

All around them, the sound of thousands of feet stomping on stone reverberated through the arena. David tried to focus, to push away the phantom sounds in his head.

He clutched Giovanni's wrist, struggling to pry the knife out of the man's hand. He could smell the stench of sweat between them, his and Giovanni's mixing in the air in a pungent odor of fear and desperation.

In the struggle, their joined hands twisted the knife around, the sharp blade disappearing in between their bodies. David felt the sickening give of flesh against steel.

Giovanni clutched at David's sleeve, a look of surprise on his stunned face. Then his eyes rolled back in his head and his grip eased, his body going limp in David's arms.

Lowering Giovanni to the ground, David released his hold on the knife protruding from the man's chest and watched helplessly as blood seeped out from around the hilt to soak the white linen of Giovanni's shirt.

David stood slowly and stared down at the blood on his hands. They seemed detached, as if they were no longer a part of his body. Thick crimson liquid dripped from his fingers to the sandy ground like red raindrops from an angry sky.

He heard the cheers of thousands echoing in his head, but when he looked up at the stands, no one was there.

Sera's gasp behind him brought him back to reality. He turned to see her standing there, her hand covering her mouth, her eyes wide as she stared at him.

"Sera. I'm sorry. I didn't mean to... I didn't want to..."

For the second time that day, David heard a gun cock behind him.

"Put your hands above your head and turn around slowly."

David did as he was told, turning to face four Italian police officers standing a few feet away, their guns aimed at his chest. Two of the men approached, each grabbing him by an arm.

As they forced his hands behind his back, David looked to Sera. She stood completely still, staring at him with a stunned expression on her pale face. The police placed handcuffs on his wrists, the click of the metal teeth ticking like a time bomb as the cuffs bit into his skin.

One of the officers knelt beside Giovanni's limp form and checked for a pulse. He raised his gaze to his comrades and shook his head, indicating what David already knew.

Giovanni was dead.

Grabbing him by each arm, two of the officers escorted David toward the tunnel. He didn't look back. He couldn't bear the sight of Sera standing in the middle of the arena, silently watching the police lead him away.

CHAPTER XXVI

The slamming of the cell door was jarring.

He'd been ready for it, bracing himself for the sounds he knew would come—the bone-grinding clash of metal upon metal, the grate of a key turning in a lock to seal his fate. But prepared though he was, the sound ripped through his body like a gunshot when the metal door finally clanked shut.

He tried not to let his anxiety show, waiting until the guard left before he let out the breath he'd been holding. The musty, stale stench of damp concrete and old urine threatened to smother him. The walls seemed to close in on him, and it took all his willpower to keep from flinging out his arms in a vain attempt to hold them back.

God, he hated confining spaces. He always had.

Looking around at the small six-by-six-foot cell, he couldn't believe how his life had turned upside down in a matter of hours. The possibility had always been in the back of his mind that he'd end up right where he was right now, only the crime would be espionage, not murder.

Italy had no death penalty for murder, just a life sentence behind bars similar to these. But David found that a small consolation.

It was only a matter of time before the authorities looked into a past that didn't exist and learned the truth about who he was.

Then he was as good as dead, because they did shoot spies here.

POMPEII

"Oh, this is terrible. What are we going to do?"

Marsha paced the length of the living room and back, her thin hands twisting in her white apron until Hershel thought she might tear the material in two.

"I don't know. It certainly throws a bit of a kink in things, doesn't it?"

"A *kink*?" Marsha looked at him with disbelieving eyes. "A man is dead, and David is in jail for murder, and you call it a *kink*?" She closed her eyes and shook her head, then resumed her frantic pacing. "It's a catastrophe, that's what it is."

"No," he softly corrected her. "I think the volcano incident was a catastrophe. This is more like a mini-disaster."

Marsha glared at him.

"Don't play semantics with me. You know what I mean." She marched over and flounced on the couch with a melodramatic flare, burying her face in her hands. "Oh, we are doomed."

Hershel felt Marsha's censure, even though she hadn't come right out and said it was his fault. But she did blame him. He could tell. She might as well get it over with and reach over and slap him on the back of the head like she usually did when he messed things up.

If he could, he'd do it himself because he probably deserved it this time. He felt guilty that he hadn't been paying close enough attention to the comings and goings at the site and had allowed Giovanni to slip past.

"It's not like I could have stopped it." Hershel tried his best to defend himself. "By the time I got there, Giovanni was already dead, and the police had arrested David."

"Oh, this not good." Marsha looked up from her lap. "Smithers is going to have a fit when he finds out about this."

The mention of their boss's name made Hershel squirm in his overstuffed easy chair. Then, as an idea came to him, his mood brightened a bit.

"Hey, you don't suppose this is another one of those tests he's been putting them through, do you? If that's the case, we might not be in too much trouble."

Marsha immediately doused all hope.

"Oh, I don't think so. He prepared us for the test when the Germans came looking for David. I certainly think he would have alerted us to something as important as Giovanni's murder."

"It wasn't murder!" Hershel felt compelled to stand up for David. "It was self-defense."

She shook her head at him again, correcting him without saying a word. He really hated when she did that.

"I know that, and you know that. But the police don't. They've arrested him for murder."

"Well, we'll just have to wait until the police figure out the truth and let him go."

"But what if they don't? They know he and Giovanni hated each other. And with Serafina the only witness to what happened in the Amphitheatre, it doesn't look good for David. If there's a trial, he could be found guilty. He might go to prison for the rest of his life. What will become of them then?"

Hershel looked at his wife. He'd never seen her look so hopeless, so fragile. She was always the strong one. She was the one who always knew what to do.

He walked over to sit beside her on the couch. Pulling her into his arms, he hugged her frail shoulders.

"There now, dear. We'll find a way to get David out. I know we will."

But in the back of his mind, Hershel worried that they might not. And if they failed again, he doubted David and Serafina would get another chance.

POMPEII

Sera perched on the small balcony outside her apartment window, the ledge so narrow she had to sit sideways to fit. The night seemed so peaceful and quiet, a stark contrast to the emotions warring inside her.

She felt numb inside. She had never watched someone die, never witnessed their life's blood pouring onto the ground around them. And yet, the surreal scene had seemed all too familiar, all too close.

A silent scream split through her head, like a long suppressed cry from the ghosts of the arena, a place where tens of thousands had died before. What was one more death to a place like that?

Sera shivered. The death was of someone she had known. Someone who, at one time, she had thought she loved.

She covered her mouth with her hand in an effort to hold back the mournful wail that threatened to rip from her throat. In spite of her efforts, the muffled sound seemed to echo down the empty street.

She took a deep breath in the warm evening air. Tears swam in her eyes again, threatening to spill down her cheeks. She fought them back, afraid if she let one go, the whole dam would burst, and she'd fall to pieces.

She worried about David. He had looked so lost, so hopeless as they led him away from the Amphitheatre. And she had been unable to speak, to tell him…

What? That it was all right? That she didn't blame him for doing what he had to do?

She knew in her heart that he'd had no choice. If he hadn't killed Giovanni, it could have just as easily been him lying there lifeless on the ground. But that didn't make it any easier.

And though Giovanni was no longer a threat, David still wasn't safe.

Sera ran a hand through her hair, pulling the damp strands away from her face. Five days had passed since his arrest, and the police still hadn't allowed her to see him. What was happening? Why wouldn't they tell her anything? She'd given the police her statement about what had happened in the Amphitheatre, telling the truth about everything.

Everything except who David really was.

Oh, David.

She squeezed her eyes shut, trying to hold back the pain. They'd had no chance to talk, to get their stories straight. Had he told the police something else? Was that why they wouldn't let her see him? Did the police suspect that there was more behind Giovanni's death than a lovers' triangle or professional jealousy?

She tried to shake off the despair and succeeded only to have it replaced with another, harsher emotion. Guilt.

The feeling assaulted Sera as she remembered Giovanni's funeral. Just that afternoon she had stood silently by as his family lowered his coffin into the ground. His parents had stared at her from across the open grave, their eyes condemning her for playing a part in their only son's death. But they didn't know the whole story. She didn't think they were even aware he'd been selling artifacts on the black market or that he'd lost his job at the ruins. They just knew that she had been there when he took his last breath, and that, somehow, she'd been at the center of it.

Hugging her knees to her chest, she tried to chase away the ever-present remorse. She didn't need their condemnation. She choked on the guilt of it every time the tragic memory played through her mind—David with the knife in his blood-covered hand, and Giovanni lying crumpled at his feet, his stunned, dead eyes staring at the open sky.

Shivering in the evening air, she wondered if the horrific image would ever fade from her memory.

Sera leaned her forehead against the wrought iron bars of the balcony railing and looked out on a town blissfully asleep in the night. But peace was not with her. She had to do something to help David before it was too late.

She finally pulled herself to her feet and dragged herself to bed. Lying down, she tossed and turned. Sleep did not want to come, but when it finally did, it gave her little relief.

She stood in the center of the arena, watching helplessly as the police led David away. Then the image wavered before her eyes, like heat rising from a sun-baked street. When it cleared, they were still in the Amphitheatre, but everything was different. The arena was no longer a crumbling ruin around her, but magnificent in the glory of its time, filled with cheering throngs of people. The two men taking David away wore ancient Roman armor. The vision seemed both strange and familiar at the same time.

But it was the sight of David that nearly brought Sera to her knees.

His bloodstained clothes were gone, replaced with a tattered loincloth about his lean hips, while bleeding, raised welts laced his proud back.

Sera wanted to go to him, but her feet were rooted to the ground. She called out to him, but her voice sounded strange, as if she were hearing it from far away. She called him by another name, one that fled her memory as quickly as it left her tongue.

David turned his head and looked at her over his bloody shoulder. He spoke, but she couldn't hear his voice. She didn't need to. As the guards led him out of the arena, the words formed by his lips seared straight into her heart.

Save me.

POMPEII

In all her life, Sera had never stepped foot into Pompei's jail-house. She'd never had to. Until now.

For the first time since they had arrested him over a week before, the police were allowing her to see David.

They led her down a narrow hallway and through a locked door. The hallway continued on, but the wall on her left was no longer made of solid block and plaster. Instead, it consisted of iron bars from floor to ceiling, stretching down the length of the building.

The large, common cell was where most of the prisoners were kept. Some of them walked the space of the confines, looking like anxious animals caged in a zoo. Others sat on wooden boards supported by concrete blocks, the crude benches serving as both bed and seating. Some of the men talked casually amongst themselves. They glanced at her as she walked by, each hoping that she was someone there to see them, before returning to their private conversations.

She looked at each of their faces, searching for the familiar one she longed to see, but David wasn't among them. The police didn't house murderers with the common criminals.

The guard led Sera further down the hallway, past several

small individual cells on her right. Stopping before a door with a single barred window, he rapped twice with the long, black stick he carried.

"Corbelli, you have a visitor."

She heard a shuffling sound, then David's tall form appeared from the hidden shadows of the cell.

He looked tired. Dark circles marked the tan skin beneath his eyes. She wanted to think she saw a brief flicker of happiness in those brown depths, but when he glanced at the guard standing beside her, the emotion vanished, if it had been there at all.

Sera turned to the guard. "Could you open the door, please?"

"No. You can only speak to him through the bars."

Disappointed, she tried again. "Then, may we have some privacy?"

The guard gave her a curt nod and took a few steps down the hallway. He stood far enough away that if they whispered, he wouldn't hear them, but close enough that if David tried to reach through the bars to harm her in any way, the guard could be there in a matter of seconds.

The thought sent a chill through her. Could he, would he, hurt her?

The man she'd come to know wouldn't. But did she know the real David? Had that been him all this time, or was he someone else entirely? The David she thought she knew wouldn't have killed anyone, yet the man standing behind the iron bars had. She'd seen him do it with her own eyes.

"I'm sorry, Sera." His low, soft voice drew her attention back to him. "I never meant to kill Giovanni. I know you cared for him."

She felt some of the tension in her body ease. Here was the David she knew, the one who'd chiseled his way into her heart.

"It wasn't your fault."

"But he's dead just the same."

Yes, that was true. All the apologies in the world were not going to change that. Instead, she tried to focus on what she could do to help David.

"Are you all right?"

He smiled, but the humor never reached his eyes. "Just peachy."

She tried to ignore his sarcasm, knowing it was his way of trying to relieve the seriousness of the situation.

"Do you need anything? Can I get something from your apartment? I think they'll let you have a book or—"

"No. You shouldn't even be here. You need to leave right now and never come back."

Hurt lanced through her. He might as well have reached through the bars and slapped her.

"Why?"

He lowered his voice to barely a whisper, and she had to step closer to the bars to hear him.

"When they find out who I really am, they might come after you."

Sera glanced at the guard standing just a few feet away to make sure he couldn't overhear their conversation.

"Maybe they won't. What about your I.D. papers? They fooled the authorities before."

"Only on the surface. When they trace them—and they will—they're going to figure out they're fakes. There is no David Corbelli from Naples."

Sera felt her throat tighten. She hadn't even thought of that possibility.

"Then, we have to get you released before they find out. It was self-defense. We have to make them believe that."

"How? You were the only witness. And so far, it doesn't appear that they believe you. They think you're protecting me." David gripped the bars set in the small, glassless opening. "Besides, I don't think there's time. They'll be sending for background information on me from Naples any day now, if they haven't already. Information that doesn't exist. It's only a matter of time before I'm found out, and when that happens, I'm a dead man."

"No!"

Sera couldn't believe how resolved David seemed to be to his fate. Where was the man who had fought for her honor? The one who, just a few days ago, defended her life with his own? He'd fought for her then. Why wasn't he fighting for himself now?

"David, let me help you," she whispered, glancing once more to make sure the guard was still far enough away. Turning back to David, she dared him to lie to her. "I know you're not alone here. I know you have someone you're working with."

The hardening of his features was barely perceptible. But she spied it in the clenching of his jaw, the narrowing of his eyes, and she knew that her hunch was right.

"Don't deny it. That's how Giovanni found out about you. He said he saw the two of you together. Tell me who it is and where you're supposed to meet him. Maybe he can get help."

"From who? The army?" He snorted and shook his head. "You forget, I'm not supposed to be here. The Allies aren't going to raise the alarm by trying to rescue one man behind enemy lines and risk blowing an entire mission. There are too many lives at stake."

Sera placed her hands on the bars, just below where David's fists gripped them with white-knuckled force.

"At least let me try."

His grip eased, and his hands slid down the bars to cover hers. Like a shock of static electricity, Sera felt a bolt of recollection travel through her body and back again, radiating from where their joined hands clasped the iron bars together.

David's sharp intake of breath told her that he felt it, too. Something more than a touch passed between them. It was a shared awareness, a brief blending of their souls into one before they were split back apart again. The sensation scared the hell out of her.

David was the first to return to the equally frightening reality at hand.

"No. It's too dangerous. I won't put you at risk like that. It's only a matter of time before they discover who I really am.

When that happens, you need to be as far away from me as you can be. I don't want to pull you any deeper into this mess."

"I'm already in it. I lov—"

"Don't!" His arm shot through the bars with the speed of a rattlesnake, startling her into silence. He pressed two fingers to her lips, stopping the words that threatened to rush from her heart. "Don't say it. Don't give me something to hope for when there's very little chance of me making it out of this alive."

The guard was instantly at her side, but Sera ignored him. Anger flared in her and with it, a desperation that seemed to come from her very soul, giving her the strength to be strong enough for the both of them.

"Damn it. I will not let you give up. I will not let you die."

ᛈᛟᛗᛈᛖᛁᛁ

Sera felt as if every eye in Pompei was on her, that every person she walked by knew where she was headed and what she was doing. Guilt tugged at her conscience for lying to Maria about going to Mass early. With what she had to do, she would probably not make it to church at all today.

At least she figured God would understand her reason. A man's life was at stake.

But the Angelicos would not understand. Although Maria already knew that David was an American spy, and she'd told Sera that she and Heberto would do all they could to help get him out of jail, they wouldn't have let Sera come here today. It was too risky. Even now, as she continued on to her destination, she wondered if she was doing something she might regret for the rest of her life.

She glanced back to make sure she wasn't being followed. All around her were faces, some familiar and some not, heading to church or on their way to visit family and friends. All doing innocent, everyday tasks.

Unlike her. With each step she took, she was one step closer to betraying her country.

But her heart didn't see it that way. With each panicked beat that hammered in her chest, she was one step closer to saving the man she loved.

And she did love him. As they had stood there with those damn bars separating them, she'd realized that she loved him with all her heart. And once she knew that, she wasn't going to let a little thing like treason stop her from saving his life.

Sera took a deep breath, knowing she clutched at her purse just a little too tight. She was probably glancing around herself just a little too much. If she didn't pull herself together soon, she might utterly fall to pieces. How did David have the nerve to take this risk every week?

It had taken two more visits to the jailhouse and some persuasive arguing on her part, but she'd finally forced him to divulge the information about his contact. And now here she was, on her way to meet with a stranger, another American spy walking among her own countrymen.

As Sera neared the edge of town, she came to the old mill which had been closed since the start of the war because of a lack of wheat to grind. This was where David told her he was supposed to rendezvous with his friend today.

The man wasn't hard to spot, sitting on the low stone wall surrounding the mill yard, smoking a cigarette. With his dark blue cap tilted slightly on his large head, he looked just as David had described him. She approached him cautiously, not sure how he might take her being here instead of David.

"Frank?"

He paused with his arm in mid-air, his smoking cigarette dangling between two stubby fingers. His dark eyes squinted at her from under the brim of his cap, the only acknowledgement that he even heard her.

Sera dared to take another step closer and cleared her throat. "Are you Frank?" She whispered the words in rusty English, causing those slitted eyes to pop open in surprise.

"Maybe. Who are you?" he asked in Italian.

"I'm a friend of David's. He sent me."

"Why didn't he come himself?"

"He couldn't. He's in jail."

If Frank had been surprised when she first approached, he now looked totally flummoxed. Glancing around them to make sure no one was within hearing distance, he returned his piercing focus to her.

"Well, that would explain why he was a no-show for our rendezvous last week. What the hell happened?"

How much to tell? Sera had gone over the speech in her head the whole way there, and she still wasn't sure how much she should reveal about Giovanni's reasons for hating David so much.

"One of the other archeologists… he suspected David was spying on the Germans."

Glancing at the numerous cigarette butts littering the ground at Frank's feet, she recalled how Giovanni said he had figured it out. She tried not to be angry at the man in front of her, the man who had inadvertently put David at risk. Right now, that same man might be David's only hope.

Continuing on, she deliberately skimmed over the facts, just as David had instructed her to do.

"He was going to turn David in. There was a fight between them, and the archeologist was killed. Now David is in jail for his murder."

"Murder? David? I don't believe it."

"We're trying to prove it was self-defense, but it's taking some time."

He arched a bushy eyebrow at her. "*We?* Just who is *we?*"

Sera silently berated herself for letting that slip out.

"Myself and two very close friends."

"You and two friends? Damn it. How many people know about him?"

"Just the three of us."

"What about the police? Do they know?"

"Not yet. So far, the forged I.D. documents have fooled them, but it won't be long before they learn the truth. The police have already sent a request to the authorities in Naples to verify them. We've got to get David out before that report comes back." Sera took a step closer to Frank and reached out to squeeze his hand. "Please. You have to help him."

Frank's expression softened a bit as he looked at her hand resting on his, then back to her face.

"You must be Sera."

Surprised that he knew her name, she nodded, pulling her hand away to return it to the death-grip she held on her purse strap.

"He told you about me?"

"Oh, yeah."

The inflection he put on those words made her wonder just what David had said about her. But now wasn't the time to think about such things.

"Can you help him?"

"I don't know." Frank rubbed his hand down his face. "This is a damn shitty situation he's gotten himself into. I'll report it to our superiors, but I can't make any promises. David might be put in more danger if too much attention is suddenly focused on him from outside sources."

"I know. That's what he told me. But we have to at least try. Maybe someone could intercept the report before it gets back to Pompei or something?"

Frank grinned at her. "Not a bad idea, if we can manage it. Say, you wouldn't be interested in working for our side, would you?"

Sera couldn't stop the stiffening of her spine.

"No. I'm only interested in saving David's life."

Frank's grin faded, and he nodded at her.

"Me too. I'll do what I can, but I won't be able to come back until next Sunday. It'll be up to you to stall the authorities on this end until then. Can you do that?"

"Yes."

How she was going to manage that, she wasn't sure. But she'd be damned if she wasn't going to try.

As she turned to walk away, Frank called after her.

"You're one heck of a woman, you know that? I guess you were worth disobeying orders for, after all."

Sera stopped and turned back to face Frank.

"What do you mean?"

Frank gave her an odd look.

"No, I don't guess he would have told you."

"Told me what?"

"Once you found out about him, David was given orders to take you out."

The thought chilled her, even though she'd wondered the same thing more than once. She swallowed hard around the lump that had suddenly formed in her throat.

"I wonder why he didn't?"

Her voice had come out in a whisper, and she wasn't sure Frank even heard her.

Frank winked and turned to leave.

"Probably for the same reason you're here right now."

CHAPTER XXVII

Sera poked her finger into one of the plaster-filled holes on the body mound. The once pasty goo felt firm under her fingertip. She sat back on her heels, staring at the earthen dome as the afternoon sun beat down on her shoulders. Completely hardened now, the plaster cast was ready to be unearthed.

But she wasn't ready.

She didn't want to do it without David. The cavity was their find, and she didn't want to finish the last part of the excavation without him.

Thankfully, Professor Moretti understood her hesitation and agreed they could wait. After all, the body had been buried here for two thousand years. It wasn't going anywhere any time soon.

Of their own volition, her eyes moved from the mound, across the excavation field, and up the stone wall to the tower where David used to sit. For a brief second, she thought she saw a shadow move, and her heart leapt, imagining he was there.

But he wasn't. He was still sitting in that tiny jail cell, where he'd been for over a month, waiting for the officials to clear him of a crime he didn't commit. Or to find out who he really was and convict him of something worse than murder, if that were even possible.

As if drawn by an invisible thread, Sera rose to her feet and walked around the mound to the base of the wall. She started climbing, as she had done several times each day since she'd been back to work without David.

Assuming his usual vantage point on the crumbling outer wall, she looked out over the German encampment, sighing heavily as she leaned back against the tower. Up here, she somehow felt closer to him, and the site didn't feel quite so lonely without him.

She watched the German soldiers moving about the camp, not really certain what she was looking for. Their numbers and activity had definitely increased since the Axis surrender of Sicily three weeks before. The army below was larger and more reinforced than ever, even to her untrained eye.

Thinking back to the day when she'd first met Frank, she remembered he had jokingly asked if she'd wanted to work for their side. At the time, the suggestion had appalled her. She had to laugh at herself, because now she was doing just that, spying on the Germans.

But she wasn't spying for Frank or for the Allies. She was doing it for David, even though he would probably wring her neck if he knew she was taking such a risk. But it was her way of helping him, since she felt so powerless otherwise. Plus, doing it kept her in touch with Frank, giving her a reason to meet with him every Sunday, just as David had been doing before he was arrested.

At the thought of Frank, she wondered how he was doing on his end. She wondered if, right at this moment, the army was devising a way to rescue David before it was too late.

Heaven knew she wasn't making much progress with the authorities herself. They kept putting her off, telling her the circuit court judge was busy in Salerno and would make a decision regarding whether or not to charge David with murder when he came to Pompei, providing the report from Naples arrived.

Sera tried to tamp down the panic creeping up inside at the thought of how much damage that one piece of paper could do. So far, David had survived two close calls with the damning report. The first never arrived from Naples, apparently lost somewhere along the road, and after two weeks of waiting, the local authorities had sent for a second report. That one had arrived a week later, but in such mangled condition, it was no longer legible. So a third request for background information on David had been sent, and the waiting had begun again.

She couldn't understand what was taking the last report so long to get there, but she was thankful for each day that it didn't arrive. Each delay offered them one more day that David was safe, even if he had to spend it behind bars.

Sera tried to hold out hope that it was a sign that everything would turn out all right. But as each day passed, the sense of hope grew weaker and weaker.

POMPEII

Riding her bicycle through town on her way home, Sera felt incredibly alone, even though she was surrounded by people she'd known all her life. Since David's arrest, she'd worked the site by herself, except for the few times Heberto or Olympia offered to help. But they had their own areas to excavate, and so she was mostly left to herself. Being alone had never bothered her before. In fact, she used to relish the solitude of the dig, the peaceful quiet of the excavations.

But that was before David came into her life. She missed his laughter, the teasing, the quiet conversations. Now the solitude she had sought so often gave her little comfort. Instead, it allowed unwanted thoughts of what might happen if they didn't get David out soon to invade her mind.

A man darted into the street in front of her bicycle, snapping her out of her daze as she nearly ran him down. It was then that she noticed the street was more crowded than usual for this time of evening.

Raised voices drew her attention to small clusters of people gathered in the street. The man she almost collided with was now standing among one such group, gesturing wildly with his arms as he talked with his friends.

Looking around, she noted they weren't the only ones in heated conversation. Anticipation filled the air, the usual talk about the weather or family pushed aside for something more important. From the bits and pieces she overheard, the excitement had to do with the war. That in itself wasn't unusual. But something was different. She could feel it.

She stopped her bicycle, straddling it in the middle of the street. Hotly spoken words bombarded her from every direction, all talking about the same thing.

"The *Presidente Americano* said it on the Allied broadcast. It must be true."

"I'll believe it when I hear it from Prime Minister Badoglio himself."

A prickling sensation raced up her spine, buzzing like a swarm of bees at the back of her head. Sera reached out and stopped a woman rushing past her.

"What has happened?"

The woman stopped and blinked in surprise at her question.

"Haven't you heard? Italy has surrendered."

POMPEII

Marsha nearly jumped out of her skin when she heard the front door slam.

Since the first rumors of Italy's surrender began to surface, she and Hershel had been glued to the BBC. As footsteps pounded down the center hallway, Hershel jumped up and stood in front of the radio in an attempt to hide it with his skinny body.

She shook her head at him. Did the fool even think to just turn it off?

Before Marsha could reach for the knob, Serafina barged into the room, her face pale and strained.

"Did you hear?"

Marsha breathed a heavy sigh of relief and relaxed.

"Yes. We were just listening to it on the radio."

Serafina stepped further into the room, coming to sit on the ottoman beside Marsha without ever taking her eyes off the small radio on the side table.

"What are they saying?"

Hershel returned his attention to the radio and attempted to tune into the Allied broadcast. Static ripped through the small speaker, interspersed with the occasional voice of a reporter or advertisement.

"Well, it appears that Italy signed an armistice with the Allies last week, agreeing to our unconditional surrender."

"Last week?" Marsha squawked, looking at Hershel in surprise. She'd somehow missed that little tidbit of information in the last announcement. "Why haven't we heard anything about it until now?"

Hershel made a grunting sound of disgust as he banged on the top of the radio with his fist, apparently trying to improve the tuning with brute force. "Probably because Badoglio didn't want Hitler to get wind of it until the Allies could take firm control of Italy. Now that the news is out, there's certainly going to be hell to pay from Germany."

"Heberto!"

He grimaced at his slip of the tongue. "Sorry, dear."

Finally giving up on getting a clear signal from the BBC station, he adjusted the knob to pick up the local Italian broadcast.

"Let's see what Italy has to say about all of this."

Huddling around the radio, the trio didn't have long to wait. Fifteen minutes into the regular broadcast, the Prime Minister's announcement broke in, his deep voice flowing out over the radio waves.

"The Italian forces will cease all acts of hostilities against the Anglo-American forces, wherever they may be. They will, however, oppose attacks of any other forces."

Serafina glanced back and forth between Hershel and Marsha, her brow creased in confusion.

"Does this mean that the war is over for Italy?"

Hershel sighed heavily.

"No. It means we've switched sides. We're fighting against Hitler now."

Marsha saw hope flash in Serafina's eyes.

"Then, does this mean that David is safe, even if they discover who he is?"

Hershel didn't answer her right away. He switched off the radio, and Marsha watched as his eyes lit on every surface in the room—anywhere but on Serafina's expectant face.

An uneasy feeling churned in the pit of Marsha's stomach. He only avoided eye contact like that when he was in trouble or trying to evade the subject.

"Heberto?" Marsha prodded.

Finally, he cleared his throat, and when he looked at Serafina, Marsha saw regret and sorrow etched in the deep lines of his face.

"I honestly don't know, sweetheart. David was spying on the Germans before the surrender. If I don't miss my guess, Hitler will be sending more troops down here to try to hold onto Italy any way he can. If the Nazis ever find out who David is and get their hands on him…"

The threat to David, trapped as he was in a jail cell, hung heavy in the air.

"Plus, there's still the problem of the murder charge against him." At Serafina's stricken look, Marsha could have bitten off her tongue. She hadn't meant to add to the girl's worry.

"Oh, God." Serafina wrapped her arms around her waist and curled in on herself. "What's going to happen to him?"

Her heartfelt plea nearly broke Marsha's heart.

"There now, dear," she crooned, taking Serafina into her arms. She looked over at Hershel, exchanging a look of helplessness with her husband. "We're doing all we can. He'll be released soon. You'll see."

Serafina held onto Marsha like a lifeline, then pulled out of the embrace and shook herself, visibly drawing on some inner reserve that was rapidly draining before Marsha's eyes.

"I should go now."

"Oh, Serafina. I'm sure you haven't eaten yet. Why don't you stay and have dinner with us?"

She shook her head. "Thank you, Maria, but no. I need to be alone right now. Please understand."

Marsha watched Serafina leave the apartment, her shoulders slumped as if the weight of the world were upon her.

She'd never seen the poor girl look so sad, so lost. Not even after her mother's death.

As the door clicked shut, she turned swiftly to her husband, drawing herself up to her full four foot, eleven-inch height.

"Hershel, we have got to do something now. This has gone on long enough. I don't know how much more of this Serafina and David can take. Frankly, I don't know how much more I can take."

"But what more can we do, dear?" Hershel plopped down in his favorite chair. "I had Harry intercept the first report on David and conveniently 'lose' it. Then Ted had his boys play field hockey with the second one until it barely resembled a letter anymore. Every time the constable phones Naples, Sam dances on the lines until the call is rendered a jumble of static. We're stalling the authorities as much as we can."

"I know." Marsha rubbed at her throbbing temples. "I've had Gertrude on double over-time hovering around that judge in Salerno, making sure his little gastro-intestinal problem stays flared up so he can't get out of bed and come here."

"So what more can we do?"

"I'm afraid we've only been delaying the inevitable. Although I believe this crisis has drawn them closer, David and Sera have been apart too long. We need to get him released soon."

If possible, Hershel sunk even deeper into his chair.

"How? If we let the judge come here, he's just going to make David wait in jail until the report comes from Naples. If we let the report come, then he'll be charged with being a spy on top of murder."

Marsha paced the living room. She hated to do this, but at this point, they really had no choice.

"We need more help."

"From who? We're running out of favors to call on. It's going to look suspicious if too many guardian angels make unplanned visits to Italy."

"I think it's time we notify Smithers."

"Noooo." Hershel shook his head in tiny jerks. "We can't

do that. Then he'll know we've botched things again."

"Well, it can't be helped. If we get demoted, we get demoted. But we need to get David out of jail now, before things get any worse."

ᛈOᛗᛈᛖII

Sera was becoming such a familiar face at the Pompei jailhouse, she was surprised they didn't give her a key. Of course, that would make getting David out of his cell a little too easy, and the fates seemed to be conspiring to make her life as difficult as possible lately.

She arrived just after visiting hours started. After a long, sleepless night worrying about how Italy's surrender might affect him, she wanted to see David as soon as she could. Judging by the dark circles under his eyes, she wasn't the only one who hadn't slept well the night before.

"I guess you've heard the news."

David stifled a yawn and tunneled his fingers through his hair, making the waves look more tousled than usual.

"It was kind of hard to miss. The guards even had themselves a little party. Of course, I wasn't invited, but I got to enjoy the noise of the merrymakers all night long."

"I know. The celebrations in the street kept me up half the night, too." Even though she worried for his safety, she couldn't help but feel some of the excitement radiating through the town. "You should have seen it. The bonfires, the people dancing in the streets. It was just like the night they arrested Mussolini."

At the shared memory of what almost happened that night, David smiled.

"At least we're on the same side now."

She reached up and held his hand where it dangled over the cross-bar of the cell door.

"Oh, David. I've been on your side for a long time. I just didn't realize it until it was—"

Familiar voices echoed down the hallway, drawing Sera's attention. She turned to find a guard escorting the Angelicos toward David's cell.

"Heberto, Maria? What are you doing here?"

"Well, we came to visit David, of course." Maria beamed a smile at David. "You're not the only friend he has in this town, you know."

Sera stood stunned. She'd had no idea they'd been visiting him at all.

Her surprise must have been evident on her face, because David started laughing.

"Don't look so shocked. They've been coming once or twice a week. Signora Angelico browbeats the guards when she doesn't think they're feeding me well enough, and Heberto's been keeping me up on all the *bocce* games." David reached through the bars and shook Heberto's hand. "How did it go on Sunday?"

Heberto grinned. "Lost the first match, but won the other two."

"Not bad. When I get out of here, I'm going to have to challenge you to a game."

"You've got yourself a match." Heberto winked at Sera, then looked back at David. "But I warn you, it's a game of skill, not brawn. Think your pride can handle an old man beating the socks off of you?"

David chuckled. "We'll just have to see about that... old man."

The sound of the outer door grating open ended the friendly banter. Sera felt her heart leap into her throat as two guards made their way toward them. Without questioning how, she knew they were coming for David.

"Signore Corbelli. The *giudice della corte di circuito* is in office and will hear your case now."

Sera didn't know whether to be excited or scared.

"But I didn't think the judge was going to make a decision until the background report came from Naples."

The guard didn't even glance her way as he unlocked David's cell.

"As a matter of coincidence, the report arrived just before

he did, about an hour ago."

Sera's heart plummeted to her stomach from where it had been lodged in her throat. Dear God, this was it. She might be only moments away from losing David forever.

Following David and the guards down the hallway, with Heberto and Maria trailing behind her, Sera felt as if she were the condemned instead of David. How did he manage to walk so tall and seem so brave when she was falling apart inside?

The officers led them through the main area at the front of the jailhouse and up a wide, wooden staircase to a large room on the second floor. Crammed bookcases lined the walls on both sides, and a large wooden desk sat in front of a row of windows allowing bright sunlight to flood the cluttered room. As she stood in the doorway, the smell of cooked onions and over-ripe olives battled with the musty odor of old books and dust. A heavy-set man sat behind the desk in his shirtsleeves, a plate with the remains of his recent malodorous lunch resting on a stack of papers.

Sera, Heberto, and Maria hovered just outside the open door as the guards brought David to stand before the judge. Sera held her breath while Maria and Heberto each clasped one of her hands. If it weren't for their support, she probably would have melted into a quivering puddle on the floor.

Judge Buscelli looked up at David and eyed him with interest.

"Signore Corbelli, you are being held under suspicion of murder in the death of Giovanni Ragusa, is that correct?"

"It was self-defense, Your Honor."

The judge patted a paper on his desk with his hand. "So it says here in your statement. Do you have anything you'd like to add to it?"

David held his back stiff, looking straight ahead.

"All I can say is what I've said before—that I acted in self-defense. Signore Ragusa shot at myself and Signorina Pisano. When he ran out of bullets, he attacked me with a knife. I had no choice but to fight back to save both our lives."

"I see." Judge Buscelli leaned back in his chair, the wooden legs groaning under the strain of his weight. "And why, exactly, was Signore Ragusa trying to kill you both?"

David didn't speak right away. The air grew heavy with expectation as everyone in the room waited for his answer.

"He was stealing artifacts from the ruins and selling them on the black market. It was because of me that he was discovered and wanted by the authorities."

The judge nodded his head. "Revenge is often a strong motive, along with greed and love." Buscelli glanced down at a paper on his desk and adjusted his dark-rimmed glasses to read it. "It says here that you and Signore Ragusa had a previous altercation, just prior to his being charged with stealing the artifacts. Did that have anything to do with the thefts?"

"No, that was over me." The words flew out of Sera's mouth before she could stop them.

Buscelli looked around David at her.

"Ah, Signorina Pisano, I presume. Please do come in."

Sera walked on shaky legs to stand before the judge, forcing one of the officers who flanked David to move to the side.

"I've read your statement also, Signorina Pisano. Care to elaborate on any of it, since you were there when this unfortunate incident took place?"

Sera looked at David standing beside her, her mouth suddenly gone dry. What if the judge's decision hinged on what she said now? What if she said the wrong thing?

"What he says is true. Giovanni was angry at David and blamed him for ruining his career."

"And was that the only reason?" the judge prompted, glancing back and forth between them as if he already knew the answer.

"No. Giovanni and I were engaged for a time. He said he wanted me back, and I refused him." She felt David stiffen by her side. She'd never told him about that.

She glanced at him out of the corner of her eye, afraid he might be angry that she'd kept it from him. She licked at her dry lips and continued on. "Giovanni knew I was developing feelings for David. I think he believed that David was taking his rightful place, in the ruins and in my life."

David turned to look at her, his brown eyes darkening ever so slightly. Sera's heart began to pound again under his scrutiny, and she wondered what he was thinking.

"*Sì*, well. Since Signore Ragusa is no longer able to tell his side of the tale, I only have your word for it."

Sera felt hope fade. The judge didn't sound convinced of David's innocence.

"Fortunately, I recently received twelve additional statements from tourists who were in the Amphitheatre at the time of the altercation."

"Witnesses? What witnesses?" Maria blurted out.

Sera was as surprised as she was. There hadn't been anyone else in the arena with them until the police arrived.

Buscelli cast Maria a quelling glance, then turned his attention back to David.

"They have each sworn an affidavit attesting to the fact that they witnessed the fight and that it did, indeed, appear to be self-defense on the part of Signore Corbelli."

"So does this mean David is free to go?" Sera asked.

"Not quite. There's still the matter of the background information the public prosecutor requested on Signore Corbelli since he is virtually unknown in Pompei." The judge looked to the officer standing beside David. "I understand the report has finally arrived?"

The officer handed Buscelli a large tan envelope.

Panic swamped Sera, and a bead of sweat trickled between her breasts. As the judge cut open the envelope with a silver letter opener, the tearing sound ripped through her already frayed nerves. Her heart pounded in her chest, and she felt a desperate need to grab David's hand and run as fast as she could.

Buscelli reached in the envelope and frowned. "What is the meaning of this?"

Sera held her breath, uncertain of what was happening.

"It's empty. The report is not in here."

Out of the corner of her eye, Sera saw Maria glance sharply

at Heberto. He shrugged his shoulders at her, obviously as perplexed as everyone else.

The judge glared back and forth between the two officers in the room as if it were somehow their fault the envelope was mailed without the report inside.

"Well, since the other witnesses corroborate your story, the report is somewhat irrelevant now. I am not going to charge you with murder."

Sera couldn't stop her quick intake of breath. Was he really going to let David go?

"However, there is a penalty for any act of self-defense that results in a death. Since you have been held past the forty-day custody limit, I'm commuting your sentence to time already served, plus a fine of three hundred thousand lira."

Three hundred thousand lira! Sweet Mother Mary, that was over three months' pay. Sera doubted David had that much money saved.

If he was surprised at the amount, David didn't show it.

"I regret, Your Honor, that I don't have the money to pay the fine."

"I'm sorry to hear that." Buscelli sighed heavily. "In that case, I'm afraid you will have to serve out the remainder of the minimum three month sentence."

"David, I'll get the money," Sera said.

"No!" He looked sharply at her. "I can't let you do that."

Damn his male pride.

"And I won't let you sit in that jail cell one minute longer than necessary. I have some money saved—"

Maria stepped forward.

"And I'm certain we can come up with the rest between us and our friends."

David looked at the three of them, an indomitable wall of determination. He shook his head as the tension in his shoulders eased.

"I'll pay all of you back as soon as I can."

Heberto patted him on the back.

"All in due time, son."

The judge cleared his voice, drawing their attention back to him. "Very well. In that case, Signore Corbelli will be released as soon as the fine is paid."

As the guards turned to take David back to his cell, Buscelli stopped them. "Signore Corbelli, one more thing. Once you are released, I'd advise you to remain in Pompei. If that missing report ever turns up and shows anything in your past to indicate this incident may have been anything other than self-defense, I may be forced to re-examine this case."

David nodded to the judge, his eyes hooded.

"I understand, Your Honor."

Sera watched as the guards led him away. At least he would be out soon if they could raise the money to pay the fine. Turning to Heberto and Maria, she hugged them both.

Maria smiled at her. "We'll help all we can, dear."

"Thank you." Pulling away, Sera turned and headed for the door.

ᛈᛟᛗᛈᛖᛁᛁ

"Signora and Signore Angelico," the judge called, stopping them as they made to follow Serafina. "I would like to speak with you a moment. Close the door, *per favore*."

Hershel and Marsha exchanged wary glances. Why did he want to talk to them?

As the door clicked shut behind Serafina, a disturbingly familiar voice spoke out of the judge's mouth.

"What did you two think you were doing?"

Hershel clutched at his chest, and Marsha had to cover her mouth to stifle a scream that could have brought every officer in the building stampeding into the room.

"Mr. Smithers?"

"Yes. Care to tell me what's been going on down here?"

Marsha fiddled nervously with the pearl buttons down the front of her dress.

"I don't know what you mean."

"Yes, you do." Smithers stood and walked around the desk, the judge's rotund body shifting into Smither's tall, lean form with each step. Crossing his arms, he leaned a hip casually on the edge of the desk and pinned them with a piercing stare from behind the familiar black-framed glasses now perched on his nose. "How about tampering with Free Will for starters? How could you poison Judge Buscelli?"

"We didn't poison him," Marsha huffed. "We merely made sure he had all his favorite foods available."

"So that his ulcer would flare up and keep him in bed for a month? You might as well have poisoned him."

Hershel came to his wife's defense.

"We had to stall things. That dratted public prosecutor insisted on poking into David's background. We couldn't let that happen."

"I realize that. And I've bought you some time with the report, once again. But the prosecutor is going to keep asking for that background information, and the real Judge Buscelli is going to recover and show up eventually." Smithers looked pointedly back and forth between them. "You need to get David and Serafina out of Italy as soon as you can."

Hershel scratched behind his ear, his brow wrinkled in confusion.

"But you just told him not to leave town."

"*That* was for the officers' benefit. It's what the real judge would have said. You two need to get them out of town, and soon."

"Why?" Marsha asked.

"Because if you don't, someone is going to die."

CHAPTER XXVIII

"What? Aren't you glad to see me?" David laughed at the surprised expression on Frank's face.

His friend visibly shook himself as he propped his bicycle against a leaning tombstone in the town's main cemetery.

"No. I am. I am. It's just that…"

"Expecting someone prettier, I suppose? Someone with gorgeous blue eyes and a fiery Italian temper?"

David crossed his arms over his chest and shifted his weight on the granite sarcophagus where he'd been sitting. The burial tomb was ancient, its carved letters erased by weather and time. Anybody who might remember who was entombed there was probably long gone, too, so he figured the old guy wouldn't mind the company. He'd been sitting here for a quarter of an hour, waiting for Frank to show up at the rendezvous he'd set up with Sera last week.

His friend smiled and shook his head.

"You'll have to admit, she is a little easier on the eye than your sorry ass."

"Don't I know it." That beautiful face haunted his every waking minute. It was all that had gotten him through the lonely nights in his jail cell.

Frank hesitated briefly, then grabbed David and pulled him into a giant bear hug. Just as quickly, he released him and stepped back.

"When did you get out?"

"Yesterday." It had taken Sera and the Angelicos two days to come up with the money to pay his fine, and for that he was eternally grateful. He couldn't believe how good it felt to be out of that stinking, cramped cell.

"But how?" Frank stammered. "The last time I talked with Sera, things looked pretty hopeless at getting you released. She said the report from Naples was due any day. A report that might just get you a one-way trip to a firing squad."

"The report still hasn't arrived."

"So, why'd they let you go? I figured your goose was as good as cooked."

"So did I. It was like waiting for a ticking bomb to explode." David blew out a heavy breath, still trying to make sense of everything that had happened. "But then the judge showed up with sworn affidavits from witnesses swearing it was self-defense. I, for the life of me, can't remember anyone else in the arena when it happened." He shook his head as the reality of what he just said hit him. "Of course, I was a little busy at the time."

Frank snorted. "That's the understatement of the year."

"Unfortunately, that report from Naples is still out there, somewhere. I'm living on borrowed time."

Frank's disposition sobered instantly. "More than you know, man."

David tensed at the seriousness in Frank's tone. "What's going on?"

"The Germans are digging their heels in deep now that Italy has surrendered. They're disarming all Italians and shooting anyone who resists. The Allies have already landed troops at Salerno and Taranto. We're trying to advance, but it's slow moving."

A sinking feeling pooled in David's gut. The time bomb started ticking louder.

"There are going to be massive air strikes to try to break the Axis hold and chase the Germans out before Hitler can get more forces down here." Frank turned to look David right in the eye. "This is to be the last rendezvous. The mission is over. I've been ordered to pull out, with or without you."

David felt momentarily confused. Too many weeks alone in the jail cell had him feeling lost. Sera hadn't been able to tell him much without risking others overhearing the reports

Frank gave her.

"If that's the case, then the German camp still needs to be kept under observation, now more than ever."

"Not for long. There's a scheduled air raid on Pompeii tomorrow night. I was told if I could get you out, you're ordered back to base, effective immediately."

"*What?*" The bomb went off. Suddenly David's borrowed time shortened to seconds. "But there aren't any munitions hidden in the ruins. I've looked. They aren't there."

"Doesn't matter. They're going to strike the camp before Hitler can mobilize them."

David shoved his fingers through his hair, nearly pulling it out by the roots.

"Shit. Does Sera know about this?"

"No. And she can't know. We can't risk it leaking to the Germans and warning them in advance of the strike."

David could already guess what Sera's reaction would be to an air raid so close to the ruins.

"But the camp is right beside Pompeii. You and I both know those flyboys aren't always on target when they drop their loads. The bombs could hit the ruins."

"Sorry. Nothing you or I can do about it. A pile of crumbling rocks and a few old statues don't mean much when it comes to winning the war."

"I have to tell Sera."

Frank shook his head. "There's no time. You shouldn't even go back to your place for your things. We have to get back to base camp right away."

David couldn't believe this was happening. Not now.

"You can't do this to me, Frank. I can't leave Sera like this. I have to get her out of danger."

"It can't be helped. The civilians will be warned right before the strike so they can evacuate in time, but just barely. She can get out with the others."

"Look, give me one more day. Tell them I haven't been released yet. Tell them I'm still in jail. *Tell them anything.*"

"I can't do that, David. It's against orders. We could both

be court-martialed."

"Not if they don't find out." He hated the pleading tone of his voice, but it couldn't be helped. Right now, he'd sell his soul to the devil if it meant one more day with Sera. "Just one day, Frank. Please."

Frank looked like he might argue. Hell, he wouldn't be surprised if Frank pulled out a forty-five and took him back at gunpoint.

"All right. It's your ass. I just hope she's worth it."

"She is."

David had never been more certain of anything in his life.

ᛈᛟᛗᛈᛖᛁᛁ

David felt cheated.

One day. He had only one day to be with Sera before he had to leave. It didn't seem fair, after all the time they'd lost with him behind bars.

As he rode his bicycle back through town, he wondered how he was going to tell her about the air raid. Hell, that was the easy part.

How was he going to tell her goodbye? As if conjured by his thoughts, Sera was suddenly there, waiting on the doorstep to his apartment building. She looked lovely in a rust-colored dress, the tailored outfit hugging feminine curves he'd only seen glimpses of in unflattering trousers. A matching hat sat cocked on her head, a stark contrast to the floppy straw one she always wore at the ruins. Having rarely seen her in anything other than dirty pants and baggy men's shirts, she never looked more beautiful to him than she did right then.

"David! I was just coming to find you."

As she approached him, her face lit up in a blinding smile that made his chest tighten. He hadn't seen her stop smiling since he walked out of that damn jail yesterday. But that would all change when she learned what the Allies planned to do so close to her precious ruins.

"You were?" He tried to act nonchalant, as if he didn't have a care in the world. The act was a hard one to pull off when it felt like the whole world was conspiring against him.

"Yes. I want to show you something. Can you spend the rest of the day with me?"

He wanted nothing more. If it were possible, his chest constricted even tighter. He figured his heart was about the size of a raisin right about now. Little did she know that it would be their last day together. Come tomorrow, she would hate him, along with all other Americans for what they were going to do to her beloved ruins.

"Sure. What is it?"

"It's a surprise."

He stowed his bicycle in his flat, and when he returned to the front stoop, she linked her arm through his and grinned like a kid on Christmas. As she towed him through the town streets, he fought back the knowledge that at some point he was going to have to tell her about the air raid. Frank could rant and rave all he wanted, but Sera had a right to know what was going to happen, even though there was nothing any of them could do to stop it. He wanted to prepare her. He wanted her to hear the news from him, even if she hated him for it.

He let her lead him through town, and before he knew it, they were on a bus bound for Naples. The ancient vehicle ground gears past vineyards and small cottages, reminding him that each passing minute was one less he had left to spend with her.

"You're very quiet today," she remarked, pulling his attention from the scenic countryside.

"Am I?" *Probably because the one thing I need to talk to you about, I can't bring myself to say.*

And even if he wanted to, the bus was crowded with people. He couldn't risk anyone overhearing their conversation. At least, that's what he kept telling himself.

In truth, he wanted to spend as much time with her as he could before he had to leave, and he didn't want her angry or upset one more minute than was necessary.

He tried to put on a happy face for her. She wanted to do something special for him today. Even if it killed him, he needed to act like he was having a good time.

"So, are you going to tell me where we're going?"

"No." She gave him a smug smile. "But I'm sure you'll figure it out soon enough."

"Soon enough" came about thirty minutes later, when the bus pulled to a stop at Pugliano. "This is our stop."

Mildly surprised that they weren't continuing on to Naples, David followed her off the bus. They walked a few steps, and she directed him toward an electric carriage waiting in the crowded street. It reminded him of the trolley cars in San Francisco, which he'd seen in pictures but never ridden. As they boarded, he noticed the sign over the driver's windshield said "Vesuvio."

"We're going to Vesuvius?" he asked as he took his place beside her on one of the long bench seats that ran the width of the car.

"Yes. You've never been, have you?"

"No. Climbing an active volcano isn't my idea of a smart thing to do."

"The volcano hasn't erupted since 1929. But there was some significant volcanic activity while you were—" She stopped herself abruptly. After all, they both knew where he'd been. He watched her attempt a forced smile to cover up the unwelcome memory. "I'm curious to see what's going on up there."

David arched a brow at her. "Curiosity killed the cat, remember?"

That brought a genuine smile to her face. She patted his hand where it rested on his thigh.

"Relax. They wouldn't allow tourists on the mountain if they thought it wasn't safe."

As the tramway lurched and started moving, he didn't miss that she kept her hand on his. He turned his over, lacing their fingers together, wanting to hold onto her as long as he could. If he could ignore the war and stay behind the walls of the ruins with her for the rest of his life, he would. But he didn't have that choice. His life belonged to the army right now.

The one-car train wound its way slowly around the lower shoulders of the mountain, zigzagging up the slight grade like a side-winding snake. Out the open window, vineyards, orchards, and vegetable gardens rolled by, no doubt benefiting from the rich volcanic ash mixed in the fertile soil on the mountainside.

Lost in the calming scenery, he was startled when the tram jolted, nearly stopping before it lurched once again on its way. He threw one arm around Sera's shoulders and the other against the seat in front of them to brace himself.

"What the hell was that?"

She laughed.

"The grade is going to get steeper from here on out, so the train just went into five-wheel drive."

"You're kidding." David had never heard of such a thing.

"The rail line has a cogged center track to help the tram make it up the slope from here to the lower station."

After a few minutes, the train slowed to a stop outside a large stone and plaster building. As they disembarked, Sera pointed out a few of the smaller buildings.

"There's a restaurant, a telegraph office, storage buildings for the equipment and trains, and a small tavern nearby."

David shook his head at the wonder of it all.

"It's like a mini-city on the side of a volcano."

Looping her arm through his, she guided him into the station.

"Yes, I suppose it is."

Once inside, they took stairs to a lower level. A single track led into the cavernous area, with a pit to the side containing giant gears and wheels attached to thick cables.

But the impressive machinations weren't what astounded him. It was the odd-looking trolley-type carriage that awaited them.

"Are we supposed to ride up the mountain in that?"

"It's called a *funicular*, and you'll see why it's made this way as soon as we start up the mountain."

Sliding onto one of the bench seats, David thought the

funicular was the oddest thing he'd ever seen. The car, painted a bright buttercup yellow, was constructed on an angle, with each bench sitting higher than the next, like seats in a stadium. After the two of them boarded the tram along with a dozen other tourists, the giant gears next to it sprang to life, groaning and straining as the cable pulled the train out of the station.

As soon as they left the building, the slope of the mountainside increased dramatically, and David understood what Sera had meant. At a steep grade of almost sixty degrees, they would have been nearly lying on their backs had they been in a normal tram carriage.

The windows had no glass, so as the car began its journey up the volcano, the fresh mountain breeze flowed freely through it. Sitting back to enjoy the ride, David could almost forget that time was slipping away.

A few hundred feet up the mountain, the track split into two separate rails. He thought nothing of it until he watched a second *funicular* pass them on its way down.

"Do you know the *funicular* doesn't have any brakes?"

David turned to stare at Sera, not quite sure he had heard her correctly.

"What do you mean, there are no brakes on this thing?"

"The two cars are connected by the cable and act as counterweights for each other. While there are hand and electric traction brakes on each tram, it's mainly the weight of each car that keeps the other one in check."

"Well, that sure makes me feel safe." David was unable to keep the sarcasm out of his voice.

After a steep climb of about a thousand feet, the tramcar pulled into the station near the top. They disembarked and walked along a narrow path to the edge of the volcano.

As they stood on the rim, David surveyed the wonder of Vesuvius. Inside, it looked like a smaller volcano sitting within a larger, wider crater, reminding him a little of a Mexican hat.

"Is Vesuvius two volcanoes in one?"

"Yes. The outer crater is called the *Somma Caldera*. It's the remains of an ancient volcano that erupted some seventeen thousand years ago. The inner cone is Vesuvius."

They walked down a well-worn trail to the black bottom valley, where they paid one of the Italian guides to escort them across the hardened volcanic crust.

Sera took David's hand and pulled him along the bed of hard, black lava.

"Watch your step. Don't go anywhere where the lava is a glossy black. That's new flow and is still very hot and unsolidified."

As they made their way across the lava field, he couldn't shake the impression that the inside of the caldera looked like an enormous pot where some mischievous Greek god had stirred up a batch of dark taffy, then left it to cool in black twists and curls.

All around them, fissures and cracks belched steam, and molten lava showed through the open vents just a few inches below where they walked. David wasn't sure if it was his imagination or real, but his feet grew uncomfortably warm. He was quick not to stand in one spot too long, just in case the crust decided to give way.

The guide stopped when they reached the base of the inner cone, and Sera looked expectantly at David.

"Do you want to go up?"

He looked up at the cinder cone, about one hundred feet high. Steam poured from the top like a chimneystack, leaving a perpetual cloud to hover over the peak. Only a fool would get that close to an active volcano.

Then again, when would he ever get another chance like this?

"Let's go."

Taking her hand, they scrambled up the cinder cone. It was like walking up a dune of grey sand, their feet sinking with each step into the ash and pumice. Looking into the opening at the top was like looking into the spout of a boiling teakettle, all steam and white smoke. Far below, David could just make out the bright orange glow of the lava, churning and bubbling in its earthen caldron.

"This is incredible!" he shouted into its fiery depths.

Sera smiled. "I thought you might be impressed."

He was. He'd never seen anything so powerful, so amazing. Standing there, on the very brink of the deadly volcano, David never felt more alive. Sera had given him a priceless gift. How many people could say they'd peered into the mouth of hell and lived to tell about it?

When the heat finally grew too intense, they made their way back down the cinder cone and across the lava crust to the trail out of the caldera. Stopping to rest on the edge of the outer crater, David stood in awe of the powerful mountain.

The view from there was beautiful, with the Bay of Naples sparkling a brilliant blue in the distance. As he looked out over the land, he could see the modern town of Pompei and her ruins just beyond. They seemed too far away for Vesuvius to have so easily reached out and touched them from here.

But she had, and probably would again someday.

Sera stood by his side, and David watched her eyes dance as she looked out on the valley, her skin glowing from the heat and exertion. Her eyes were so full of wonder and delight, as if her life force was fed by the power of the dozing giant under their feet.

She drew her strength from this mountain. Her blood flowed hot, like the lava just under the volcano's crust, and every breath she took came from the soft breezes flowing off the Mediterranean Sea.

He put his arm around her and pulled her close, wanting desperately to hold onto her, even as he knew she would all too soon slip through his hands.

This was her world, her life. And, now more than ever, David realized that he had no place in it.

CHAPTER XXIX

Sera watched David prowl the dig area.

He'd been acting strangely since yesterday when they returned from the volcano. Today had been no different while they worked at the dig. Throughout the morning, she'd glance over at him and catch him with a faraway look in his eyes, staring at nothing in particular. Then, several times, she found him looking at her with the strangest expression on his face, as if being back at the ruins with her pained him somehow.

She wanted to think it was just a natural reaction to being locked up for so long. She kept telling herself that maybe he just needed some time to readjust.

He stopped before the body mound, examining the earthen sarcophagus as if seeing it for the first time.

"Why haven't you finished it?"

"I wanted to wait for you."

He looked at her, and sadness clouded his features.

"Thanks. That means a lot to me."

"The professor said we could begin removing the outer shell tomorrow."

"Tomorrow."

He said the word as if it had a different meaning to him. He looked like he wanted to say something more, but changed his mind.

"You look tired. Why don't we call it a day?"

"All right."

They gathered up their packs and rode back in silence to the Angelicos' villa. He'd never escorted her home before, but she didn't question why. She was just happy to have him with her.

They stopped on the walk outside the front door, and Sera reached out and put her hand on his sleeve. She could feel the tension in his arm, the muscles under his shirtsleeve bunching under her hand. He looked nervous, uneasy. And that made her nervous and uneasy, too.

"What's wrong, David?"

He looked at her, and the emotions swirling in his eyes scared her. Something was wrong.

He opened his mouth and started to speak, but he never got the chance.

The blare of air raid sirens filled the air.

It took a second for the sound to register. People passing in the street stood motionless, and dogs answered the high whine of the sirens with baying howls. Then, everyone started moving at once, crowding and pushing each other to get to the safety of the bomb shelters.

"Oh, my God. It's an air raid." Sera grabbed David's hand, toppling their bicycles as she pulled him down the street.

"Sera, wait."

She ignored him. The sound of the sirens screamed through her brain, cranking up the urgency to get to safety.

"Hurry. We have to get to the shelter."

Out in the street, people were everywhere, rushing to get to the designated shelters in the neighborhood. Women were screaming, carrying crying children in their arms, while men carried boxes filled with the family's most precious possessions.

The roar of planes overhead sounded like they were already upon them. Why weren't the citizens warned earlier? Fear pumped through her veins. Why were they bombing Pompei?

As they ran through the streets, paper started to rain down from the sky, floating like ashes in the wind. Sera slowed, watching the white sheets flutter to the ground, relief washing over her.

The planes weren't bombers. They were dropping leaflets. People stopped on the street to pick them up. Sera reached out and caught one herself as it drifted down. She had a hard time reading it as people continued to jostle past her.

"Sera, don't."

She dug in her heels as David tried to urge her on to the shelter and jerked her hand from his grasp. She didn't want to believe what she was reading.

"The Allies are going to bomb the German encampment within the hour. It says that all citizens should evacuate to avoid being injured by stray bombs that may fall on the city."

Her hands shook as she gripped the paper. They were going to bomb the Germans, the ones camped right next to the ruins.

"How can they do this? How could they risk hitting the ruins? They're irreplaceable." She lowered the paper and looked to David for support.

Instead, an ice cold knife of betrayal sliced through her. The look on his face told her everything.

He already knew.

"You knew about this?" She waved the crumpled paper in her fist at him. "You knew they were going to bomb the German camp, didn't you?"

"Sera, let me explain—"

She waved him off. She didn't want to hear excuses. "How long? How long have you known about this?"

"Frank told me yesterday."

"Why didn't you tell me?" She couldn't believe how much his admission hurt her. "You knew the whole time we were at Vesuvius and then today at the ruins, and you didn't bother to tell me an air raid was coming?"

David lifted his hands to her, then dropped them to his sides in frustration.

"What was I supposed to say? That everything you love was at risk of being destroyed by the Allies? What good would it have done?"

"I don't know." She stalked a few steps away and then turned back on him. "But you could have warned us. We might have been able to save some of the artifacts."

"How?" The word came out on a humorless laugh. "You

can't carry stone buildings away. Most of the statues weigh tons. Sure, you might have been able to save a few urns, some pieces of pottery, but you can't move a whole goddamn city."

The truth of his words didn't make the fact that he'd kept this from her any easier to take.

"Why didn't you try to stop this? Couldn't you have told someone? You know how important it is. You know how priceless the ruins are. You've been there. You've dug in that dirt with your own hands. You should've—"

"I can't change their minds. This goes way beyond me. I'm just one soldier in this godforsaken war. There's nothing I could have done to stop this."

She knew he was right, but she still felt betrayed. If he had only told her sooner, she could have had time to do something. She felt so helpless, defeated. So small and insignificant. All she could do was stand there and stare at him as people rushed past.

"Sera, I've been ordered to return to my unit."

Those words seeped through her dazed mind and crushed her like no others could.

"You're going to leave me alone, to face this by myself?"

"No, I'm going to get you to the bomb shelter where you'll be safe."

"And then you're going to leave?" Her voice sounded so small, so frail, even to her own ears.

"I have to. I don't have a choice."

She started backing away from him. "Well, maybe you don't have a choice, but I do."

"Sera, wait. There's no time." David reached for her, but she pulled away before he could grab her.

"Go, David. Go back to the army. Be a good soldier. That's what you came here for anyway."

Sera turned and ran, leaving David standing in the street as the white leaflets fluttered down around him.

POMPEII

Sera returned to the villa, going straight to the Angelicos' apartment instead of her own. Heberto nearly ran her down as he came out their door.

He looked completely surprised to see her standing there.

"Serafina? What are you doing here? Where is David?"

She tried to ignore the pain that knifed through her at the mention of his name.

"He's gone. Probably for good. But that doesn't matter." *Yes, it does*, a little voice whispered to her. *Otherwise, your heart wouldn't be breaking in two right now.* "Have you heard about the air raid?"

"Yes, yes. I just got a call from Professor Moretti. He wants everyone to meet at his villa now to figure out what to do."

Sera nodded, eager for someone to tell her what to do, because her mind wasn't cooperating. It was too busy trying to deal with the fact that her entire world seemed to be falling apart around her.

Maria's small head appeared over Heberto's shoulder. She craned her neck like an inquisitive ostrich to look behind Sera.

"Where's David?"

Sera couldn't stop the gritting of her teeth. Why were they so concerned about David when the ruins were at risk of being destroyed?

"Probably half way back to his unit by now."

"What? Why?"

"He was called back. He knew about the air raid and didn't tell anyone." *Me.*

"I don't believe it." Maria shook her head. "How long has he known?"

"Since yesterday."

"Yesterday?" Maria blinked several times. "Why are you so angry at him? That doesn't seem to be too horrible a crime."

"It is." Sera defended her anger towards him. She knew it was unjustified, but it was the only thing keeping her going. Otherwise, the hurt would seep in and crush her. "It's twenty-four hours we could have used to appeal to the authorities to do something to stop this. Twenty-four hours more we would have had to save the ruins than we have now."

"Come, Serafina. He was probably afraid to tell you, knowing you'd react the way you are now."

"That shouldn't have mattered." She wanted to scream. "If he cared about me, he would have told me. If he loved me…" She bit back the words. They were too painful to think of, much less utter aloud.

"He would have stayed?" Maria finished for her.

Sera didn't answer. The reality of the truth was too hard to face.

Instead, she turned and went back outside to retrieve her bicycle, leaving the Angelicos standing in the hall to stare after her.

Marsha shoved at Hershel's shoulders.

"Well, go with her."

Hershel sputtered, suddenly called upon to act when he had been a silent bystander just moments before.

"And what am I supposed to do?"

"Your job. Watch over her. Keep her safe. In the meantime, I'll do what I can to find David."

POMPEII

David was almost to the edge of town when he turned back.

Thousands of small pieces of paper littered the street, floating on the evening breeze like confetti after a parade, remnants of the Allies' warning only an hour before. The sirens continued to blare through the darkening night sky, wailing a warning for all who could hear.

Get out. Get out.

But another sound droned inside his head, a voice telling him to go back.

He understood Sera's anger. He cursed her stubborn streak with every pump of his foot on the bicycle pedal. He knew she was hurt and upset, taking it out on the closest person—him. But that didn't make it right.

He'd tried, damn it. Tried to tell her a thousand times, but the words always stuck in his throat. And then it was too late.

But he couldn't leave it like this. He couldn't go until he

made her understand that he was doing what he had to do. He didn't want it to end with her being angry at him.

And he damn well wanted to make sure she was safe.

Fighting his way through the throngs of people leaving the town, David made his way back to Sera's. He took the stairs to her apartment two at a time. No one answered her door. Perhaps she'd already fled the city with everyone else.

Cursing his luck, he rushed back down the stairs, wondering if he had somehow passed her on the street. He couldn't leave Pompei without seeing her one more time. He had to find her. He had to tell her—

David nearly stumbled on the bottom step, surprised to find Maria Angelico standing in her doorway, looking at him with a quiet reserve that set his nerves on edge.

"Signora Angelico, what are you still doing here? It's too dangerous. You should already be in one of the shelters outside town."

She tilted her nose up at him, managing to look brave and haughty at the same time.

"I'm waiting for Heberto and Serafina. I won't leave without them."

So, why did you? Her unspoken accusation hung in the air, pinning him to the spot like nails driven through his shoes.

A cold chill raced down his spine.

"Where are they?" But he was afraid he already knew the answer.

"They went to the ruins with the others to save what they could."

"Of all the stupid…" David cursed under his breath. He stopped his tirade when he saw Maria's terrified eyes. Gone was the brave matriarch of the Angelico household, replaced instantly by a frail old woman worried for her husband and a young girl with more determination than common sense.

Dropping his pack at Maria's feet, he headed for the door.

"Don't worry, Signora. I'll bring them both home."

As soon as he was outside, David jumped on his bicycle like a rodeo star vaulting into the saddle. He pumped the pedals for all he was worth, his ass never touching the seat as he flew down the road to the ruins.

He just prayed he'd get to Sera and Heberto before the bombs started falling.

POMPEII

When Sera and Heberto arrived at Professor Moretti's villa, he was on the phone, arguing with Italian officials about the threat to the ruins, begging them to intercede with the Allied powers and try to stop the impending destruction. It was no use. They wouldn't listen to his fervent pleas, so it now fell to a rag-tag group of archeologists to save Pompeii's priceless legacy.

Sera now found herself racing toward the ruins on her bicycle. Olympia was beside her, with the Professor and Heberto close behind. About a half dozen of the other archeologists accompanied them, the few who had decided to stay behind and save what they could.

The drone of airplanes drowned out the frantic beating of her heart. Looking to the darkening sky behind her, she knew these weren't the peaceful Allied planes that had dropped the warning leaflets less than two hours ago. These planes carried a lethal cargo, and she nearly cried out as they flew over her head toward the ruins.

An ear-piercing whistle cut through the air, followed by a hollow thump. A blinding flash of light filled the sky in front of her.

Dear God, it had started.

Without speaking, they all began to pedal faster. Being younger and stronger, Olympia and Sera pulled ahead of Heberto and the Professor.

Another whistle began overhead, the whine growing louder until she thought her eardrums would rupture from the piercing sound. The bomb hit a hundred yards in front of them, showering them with dirt and rocks. They slowed as they entered the cloud of dust left behind, careful to navigate around the crater left in the road.

From behind her, Sera heard a thunk and a crash, followed

by a muffled curse. Obviously, one of the other archeologists had not been as careful.

Glancing back, she saw Heberto and Moretti still pedaling behind her, although they'd dropped further back. She worried that the two older men might not be able to handle the stress and exertion.

She didn't have time to worry too much. The telltale whistle filled the air again. She refused to look overhead. If a bomb was going to kill her, she'd prefer not to see it coming.

The whine increased in intensity until it sounded like the very heavens were screaming out in pain. The impact came from behind, the concussion blowing Sera from her bicycle into the brush at the side of the road. She curled into a ball to protect herself and waited for the rain of rocks to stop.

When it seemed safe, she got to her feet and climbed back up to the road. The settling dust stung at her eyes and choked her throat. She could hear someone coughing nearby, but couldn't see who it was. She felt as if she were walking in the middle of a dirty brown cloud, with no way of knowing which way to go.

A cry of pain to her left startled her. Someone was hurt. Who?

She made her way down the road. Dark forms started emerging from the dirt cloud, taking on human form as the dust continued to settle. She zeroed in on the one body that didn't rise. As she drew closer, she saw Professor Moretti clutching his leg as he lay sprawled on the road.

"Professor! Are you hurt?"

"My leg. I think it's broken."

Kneeling down beside him, Sera tried to comfort the injured man.

"Lie still. We'll get you to a hospital."

"There's no time." The professor tried to move, but even that slight shift of his body caused him obvious pain.

She looked around desperately for help. It came in the form of Olympia.

"The professor's hurt," Sera informed her. "We need to get

him to the hospital."

"No!" he protested as the other archeologists gathered around him. "We need to get to the ruins. The damage has already begun."

"You're in no shape to go anywhere," Olympia said, taking on the role of mother hen. Looking around at the people standing with her, she started issuing orders. "I'll stay with the professor. Enrique, you go call for an ambulance. Serafina, you, Heberto, and the others go on to the ruins as planned."

At the mention of Heberto's name, Sera glanced around.

He wasn't there.

Her eyes were drawn to the large crater left in the road by the bomb. She felt her stomach bunch in a knot, threatening to relieve itself of its contents. A buzzing started in her ears as she made her way to it on shaky legs, the crowd of archeologists behind her growing conspicuously quiet.

As she stood on the edge, the wide hole gaped up at her like a giant's empty bowl sunk to the brim in the dirt. Inside lay the crumpled remains of Heberto's bicycle, the blue frame twisted and contorted into a mangled metal pretzel. His hat rested at the edge of the crater covered in dust. It was all that indicated he had even been there at all.

Sera felt her heart break into a thousand tiny pieces.

"Noooo!"

POMPEII

David found her just as another bomb detonated on the other side of the wall. She was covering the mound with her own body, shielding it as if flesh and bone had any power against exploding bombs and flying debris.

"Sera!"

He ran to her, grabbing her shoulders and pulling her around to face him. Any reprimand he may have had died on his lips as he saw her tear-streaked face. He'd never seen such sorrow in her brilliant blue eyes. The sight tore his heart apart.

"Heberto," she sobbed and flung herself into his arms.

He cradled her, letting her absorb his strength when she

needed it most.

"I know. I saw the others as I came in. They told me." He squeezed her tighter, wanting to take away all her pain. "I'm so sorry."

"It's my fault."

"No, it's not." He rocked her like a child, brushing his hand through the dust and dirt matting her hair. "Heberto made his choice to come here, just as all the others did. It was his decision to make, and there was little you could do to stop him." *Just as I couldn't stop you.*

"How will I ever be able to face Maria?"

"You will." He tried to speak around the sorrow that threatened to choke him as he thought of the brave old woman waiting at home for a husband who would never return. "And you'll be strong for her, because she's going to need you now more than ever."

An explosion detonated on the other side of the wall, sending small bits of rock flying in the air around them.

The tender moment was gone. There was no more time for solace or regrets.

"We've got to get out of here."

Sera stiffened in his arms and pulled back, her eyes full of determination and fire.

"No."

"No?" He couldn't believe what she was saying. She'd seen with her own eyes what a five-hundred pound bomb could do.

He jerked her to her feet, prepared to sling her over his shoulder and carry her out if he had to.

She pulled against the vise-like grip he held on her arms.

"I'm not leaving."

"Damn it, Sera. It's not worth your life."

She struggled within his grasp.

"I won't let Heberto's death be in vain. It's more important now than ever to save the cast. I have to."

"Are you crazy? You can't stop bombs from falling from the sky."

She looked back over her shoulder at the mound, exposed

and unprotected out in the open.

"But it's been preserved for two thousand years. I can't let it be destroyed now."

"If it's going to be destroyed, there's nothing you can do to stop it."

"I have to try."

"And get yourself killed in the process? You're worth more than that."

She shook her head.

"Pompeii is irreplaceable. Every statue and building here is priceless."

"No, Sera." David grabbed her face with his hands, the swiftness of the movement startling her. He forced her to look at him, as if he could imbed the meaning of his words into her mind by force of will. "They're just stones and ash, things long dead and forgotten. You're flesh and blood and alive." He paused, his eyes boring deep into her soul. "Oh, so very alive."

She stopped fighting him. Looking into his eyes, she saw the truth for the first time.

He loved her.

He hadn't said the words, but he didn't have to. She knew it with every fiber of her being.

The fight left her, and, for the first time in her life, the desire to hold onto the past was replaced by dreams of the future.

A future with David.

"All right. I'll come with you." The words came easily, even though she knew to say them meant it was to leave all she cherished behind.

The drone of the second wave of bombers flying overhead drew David's attention to the sky.

"Run!"

He grabbed her hand, practically dragging her behind him.

A distant whistle behind them turned into an ear-piercing whine followed by a blinding flash. The thundering concussion that followed slammed them both on the ground.

CHAPTER XXX

As the debris sifted down around her and the hail of pebbles slowed to an occasional plink on the ground, Sera pushed herself up and scoured the area for David.

The anguish she had felt when Heberto disappeared before her eyes resurfaced tenfold.

She couldn't lose David, too. Not now.

The fog of dust finally settled, and she spied his body sprawled a few feet away from her. The distance seemed to stretch out to miles as she crawled her way toward him, not caring as the rough ground cut into her hands and knees.

He was so still, so pale. Dust covered his entire body like a death shroud.

"No!" she screamed, feeling the words rip from her heart.

She laid her head on his chest and heard the wonderful sound of his heart beating. He was alive.

Sera gently cradled his head in her hands, praying for him to be all right. A warm, wetness seeped through her fingers, and when she pulled her hand away, crimson blood covered the palm.

"Oh, David, no."

He was bleeding, either from the flying debris of the blast or from the fall, she couldn't be sure which. All she knew was he was hurt badly, and she needed to get him out of there.

"Wake up. Oh, please, wake up."

She shook him by the shoulders, and his head rolled from side to side like a ragdoll's.

Then his eyes fluttered open.

"That's really not helping my head very much."

Sera stared in disbelief at him for a moment.

"How can you joke at a moment like this?" If he weren't already hurt, she was tempted to punch him until he was.

"I wasn't kidding. It hurts like hell." David touched behind his ear and brought back his fingers covered in blood.

"Is it bad?"

He shook his head, then winced.

"No, it's just a scalp wound. They tend to bleed like crazy."

Another whistle cut through the air right before a bomb landed just on the other side of the wall, sending a shower of debris to rain down on them. Sera threw herself over David, covering his body with hers, shielding him just as she had tried to protect the body mound.

As the dust settled, she raised her head and pulled back to find David's eyes piercing her own. He reached up and pulled her face down to his, crushing her mouth in a forceful kiss. Only the shaking of the ground beneath their bodies from the impact of another bomb succeeded in pulling them apart.

"We have to get out of here."

Sera nodded, pushed herself off David. He tried to stand, but as soon as he got his feet under him, his leg buckled, and he crumbled to the ground, rolling in obvious pain.

"Holy shit!"

"What is it?" She was instantly kneeling on the ground by his side.

"My leg."

Her gaze shot to where he clutched at his thigh. A jagged tear ripped through the fabric of his trousers, and blood had turned the dark green material nearly black from hip to knee.

She had to pry his hands away to see how bad it was. Grabbing the edges of his torn pants leg, she ripped it open wider. Bright red blood oozed from a deep gash in his thigh, making the flesh look like a tomato split open in the hot sun.

Sera's hand flew to her mouth as a wave of nausea hit her. She was accustomed to the dry bones of the dead, not the fresh wounds of the living as their life-blood pulsed out of gaping wounds.

She looked up to David's face. Sweat dampened his brow,

turning the fine dust on his skin to tiny rivers of liquid mud dripping down his temples. She had to stop the blood, or he could bleed to death.

The hum of fighter engines filled the air overhead, while sirens and machine-gun fire from the German camp on the other side of the wall joined the symphony of battle. The now-familiar whistle of incoming bombs broke through the deafening noise. A thud landed just on the other side of the wall, followed seconds later by the rattling concussion of the explosion.

Small stones and large chunks of the ancient wall flew over their heads and rained down around them. They couldn't stay here, out in the open like this. They needed to get out of the ruins.

Sera moved behind David and shoved her arms underneath his. Even though he tried to help her move with his good leg, he felt like dead weight. Hobbling just a few feet had him shaking from the strain and leaning heavily on her. Three more feet, and they both tumbled to the ground.

It was hopeless. She'd never get him all the way to the main gate. They had no choice but to find cover close by.

The dark opening of a ruined merchant's shop beckoned, and she used all the strength she had to get David into the safety of its shadows. Sera guided him to the back corner of the shop, where she eased him carefully to the ground.

As with the majority of the ruins, there was no roof over their heads to shield them, but the stone walls did offer some protection. The detonating bombs sounded like thunder on the horizon, only it wasn't rain falling down on them, but small bits of rock and dust carried on the wind from the blasts over the wall.

David pushed himself to a semi-sitting position with his back propped against the stone wall. Crawling to his side, she examined the jagged wound once more. Fresh blood oozed from the gash every time he moved, the red droplets falling on the parched ground beneath him, soaking in like drops of rain. She took a deep breath, willing herself to be strong. She couldn't afford to faint right now. She was the only one who could help him.

"What should I do? Should I make a tourniquet?"

He seemed to sense her alarm.

"Don't panic. It's not that bad. I don't think it hit an artery, or I'd be dead already. But we do need to stop the bleeding."

"That's what you think. You haven't had a good look at it."

Even to her untrained eye, the wound needed stitches. But there was no chance of her being able to sew it up, even if she had the needle and thread to do it. The best she could do would be to bandage it tight enough to stop the bleeding until they could get him to the hospital. But with what?

"I need your shirt to use as a bandage."

David made no comment as she reached up and started unbuttoning his shirt. He leaned from side to side to help her pull it off his broad shoulders and peel it down his arms. He winced every time he moved, and she hated that she was causing him pain.

The earthen floor exhaled dust whenever either one of them moved, threatening to invade the wound and make the situation worse. She needed something to lay him on to keep the dust down, but they had nothing but the clothes on their backs. Sera thought desperately about what she might be able to use, then remembered the excavation site and all the equipment just a few feet away.

She grabbed David's hand and pressed it to the wound.

"Keep pressure on this, and don't move. I'll be right back."

"Sera, don't go out there!"

He tried to reach for her, but she was already out the door.

She ran down the road with her hands covering her head, jumping over rocks and fallen stones from crumbling walls littering the street. Dashing under the tent, she scoured the table for anything she might be able to use. She had picks and scrapers, trowels and brushes, but nothing that could be used to tend a wound.

The canvas over her head flapped in the breeze as she struggled to think. She glanced up at the source of the noise.

The tent. At least they could put it on the ground and maybe even wrap up in it to shield themselves from the dust and debris.

Sera ran to one of the poles and untied the ropes staking it into the ground. She kicked the pole away, and one end of the tent collapsed. The others followed, landing on the ground with the hump of the screening table draped in the middle. She tugged at the canvas, not caring as the material pulled the table over, toppling all her tools and supplies on the ground.

She wadded the canvas up in her arms, pausing for one brief moment to glance at the body mound exposed in the middle of the road. It would have to fend for itself. David needed her more.

Grabbing some of the tools and a few loose stakes, she turned and ran back to their ruined shelter.

His look of relief was quickly followed by censure. "Don't you ever do something so stupid again. You could have been killed."

Sera ignored him and dropped the supplies on the ground. She knelt beside him and spread the canvas on the ground.

"Here, let's get you on this. It's not ideal, but it'll help keep the dust down."

He cocked a brow at the discarded tools and shovel.

"Planning on doing some excavating work while we wait it out?"

Sera sat back on her heels and glared at him. She wanted to smack him. How could he joke at a time like this?

"Very funny. I thought we might be able to use something as a splint for your leg." She fought hard to hold back the tears that threatened to come. She had to be strong if she was going to save David's life in spite of himself. "But if you'd rather lie there and bleed to death, I'll be more than happy to—"

"Hey, hey." He reached over and grabbed her fist held curled in tight on top of her thigh. "I'm sorry. I know you're trying to help. I was just kidding."

"Well, now's not the time to be making jokes."

"I know. I'm sorry." He nodded at the stakes. "It was good

thinking, but I don't think it's broken, so we probably don't need to put a splint on it. We just need to bandage it up tight."

"All right." Sera chewed on her lip. She knew next to nothing about field-dressing a wound.

She helped him shift onto the makeshift bed, wincing herself as she heard the muffled groan he tried to hold back. Kneeling beside him once more, she tried to think methodically about what she needed to do.

"Do you still have your knife?"

David pointed to his right boot. She pulled the knife from the sheath around his lower calf. Inserting the point into the tear in his pants, she cut the material all the way down to the ankle and spread it apart. Peeling his blood-soaked shirt away, Sera used the cleanest parts of it to wipe away the blood around the gash. The bleeding had slowed, but still hadn't completely stopped. She chastised herself for not thinking to use the shirt as a bandage first.

Without stopping to think, she began unbuttoning the front of her shirt and shrugged it off. She stood, kicked off her shoes, and shimmied out of her pants.

"What are you doing?" She didn't miss the heated flare in David's eyes.

Sera shook her head at him. How typically male. He was bleeding to death and still thinking about sex.

"We need bandages. The tarp is too dirty and rough. My clothes are all that we've got."

Sitting in her white cotton bra and panties, she used his knife to cut her pants in two. She folded one leg into a square big enough to cover the gash on his thigh. The other half she eased under his leg, wrapping it around once, then pulling the ends as tight as she could and tying them together.

She felt the muscles of his thigh tense under her hands.

"Is it too tight?"

"Yes," he grimaced, then relaxed. "But it needs to be."

Next, she tied her shirt around his head. Although the wound had almost stopped bleeding, she didn't want any dirt to get into it.

She sat back to examine the makeshift dressings, and frustration at her own ineptitude swamped her. He looked ridiculous, with her pants wrapped around his thigh and her shirt tied lopsided on his head.

"I don't know what else to do."

"It'll be fine." He reached up and cupped her cheek, startling her attention away from his wounded leg. "Don't worry. We're going to make it."

"Are we?"

As if to emphasize the point, another bomb detonated nearby. The walls around them shook, and the explosion felt as if it had landed right outside the door.

David grabbed Sera's hand and pulled her down beside him. He held her tightly by his side as bombs dropped around them, the booming vibrations that followed causing ancient stones to fall as centuries-old mortar released its hold.

She snuggled deeper into his embrace. For some reason, even though hell seemed to be unleashing its wrath all around them, she felt safe here with David.

They held each other for what seemed like hours, watching the sky darken above them, the flash of exploding bombs illuminating the clouds like lightning in a summer storm.

"I'm sorry." She spoke the words against his bare chest, not sure if he could hear her whispered apology over the deafening noise outside.

He squeezed her shoulder gently. "For what?"

"For getting you in this mess. If you hadn't followed me here, you wouldn't have gotten hurt. If it weren't for me—"

"Shush." David stopped her with the simple command.

He lifted her chin gently with the pressure of his fingertips, drawing her head away from its hiding place against his shoulder.

"God, Sera. There are a lot of things I would change if I could. I wish I could take away all the hurt your father did to you by not being there for you. I wish I could change the fact that you ever loved a man like Giovanni, who made you feel like you weren't worth waiting for. I wish I could bring back

Heberto so the sadness would leave those beautiful blue eyes."

He paused and took a deep breath.

"But I wouldn't, even for one minute, wish that I had never met you, and that I wasn't here with you right now." Leaning down, he softly kissed her lips. "Don't you know, for the first time in my life, I've found something—someone—worth dying for."

"No, David. Don't say that."

"Why not? It's the truth. If my life were to end right here, right now, I'd die happy because I got to hold you in my arms in these last moments."

A tiny tear slipped down her cheek, and he caught it on his fingertips.

"I love you, Sera. I pray to God that He doesn't take you from me just when I've found you."

She cupped his cheek. Never before had she seen such love in anyone's eyes. Love for her. It was as though he'd been a part of her for a lifetime, maybe more. She couldn't imagine living without him.

"Then let's make this moment last forever."

She watched his eyes darken as she pulled his face down for a kiss. His lips touched hers gently, the tip of his tongue teasing the sensitive skin like the brush of a feather. She shivered in his arms, wanting to crawl up his body to get closer until she became so much a part of him that they could never be separate again. She opened her mouth to him, allowing him entry. He deepened the kiss, pulling her tighter against him until she thought she couldn't breathe unless he did it for her.

David shifted and slowly pressed her down onto the canvas, covering her body with his. He slipped his knee in between her thighs and she cradled him, squeezing his hips to hold him to her.

He let out a yelp and rolled away, his face contorting in pain as he clutched at his leg.

"Oh, David. I'm sorry. I didn't mean to hurt you." Sera sat up, wanting to put her hands on him, but afraid she'd hurt him more. "Maybe we shouldn't—"

"No!" he barked, startling her with his vehemence. Then his features softened. "If you stop now, it will kill me for sure."

"But I don't want to hurt you."

"If you do, it'll be worth it, I'm sure."

Sera looked at his bandaged leg, held stiffly out in front of him.

"But how?"

David smiled. "I think we can find a way to work around it."

He pulled her face down to his, silencing any more protests with his kiss.

She melted into him. How could she ever refuse this man? How could she ever deny her heart? Deep inside, she knew this moment was meant to be, even as the war raged all around them.

Pushing herself up off his chest, Sera eased her leg over his body so that she straddled his hips, careful not to touch his leg. He looked up at her with so much love in his eyes she thought she might explode from the force of it.

His hands skimmed up her thighs, pushing the loose bottom of her panties up to bunch at her hips. Sera clasped his hands, stopping him before he could expose her completely. Instead, she brought his hands up to cup her breasts. David kneaded them gently, guided by the squeeze of her hands on his. Finally, she released his hands to let them do their magic on her body.

Every touch made her body sing, every stroke made her senses soar. Her hands traced down his strong forearms, feeling the muscles beneath his warm skin bunch and tense. She threw her head back, acutely aware of the soft feel of her hair on the skin of her back.

She felt him slide the straps of her bra off her shoulders. The thin barrier disappeared and the heat of David's hands seared her sensitive skin. She looked down at him, his eyes intense on her face in the brief flashes of light from the exploding shells.

A bomb exploded close by, sending several stones from the

wall across from them toppling to the ground. David pulled her down on top of himself, protecting her head and back with his hands as best he could. As the shower of dust settled, Sera pulled back and looked deep into his eyes. She trembled with fear and with love for this man.

He pulled her down again, kissing her lips with the joy of life. They might not make it through the night, but at least they were alive for now.

With gentle pressure, he urged her to move up his body, kissing her neck, her collarbone, until his questing lips found her breast. White, hot fire shot through her body as he pulled her nipple into the moist heat of his mouth. She bucked and arched against him. Running her fingers through the dark waves of his hair, she pressed him to her, begging without words that he take more of her. David caught the rigid tip of her nipple in between his teeth and gently tugged. She jerked from the pleasure-pain of it. Then he soothed her with his tongue.

"Oh, David."

When she thought she could stand no more, he moved to the other breast and continued his slow torture there. She arched and started grinding her hips against his in an effort to alleviate the throbbing ache, but it only served to stoke the fires to blazing.

"Oh, God."

David groaned, too. He stopped his relentless assault on her body and pushed her up until she once again straddled his thighs.

What was he doing? Why was he stopping?

He took her hands and guided them to the waistband of his trousers, then let go. He didn't have to speak the words. His eyes asked the question for him. He was letting her decide, letting her determine if they would go any further.

In answer, Sera's trembling fingers unfastened the first button, then the next, until all were undone. That task completed, she looked to David, not sure what to do next. He arched his back off the ground using his uninjured leg and pushed his trousers down his lean hips. Sera followed his lead, helping him ease his torn pants over the bandage.

In the darkness, she could just barely make him out, naked except for the bandages. Crawling up to kneel beside him, she took in his reclining form with hungry eyes. Undoing the clasp of her bra, she slid it off her arms. She shimmied out of her panties, until she was as naked as he was. With an animalistic growl, David pulled her down across his chest, crushing her to him. He took her lips in a kiss meant to brand her, claim her as his, for now and always.

And she was his. Body and soul.

His hands roamed down her back, burning a trail of fire on her skin. David positioned her legs so that she once again straddled his waist. She could feel the long, hard ridge of him pressed against her stomach. With one shift of his hips, he was poised at the entrance of her, waiting like an eager traveler to be allowed inside.

Grasping her hips, he eased himself slowly into her. She felt herself stretch to accommodate the intrusion, a hot burn traveling up inside her body. She hissed, closing her eyes to the unfamiliar feeling.

"Sera?" David stopped, holding her hips in his hands, half in and half outside of her. She saw the shock on his face, the sudden realization of the resistance met inside her.

"For heaven's sake, don't stop now!"

Gripping her hips tighter, he pulled her down in one swift motion, filling her completely. Their mingled moans filled the air, his of pleasure, hers of pain.

Ever so slowly, David guided her hips up and down. The motion burned at first, but then her tense muscles eased, and her body flowed to accept him.

He urged her to go faster, and soon she was riding him of her own volition, trying to ease the rising ache within her. No longer able to support herself with her hands on his chest, she leaned forward and placed one hand against the wall behind his head, the stones rough under her palm. At that angle, his mouth easily found her breast, sending bolts of electricity from her nipple to between her legs and back again.

"Oh, God. David!"

His hands gripped her buttocks, pushing her down, driving himself deeper with each thrust. She could feel the pressure building inside her, like a volcano about to erupt.

He must have felt it, too. He released his hold on her hips and cupped her face in his hands.

"Look at me, Sera."

And when she did, the world exploded around her.

Through the pounding of her heart, she could feel him pulsing inside her, filling her with an essence more powerful than life itself. As the last shudders rippled through her body, she collapsed against his.

David wrapped his arms around her and kissed the top of her head.

"I love you."

"I love you, too." She was so shaky, she could barely utter the words.

He rubbed his hands up and down her arms, across her back, slick with sweat and the heat of the night. She felt sated and exhausted at the same time.

"Are you sore?"

She smiled against his damp skin. "A little."

There was a pause, then David finally spoke. "Sera, didn't you and Giovanni ever…? I mean, weren't you two…?"

She didn't answer for the longest time.

"No," she finally sighed, blowing her soft breath across his bare chest. "I didn't want to repeat my mother's mistake. I wanted to make sure when it happened, it was with the man I loved."

"But you loved him, didn't you?"

She felt him hold his breath, waiting to hear her answer.

"I'll admit I was attracted to him. Maybe I even thought I loved him, but something always held me back. Something always stopped me."

"What?"

The question hung in the air between them.

"I've asked myself that same question many times." Finally, her eyes rose to meet his. "Now, for the first time, I know the answer."

She placed her hand over his heart, the beat within his chest echoing her own.

"I was waiting for you."

CHAPTER XXXI

With the dawn came a calmness of spirit, both inside and out.

Outside, the bombing had stopped hours before, while inside the heat of passion had ebbed into a serenity of what was to come.

David watched Sera sleep. She seemed so peaceful that he hated to wake her. He didn't want to see her sorrow at what the Allies had wrought on everything she loved. Unfortunately, he knew reality would intrude on their hiding place sooner or later.

He bent down and gently kissed her soft lips.

"It's morning."

Sera blinked groggily as she came awake.

"It is?"

He watched her glance up at the sky, the dawn clouds above them just beginning to lighten with the first rays of the rising sun.

She smiled. "We made it through the night."

"It appears so."

"It's over, then?"

"The air raid? Yes, it's been over for hours." David looked at her. She seemed so small and vulnerable, wrapped up in the canvas tarp by his side. "But it's only just started for us."

Sera shook her head.

"David, I'm a big girl. You don't have to—"

"Yes, I do." He stopped her with a bone-melting kiss. He pulled away before things got out of hand—again—and rested his hand on her belly. "I, for one, do not intend to leave any souvenirs behind."

The idea moved him in a way he never thought possible.

He watched tears well in her eyes, and he could tell the tender gesture touched her, too.

She covered his hand with her own, cradling her womb where even now a new life might have already started to grow.

"You don't have to make any promises."

"Yes, I do." He stopped her from saying more. Now that he'd started down this path, he was determined that there would be no room for doubt for either of them. "Now that I've found you, I don't ever intend to let you go."

"But there are so many things in the way. You're from America, I live in Italy. The war…"

"It doesn't matter. None of it matters. We'll find a way. I love you, Sera. I'm not going to ever risk losing you again."

Sera reached up and touched his face.

"I love you, David." She drew in a deep breath, as if drawing on some inner courage. "From the moment we first met, I felt like I'd known you my entire life. That, somehow, you've always been a part of me."

In saying those words, she gave David her heart. He cupped her face in his hands, realizing what a precious gift she had given him. He bent down and kissed her with all the love he had in him.

He sighed heavily when he finally broke the kiss.

"As much as I'd like to stay here and make love to you all day long, we should probably get going."

Sera tossed back the canvas tarp that had shielded them throughout the night and stood. With her back to him, David admired her shapely form, naked in the dawn. She looked so beautiful to him in that moment. All too soon, she covered herself with her bra and panties, the white cotton now smudged with dirt and stained with his blood.

She found his pants and helped him pull them on over his bandaged thigh. Their shoes followed, and soon they were both as dressed as they could be.

Sera plucked at the loose leg of her dirty panties.

"I can just imagine the tongues wagging when they see me walking through town dressed like this."

"I'm not looking much better."

"Yes, but at least you being shirtless is socially acceptable. Me in my underwear is a totally different matter."

She was right. One look at her half-naked appearance, and the busybodies in town would assume the worse. Like mother, like daughter. It wouldn't matter if he married her or not. Sera's reputation would be ruined.

David scooted himself to a sitting position against the wall.

"Hand me my knife."

Sera picked the weapon up off the ground and handed it to him without comment. It was only after he pulled the canvas onto his lap and started cutting at the material that she questioned him.

"What are you doing?"

"Making you a dress."

"You're kidding, right?"

"Nope." When he finished slicing a long strip several yards long, he cut one of the remaining ropes off the corner. He tucked his knife back in its sheath and held out his hand to her. "Now, if you don't mind helping me up?"

She took his hand and pulled him to his feet. David wobbled a bit until he found his balance.

Taking the piece of canvas he'd cut, he draped it over her left shoulder, overlapping the sides at her waist.

"If you will hold the sides together, madam?"

He felt a small tremor race through Sera's body as he reached around her to tie the rope around her waist. He wasn't immune to her, either. As he drew back, he couldn't resist stealing a small kiss. But once their lips touched, it was as if they hadn't made love all night long. He couldn't believe he could want her again so soon, but he did.

With a groan, he pulled back and took in the makeshift dress. For the moment, he just watched her standing there. Then the sun broke over the wall and a brilliant ray of light temporarily blinded him.

Blinking through the glare, he couldn't believe his eyes. Instead of the coarse rope around her waist, she wore an ornate belt of small golden links. Instead of brown hair falling in tangled waves about her shoulders, the locks were pulled up and styled in soft curls around her beautiful face. And instead of a filthy piece of bleached canvas, a white Roman gown draped her slim figure.

He closed his eyes, trying to make sense of what he saw.

"David? Is something wrong?"

When he opened his eyes, she was back, just as she should be, his Sera.

"No, it's just that…" She wouldn't believe him if he told her. "You look like you were born to wear a toga."

She ran her hand down the canvas, smoothing out the folds as if it were a gown made of the finest silk.

"It's not half bad, but I don't think I'll be able to work in the ruins in something like this."

She turned then and looked out the doorway.

"Speaking of the ruins, I guess it's time to leave."

POMPEII

Sera was almost afraid to walk through the opening.

It was too silent outside.

Letting David lean on her, they stepped out into a very different Pompeii. The once cleared street was now a minefield of rubble, scattered with stones shaken loose from fragile walls by the vibrations of the bombs. Bits and pieces of wood, plastic, and even some metal littered the ground, tossed over the wall from the German camp by the force of the blasts. She didn't want to examine the debris too closely, afraid of what she might find. No doubt, many of the German soldiers had not survived the night, and she didn't want to see evidence of what was left of them under her feet.

Finally, she dared to look at the excavation site, and her heart nearly broke at what she saw.

The tent over the body cavity was ripped to shreds. A large, gaping hole was torn in the middle of the fabric, the edges of white canvas still attached to the supports waving in the breeze like tiny flags of surrender. A beam of sunlight pierced through the opening, casting a glow over the mound like a spotlight on the stage.

Gone was the rounded, earthen dome dotted with white spots of dried plaster. Instead, jagged lines and fissures fractured the hard volcanic crust, revealing glimpses of its white interior.

"Oh, no." It looked worse than she could have imagined.

She had taken only one step toward it before David stopped her with a hand around her upper arm. It wasn't a forceful restraint, but more like a caress, like the touch of a bracelet on the skin.

"Sera, wait."

The concern in his eyes warmed her heart. His hand on her arm felt comforting, natural. Was he trying to stop her? To prevent her from seeing what the Allies had done to the plaster cast? What did it matter? She would have to see it sooner or later.

He seemed to read her thoughts and released her.

"Are you sure you want to do this?"

She smiled, but it felt pained.

"Better to do it now, while we're alone, than reveal our greatest discovery destroyed in front of the others."

She turned and took first one, then another step toward the mound, afraid of what she might find when she drew near. She stopped and looked back to him once more, reaching out her hand to him.

"Come with me."

He hobbled up to her, and together they approached the mound.

"Is it ruined?"

At first glance, it looked as though it was. Then Sera knelt to examine it closer. She pried one of the chunks off in her hand and lifted it carefully from the mound. Beneath, the stark white of the plaster cast glared up at her. She reached out and removed another, then another.

Unlike the plaster cast of the child, where they'd had to painstakingly chip the volcanic matter away, the pieces of the mound peeled away easily, like the cracked shell of a hard-boiled egg. With each chunk that fell away, more of the cast was slowly revealed.

Her heart began to pound. The cast underneath seemed to be untouched, perfectly preserved.

"I think it's okay."

David struggled to lower himself down beside her.

Her hands shook with each piece of hard ash she removed. What should have taken them hours seemed to take only minutes as the hard shell fell away to reveal the white plaster cast beneath.

"I think I found a leg over here," David said.

"I've got a head."

"Here's a hand. It looks like he's holding onto something."

"No." Sera sat back as the mid-section was revealed. Her stomach tightened in knots as the reality of what lay beneath set in. "He's holding onto *someone*. It looks like there are two of them in here."

Surprised, David glanced from the cast, to Sera and back again.

"Are you sure?"

"Look," she pointed to a raised area. "There's the form of an arm here. And here," she indicated a hump on the smaller figure, just below the other's arm. "It looks like the curve of a hip."

"So what do you think?"

Sera swallowed, her mouth suddenly gone dry.

"I can't be sure until we uncover more of it."

Her fingers itched to pull another chunk from the pile, but then she looked at David, sitting on the ground with his injured leg stretched out beside him, and guilt tugged at her conscience.

"But we should get you to a hospital first."

"Are you kidding? And leave this half-finished?" He shook his head and smiled at her. "I made it through the night. I think I can handle a few more minutes here. I'm not about to let you do this without me."

Sera grinned. He was going to make a fine archeologist yet.

She retrieved some of the tools to carefully chip away at the more stubborn pieces of the volcanic casing. The minutes turned into hours as the sun slowly rose up over the walls of the ruins. By the time they were done, the glowing orb sat high in the sky.

David used one of the tent poles to pull himself to his feet. Although she was sweaty and dirty, a shiver raced through Sera as she removed the last of the hardened ash from around the heads of the victims. Below were two faces, looking so peaceful and calm, like two lovers asleep in each other's arms.

Excitement and sorrow blended together, threatening to overwhelm her.

"Can you tell what… who they were?"

Sera shook herself, trying to bring herself back to the detached archeologist she needed to be. She examined the figures more closely.

"This one over here," she pointed to the larger one on its side, "is definitely a man." She cocked her head, noticing the impression of a wide belt at his waist. "By the looks of him, he was a slave."

"How can you tell?"

"See the wide belt he was wearing? It's likely a slave belt. And the impression of the weave of his garment is very course, low quality."

"And the other one? It looks smaller. Is it a woman?"

Sera looked at the other figure, partially covered by the man's body.

"It is." Then she looked closer. "This is interesting."

"What?"

"Well, like I said, he's obviously a slave, but she appears to be from the upper classes. The style of her garment is much finer than his, and instead of a slave belt, it looks like she was wearing one of metal or maybe even gold links. It's odd to find them together like this."

She looked up and noticed his face had gone rather pale.

"David, what's wrong? Is your leg hurting you?"

"What? No. What else can you tell about them?"

Sera nodded, wondering why what she'd said seemed to bother him so much.

She stood and walked around the figures until she stood beside him, and he wrapped his arms around her, much like the man held the woman before them. In that instant, a wave of energy coursed through her, beginning in her toes and traveling up through her body to tingle along her scalp. It was as if a connection from the past reached out from the plaster cast and suddenly linked her to the tragedy of centuries ago, now lying revealed before her eyes.

David's arms tightened around her, and she heard his swift intake of breath, as if he, too, felt the emotions that suddenly seemed to swirl in the air around them.

"It looks like he was trying to shield her, to protect her from the falling debris." She felt her eyes well up with unshed tears. "He must have loved her very much."

David softly kissed her temple.

"Yes, I think he did."

Staring at the tragic lovers, Sera knew deep in her soul that it was true.

Whoever they were, they had loved each other to the very end.

CHAPTER XXXII

"They were supposed to get married first, then procreate."

Smithers clicked the remote control and the white screen disappeared into the clouds, taking the image of David and Sera with them.

"Got things a little backwards, didn't you?"

"Perhaps," Marsha sniffed. "The end result's the same. They're finally together, like they were always meant to be."

"Besides," Hershel coughed into his fist. "It was such a beautiful moment, I couldn't resist letting it happen."

"Hershel!" Marsha's eyes nearly bugged out of their sockets. "You watched?"

"Of course not." He looked insulted, then squirmed slightly in his chair. "At least not all of it. Once I was certain they were safe, and David wasn't going to bleed to death, I gave them their privacy."

"Good." Marsha fanned herself with her hand. "After all, there's only so much this old heart of mine can handle."

"Marsha, you haven't had a real heart for over twenty-five centuries."

She glared at him. "Well, I did for a while, and it nearly stopped beating when you died."

"I'm sorry, dear. I don't know how it happened." As Marsha continued to glare at him, Hershel searched to find a silver lining to appease her. "Besides, being an angel again enabled me to protect the plaster cast. Serafina would have been devastated if it had been destroyed."

"But you didn't worry that I would be devastated? I had to finish everything—help David recover, host their wedding before he was shipped back to the States, arrange *your* funeral.

How could you do that to me?" Marsha turned and continued to vent her anger on Smithers. "And why didn't you warn me?"

"I did." Smithers sat back in his chair. He had begun to wonder when they would realize they were still in his office. "That day I came to the jailhouse."

Marsha and Hershel exchanged confused looks as they tried to recall the conversation that day.

Seeing they were never going to figure it out for themselves, Smithers enlightened them. "I said, if you didn't get David and Serafina out of Italy, someone was going to die."

"Oh, for heaven's sake," Marsha huffed. "We thought you meant David or Serafina, not one of us."

Smithers shrugged. "Obviously, you thought wrong."

"Well," Marsha sighed as she rose to her feet and smoothed the wrinkles from her skirt. "At least everything worked out in the end."

"Not so fast." Smithers held up a hand that effectively halted Hershel's rising rear end in mid-air. "Your jobs are not over yet."

"They're not?" They both sank back down into their chairs.

"Yes. You've only just succeeded in bringing your two clients together. Now, as their guardian angels, you must see them through the rest of their natural lives." He handed each of them a packet of papers. "It's your responsibility to watch over them, and their children, and their children's children."

"Oh." Marsha flipped through the pages. "But we can do that from up here, can't we? I mean, we don't have to go on location again, do we?"

"No, as long as we don't have any more *incidents* that need your personal attention."

Hershel's face took on a puzzled look, and he glanced at his wife.

"By the way, how is it that you're here now? You didn't die. Won't Serafina and David notice you're gone?"

"No." Marsha crossed her arms and gave her husband a cold shoulder. "Since you left me all alone, I sold them the villa and told them I was going to live with my niece in Salerno."

"But we don't have a niece." Hershel looked more confused than ever. "Do we?"

"Of course not, Hershel. But they don't know that. Besides, they're going to live in America until the war is over. The army is sending David home to recover, and Serafina is going with him. Plus, it's much safer for the baby, you know."

"Baby? What baby?" Hershel and Smithers questioned in unison.

"The baby they conceived that night." Marsha smiled smugly at the two shocked angels. "See, neither of you know *everything*."

"I love my mountain. She and I dwell together in solitude mysterious and terrible... I could not leave her. I am wedded to her forever; my few friends say that her breath will scorch and wither my poor life one of these days; that she will bury my house in streams of liquid metal or raze it to its very foundation. Already she has hurt me, has injured me sorely. Yet I forgive her, I wait upon her, I am hers always."

Professor R.V. Matteucci,
Director of the Vesuvian Observatory,
as quoted in *The Cosmopolitan* magazine, @ 1900

Epilogue

Six decades later

The room was filled with light, the curtains thrown open to let in the first glorious rays of dawn. David sat beside the bed, holding onto Sera's weathered, blue-veined hand as if he could pull her back from the angels that had surely come to claim her.

As hard as it was for him, he knew he had to let her go.

"You've fought long and hard, *cara mia*. It's time."

The frail chest under the crisp white sheet rose and fell steadily, and he swore each breath would be her last.

"Don't you worry about me, sweetheart. I'll be fine. After all, I've got the kids to keep me company, now don't I?"

He squeezed Sera's hand, as he'd often done every time he walked past her. Always a gentle touch, a loving caress to let her know that even after all these years, he still loved her.

"We've had a wonderful life together, haven't we? And we've been blessed with two wonderful children and five beautiful grandchildren to show for it. I'd say we didn't do too bad for ourselves."

Sera's breathing became ragged, and David panicked, almost reaching for the buzzer that would bring the hospice nurse running into the room.

He stopped himself. No, it was better this way. It was what she wanted—to go now, peacefully in her sleep, in the comfort of their home. After moving heaven and earth to get her released from the hospital, he couldn't risk them taking her back now. If she was going to leave him, then she would want to do it here, where they had spent most of their lives together.

347

As he watched, Sera drew in one last breath, and with what David could have sworn was a gentle squeeze of his hand, she quietly slipped away.

POMPEII

Sitting on the edge of the bed, David gazed out the window at the quaint town of Pompeii. It was a view he'd shared with Sera for over sixty years.

Oh, Sera, how am I to go on without you now?

A soft knock rapped on his door, and he turned to see his family crowded in the hallway. His oldest, Marie, stood in the doorway with her husband and their two kids. Behind her stood his son, Bert, with his wife and their three. Named after Maria and Heberto, the kids, as he called them, were both in their fifties, and the grandchildren were grown with busy lives of their own. Old habits died hard, he supposed.

"*Papà*," Marie said. "We're going down to the *piazza* for lunch. Are you coming?"

"No, you go on without me. I'm not hungry."

Marie looked as if she was about to argue with him, and then seemed to change her mind. She was so much like her mother, sometimes it made his heart ache.

She stepped into the room and came to sit beside him.

"Are you all right, *papà*?"

David breathed in deeply and stared at the brass urn sitting on the table by the window.

"I'll be fine, honey. Just as soon as I do what I have to do."

Marie squeezed his shoulder, shaking her head. "I'll never understand why *mamma* wanted to be cremated."

"When I first met your mother, she was knee deep in the ashes of Pompeii." David chuckled at the memory. "She didn't seem to mind them then, so I don't think she'll mind being a part of them now." He patted Marie's knee. "It's what she wanted. Besides, she always loved working outdoors, so I don't think a coffin would have suited her anyhow."

"No, I don't suppose it would have. She always was a free spirit, right up to the end."

"Yes, she was. It was one of the things I loved most about her."

Marie kissed him on his cheek.

"Call my cell phone if you need us. We won't be long."

"Take your time. I'll be fine."

As his family left, David turned and stared out the window once more, looking through the clouds to the mountain of Vesuvius in the distance.

When the villa grew too silent, he stood up and walked over to the table. He picked up the brass urn with Sera's ashes, caressing its smooth polished surface with his thumb.

"Care to go for a walk, *cara mia*? Take one last look at Pompeii before..." The words caught in his throat. Tomorrow the family would scatter her ashes over the ruins—new ashes to mingle with those of the people who had perished nearly two thousand years before. It was what she wanted. It was where she belonged.

He took solace in the thought that for today he still had her and their memories. He needed this time to be alone with her, to say goodbye.

David tucked the urn into its leather carrying case and pulled the strap over his shoulder. The walk to the ruins from the villa they'd bought from Maria after Heberto's death took about twenty minutes, but he didn't mind. After paying the admission fee, he joined the other tourists in the walk up the ramp through the *Porta Marina*, the same stone arch he had walked through over sixty years before.

He gazed down the stone-paved street past the skeletons of buildings still familiar from the past. Sixty years was nothing compared to the history this city had known.

He found it hard to believe almost two decades had passed since the last time he and Sera had worked in the ruins together. Even after they'd officially retired, she'd spent each summer helping archeology students at the site, until the grueling work had gotten too hard on her.

The place still looked the same, and yet some things had changed. Grass and weeds were creeping into crevices, trying to reclaim the stone roads, and walls that had stood for centuries supported by Vesuvius's ashes were starting to crumble from exposure to the sun and rain.

As he walked along the street, he saw that many areas had been closed to the public. These were places he had once moved freely around in, places he had spent hours exploring with Sera.

Sera. Everywhere he looked, he saw her. He remembered every stone she had touched, every hole she had dug. The very ruins themselves seemed to echo with her presence.

Pushing on through the crowds, David made his way down the *Via dell'Abbondanza*. He passed by the Stabian Baths and the House of the Orchard, both popular sites for the tourists. But he didn't stop to pay them much attention. There was only one thing here that he needed to see.

David skirted around a wooden barricade with more agility than an old man should have. The small side street was empty, and as he walked down it, he felt himself travel back in time, back to 1943 when he and Sera first started working in this area of the ruins.

At the end of the lane, a section of volcanic rock and ash rose nine feet above street level, looking like a grey plateau between the ruined buildings and the old city wall.

Stepping carefully on the make-shift stairs, he climbed to the top. Metal scaffolding supporting large panes of glass formed a roof over the raised area. In later excavations, more bodies had been found in the area—a young family with three small children, all tragically dying within feet of each other. Rather than move any of them as had been done with many of the other plaster casts, the archaeologists had decided to leave these poor souls where they were found. Thus, the area beneath them had never been excavated down to the street level.

David skirted around the family and came to stand beside the cast of the slave gladiator and his lady, lying just as they had died—on a bed of stone, in each other's arms.

He found a shady spot nearby and eased himself down to sit on a low ridge where he could lean against the wall. Hidden here in the back of the ruins, the body casts were protected from over-zealous tourists, vandals, and, thanks to the glass canopy, the elements.

Pulling the urn from the leather pouch, he cradled it in his lap as he stared at the cast. For long moments, he never moved, never took his eyes off the couple.

He felt so proud. It was Sera's greatest find, still perfectly preserved—two lovers frozen in time, just as the volcano had left them so long ago.

At times, he almost could've sworn they moved—that maybe the gladiator's hand caressed the girl's face ever so slightly.

David laughed at himself. He was getting senile, as the grandkids would say. Either that or the light was playing tricks on his old eyes.

Time slipped away, and the day grew late. He was reluctant to go, but the last of the tourists would be leaving, and the employees would be closing the ruins for the night. Still, he felt desperate to have just a few more moments with the cast, knowing this would probably be the last time he ever saw it.

He closed his eyes and absently caressed the urn, its metal warm from the last rays of the setting Mediterranean sun. Then he rose and stepped up to the cast to get one final, closer look. Sighing heavily, he felt a sense of peace for the first time since Sera had died.

He reached out and touched the plaster man on the shoulder.

"Goodbye, old friends."

Turning away, he left the gladiator and his lady to their eternal sleep.

With a start, David suddenly realized he wasn't alone.

A young girl stood on the other side of the body casts, a strange, ethereal glow hovering about her. Dressed as she was in flowing Roman robes, he thought at first she was a statue. Then she moved toward him, appearing to glide across the ground, not even glancing down as she passed the plaster lovers frozen in time.

"David. It's me, Sera."

He felt rooted to the spot. As she approached, she changed from the young girl to a dark, Mongol-looking woman wearing a fine ornamental tunic and furs. Drawing closer, she materialized from a medieval peasant into an older woman with a white powdered wig and a wide bustled gown. Finally, she stood before him looking like Sera as he last saw her, old and frail.

"Sera?"

As she reached out to touch his cheek, she changed yet again. Right before his eyes, she became young again, just as she'd looked the first time he laid eyes on her over sixty years before.

With her gentle touch, something within him shifted and changed. He suddenly felt more alive than he had in years. There was no pain of old age, no aching of brittle bones.

"Sera? I don't understand. What's happening?"

"Look." She turned him around. David saw himself, still sitting against the wall, his head with its thin gray hair resting on his chest as if in a gentle slumber, his arms cradling the urn with her ashes inside.

Then he looked down at his hands. Gone were the brown spots and painful, swollen joints. His hands looked like those of a young man, healthy and strong in his prime.

He turned back to Sera, unable to voice the many questions that came to his mind. Somehow, she seemed to read his thoughts and answered him.

"You see me as your heart remembers me, and I see you as my heart remembers you. Young and strong, and oh, so brave. When the children's time comes, they will see us a bit older, as their memories of a mother and father should be. Where we're going, you only see through the eyes of love."

"Where are we going?"

"Home. It's time to go, David."

She reached down and took his hand. They started moving toward a ray of bright light floating on the gentle Mediterranean breeze.

"But what about the kids? The grandchildren?"

She smiled, her big blue eyes shining with all the love in her heart.

"They'll be fine. After all, they'll have us up there looking out for them."

He glanced back once more at the shell of the old man he used to be, the reality of what was happening just beginning to dawn on him.

He watched, detached, as the weathered hand dropped limply to his side and the urn slipped out of his slack grasp, tumbling to the ground.

A sense of love and completion filled David as he watched Sera's ashes spill silently on the ground near the plaster cast, only to be picked up and carried away on the wind.

AUTHOR'S NOTES

David and Sera's story came to me when I saw a *National Geographic* photograph of a plaster cast of a couple from Pompeii. The man and woman died in each other's arms as they tried to flee the city, forever frozen in time, his hand shielding her face in a vain attempt to protect her.

The cast is beautiful, touching, and heartbreaking. I began to wonder what their story might have been, and the tragic couple eventually evolved into a young Pompeian girl and the slave gladiator she loved. Then I wondered what might have happened if they were given a second chance.

The process of making plaster casts of the victims was invented by Giuseppe Fiorelli in 1863 after it was discovered that hollow spaces in the hardened ashes were the impressions left by the dead after their bodies decayed. Over eleven hundred plaster casts have been made of the victims of Pompeii, all captured at the exact moment they died.

In September of 1943, Allied planes dropped 163 bombs on the German encampment set up outside the walls of Pompeii, believing that they were hiding artillery within the ruins. As incredible as it sounds, on that fateful evening, the archeologists rushed to the ruins to try to save what artifacts they could. On their way there, the Director of Excavations, Amedeo Maiuri, and his assistant were blown off their bicycles by a stray bomb. Maiuri's leg was broken and, tragically, his assistant's body was never found. The bombing severely damaged some parts of the ruins, including the Great Palaestra, the Antiquarium, and the gladiator barracks.

Mount Vesuvius last erupted in March 1944, spewing lava down the mountainside and destroying three small villages in its path. That time Pompeii was spared from destruction, and the mountain sleeps silently now, waiting.

By all estimates, nearly two thousand Pompeians died in the A.D. 79 eruption. However, only about sixty percent of the ruins have been excavated so far.

Who knows what lies beneath the remaining ashes, and what their story may be?

ABOUT THE AUTHOR

In a previous life, Lori was a graphic designer for fourteen years. In her current existence, she lives in Virginia with her engineering geek/hero husband, two kids who test her sanity on a daily basis, a dog named Hokie (named after the Virginia Tech Hokies, of course), and various other critters of the furred and finned variety.

Out of the Ashes is her first published novel. If you enjoyed Sera and David's story, please consider posting a review on Amazon, Barnes and Noble, Goodreads, or any other book review site. Good word of mouth from readers is the life blood for an independent author.

Lori loves to hear from her readers.
You can contact her at lori@loridillon.com
or visit her at www.loridillon.com